Pra

"*Her Husband's* ... .nary read."--*Dear Author*

"Erotic historical romance isn't as plentiful as many would think, but here you have a very well-written example of this genre. It's entertaining and fun and a darn good read."--*The Book Binge*

"I devoured this book in a couple of hours! .... If you love a story with a heroine who is a wallflower with a backbone of steel or a damaged hero then you will love this one too."--5 star review from *LoveRomancePassion.com* on *Her Wanton Wager*

"I found this to be an exceptional novel. I recommend it to anyone who wants to get lost in a good book, because I certainly was."--A Top Pick from *NightOwlReviews.com*

"I thoroughly enjoyed this story. Grace Callaway is a remarkable writer."--*LoveRomancePassion.com* on *Her Prodigal Passion*

"The depth of the characters was wonderful and I was immediately cheering for both of them."--*Buried Under Romance*

"Grace Callaway is one of my favorite authors because of her fearlessness in writing love scenes that truly get the blood pumping."--*Juicy Reviews*

Books by Grace Callaway

HEART OF ENQUIRY
The Widow Vanishes
The Duke Who Knew Too Much
M is for Marquess
The Viscount Always Knocks Twice

MAYHEM IN MAYFAIR
Her Husband's Harlot
Her Wanton Wager
Her Protector's Pleasure
Her Prodigal Passion

CHRONICLES OF ABIGAIL JONES
Abigail Jones

M IS FOR MARQUESS

Heart of Enquiry Book Two

GRACE CALLAWAY

M is for Marquess is a work of fiction. Names, characters, places, and incidents are the products of the author's imagination and are used fictitiously. Any resemblance to actual events, locales, or persons, living or dead, is entirely coincidental.

Cover design: © Seductive Musings Designs
Images: © Period Images

Printed in the United States of America

Acknowledgements

To my readers, thank you for your support of the Kents. This family's saga continues because of you, and I hope you will enjoy their adventures to come. Many hugs.

To my peeps who keep it real. Tina Folsom, BFF to the gazillionth degree, who shares the bumps and thrills of this writing journey with me—I couldn't do this without you (or your espresso maker). Jess Michaels, you're an inspiration. Diane Pershing, thank you for always seeing where the story needs to go. Carrie, you inspire me to write stories worthy of your gorgeous covers. The Montauk Eight, let's keep those good times rollin'.

To Brian, husband and editor, equally brilliant at both. Love you to pieces.

To Brendan, the reason I wrote this story and the reason for most everything.

Chapter One

At the stone gate, Gabriel Ridgley, the Marquess of Tremont, pulled his stallion to a stop.

"Easy, Shadow," he murmured as the animal's muscles quivered beneath him.

He didn't blame the steed. At midnight, the moon's spectral glow and the swirling shroud of mist transformed the Yorkshire moors into an eerie, forbidding landscape. Which was likely what drew Sir August Mondale, former spymaster and Gabriel's mentor, to build a home here.

Spies, even retired ones, were drawn to obscurity. Gabriel, himself, chose to cloak himself in respectability. It was a source of private amusement that the sticklers of the *ton* had dubbed him *The Angel* for what they perceived to be his proper, faultless behavior. Their tongues would wag up a damned storm if they knew the truth. But they wouldn't— because he didn't want them to. Concealing his thoughts and desires was second nature to him.

Keep your guard up, and trust no one.

His mentor's motto and the first lesson of being a spy.

Gabriel dismounted and secured his horse. He scaled the gate with ease, landing soundlessly on the other side. The rear windows of the manor house were dark, but he knew the spymaster was waiting for him. Mondale, known in the old days as Octavian, had sent Gabriel a summons written in the old code. After more than a decade out of the profession, deciphering the message had still come as naturally to Gabriel as breathing.

My study Friday at midnight. Tell no one. Do not be seen.

He made his way through overgrown hedges, his boot steps muffled by the carpet of moss and weeds. Clearly, Octavian hadn't taken to gardening after retirement... if indeed the old codger had retired at all. Since the disbanding of the Quorum—the spy ring that Octavian had created and recruited Gabriel to—Gabriel had heard nothing from the other. Not surprising as the spymaster had been in high dudgeon at their final meeting.

"What do you mean you want to quit? Over a setback?" Octavian's rough-hewn features had evinced disbelief.

"Marius' death was more than a setback." Though Gabriel's voice had been quiet, his chest had been tight with rage and guilt. Marius had been his comrade and friend, more of a brother than his own had ever been. "He died protecting me."

"Missions don't always go as planned. 'Tis part of the game, Trajan."

Trajan. Gabriel's old code name. A good soldier, an obedient killer. A reminder that Octavian had trained him, giving him purpose and discipline, the lethal tools to pursue a higher cause.

But that last mission in Normandy had changed all that. Being captured and tortured, seeing your best friend die for you and being helpless to do anything—that made you see clearly.

"The war's been over for two years," Gabriel said.

"War is *never* over." Octavian's fist pounded the desk.

"We may have defeated Bonaparte, but enemies of England continue to conspire. The Spectre may still live—"

"I killed him," Gabriel said. "During the escape."

Flame and mayhem flashed in his mind's eye. The cloaked figure had stood twenty yards away, shrouded by the billowing grey smoke, but Gabriel's gut had identified his nemesis. *Le Spectre.* The French spymaster so called because he was a ghost who eluded capture, who'd kept his identity hidden in the shadows.

Although bloodied and injured, Gabriel had aimed with a steady hand. He'd sent his dagger—one of six forged from Damascus steel—on a lethal flight through the smoke. He'd seen his target fall the instant before an explosion had ripped through the fortress and sent the world crashing down.

"We never found his body. Or your blade." Shaking his grizzled mane, Octavian said, "Without proof, we don't know he's dead. He has survived blades, fire, and explosions before. He's walked away from death more times than I can count."

"Chase phantom spymasters if you wish. I'm done."

Gabriel had walked out of his mentor's study a dozen years ago. He hadn't looked back.

Then what the devil are you doing returning here now?

As he approached the back of the manor, his trepidation grew. He'd sensed an underlying urgency in the spymaster's summons. Loyalty was in his nature; he couldn't forget Octavian any more than he could forgive him.

Further proof that he could never leave his past behind. That mistakes, despite one's best efforts, had a way of repeating themselves. Unbidden, his most recent error unfolded in his mind's eye. From the first, Dorothea Kent's steady hazel gaze had captivated him, seeming to see straight into his soul. Her fine-boned beauty and lustrous gilded brown hair had reminded him of an etching in one of his son's storybooks, the one of the princess locked in an ivory tower.

He couldn't recall if that drawing had possessed Thea's sweetly formed breasts or her nicely rounded bottom. Or if the princess in the story had smelled of honeysuckle, her skin smoother than cream. Or if one kiss had made the hero of the story harder than a steel pike.

He shut down that line of thought, which would only lead to trouble. He'd been right in putting distance between himself and Thea; in truth, he'd allowed things to go too far. Getting involved with a virgin—and one with a delicate constitution at that—was the last thing he needed. He'd gone down that road before, and it'd led to disastrous consequences for all involved.

Besides, he had more pressing considerations: an estate to run... a son to raise.

Jaw tautening, he focused on the task at hand. His gloved fingers found the seam of a window left ajar. He saw a faint glow through a slit in the drapes, a flash of leather spines that told him he'd found the study. He lifted the pane, eased silently inside, brushing aside velvet as he assessed the room at a glance.

Lamp on the desk, half-burned. Scent of Octavian's favorite tobacco. And something else...

Gabriel unsheathed his blades, the metal glinting. He scanned the room. No movement. No hiding place. Keeping close to the wall, he crept forward—and saw the hand on the ground by the bookshelves. Another three steps brought the body, which had been obscured by the desk, into full view. A grey-haired figure lying on his belly, one arm outstretched, his face turned to the side and pale eyes unseeing.

Octavian.

Emotion welled; at the same time, Gabriel's training kicked in. Sleet coated his insides, blocking out sentiment as his brain analyzed details with detached clarity. The spymaster's throat had been slit. From behind and without warning, judging from the clean incision. The poor bastard hadn't seen it coming, hadn't struggled. There were no signs of forced entry. The murderer had come and gone like a ghost.

Clinging to the last thread of life, Octavian had had perhaps a minute or two before he'd suffocated in his own blood. The trail of scarlet indicated that he'd taken that precious time, used monumental effort, to drag himself the distance from the desk to the bookshelf.

Why?

Crouching, Gabriel rolled the body over. Saw the book clutched in his mentor's hand, fingers curled between the pages. With care, he freed the leather volume from Octavian's death grip.

Shakespeare's *Julius Caesar*. Gabriel scanned the marked page. Act III, Scene I, Caesar's words anointed with Octavian's blood. *Et tu, Brute? Then fall, Caesar!*

Caesar's famous words denouncing the ultimate betrayal by a member of his inner circle. Had Octavian, too, been deceived by someone close to him? The spymaster had no surviving relatives or friends and over the past years had become a virtual recluse. He belonged to no group, except the one that, like Caesar, he'd led.

The Quorum.

Ice ran through Gabriel's veins. Why would one of the Quorum—one of Gabriel's former colleagues—want Octavian dead? Had the old spymaster known that danger was coming? Was that the reason behind his mysterious summons to Gabriel this eve?

Gabriel ran a gloved hand over his mentor's eyes, closing them.

"Rest now, old friend," he said quietly. "Your travails are over."

His own had just begun. He left the way he came, through the window and into the garden. Blending into the shadows, he went in search of answers.

Chapter Two

Three weeks later

Passing the entrance gate, Dorothea Kent took in the gardens of the Zoological Society with wide-eyed wonder. Located at the eastern edge of Regent's Park, the collection of animals stretched as far as the eye could see. All around her, creatures sporting fur, feathers, or scales roamed in pens of sun-gilded grass. Up ahead, she spied fluttering shapes within a glass-domed aviary and, to the left of it, exotic beasts of burden grazing around an Arabian-styled house.

"This is the *tops*." Violet, Thea's middle sister, stood on tiptoe, chestnut curls bobbing as she craned her neck to get a better view. "Let's see the leopards first. No, make that the bears."

"We've all afternoon, Vi." Their eldest sister Emma shook out the map she'd purchased at the entry hut. "If we follow the walking path in a clockwise manner, then we'll be sure to see everything—"

"Gadzooks, are those *llamas*?" With a shriek of excitement, Vi bounded off.

"Shall I follow her, pet?" the Duke of Strathaven quirked an eyebrow.

Tall, dark, and wickedly handsome, Strathaven had married Emma last year. It was clear to all—and a source of some amusement amongst the *ton*—that the former rake adored his bride. Emma had recently given birth to their daughter, Olivia, and Thea had never seen her sister happier.

"I suppose you'd better," Emma said, wrinkling her nose, "before someone mistakes Vi for a wild creature and locks her in a cage."

With a lazy grin, Strathaven kissed his duchess before striding off after Violet.

Cheeks pink, Emma adjusted her cottage bonnet. "Shall we, girls?"

Their youngest sister Polly and niece Primrose, both seventeen, chorused, "Yes, please," and wandered ahead on the path arm-in-arm, white muslin skirts swaying as they took in the live exhibits. Strolling behind with Emma, Thea noted more than one gentleman casting looks in the girls' direction. Polly didn't seem to notice the attention whilst Rosie's dimples deepened. A blond beauty possessed of a vivacious temperament, the latter was well accustomed to admiration.

Thea wondered what it would be like to draw such attention. She was an observer by nature, more comfortable watching than being watched. The sole exception was when there was a pianoforte in front of her. Then everything—the audience, the world—melted away to the smooth glide of ivory beneath her fingertips, the immersion into a realm beyond the ordinary, where only soul-deep sensation existed.

She often got so lost in the music that the applause startled her out of her reverie. At times, guests called for an encore. But only one man had ever truly heard her.

Her hands curled in her gloves, her fingers tingling with the memory of thick, tawny locks sliding between them. The dark, delicious flavor of her first kiss drenched her senses.

The familiar mix of longing and humiliation rushed through her.

Don't be a ninny, she chided herself. *If he wanted you, he would not have left. He would not have disappeared without a word for three months.*

"Tired, dear?"

Thea looked up into Emma's concerned brown eyes. She managed a smile. The last thing she wanted was to worry her sister, who tended to be overprotective as it was.

"I'm fine," she said.

"It was quite the walk in from the promenade. And you were up early with Olivia this morning—"

"There's no need to fuss." She cut Em off gently. "You know I love to play the doting aunt."

Married to a duke, Emma could have an army of nursemaids at her disposal if she wished. But that wasn't the Kent way. They were country-bred middling class folk, and despite Ambrose, the eldest brother, and Emma both marrying into the upper classes, the siblings retained much of their original outlook on life.

Family stuck together through thick and thin. Older Kents watched over the younger ones. Thus, after Olivia's birth, Thea had gone from her brother's home to her sister's to help care for the newest member of the family.

Emma frowned. "It rained yesterday, and you know how your lungs get after the rain."

At the mention of her health, Thea tamped down a spark of frustration. It wasn't fair of her to be annoyed at Emma, whose habitual fretting stemmed from years of looking after all the Kents—and her especially. At age five, Thea had contracted the croup, the coughing and fever lasting nearly a fortnight. Others of her family had gotten ill, too, but everyone else had recovered fully.

She, however, remained vulnerable to coughing fits, the sudden spasm of her lungs. For years, the breathing ailment had stolen her energy and restricted her activity, and she'd faced the prospect of living life as an invalid. Then a miracle had occurred. She'd come under the care of Dr. Abernathy, a brilliant Scottish physician, and he'd prescribed a novel treatment of exercises and salt water rinses to strengthen her respiratory system. Over the past year, her constitution had gradually improved, and hope blossomed within her.

Physically, she knew she'd never be as robust as her siblings, but her will was as strong as theirs. She would give anything to live a full life, one unhindered by her body's limitations. One in which she would know the kind of passion she'd thus far only experienced through music.

"I do appreciate all that you've done, Thea. Olivia is rather a handful—even more so than Polly was at that age." Emma tipped her head, her sable curls glinting where they caught the light. "It must come from Strathaven's side of the family."

Thea smothered a grin. "I think His Grace has settled in nicely."

"He has, hasn't he?" Smiling, Emma paused to look at enormous birds labeled as "Emus" chasing each other around a gated pen. "Marriage has been good for both of us."

Feeling an insufferable pang of self-pity, Thea inwardly sighed. *What's wrong with me?* She was so happy that Emma and Ambrose had both found worthy partners—no one deserved love more than her siblings. Yet being around people in love made her crave a taste of that intensity, that life-altering ardor. And at four-and-twenty, she was running out of time.

By Season's end, she would be firmly on the shelf. After that, she'd be like an apple that had rolled out of view, growing wrinkly and moldy in some dark corner with no one to notice... except perhaps ants. But who wanted to be noticed by ants? The things she wanted—a passionate love match, a husband and children of her own—would be out of her reach forever.

Apparently, Emma caught wind of her thoughts. "On the topic of marriage, I've been thinking about you."

"Me?" Thea kept her eyes on the prancing birds, the flutter of brown and black feathers.

Emma's expression turned resolute, a familiar crease deepening between her brows. "You've been in the doldrums ever since the Marquess of Tremont left Town. Strathaven does business with Tremont, and they're friendly, as you know. I can ask him to—"

"*No*, Emma." Thea's lungs constricted at the notion. "You promised you wouldn't interfere. Please don't make me regret sharing my feelings with you—feelings which have faded, I assure you."

The last part was a lie but better than the alternative. Of all her siblings, Thea felt closest to Emma, who was older by just a year. But Em had a tendency to think that she knew best for everyone and, as a result, could be a bit managing.

Em gnawed on her lower lip. "I'm still convinced that the marquess was interested in you. For months, he was so attentive. I don't understand his sudden departure."

Though her habit was to confide in her sister, Thea had

kept one secret to herself: the kiss she'd shared with Tremont. After all, what woman wanted to divulge that she'd wantonly thrown herself into a gentleman's arms, experienced moments of heavenly pleasure… only to be summarily rebuffed?

Trying for an offhanded tone, she said, "Perhaps he had things to attend to at his estate."

"But to leave in the middle of the Season? And without a word to anyone? After the time he spent in your company," Emma said with an indignant huff, "he could have at least sent a note."

Her sister did have a point. Since last Season, Tremont had been paying respects to Thea. Nothing that would raise eyebrows, just the occasional dance or turn around the ballroom. She'd found herself drawn to the enigmatic widower. Not merely because he was attractive—which he certainly was with his classical features and virile physique—but because she sensed in him a kindred spirit.

On the surface, he was the perfect gentleman—*The Angel*, as the ton liked to call him. He didn't gamble, drink much, or indulge in the other excesses common to men of his station. His manner was polite to the point of being devoid of any emotion. He favored austere fashions, his crisp cravat and gleaming boots as spotless as his reputation.

Yet beneath all that masculine restraint, she sensed passion, potent and yearning.

She'd never forget his first words to her. She'd just finished performing her favorite piano sonata at Emma's engagement party, and guests had approached to offer accolades on her playing. The last in line had been a tall, broad-shouldered stranger. He'd looked to be in his mid-thirties, a man in his prime. The chandelier had glinted off the gold in his hair, cast shadows over a face of stark male beauty.

"It began like a gentle rain," he'd said, his deep voice lifting the hairs on her skin, "and ended like a thunderstorm. Thank you for reminding me of the human spirit. Of its passion and folly, its ability to endure."

Breathless awareness had gripped her. The fibers of her being tautened, quivering with the readiness of an instrument about to be plucked. A feeling she'd waited a lifetime for.

Mesmerized by the intensity of his slate grey eyes, she'd whispered, "Thank you... um, *who* are you?"

His slow, self-deprecating smile devastated her senses. "My manners aren't usually this shoddy. Forgive me. Gabriel Ridgley, Marquess of Tremont, at your service."

And so her feverish infatuation had begun.

For his part, he'd never actively encouraged her attachment, nor had he discouraged it. They'd talked, danced, strolled in the garden, all of it properly chaperoned. All of it friendly and polite. At times, she'd thought that they were about to turn a corner—that he might declare his feelings—only to have him withdraw, his eyes opaque as steel. As cool and impassive.

Finally, she hadn't been able to stand it any longer. For the first time in her life, she'd acted recklessly. She'd grabbed life by the horns—and been flung aside.

"He doesn't owe me anything." Then, because it had to be said, "Please don't meddle, Em. It'll only make matters awkward if he and I cross paths in the future."

"Fine. You're better off without him, if you ask me," her

sister declared. "Tremont always struck me as a bit of a cold fish."

If only his kiss *had* been cold, then she might have forgotten him more easily. But in those few precious moments before he'd rejected her, his lips had set fire to her blood, awakening dormant yearnings. Desires that now infused her dreams, made her toss restlessly in her bed...

"And speaking of fish, he's not the only one in the sea. Instead of moping, you ought to make the most of the remaining Season. Meet potential suitors. You've been so preoccupied with that blasted Tremont that you haven't noticed anyone else."

Actually, Thea had noticed the handful of gentlemen who'd shown her attention... who might have even courted her, had she encouraged them. They were all substantially older than she was, widowers with heirs securely in place. Men who could afford to take on a fragile wife to be a companion in their dotage or an ornament in their drawing room. Men who would peck her on the cheek, pat her head, and send her off to her separate bedchamber.

Men who didn't understand her at all.

Yet the one man who did—who'd seemed to see to the vital, pulsing heart of her desires—didn't want her. For weeks, the reasons for Tremont's rejection kept her mind spinning like a top. Was it because her constitution seemed too weak? Was she too old? Not pretty enough? Perhaps it had been her kiss—too brazen or too inexperienced?

Or maybe he'd never reciprocated her feelings at all. Maybe he'd seen her only as a platonic companion. Maybe his heart still belonged to Lady Sylvia, his departed wife whom everyone said had been a paragon of virtue...

Stop it, Thea told herself firmly. The answer lay as out of reach as a mirage. Which meant she must cease obsessing over it or she would be driven to Bedlam.

"If I meet anyone of interest, you will be the first to know." She gave her sister a pleading look. "Now can we *please* drop the subject?"

Emma huffed out a breath. "I only pester because I care, you know."

"I know." Drawing her shawl more tightly around her shoulders, Thea forced a smile. "We'd better catch up to the girls." By the camel house, two bold dandies were bowing before Rosie. "They're getting more attention than the menagerie."

"That's Quality for you," Emma said, sighing. "They're here to watch each other not the animals."

A lady sporting a full plumage of peacock feathers in her hat strolled by.

Thea murmured, "How can you tell the difference?"

Her sister laughed, dispelling any lingering tension.

The next hour passed quickly given the distractions of the various displays. They met up with Strathaven and Violet, the latter chomping at the bit to see the kangaroos. The other girls wanted to go too; feeling the familiar fatigue creep over her like fog over the Thames, Thea scanned the bustling environs for a bench and proposed to wait there.

"I'll stay with you," Emma said.

"No, go and enjoy yourself. I'd like a few moments of quiet. Truly I would."

Emma looked ready to argue, but Strathaven put an arm around her waist. "Don't fuss, love. Let Dorothea enjoy a respite from the mayhem. We won't be gone long."

Thea gave her brother-in-law a grateful look.

With a wink, he led Emma and the others away.

Thea made her way to the seat. But a pair of ladies beat her to it, forcing her to look for another. She spied one in the distance; away from the main walk, the bench was set by a sparkling pond, partially hidden by a cluster of trees. Lured by the promise of solitude, she headed over.

A few minutes later, she sat in the enveloping shade. The leaf-scented coolness was a balm to her senses, and she smiled at the frolics of the water fowl honking and flapping their wings, splashing diamonds across the water's surface. Just as she began to relax, a boy's voice cut through the calm.

"Please, Mademoiselle Fournier, I cannot keep up."

"You do not wish to miss the feeding of the bears, do you?" The female voice bore a crisp French accent. "You must hurry, or we will miss it."

Shading her eyes, Thea spotted the pair: a small, tawny-haired boy, simply and expensively dressed, led by the arm by a woman whose drab gown and bonnet pronounced her as his governess. They were on the other side of the pond, heading toward the trees along the perimeter of the gardens.

The child dug in his heels. "I do not think that this is the way to the bears. And what about Papa? He said he would be right back—"

"Your papa will find us. You must listen to me. *Allons-y*."

The governess yanked impatiently at her charge's arm, and the boy whimpered, "Stop, please, you're hurting me!"

Thea found herself on her feet, dashing over. "Pardon," she said between breaths, "what is going on?"

The govern' head whipped in her direction. The woman was in her twenties, exceptionally pretty, with even features and a slim figure. Her dark shrewd eyes roved over Thea, and her expression smoothed like a sheet over a bed.

"Nothing to concern you, *mademoiselle*," she said.

"Your treatment of this child concerns me." Thea turned to the boy, whose blue-grey eyes took up much of his thin face. Freckles stood out against the paleness of his skin. Gentling her voice, she said, "Are you all right, dear?"

"Y-yes, miss."

The boy's quivering reply indicated that he wasn't fine. Not by a long shot.

"Are you being taken against your will?" she said.

"I am his governess," the Frenchwoman snapped. "You are interfering in business that does not concern you. Come, Frederick, we must go."

Thea tensed as the boy resisted, pulling against the other's grip.

"I want Papa," he said, his lower lip trembling. "He told us to wait whilst he went to purchase tickets for the camel rides."

"We are leaving *now*." The governess twisted his arm, and he cried out.

"Stop hurting him!" With a desperate lunge, Thea grabbed onto the governess' arm, managing to shake the other's grip off the boy. She pushed the child behind her, shielding him as best she could.

Desperation lit the Frenchwoman's eyes. She shoved her hand into the side of her skirts, removing a glinting object. Stunned, Thea found herself staring at the barrel of a small pistol.

"Give him to me," the governess said.

Thea could feel the child shaking behind her skirts—or

was it her own limbs quivering?

"You'll have to shoot me first." She hated how winded she sounded, the shortness of her breath. *Keep calm, breathe slowly* … "If that pistol goes off, everyone will hear," she managed. "You won't get away."

The woman leveled her weapon. "This is your last warning—"

"Frederick!" The masculine roar came from a distance. "Where are you?"

"Papa!" the boy shouted. "Over here!"

Thea kept her gaze on the governess. Panic flared in the other's dark eyes, her knuckles bone-white against the gun. Thea braced, her heart thudding in her ears—

The governess turned and raced toward the trees. Dazed, Thea stared after the retreating figure. Something white fluttered from the dark skirts, landing on the grass, but the woman took no notice. She continued running, reaching the copse at the perimeter of the gardens and vanishing into the dense brush.

Thea took the few steps over to the fallen object. Bent to pick it up. It was an ordinary white handkerchief, the initials "M. F." embroidered prominently at the center.

"Frederick! Are you all right?"

At the familiar deep male voice, Thea jerked around. Her disordered breath hitched further. *Tremont?* For an instant, their gazes locked; she saw her own shock reflected in those tempestuous grey depths.

Then he looked back to the boy. Was that… *his son?*

"I'm fine, Papa," Frederick said in a trembling voice.

"What the devil do you think you're doing?" The marquess' features set into foreboding lines. "I told you to stay put. Where's Mademoiselle Fournier?"

"She wanted m-me to see the bears. I didn't want to." Frederick's eyes welled.

Coming to her senses, Thea blurted, "It wasn't his fault. The governess was trying to abduct him. She had a *pistol*."

"What?" Tremont's voice turned dangerously hushed.

"She ran off in that direction." Thea pointed toward the trees—and realized she still held the governess' handkerchief. "She dropped this."

He took it from her, his jaw tightening. His muscles bunched beneath the blue superfine of his jacket. "Stay here with Frederick," he said tersely. "I'll take a look—"

"Papa, I don't feel well..."

Thea's gaze flew to Frederick. An alarming flush had crept over the boy's face. He weaved unsteadily on his feet, and Tremont caught him before he hit the ground. Cradled in his father's arms, the boy gasped, his head turning to one side, eyes rolling back in his head. His thin limbs began to shake.

Chapter Three

"Hang in there." Gabriel walled off his inner chaos, keeping his voice calm and steady even though he knew his son couldn't hear him. He held on tightly to Freddy's small, jerking body. "It'll be over soon, I promise."

"What can I do?" Thea's gentle voice reached him. She'd knelt on Freddy's other side. Beneath the brim of her bonnet, her hazel eyes were bright with worry.

"There's nothing to do but wait," Gabriel said tersely.

Silently, she kept vigil with him, holding Freddy's hand. His thudding pulse measured the passing seconds. *This fit is lasting too long. Why the devil hasn't it stopped?*

An eternity dragged by before the shaking finally ceased.

"P-papa?" Freddy mumbled, his lashes fluttering.

Relief scalded Gabriel's insides. "I'm here. Rest. You've had another spell."

A feeble moan broke from Freddy's lips, his chest rising and falling on shallow breaths.

"Thea! We've been looking all over—*Lord Tremont?*" The Duchess of Strathaven approached, followed by her husband and sisters. Her gaze landed on Freddy's prone figure. "Heavens, what is going on?"

"This is Lord Frederick, Tremont's son. He isn't feeling well," Thea said, her manner blessedly discreet. "We must get him to safety as soon as possible."

"I'll get the carriage." Strathaven paused, frowning. "Tremont, when did you return to Town? Where are you staying?"

To fund much-needed improvements to his country estate, Gabriel had sold his townhouse in London a while back. Strathaven, being his business partner and friend, knew about his financial circumstances. In fact, it was thanks to the duke's brilliant investment schemes that Gabriel had made significant strides toward recovering his fortune in the last year.

"I've taken rooms at Mivart's. We were only to stay for the weekend." His chest tightened. "It is Frederick's birthday, you see, and he wanted to see the gardens."

"A hotel's no place for a convalescence. You'll come stay with us." Strathaven's ducal tone brooked no refusal. "I'll send for my personal physician to see to your boy."

"I don't wish to inconvenience—"

To Gabriel's consternation, Strathaven's broad back was already fading into the distance.

"Don't mind him. His Grace likes to have the last word," the duchess said.

"I'm s-sorry to cause trouble," Freddy said. "Please don't be angry, Papa."

"I am not angry." *Not at you.*

Thea smiled, giving his son's hand a squeeze. "It's no trouble at all. In fact, we would welcome the company."

"I'm not much company, miss," Freddy mumbled.

The forlorn admission made Gabriel want to punch something. It was damnably true. Frederick's affliction made him unable to tolerate stimulation of any kind. When Sylvia had been alive, she'd made sure that their son remained in secluded and tranquil environments, keeping him safe from the world.

Yet Gabriel had exposed the boy to danger by bringing him to a public place—and by failing to protect him. Anger blazed as he thought of Mademoiselle Fournier. Why had the governess tried to kidnap his son? Possibilities proliferated... he pushed them aside.

Time to hunt the bitch down later. Get Freddy to safety first.

"Well, it *is* difficult to be good company when one hasn't been properly introduced." Thea was smiling at Frederick. "I'm Dorothea Kent."

Christ, three months away from her and nothing has changed, Gabriel thought savagely. Just the sound of her voice, one bloody glance at her coral pink lips and shining hair, and he was filled with need. With the desire to do unspeakable things to her. To possess her completely.

"Pleased to meet you, Miss Kent," Freddy said shyly.

"Would you like to meet the rest of my family?" she asked.

Freddy gave a tentative nod. As she introduced her sisters and niece, the poor lad blushed, stammering out his hellos. One could hardly blame him. It required all of Gabriel's discipline to keep his gaze vigilantly scanning the field for signs of threat. Even so, his senses hungrily absorbed Thea. Her honeysuckle scent curled into his nostrils, unleashing a ravening need.

The potent mix of danger and desire made him ready to fight, to fuck. For him, those base urges had always been two sides of the same coin, feeding off one another. When her gaze met his, softly inquiring, lust punched him in the gut.

Strathaven arrived soon thereafter with a spacious

equipage, and they all bundled aboard, Gabriel carrying his son. Thea took the seat beside him. At every dip in the road, her body brushed with innocent sensuality against his, and he clenched his jaw against the sweet torture.

It's not going to happen, you bastard. Get used to that fact.

Once, pursued by enemies through the crooked streets of Marseilles, he'd taken to the rooftops, leaping from one tiled surface to another. On the last jump, he'd nearly missed. The same sensations assailed him now. The desperate bid to regain balance, the instinct to hold on. The need to resist a greater force—because you knew what would happen if you didn't.

Tremont paced before the fireplace like a caged lion. To Thea, who watched him discreetly from a nearby curricle chair, the plush green and gold backdrop of the sitting room furthered the illusion of him being some exotic beast of prey prowling through jungle territory, his muscles sleek and rippling beneath his coat. Seated on an adjacent settee, Emma and Strathaven made attempts at conversation as they all waited for Dr. Abernathy to finish the examination of Lord Frederick.

In the months of their acquaintance, Tremont had mentioned his boy, of course, but only in passing. Whenever Thea had tried to ask more about the child, he'd turned reticent. According to Emma, the *ton* knew little about the marquess' heir, and even Strathaven had never met the boy, who lived year round at Tremont's seat in Hampshire.

Thea had assumed that Tremont's reluctance to speak of

the child was due to his natural desire for privacy... or perhaps lingering grief over the boy's mama. It was common knowledge that he'd been grief-stricken by the loss of his marchioness, who'd passed away four years ago whilst giving birth to their stillborn child.

Everyone said that Lady Sylvia had been the ideal wife: beautiful and kind, the pinnacle of femininity. How could a spinster with a frail constitution hold a candle to such perfection?

Stop it, Thea chided herself. *That's over. Focus on the present.*

Thinking of Freddy, she felt worry mingled with admiration. With his ailment, the little fellow carried a heavy burden and yet he'd shown such courage in standing up to the villainess who'd tried to abduct him. The boy was stronger than he looked, Thea thought, a true warrior. She prayed that his resilience would lead to a speedy recovery.

The door to the adjoining suite opened, and Dr. Abernathy, a beetled-browed Scotsman, entered. He bent his steely grey head in a precise bow. Thea smiled at him; she owed much to the gruff physician, whose unorthodox treatments had led to significant improvements in her own condition.

"How is he?" Tremont said tersely.

"My professional opinion, my lord, is that the lad has suffered from an overstimulation of the nerves. He requires rest." The doctor's brogue gave added emphasis to the advice. "I've given him a few drops of laudanum to help him sleep, and I'm confident he will recover completely."

Some of the starkness eased from Tremont's features. "I am in your debt, sir."

"That is excellent news," Strathaven said.

"Indeed." Dr. Abernathy nodded. "A sennight or so abed and the lad should be right as rain."

Tremont went still. "A week? He has to remain here that long?"

"Best to err on the side of caution," the doctor said. "Today's events have undoubtedly unbalanced Lord Frederick's nervous system, which is sensitively calibrated due to his illness. He needs time to stabilize."

Tremont's stormy grey gaze suddenly swung to Thea, and awareness forked through her like lightning. Her breath hitched; her pulse raced. After these months apart, why did he still have such an effect on her?

"You're welcome to stay as long as you like, my lord," Emma said from the settee. "Strathaven would love to catch up with you, wouldn't he?"

Thea's brother-in-law looked amused—a common expression when he was dealing with Em.

"You know best, my love," he drawled.

"I apologize for the inconvenience." Lines deepened around Tremont's mouth. "I should have known better than to take Frederick to the gardens. The fault is mine."

"'Tis no one's fault," Thea couldn't help but protest. "You wanted only to grant your son's birthday wish. Why should he not enjoy the same delights as any other child?"

"I've been advised repeatedly to keep him away from public settings. To protect him from the stresses induced by boisterous environments." Though his expression was stoic, torrents raged in his eyes. "As the doctor said, my decision triggered Frederick's spell."

"I said no such thing." Dr. Abernathy frowned.

"You said today's events unbalanced Frederick's system."

"I was referring to the attempted kidnapping, not your decision to take your son to the gardens." The physician paused. "I know some of my colleagues advocate quarantining patients with falling sickness, but I disagree. Strongly. In my opinion, seclusion oft does more harm than good—"

"It doesn't matter," Tremont said flatly. "If I'd kept Freddy safe in the country, none of this would have happened."

Thea wanted to point out that safety was its own prison. Having been an invalid herself, she knew the cruelty of being trapped in one's own bed, watching as life passed by. Seeing the hard set of Tremont's features, however, she decided not to waste her breath. She'd never been one to argue—in her family, she oft played the role of peacekeeper—and, in this situation, it wasn't her place. The marquess had made it abundantly clear months ago that he didn't want her in his life.

Then why do I want to know him? Why do I feel this connection between us?

From the start, she'd sensed the passion beneath his aloof exterior. His eyes held an enigma that called to her, even when she knew that pursuing him would only lead to another rejection. Her hands twisted together in her lap.

The physician sighed. "I'll take my leave, then. I'll be back to see the patient tomorrow."

"Thank you, sir." Tremont bowed. "I am in your debt."

After the Scotsman departed, Emma said, "What's done is done. We must focus on the next steps to take. Have you any inkling why the governess tried to abduct your son?"

"I have no idea, Your Grace. The most obvious motive, however, would be ransom." Tremont's gaze iced over. "Rest assured, I will do everything in my power to hunt her down."

"Kent and Associates could help," Emma said with predictable eagerness. "We specialize in difficult cases."

Last year, Em had gotten involved in the private enquiry firm owned by their brother Ambrose and his partners. It was during the course of her first investigation that she'd met Strathaven. After their marriage, the duke had supported her work as long as he accompanied her and the cases weren't too dangerous. Thea suspected that he'd chosen the path of least resistance. Trying to stop Emma from pursuing her desired goal was like jumping in front of a runaway carriage.

"Thank you, no. I have my own resources," Tremont said.

"Yes but finding criminals is our bread and butter—"

"I am in your debt as it is, Your Grace. For the accommodations as well as the protection of the footmen you've posted outside. On the morrow, I shall look into retaining my own guards."

"All the more reason to hire Kent and Associates," Emma persisted. "Strathaven's brother, Mr. McLeod, oversees the firm's security cases, and he was once part of the 95th Rifles—"

"It isn't *comme il faut* to badger one's guest, darling," Strathaven said mildly.

Thea had to agree with the duke. She knew that Em's perseverance would achieve nothing other than friction with Tremont.

"Why don't we check in on Olivia?" she suggested

before her sister could argue further. "We haven't seen the poppet for hours, and she's probably wondering where everyone's gone."

If there was anything Emma couldn't resist, it was the pull of her infant daughter.

"Oh, all right. I was only trying to help." Emma rose to her feet, Strathaven politely following suit. "Tremont, talk to the duke here if you won't take my word for it. My brother Ambrose and his partners are the best investigators in the business."

"I do not doubt it, your grace," Tremont said with a bow.

Thea followed her sister out. As she passed Tremont, she made the mistake of looking him straight in the eyes. The flash of yearning she saw—the white-hot of molten steel—made her stumble. He caught her, steadying her against him. His subtle scent pervaded her senses; he wore no perfume, smelling of clean soap and his own male musk, an ineffably arousing combination. His heat and sinewy strength melted her insides. Their gazes held.

Heart thumping, she said, "I—I beg your pardon."

"No need, Miss Kent. 'Tis my pleasure to be of assistance."

The raw edge to his voice heightened her giddiness.

"Coming, Thea?" Her sister's voice broke the moment.

Immediately, Tremont released her, the warmth vanishing like quicksilver from his eyes. Making her wonder if she'd imagined it—if those cool grey depths had ever held anything more than polite regard for her.

Don't mistake kindness for more. He's already rejected you once.

Dash it all… why?

Swallowing, she said, "Good afternoon, my lord."

She walked away before she did something else to regret.

Chapter Four

Half-past midnight, Thea gave up on trying to sleep. Donning a chintz wrapper over her night rail, she took a lamp and left her bedchamber, heading to the stairwell. There she paused, her gaze drawn down the flickering corridor that led to the wing of guest rooms. An image flashed in her head of Tremont in bed…

Awareness shivered over her. 'Twas this type of thinking that had led to her insomnia in the first place. Tremont's proximity was tinder to her senses, inflaming them and clouding her judgment. Thankfully, he'd taken supper on a tray in his son's room, and she hadn't seen him all evening.

As she descended the wide, curving steps, however, she couldn't help but wonder what kind of trouble Tremont was mired in. She sensed that there was more to the attempted kidnapping than he was letting on. What secrets was he harboring?

Don't meddle. His business doesn't concern you. He's made that clear enough.

In search of distraction, she entered the dimly lit library. The duke's collection of books occupied shelves spanning from the floor to the high ceiling; one could spend a lifetime exploring the literary hedgerows. Plush seating clustered around the hearth flickering at the center of the room, and, at the far end, tall bow windows overlooked the moonlit gardens. The scent of wood smoke and vellum stirred up memories of the cozy cottage where Thea had grown up. Papa had been the village schoolmaster and a dedicated scholar; although her family had known lean times, the one thing she and her siblings had never lacked for was books.

She recalled coming down with a head cold at age eleven, which had led to yet another relapse of her lungs. Weak and listless, she'd been forced to remain in bed; from the window, she'd watched with longing as her siblings worked and chattered away in the garden. How she'd wanted to share in the travails. To carry her own weight, be a full participant in the family.

When her mama had asked what the matter was, she'd blurted, "Why can't I be like Emma and the others? Why am I so weak?"

"Everyone has different strengths, dear," Mama had said. "You simply have to find yours."

That night, Papa had given Thea a leather volume, his blue eyes twinkling behind his spectacles. "The mind can explore even when the body cannot, my girl."

Thanks to the adventures of Captain Gulliver, Thea's convalescence had passed more quickly. Wistfully, she wished her parents were alive to see how the family was thriving—even her, the runt of the litter. She'd never scale a tree like Violet or manage a household with Emma's alacrity, but thanks to Dr. Abernathy's treatments she could now practice at the pianoforte for hours without tiring.

She had enough energy to pursue what she truly wanted: passion and love. The kind she'd read about in novels when she'd been too ill to leave her room. She wanted to experience those vital feelings for herself before it was too late—which meant that she had to get over Tremont. Her best years were already behind her, and she couldn't afford to waste any more time.

With a frustrated sigh, she browsed the shelves for a sensation novel and went to curl up by the fire. She saw a tea tray and an empty snifter of brandy on the coffee table in front of her. Odd. The staff was typically relentless in their efficiency.

"Good evening, Miss Kent."

Her head jerked up. Heart thudding, she found herself staring up at Tremont's austere face. He'd emerged noiselessly from the shelves.

"Goodness," she said, "you startled me. You move like a ghost."

"An unfortunate habit." His mouth lifted at the corners—to some inner source of amusement? "I apologize for treading too lightly."

"Fools rush in where The Angel fears to tread?"

His smile deepened at her quip, transforming him from his celestial namesake to a flesh and blood man. Indeed, in his shirtsleeves and sans cravat, he was even more disturbingly masculine than usual. His lean cheeks bore the shadow of bronze scruff, which accented the sensual line of his lips. Against the snowy linen of his shirt, his throat was strong and bronzed, the open collar offering a tantalizing glimpse of his muscled, hair-dusted chest...

"What are you doing up at this hour, Miss Kent?" he asked.

Hastily, she pulled her gaze up. "I couldn't sleep."

"Neither could I. All the excitement, I suppose."

She did not reply. Not because she couldn't think of

anything to say but because of the abundance of words suddenly cluttering her brain. *Did I imagine the attraction between us? Why did you leave without a word? Was my kiss that repugnant?* Yet she'd never been one to confront, and so she sat there, steeped in silent tension.

Logs crackled in the fireplace. Tremont ran a hand through his hair, a sign of his own unease perhaps. It *was* an improper situation; when he opened his mouth, she fully expected him to take his leave.

Instead, he gestured to the adjacent wingchair. "May I?"

She blinked. "If you like. It seems you were here first."

He settled his long, lean frame against the leather. With the ankle of one boot propped against the opposite knee, he regarded her. Master of the house, even if he was only a guest. Power, understated yet palpable, emanated from him. She wished she didn't find his natural air of command and self-assurance so very attractive.

"I am in your debt," he said, "for rescuing Frederick today."

"I did as anyone would have done in those circumstances."

"I disagree. Your actions showed uncommon courage, particularly given your constitution."

The qualification burst the bubble of pleasure that his praise had given rise to. An edge crept into her tone. "I'm not as delicate as I appear."

"I know few ladies, delicate or otherwise, who would have dared to intervene with a kidnapping."

Obviously, he was not well acquainted with the females of her family.

"How is Lord Frederick faring?" she said politely.

"He was sound asleep when I checked in on him. The doctor's potion seems to be working." Lines deepened around his mouth. "I can only hope today's trauma has no lasting effects."

"How often does Lord Frederick have falling spells?"

She asked without thinking: it was a natural question, after all. Yet Tremont's eyes turned steely, as hard as a blade. It was an impenetrable barrier, the kind only a foolish miss would try to overcome. She'd deluded herself once; she didn't fancy repeating the experience.

"I didn't mean to pry." She rose. "If you'll excuse me—"

He was on his feet in an instant, his hand circling her wrist. "No, please. Don't go."

The heat of his touch jolted her. His fingers were strong, callused against the sensitive underside of her wrist. Awareness spread from the point of contact, goose pimples tingling over her skin, the tips of her breasts stiffening, rising beneath her nightclothes. Warmth liquefied and pooled in her belly. Her heart thumping, she forced herself to meet his gaze.

"I don't enjoy games, my lord," she said.

"Games?"

"Mixed messages. Uncertainty." Her voice trembled. "Hot and cold leaves me lukewarm."

His hold on her tightened subtly. "I find you anything but lukewarm, Miss Kent."

"I'm not the problem." Frustration strung her nerves as tautly as piano strings. "*You* are."

Something dangerous flashed in his eyes. "Meaning?"

Like a catapult cut loose, suppressed emotions surged from her. "You toyed with my affections for months, and I never knew if you were courting me or merely passing the time. You were never clear with your intentions. If you didn't want me to kiss you, then you should have just said so instead of leaving without a word." Her breath surged in agitated waves. "And now you are back and your behavior is more confusing than ever. I don't know why you left. I have no idea what you want now—"

"I know what I want, Thea," he rasped. "What I have *always* wanted from you."

He yanked her against him. A shocking collision of softness against hardness. Before she could gather her wits, his mouth sealed over hers, his kiss stealing her breath.

She tasted exactly as he remembered.

Sweetness with a hint of spice. The addicting essence that had fueled his fantasies since he'd last sampled temptation in her arms.

Even through the haze of brandy and desire, he knew that this was foolish. Reckless in the extreme. His mentor had been killed, his son nearly kidnapped, the fog of mayhem and murder growing thicker with each passing moment. Even if it weren't for the dangers, he had no right to start this. No right to feel her mouth blossoming beneath his, her tongue a silken petal that made the dark needs in him quiver and burgeon.

Desire blazed through his veins like wildfire.

At the same time, Sylvia's trembling voice slashed through him. *I've given you an heir. I love you, and if you love me in return, you'll do as I ask. Spare my sensibilities, I beg of you.*

What the hell was he doing? He was no husband for a virginal miss. And she would not be able to give him what he needed... what he craved. He'd vowed never again to place himself in the torturous state of wanting someone who didn't want him back. Of loving someone who couldn't stand his touch.

He dragged his mouth away. Yet he couldn't tear his gaze from Thea's upturned face: her kiss-ripened lips, her golden hazel eyes both sultry and pure... and he registered that she didn't look afraid. No, she looked *desirous*.

Then her hands darted out. Gripped the back of his head.

Lord Almighty, she *tugged* on his hair to bring his mouth back to hers.

Her sweet, feminine aggression snapped his restraint. A growl rose in his throat, and then he was kissing her again. His hand knotted in the fine silk of her hair, holding her steady as he plundered her mouth. He drove his tongue into the honeyed cove. Her taste infused his senses, fed his hunger, the need to take more of her. When her hand slipped inside his collar, his vision blurred at the edges.

Before he knew it, he had her in his arms, on his lap on the settee. His kiss was hard, demanding, yet she didn't push him away. Her fingernails grazed gently against the rigid muscles of his chest, and the beast in him reared in startled delight. Beneath her soft bottom, his cock was harder than steel, throbbing with an intensity that bordered on pain. When she squirmed, he knew an agonizing pleasure.

The warning bells of his conscience faded to the roar of his blood. His hands roved with a marauder's touch, parting the panels of her robe to reveal the voluminous shift beneath. Swathed in snowy linen, she was the quintessence of femininity. He traced the elegant slope of her collarbone beneath the thin fabric, her heart fluttering like a hummingbird beneath his palm. When he cradled one perfect breast, his thumb whispering over its stiffened peak, her gasp heated his lips.

"I've dreamed of this," he rasped. "Of touching you."

Her thick golden lashes swept up. She whispered, "Do it again. Please."

The innocent longing in her eyes shook him to the core. He repeated the caress, strumming her nipple through the linen, arousal scorching him as her neck arched over his other arm. The graceful curve tempted him beyond bearing. He bent and nuzzled her throat. Lust became the scent of honeysuckle and soap, the sweep of his tongue over the softest, smoothest skin.

The breathless sounds she made maddened him. His kisses roved lower and lower, and then he was suckling her breast through the linen. His nostrils flared at the sight of her nipple jutting against the wetted barrier. Groaning, he drew her back into his mouth, swirling his tongue over the stiff crest. Blood pounded in his ears, in his turgid shaft. Darkness flooded his veins, and he grazed her with his teeth—

"Tremont. Wait."

Her panting words barely permeated his haze of lust.

"I can't—I can't breathe."

His head snapped up. Thea's face was pale, her chest moving up and down in quick, shallow waves. Her pupils were dilated—with fear?

His gut recoiled as if punched. "What's the matter?"

"My lungs... tight..."

Understanding dawned. "Tell me what to do," he said tersely.

"Tea," she said between gasped breaths. "Helps..."

He snatched the pot off the coffee table, sloshing some of the liquid into a cup. He held it to her lips. "Here. Drink slowly."

She obeyed, taking small sips. Gradually, her respiration steadied.

Pushing away the cup, she said, "I'm fine now."

In the firelight, he saw that some color had returned to her fine-boned features. Her bosom rose and fell in a regular cadence. He felt relief, followed by a swift undertow of anger. At himself.

"I apologize," he said stiffly. "I should never have—"

"It's not your fault. It just happens sometimes." Her cheeks were pink now. "Excitement can trigger an episode, and, well, there's been plenty of that today, hasn't there?"

Her attempt at levity did nothing to assuage his guilt.

"It's late," he said curtly. "If you're feeling better, you should go to bed."

She blinked. "I am not a child, Tremont."

Devil and damn, he was all too aware of that fact. Now that the danger had passed, he saw the peril of what had almost transpired. How despicably he'd behaved. He was disgusted at himself for trespassing on territory he'd known was forbidden.

One didn't kiss virgins without consequences. Consequences he was not prepared to face.

Thea was not only a virgin but one whose health was fragile. Though he'd barely touched her, he'd caused her to have an attack. What would happen if he unleashed his true, aberrant desires on her? The shock would probably kill her.

Shame twisted his gut. "No, you're a lady. And you shouldn't be alone with a man at midnight. At any time." He shoved a hand through his hair. "Damnit, this was a bloody mistake."

Silence stretched. She rose, forcing him to follow.

"A mistake." Her eyes blazed with golden fire. "That is what just happened between us?"

"The fault is mine entirely. I should not have—"

"Just tell me this, Tremont," she said in a trembling voice. "Do you or don't you want me?"

I want to strip you bare and fuck you until neither of us can move. I want to own your pleasure, possess you completely. I want my fingerprints on your bloody soul.

"I'm not right for you," he bit out.

"Why?" Her voice quivered.

"I wouldn't make a good husband." The understatement of the century, he thought darkly.

"But you were married before. Everyone says you were happy."

Because they don't know the truth.

"My wife was a paragon," he said in flat tones, "and I would not ask the same of anyone else. You're too delicate and innocent for someone like me. Find a husband who will give you what you deserve."

Pain rippled through the depths of her eyes. Her throat worked.

"From now on," she whispered, "stay away from me."

Turning, she ran from the room.

Chapter Five

Thea opened her eyes the next morning to a surge of energy.

Sometimes it happened this way: after an asthmatic attack, she slept deeply and woke refreshed. Or perhaps the interlude with Tremont had wiped the slate clean, relieving her of the burden of uncertainty and hope. She pushed aside the covers and the stab of longing.

The memory of pleasure and humiliation burned through her. She didn't know who she was more frustrated with: him or herself. For once, why couldn't her body function in a normal manner? Why did her dashed lungs have to seize at the most inopportune moment? Why didn't he at least give them a chance to discuss matters?

Because, apparently, I'm not a "paragon" like his first wife. I'm too delicate. Weak.

At least she had her answer now. The truth was what she'd expected. He was still in love with his dead wife, and Thea could never compete with a ghost, nor did she want to. And his excuse that it wasn't her, but him, that was the problem?

She might be a middling class spinster and recovering invalid, but she wasn't a fool.

Drawing a resolute breath, she tamped down the morass of emotions. As Mama had been wont to say, *No use crying over spilt milk*. Feeling sorry for oneself had never achieved anything; what she needed was to learn from the rejection and carry on.

Rising, she went to part the heavy brocade drapes. Sunshine dazzled her pupils, the blue sky stretching over the leafy square outside. Pastel parasols dotted the park's paths. Determined not to waste the morning's rare beauty, she set about performing her morning ablutions, which included the series of nasal and throat rinses prescribed by Dr. Abernathy. When she was done, she rang for her lady's maid to help her dress.

A half-hour later, garbed in a light pink walking dress with fashionably full sleeves, Thea made her first stop at Lord Frederick's room. Despite her jangled feelings toward Tremont, his son tugged at her heartstrings. She wanted to see how Frederick was faring after yesterday's harrowing episode, and she had a book she wished to give him.

Tucking the volume under her arm, she knocked softly on the door. "Good morning. It's Miss Kent. May I come in?"

At his affirmative, she entered and smiled at the boy sitting upright against a mound of pillows. Thankfully, he looked none too worse for the wear. He inclined his head in a formal nod, the effect somewhat spoiled by the fact that his golden hair was tousled, a cowlick springing up at the back of his head.

She approached the bed. "Good morning, Lord Frederick. Feeling better, I hope?"

"Yes, thank you. And I give you leave to call me Frederick. Or Freddy, if you prefer."

She hid a smile at his solemn manners and sat by the side

of his bed. "Then you must call me Dorothea or Thea, as my friends do."

"Miss Thea," he said gravely, "I am in your debt for your assistance yesterday."

"I was glad to lend a hand. Not that you needed it. You showed uncommon courage refusing to obey your governess' commands."

"I was obeying Papa. He told us to stay put." A nearly imperceptible breath escaped Freddy. "And I disappointed him."

"Disappointed? Why would you say that?" Thea said in surprise.

"He was angry," the boy mumbled to the sheets. "I could tell."

"If he was, I'm certain it wasn't at you."

She hesitated. It wasn't her place to translate Tremont's behavior to his own son. Actually, it was rather ironic that she should decipher his actions to another when she couldn't figure out what he wanted from her. Yet seeing him with his boy—the depth of emotion in his eyes—she had no doubt of his fatherly concern, even if he didn't express it in so many words.

"If not me, then who? I'm the one who caused the problem yesterday."

Goodness, misery was written all over the boy's little face.

"You didn't cause the problem. Your governess did." Brow furrowing, Thea asked, "Had she been acting strangely before this?"

Freddy shook his head. "She only started with us recently. My old governess received an inheritance out of the blue, you see, and left us with little warning. Mademoiselle Fournier applied for the post." His thin shoulders went back. "I'm sure her references were exemplary as Papa is always thorough."

"I'm sure," Thea murmured. "All the same, her behavior left something to be desired."

"One moment she was fine and the next she was insisting that we see the bears. I'm not even partial to bears." A bewildered wobble entered Freddy's voice, his façade of maturity slipping. "I tried telling her so, but she wouldn't listen."

"You certainly did your best, and the most important thing is that you're safe."

He raised his knees, his arms curling around them. "Do—do you think she'll come back?"

Thea thought it prudent to be honest. "I don't know. But if she does, we'll be prepared. There are footmen guarding the premises as we speak, and your father plans to hire on more men to protect you."

"This is my fault." Freddy's blue-grey eyes had a sudden glimmer. "Papa didn't want to take me to London, but I badgered him into it. He was right: I *am* too sickly to go anywhere. Now we can't leave because Dr. Abernathy says I'm too weak to be moved—"

"None of that is your fault. You did nothing wrong, dear."

"But I had a spell. In public." Moisture spiked the boy's eyelashes, and his chest surged on uneven breaths. "Now everyone will know that I'm an odd-oddity. I em-embarrassed Papa."

Thea's heart clenched with sudden anger. Had Tremont

hidden the boy in the country, kept him from Society, because he was ashamed of his beautiful son? Because he thought Freddy too imperfect, too *delicate* for the eyes of the world?

"You are not an oddity," she said firmly, "and you've nothing to be ashamed of. You can no more help your spells than I can mine."

Freddy blinked. "You have spells too?"

"I do. Not the same sort, precisely, but I've had a respiratory ailment since I was a little girl. My lungs are prone to spasms—and often at the most inopportune times." Flashing to the inopportune attack the night before, she felt her cheeks heat. "My episodes, like yours, can be unpredictable. That is nature's fault, not ours."

"Even if that were true, I'd give anything to be like other boys." Freddy's shoulders slumped. "To be able to ride with Papa and play sports and have friends. To be... normal."

You can do anything you put your heart to, Freddy, she thought fiercely. *Anything at all.*

Yet she understood from the boy's resigned expression that words would do little to alter his opinion of himself. After all, she struggled with her own self-doubts. In her own situation, what had helped most was being around her family. They'd brought normalcy into her confinement, entertaining her with conversation and games when she was too weak to leave her bed. Their loving, rambunctious presence had buoyed her through her darkest moments. Perhaps Freddy's spirits would be lifted by being with children his own age. And she knew just the companion for him.

On impulse, she said, "When you're up to it, would you

like to meet my nephew? Edward is around your age, and I think the two of you would rub along famously."

"I don't know," he said doubtfully. "The doctor said I mustn't leave the bed. And I haven't much experience with friends—"

"Friends?" Tremont's deep voice cut in.

Thea swung around in her chair. Once again, he'd approached as soundlessly as a shadow, and this morning she found the habit irritating. That and the fact that he was so dashed attractive. Why couldn't he be missing a few teeth or losing his hair? But, oh no, he had to look perfect. Like a sculpture, his angelic features were schooled to an impeccable sternness. His hair, the same tawny shade as his son's, lay neatly against his head. His eyes were as somber as the charcoal coat and buff trousers that fit like a glove over his lean muscularity.

"Good morning, Papa," Freddy said tentatively. "I'm feeling so much better today."

"I'm relieved to hear it. Now what is this about friends?"

The boy bit his lip, so Thea said, "That was my idea, my lord."

At Tremont's inquiring look, she repeated her proposal.

"That is not possible," he said. "My son is not well enough for a social call."

Freddy's face fell like a soufflé.

"We could consult Dr. Abernathy," she said swiftly. "I am sure he will approve of the distraction. In addition, I could make sure my nephew knows not to overtire Freddy. Edward is a quiet boy by nature and much prefers games like chess to Oranges and Lemons or Hide the Slipper."

At length, Tremont said, "I will consider it—if the

doctor approves."

"Thank you, Papa," Freddy said tremulously.

Tremont's gaze remained on hers, the grey depths turbulent, disconcertingly warm. Thea told herself that she was glad for the boy's sake alone. She didn't care what his father thought.

She rose to leave—and remembered the book in her hands. Holding out the leather volume, she said, "I almost forgot. I brought this for you."

"For me?" Freddy took it, his eyes as big as dinner plates.

"A belated birthday gift. My papa gave it to me when I was bedbound, and Captain Gulliver's adventures made the time pass more quickly." She smiled at the fervent way the boy opened the cover. "I hope you'll enjoy it as much as I have."

She almost made it to the door when Tremont blocked her path. She ignored the jolt that his gentle touch on her arm elicited. Lifting her chin, she said, "My lord?"

"I wanted to inquire after your health." His high cheekbones turned ruddy. "After, ahem, yesterday's events."

His solicitous tone made her grind her teeth.

"I'm no porcelain doll," she said tartly. "I'm perfectly well and stronger than I look."

"Did you know Miss Thea has an illness too? I would not have guessed," Freddy piped up from the bed. "She was fearless yesterday and didn't stand down."

"Miss Kent's vigor is indeed a thing of wonder," Tremont said.

Cheeks flushing, Thea told herself to ignore the husky edge to his voice, the hungry gleam in his eyes. Frustration filled her. Why was he toying with her, flirting with her when he'd made clear not once, but *twice*, that he didn't want her?

There was, she supposed, a freedom that came from knowing that one has been rejected. She had enough pride not to ask him to reconsider. If Tremont couldn't recognize the strength of her passion—couldn't see her for who she was—then she would find someone else who would.

She refused to languish away like some piece of forgotten fruit. No, she would search out someone who would return her love. Who would kiss her, touch her, desire her as a flesh and blood woman. Who would make her feel as alive as she did when she was in Tremont's arms...

Stop it. Don't let him play with your emotions like a cat with a ball of string.

"I have errands to attend to, my lord," she said coolly.

The steel curtain dropped over his gaze.

An instant later, he moved out of the way and let her go.

What a surprise.

Chapter Six

After ensuring that Freddy was settled, Gabriel descended the steps to the main floor.

What the devil are you doing flirting with her?

He had urgent business to take care of—and that didn't include dallying further with an innocent miss he couldn't have. Yet in Thea's presence his principles seemed to fade, the compulsion to be near her, to possess every glowing inch of her, making him act like a damned cad.

God help him, her passion had burned so brightly at their midnight encounter, illuminating his darkest fantasies. He'd stared at her lustrous hair, knotted in his fist, and the beast in him had hungered to use that silken skein like a *rein*. To flip her onto her knees, tear off her shift, and plow her until she screamed his name—until she let him do anything. Everything.

Instead, he'd hurt her. Caused her to have an attack.

He passed the landing, his shoulders rigid.

He knew better than to get involved with a woman who couldn't give him what he needed. And whom he couldn't please no matter how hard he tried. Memories of his marriage fell over him like a shadow.

Fresh from leaving the Quorum, he'd met Sylvia at a society ball, the first he'd attended as a newly minted marquess. After the life he'd led, he'd felt out of rhythm with the carefree dance of the *ton*, but from the moment he'd been introduced to Sylvia, her delicate brunette beauty and ladylike graces had anchored something inside him. Over the next few weeks, they'd fallen in love. He'd asked for and received her hand in marriage.

He'd been certain that he'd finally found what had been missing in his life. Sylvia had been like a shining torch: her lightness and beauty, her tranquil presence, had promised to chase away his shadows. For the first time, his future had seemed bright.

Their marital relations had come as a shock—to both of them. Having spent his adult life immersed in the murky world of espionage, he'd never been with a lady before. He hadn't realized how debauched his sexual preferences were. The whores he'd bedded prior to his marriage had never complained; in fact, they'd urged on his depraved demands the way a jockey does a mount.

But Sylvia was no trollop. She was his bride, an innocent. He'd made every effort to tame his lovemaking, to change his needs and see to her pleasure—but nothing changed.

She didn't enjoy his touch. Every time, she lay there, tense and stiff as a board, waiting for it to be over. When his hope began to fade and his visits to her bedchamber became less frequent, he could see the relief, the sense of reprieve in her blue eyes, and it was like throwing sand on the flames of his soul.

After she gave birth to their son, she'd finally told him what she wanted. For him to do what every considerate gentleman did: take a mistress. *Please, you can't expect me to see to all your needs. You want too much.* Tears had leaked down her beautiful face. *Isn't it enough that I've given you an heir and a peaceful home?*

Shame crept over him, thinking of that accusation. That he was too... needful. He knew that she'd meant not just sexually but emotionally as well. He cringed to think of how, in those early days of their marriage, he'd let down his guard for the first time in his life. He'd been so damned eager to put his dark past behind him, to start life over as a new man. The humiliating truth was that he'd been like a foolish puppy, annoying and pathetically eager for his new bride's attention.

A sinful, needful bastard. No wonder Sylvia had found him tiresome.

His mama's deathbed words had risen to haunt him. *'Tis the curse of the Tremont blood.* Her beautiful, pious face etched by years of suffering, she'd whispered, *All of you, beasts of excessive appetites. I've prayed for your soul, son. That you will not become a degenerate like your father.*

At age twelve, he hadn't understood her words. By the time he had, it'd been too late. His tainted blood had won out, the beast's hungry presence pulsing within him. Yet despite everything, his heart had belonged to his wife. He couldn't betray her, so he'd lived in limbo, wanting the woman he loved and knowing that she didn't want him back.

Hell had been staring at the closed door between their bedchambers night after night. Sitting at the breakfast table, making polite conversation with his dutiful marchioness who despised his touch. Pretending to be happy for her sake and their son's.

He would never put himself in that situation again. He knew what he was and the bitter futility of wanting what could never be his. In the unlikely event that he should remarry, he would base the match on things that might at least be attainable. Sexual compatibility. Honesty. There would be no talk of love or such other nonsense.

Even so, the first criterion made finding a suitable mate nigh impossible. How could one ascertain one's sexual fit with another prior to marriage, after all? The kind of well-bred female he desired for a wife was not the sort of filly one could take for a test ride and decide whether to buy. You didn't get to try out a potential bride to see if you could make each other happy in bed. And what were the chances that that could happen anyway? His own sexual tastes were dark, filthy, and likely to send any virgin into a dead faint.

So there it was. He wanted a gentle lady by his side, a submissive wanton in his marriage bed, and no complicating emotions between them. In other words, he wanted the moon, stars, and all the heavens in between.

You're a great bloody fool, aren't you? And a bastard. From now on, he had to stay away from Thea, for both their sakes. Last night had demonstrated that his desire for her was a madness in his blood. His loins stirred at the memory of how fervently she'd returned his kisses.

But Sylvia, too, had seemed to enjoy kisses during their courtship. It wasn't enough to predict a true sensual connection, which for him would involve more than kisses. He expelled a breath. *A hell of a lot more.*

"On your way out, Tremont?"

Reaching the foyer, he was greeted by his host—and was surprised to see the duke cradling an infant in the crook of his arm.

"This is my daughter Olivia," Strathaven said. "Poppet, say hello to our guest."

"The pleasure is mine, my lady," Gabriel said.

The babe stared up at him with big green eyes. Her tiny rosebud mouth opened, and a silvery line of spit dangled before landing on the arm of the duke's pristine jacket. A dark spot gathered and spread.

"She likes to drool over me. Gets it from her mama, I expect," Strathaven said complacently.

"You're quite reformed, my friend." In truth, Gabriel could scarcely credit the changes in the former rake.

"The influence of my women. They civilize me." The duke cocked his head. "Or, quite possibly, the reverse is true."

"You civilize them?"

"No, my wildness rubs off on them," the duke said in rueful tones. "Over breakfast, Her Grace continued deliberating the merits of her plan. She means to convince you to hire on her brother's firm."

Icicles prickled Gabriel's muscles. He couldn't afford to have investigators poking into his business. If his instincts were right—and they tended to be a reliable compass when it came to murder and mayhem—the attempted kidnapping had been triggered by his enquiry into Octavian's murder. In the past three weeks, he'd been tracking down information on his mentor's last mission, trying to discover what had gotten the other assassinated.

His intuition told him that he was getting closer to the killer, and the latter had struck out at Freddy as a warning. Rage simmered. *No one hurts what's mine.*

This was spy business, and civilians would only get in the way. He couldn't risk exposing his past activities or those of his former colleagues. Intelligence agents might not have many scruples, but, like thieves, they had their own code of honor. Respecting the anonymity of the game and its players was one of them.

"I appreciate her concern," he said, "but I must do as I see fit."

"I told her as much. Won't stop her from trying." Strathaven rocked his daughter, his expression serious. "Far be it for me to interfere, but as you know, I had troubles of my own last year. If it weren't for Kent and my brother William, I might not be standing here today. They have my highest recommendation—and not just because I happen to be related to both of them."

"I'll keep that in mind. Thank you, my friend, for everything." Gabriel hesitated. "Would you keep an eye on Frederick while I attend to some business?"

"Of course." The duke looked down at his sleeve and sighed. "As it appears I've been reduced into a napkin, I'd best return this sprite to her nurse and summon my valet."

The two exchanged farewells, and Gabriel called for his carriage. As the conveyance headed eastward into the city, his mind worked over the facts. Since Octavian's murder, he'd been retracing his mentor's steps, searching for clues. What had Octavian done or discovered that had gotten him killed?

Et tu, Brute.

Octavian's last act on this earth had been to communicate that he'd known his killer, an intimate from his innermost circle. The faces of Gabriel's fellow agents in the Quorum flashed through his head, as familiar as the passing streets.

Cicero. The statesman of the group, his silver tongue had

gotten them out of trouble more than once. One could never tell if Cicero was telling the truth or lying. The former agent had taken up his seat in the House of Lords and now occupied a place of importance in politics.

Tiberius. Aristotle had written that there was no great genius without a mixture of madness, and nowhere was this more apparent than with this particular colleague. Rumor had it that Tiberius' tenuous grip on sanity had slipped even further, thanks to the use of opium. According to Gabriel's recent reconnaissance, Tiberius had joined a radical group that supported tenets bordering on treason.

Pompeia. Beautiful and deadly, she was a lady now, moving in glittering circles that belied her true beginnings. She had a talent for playing any role, inventing any identity she pleased. Clever and cold, she'd abandoned the Quorum in a time of need, leaving them shorthanded and vulnerable during that last fateful mission.

Gabriel's back tautened at the thought of Normandy... and his final comrade. Marius had been the brilliant strategist and thinker; if there had been one person in the Quorum who could be trusted, it'd been Marius. The latter had been the true leader of the group, the glue that held them together when mistrust, jealousy, and self-gain threatened to pull them apart.

To Gabriel, Marius had been like an older brother—except, unlike his blood sibling, Marius hadn't beaten him to a pulp at every opportunity. Marius could outtalk Cicero, outwit Pompeia, outthink Tiberius, and occasionally outfight Gabriel. Yet he'd always employed his abilities for the greater good.

For an instant, Gabriel returned to the edge of the

chalky cliffs, sea air abrading his lungs, moonlight shattering over the dark waters below. His chest tightened on the name he'd shouted again and again that night to the raging waves. If only he hadn't lost control, if only he hadn't been hell-bent upon slaying every last enemy, if only he'd moved faster to save his friend…

But *if only* changed nothing. There was no going back, and Marius was not a suspect. Death had relieved him of that one burden at least.

Near Temple Bar the carriage slowed to the glut of people and vehicles outside. Rapping on the ceiling, Gabriel had his driver deposit him on the street, with instructions to reconvene in the same place in an hour's time. He set off on foot toward his destination; just before he passed beneath Sir Wren's arched gate, he glanced up. The Portland stone monument, crowned by statues of Tudor monarchs, appeared innocuous enough now, yet heads of traitors had once been displayed on spikes upon the arch's roof.

Britain showed no mercy for those who betrayed her. Even those who worked in clandestine service for her welfare walked a thin line. Octavian had liked to put it this way: *If you succeed, no one will ever know what you did. If you fail, treason may claim your head.*

His mentor had always had a way with motivation.

Gabriel continued along Fleet Street toward his destination. His taste for simple clothing was not purely aesthetic; somber colors and clean lines enabled him to blend into the surroundings. Beneath the low brim of his hat, he monitored the environs. Printing shops and booksellers flourished in this area, customers leaving the tidy establishments with paper-wrapped packages. He saw nothing to rouse his suspicion, yet one could never be too careful.

He felt the slight weight concealed in the inner pocket of his coat. He'd received the letter the day before he was to take Freddy to London. With prickling premonition, he'd read the enigmatic lines:

I am writing to carry out the instructions left by a mutual friend. Upon his death, he instructed that his subscription to my services be passed onto you, and as such I must inform you that I am now in possession of the rare item he ordered. My only regret is that I was not able to obtain it prior to my patron's passing.

The item awaits you at your earliest convenience. All that is required is the enclosed card of membership and the name given to you by our mutual friend.

Respectfully yours,
Theodore Cruiks

As Gabriel had been bound for Town the next day, he'd planned to kill two birds with one stone: grant his son's birthday wish and collect whatever item Octavian had left for him. The need to find the culprit behind his mentor's death had been rooted in a sense of duty and loyalty tarnished but not destroyed by bad blood and the passing years.

The attack on Frederick, however, had made things personal. Whoever had tried to hurt his boy was going to pay.

Gabriel arrived at the appointed address, a brick storefront with a sign that identified it as Cruiks Circulating Library. He entered the premises to the soft tinkle of a bell; several patrons glanced his way before returning to their perusal of magazines and newspapers. A clerk stood behind the counter assisting customers. A lady with a flower-trimmed bonnet handed over a white card; after a quick exchange, the clerk exited through a green curtain and re-emerged minutes later with a book in hand.

Pretending to browse, Gabriel waited until the clerk was free before approaching the counter.

"Good day, sir," the clerk said. "How may I be of service?"

Withdrawing the subscription card from his pocket, Gabriel laid it down upon the gleaming wood surface. The white card bore his name in elegant flourish.

"I believe you have an item of mine," he said.

The clerk bowed low. "Very good, my lord."

He made a trip through the curtain, returning moments later with a short fellow with wire-rimmed spectacles and brown hair greying at the temples.

"Welcome. I am Theodore Cruiks," the proprietor said. "I understand you are inquiring about a biography. Any particular one you are interested in?"

Gabriel recognized the underlying request.

"Yes, I'm reading up on the Romans." For the benefit of any eavesdroppers, he adopted the bored drawl of a gentleman with too much time on his hands. "Do you have anything on that old boy... the soldier who became an emperor? What *was* his name, by Jove?" He drummed his fingers. "Ah, yes. Trajan. That's it."

"Indeed. A moment, if you please." Cruiks went to the back of the store, returning with a plain brown volume which he placed on the counter. "This is a rare item, obtained through special auction from an anonymous source.

The cost was significant. There was no way to trace its origins."

Translation: a high-end fence. Cost: in the thousands of pounds. Seller unknown.

"Although it took many years to find, our mutual friend always believed it would resurface," Cruiks went on. "I regret that he did not live to see it. The reading room is to the left if you wish to examine the item."

Gabriel thanked the dealer. He found the reading area, empty save for a pair of ladies flirting with a dandy. They paid Gabriel no attention. He found a desk in the corner which put a wall against his back and a full view of the room before his eyes. Then he went to work opening the "book."

His fingers skimmed the edges of the pages—wood carved to give the appearance of paper. He'd dealt with more than a few of these in his time. Within seconds, he located the hidden mechanism in the spine. A soft click and the cover released.

Gabriel's heart thudded in recognition.

He ran a finger over the blade's distinctive pattern, flowing water captured in steel. He knew that his hand and the hilt would fit together like puzzle pieces. If he removed the two knives from the halter beneath his jacket and put it next to this one, the three would be a perfect, lethal match.

This was his missing dagger. From the set of six Octavian had given him years ago, before his first mission. *Damascus steel is a lost art, and this is a rare surviving set. Use it well, Trajan.* His mentor had spoken with a gruffness that might have been pride. *You're ready now to defend your country.*

Gabriel's mind whirred, buffering shock, distilling the facts. The last time he'd seen this knife was Normandy.

When he'd sent it flying into the Spectre's chest. Somehow this dagger had survived the explosion and gotten out of the inferno.

His mentor's voice played in his head. *Without proof, we don't know he's dead... he's survived blades, fire, explosions before... he's walked away from death more times than I can count...*

This was what Octavian had been after the whole time: the proof that now lay in front of Gabriel. The French spymaster who was ultimately responsible for the death of countless British officers and agents—including Marius—was still alive.

Et tu, Brute?

The chill settled deep in Gabriel's bones. Only one kind of betrayal would cut Octavian that deeply. It explained so much. How the Spectre had been able to get access to secrets. How the other had seemed to know British intelligence inside out. How the bastard had always been able to stay one step ahead.

The grim conclusion stared Gabriel in the face.

Not only did the Spectre live, he—or she—was a double agent.

One of the Quorum.

Chapter Seven

The next morning, Thea and her sisters arrived for an appointment with Madame Rousseau, a fashionable modiste. The shop on Bond Street had recently expanded its premises in order to accommodate its ever-growing legion of devotees. The spacious atelier, done up in fresh shades of spring green and pale bronze, was brimming with patrons rhapsodizing over Madame's exquisite creations. An assistant dressed in black led Thea and her sisters back into a large private dressing room.

Thea and Polly shared the cozy loveseat while Em occupied the cream velvet chaise longue. Not one for sitting still, Violet wandered around the room, inspecting things.

"*Madame* will be in shortly," the assistant said. "May I bring some tea while you wait?"

They all declined, except for Violet, who asked if a biscuit could be had as well.

"Didn't you have breakfast this morning?" Thea said after the assistant left to fetch the refreshments.

"That was ages ago." Violet sifted through bolts of fabric on the worktable. "I get hungry."

"I wonder why," Emma said in dry tones. Their middle sister had moved on, investigating a grid of colorful bobbins that hung on the wall. "Sitting still isn't a crime, you know."

Vi spun a spool on its hook. "But it feels like

punishment. It's so boring."

If there was anything Violet couldn't abide, it was boredom.

"You're about to have your final fitting for a masquerade," Em said in exasperation. "That should be exciting enough, even for you."

This Friday night, Emma, Thea, and Violet were to attend a costume party given by the Marquess and Marchioness of Blackwood. The annual event coincided with the winding down of the Season, and, with unattached ladies and gentlemen still searching for mates, it was guaranteed to be a crush.

For once, Thea was looking forward to a social event. She was determined to get her mind off Tremont and start afresh. Mama had always said that the important things in life were worth working for. If Thea wanted love and marriage, she couldn't let one disappointment stop her from pursuing her goal. She refused to rot away like forgotten fruit. No, she would dedicate herself to meeting possible candidates and, if necessary, learn to play the marriage mart game.

But why did the notion make her heart feel as heavy as lead? Tremont, for his part, seemed unaffected by what had passed between them. Actually, he'd been avoiding her; she hadn't seen him since yesterday morning in Freddy's room.

"I wish I could go." Polly's aquamarine eyes were wistful. "The costumes will be so beautiful."

"You'll get to go next year, dear. After you've had your come out," Emma said.

Now that their sister was a duchess, the Kent girls were being introduced at Court. It was a far cry from their previous lives, where the most esteemed personage they'd met had been the local mayor. Polly bit her lip, her gaze lowering to her hands. Guessing her youngest sister's fears, Thea set aside her own turmoil and gave the other's arm a reassuring squeeze.

"It wasn't all that bad, Polly," she said. "It's mostly standing around waiting. The actual presentation itself only takes a minute. And since Rosie will be making her curtsy too, you'll have her by your side."

"Rosie's not afraid of anything," Polly said with a relieved nod.

"Exactly. Between her exuberance and your gentle charm, the two of you will take Court by storm," Thea said.

Polly's slow smile transformed her little face into a thing of beauty.

The door opened, and the *modiste* entered. A slight French woman with dark coloring and pale skin, Madame Rousseau managed to look utterly chic in severe black. The pair of assistants behind her scurried over to the dressing screens and carefully hung up the dresses.

"*Bienvenue*, Your Grace. Misses Kent." Madame Rousseau's skirts rustled crisply as she curtsied. "I am most eager for you to view my finished creations."

"Thank you, Madame," Emma said. "We're grateful that you expedited our order."

"You are family to Mrs. Kent," the modiste said simply.

Marianne Kent, their sister-in-law, had been one of Madame Rousseau's first patrons, helping to launch the dressmaker's star. The two women were confidantes, and Marianne had brought the Kent sisters into their realm of high fashion and impeccable taste.

Which had been no small feat, Thea thought with amusement. Growing up in Chudleigh Crest, she and her siblings had not only been lacking in Town polish, they hadn't even known what polish *was*. For most of their life, they'd sewn their own clothes, many of which had been passed down, patched over, and remade.

Yet here they all were now, looking as shiny as buffed apples. The fact never ceased to amaze her. How far her family had come; she had so much to be grateful for.

"Who would like to go first?" Madame said.

Violet jumped at the opportunity. When she emerged from behind the dressing screen in a bright yellow gown, Thea smiled. Madame had made Violet into a daffodil. Exquisite leaves of emerald green decorated the bodice, matched by long satin gloves of the same shade. The bold, fresh colors perfectly captured Vi's vibrant spirit and the long, clean lines clung to her lithe figure, emphasizing her femininity.

"Lovely," Em approved. "You put me in mind of that poem by Mr. Wordsworth."

"*Ten thousand saw I at a glance, tossing their heads in a spritely dance,*" Thea quoted softly.

"*And then my heart with pleasure fills,*" Polly chimed in, "*and dances with the daffodils.*"

Grinning, Vi swung this way and that in front of the looking glass. "This daffodil definitely plans to waltz the night away."

"Now, Vi, you do know the rules about waltzing—" Em began.

Violet directed her tawny eyes at her hairline. "Not to worry, mother hen. 'Tis only a figure of speech."

Emma exchanged looks with Thea, who shared the other's concern. As a young girl, Vi's high-spirited nature had landed her into plenty of scrapes; luckily, most had proved harmless. Now that she was older, however, and circulating in London's higher circles, her impulsiveness could lead to more damaging consequences.

"Even so, you must have a care, Vi," Thea said. "You know how sticklers can be."

"If sticklers are anything like *sisters*, I'll be in suds for certain." Violet snorted. "Don't worry, I'll be so proper and demure they'll mistake me for my shrinking namesake."

She trotted off to change, snatching a biscuit along the way.

"Who would like to go next?" Madame Rousseau waved at the second dressing screen.

Emma volunteered, and when she returned Thea and Polly applauded her appearance. The modiste had transformed their eldest sister into a sleek feline with luxurious ermine trimming the bodice and hem of her dove grey gown. The cleverly designed headpiece gave the appearance of two small pointed ears protruding from Emma's dark curls.

"How adorable you look," Thea said.

"It was Strathaven's idea." Emma blushed. "But never mind me. It's your turn, Thea."

Thea took her turn behind the dressing screen. Madame helped her to don her outfit, and when they were finished, she regarded the image in the looking glass. She'd seen the unfinished costume before at previous fittings and approved the elegant design.

Yet looking at herself now, emotion hit her like a wave.

A tear leaked and slipped down her cheek.

"*Alors*, what is this?" the modiste said, frowning. "You do not like the ensemble, *mademoiselle*?"

"N-no. It's l-lovely."

In vain, Thea tried to control the quiver in her voice. But it was as if a hidden dam had broken inside her and the tide of emotions she'd been holding back came rushing to the fore. She thought of her sisters so vivid and hale in their costumes, and despair filled her. *Why can't I be like them?* Her own feathery white image blurred.

Instead, I'm a stupid swan. Pallid and useless. An ornamental creature.

"Ah, *je comprends*. The dress, it is not how you envision yourself, Miss Kent?"

Looking into the Frenchwoman's shrewd eyes, Thea said helplessly, "I-I'm sorry. I don't know what's come over me. You've done a splendid job, and I am ever so grateful—"

The modiste cut her off with a hand. "We must begin anew."

"Oh no," Thea said, horrified, "there's nothing wrong—"

"If it is not right, then it is wrong," Madame Rousseau said simply.

"Thea,"—Em's voice drifted from the other side—"is everything all right? Shall I come and help you?"

Why do I always need help? Why can't I be strong? Why can't I even kiss a man without my lungs giving out on me?

One after another, thoughts tumbled through Thea's head. Heat pushed behind her eyes.

The modiste murmured, "I'll be right back."

Numbly, Thea heard the proprietress saying to Emma

and the others that Thea's fitting required more time. She instructed her assistants to show the Kents some accessories in the main shop.

"Are you certain you don't need me?" Emma called out.

"Don't worry about me," Thea managed. "I'll be right out."

The doors closed behind the others, and Madame Rousseau returned.

"Thank you, Madame." Embarrassed, Thea said, "I'm usually not a watering pot."

"In my profession, tears are as common as pins. And like pins, they are useful if one knows what to do with them." The modiste passed Thea a handkerchief, her manner matter-of-fact. "In your case, *mademoiselle*, tears may yet lead us to the truth."

"The truth is that I'm being an idiot." Thea dabbed at her eyes. "This dress is lovely. It will suffice, truly—"

"In my shop, sufficient is not a goal one aims for. Do you wish to tell me what troubles you, Miss Kent? A modiste cannot properly dress a client without understanding her. And of my discretion, you may be assured."

"That is very kind of you." Blowing into the linen, Thea wondered why it was easier to talk to the dressmaker than to her own sisters. Perhaps it was the lack of judgement, the no-nonsense objectivity she sensed in the other. She exhaled a shaky breath. "There is... a gentleman."

"Ah, *chérie*, there almost always is."

"He thinks I'm fragile and weak," she blurted.

Madame shrugged. An infinitely Gallic gesture. "Gentlemen, they like to believe we are the weaker sex, *non*?"

"I thought we had an attraction." Releasing a breath, she

said haltingly, "He's a widower, you see, and his departed wife was a paragon. Everything a lady ought to be. I'll never be as perfect as she was."

"No two gowns can ever be alike," the modiste said philosophically. "In fashion, as in life, the goal must be to accentuate one's unique gifts rather than emulate another's. That, *ma petite*, is true art."

Her chest clenched. "But what if one doesn't have any gifts?"

Madame arched a dark brow. "Then I would say begin with that belief."

"Pardon?"

"If you see yourself as lacking, then the world will see what you see."

Did she see herself as lacking? Was that the problem?

"I *want* to be strong," she whispered.

"*Alors*, aspiration is the first step to success." A glint in her eye, the modiste circled Thea slowly. "Go on. What else do you wish for?"

"I don't want to be held back by my illness. I don't want to be frail, to miss out on life while it happens around me." Her voice grew steadier as she faced herself in the mirror. She saw a slender woman clad in ashen feathers, colorless cloth, and her hands balled. "I want to fall in love and have a family of my own."

Madame Rousseau tapped a finger against her chin. "And?"

"I want to know passion," Thea said in a rush.

To feel the way I do when I'm in Tremont's arms. Dash it all, why can't I forget him?

"Ah, I begin to understand. It is not the calm, serene

waters you seek but a new adventure. You wish to feel alive, to be vibrant... aflame with the *joie de vivre*." The artiste's eyes blazed. "*Mais oui.* I know *exactement* the costume for you."

"You do?"

"Yes. I shall make you the dress of your dreams, but only you can make your dreams become a reality." The modiste's gaze seemed to see straight through her. "If you wish others to see you as strong, *you* must first believe that you are so."

"I will try," she said earnestly.

"Then I will promise you this: when you wear my creation two days hence, the world shall see you as you were meant to be seen. As for the feat of transforming yourself truly into this vision, *chérie*,"—the modiste lifted her brows—"that will be up to you."

Chapter Eight

Madame Rousseau's words lingered with Thea that day and the next. Whenever she tried to guess what kind of costume the other was designing for her, she felt a charge of excitement and hope. Whatever form the creation took, she vowed that she would do it justice. For the modiste's words had resonated with a truth she hadn't considered before.

It wasn't enough to want others to believe that she was strong—*she* had to believe it too. Her first task, then, was to prove the depth of her resolve to herself… and there was no better place than at the Blackwood masquerade.

Tomorrow night, she wouldn't sit on the fringes of the ballroom like a frail invalid or dejected spinster. She wouldn't just watch the world go by as the old Thea used to do. No, her new self would dance and flirt and make new acquaintances. She would behave like any woman in search of a spouse. She would work toward finding the love she wanted.

Her plans for the ball took a backseat, however, when Freddy developed a megrim that afternoon. As worried as she was for the boy, she was also surprised and touched when he asked for her personally. She kept him company, placing cool towels on his forehead and distracting him with Captain Gulliver's exciting adventures with the Lilliputians until Dr. Abernathy arrived. During the physician's examination,

Freddy's small hand clung to hers, and she didn't let go until after the laudanum had taken effect and he drifted into sleep.

"How is my son, Dr. Abernathy?"

Tremont had remained at the foot of the bed while the doctor treated Freddy. Despite his stoic demeanor, Thea saw his tight grip on the bedpost. The wags of the *ton* oft made note of his lack of emotion, but Thea suspected there was a surfeit, rather than lack, where he was concerned. From her observations, he was a man who guarded his feelings and secrets tightly.

His feelings are none of your business. You've moved on, remember?

Right. Her gaze returned to Freddy's face, and a *frisson* of anxiety coursed through her. His freckles stood out in stark relief against the pallor of his cheeks. She brushed a damp lock of hair off his forehead.

"The willow bark will help with the pain," Dr. Abernathy said. "Let's leave him to his rest and talk outside."

The three of them removed to the sitting room. Thea and Dr. Abernathy sat near the hearth while Tremont remained standing, his arm propped on the mantel next to a vase filled with damask roses. With any other gentleman, the posture would be indolent. Yet Thea noted the taut ridges of muscle straining against his tailored waistcoat and trousers. The morning light cast a metallic sheen over his hair and illuminated the sculpted angles of his face.

If Tremont was an angel, it certainly wasn't the cherubic sort that lounged about on clouds. Or the ones whose voices lifted in heavenly song. No, he was the kind that carried a sword and avenged trespasses.

"Well?" His tone held polite menace.

"Your son has suffered a mild aftershock," the physician said without preamble. "His complaint of a headache is not uncommon after a prolonged spell such as the one he suffered at the gardens. Has he complained of such symptoms before?"

"No."

"The situation was extraordinary, so I'm not surprised it overset his nerves. I wouldn't worry about it. He should be right as rain by the morrow."

While Tremont remained still, Thea sensed some of the tension leaving him.

Dr. Abernathy stroked his sideburns. "If I may, I'd like to get a further history of your son's ailment. How old was he when the spells began?"

"Less than a year old," Tremont said curtly.

A clamp closed around Thea's heart. *Poor little fellow.*

"And what is the frequency of the seizures?"

"It waxes and wanes. Four to twelve episodes a month."

"Have you tried any treatments?" the physician asked.

Tremont's laugh held no humor. "We have tried all the treatments, sir. My late wife had great faith in your profession. Freddy has been thoroughly poked and prodded and has tried every herb, root, and snake oil concoction under the sun. When one quack proposed to drill a hole in his skull to release the unnatural forces, I put my foot down."

Thea's fingernails bit into her palm. With her own ailment, she knew that sometimes the so-called cure could be worse than the cause, and it pained her to think of Freddy undergoing so much and since such a tender age. The lump in her throat grew, as did her admiration for the lad: how strong he was to survive such ordeals.

"As a man of science, I can offer no excuse for such ignorance," Dr. Abernathy said, his burr deepening with disgust. "There are charlatans in every profession, and unfortunately mine is no different. One must not throw the baby out with the bathwater, however. There are newer, scientific treatments being studied that may—"

"My wife consulted the most prominent physicians in London. They were unanimous in prescribing bed rest and a quiet environment to calm Frederick's nerves."

"I don't wish to disagree with my learned colleagues, my lord, yet in my own practice I have seen that cloistering a patient can have adverse effects. Especially for children." Dr. Abernathy leaned forward, his elbows on his knees, expression earnest. "As such, I have been researching experimental treatments including—"

"My son's health is not an experiment." Tremont's words hovered over the room as ominously as thunderclouds. "Had I not taken Freddy on this trip, none of this would have happened. As soon as he has recovered, I will return him to my estate and see that he suffers no further disturbances."

I'd give anything to be like other boys. Freddy's forlorn voice wound like a vine around Thea's heart, squeezing. *To be… normal.*

How well she understood.

"He has spells there, too," she said quietly.

Tremont turned to her. "I beg your pardon?"

She held herself steady in the wake of his stormy gaze, the tempest of frustration and anguish that he was clearly struggling to hold in check. Strangely, his potent emotions didn't intimidate her. The knowledge that he didn't want her—that she had nothing to lose in terms of his esteem—allowed her to speak with new freedom.

"Just now you said that Freddy has two to six falling spells even at your estate," she pointed out. "What have you to lose by trying Dr. Abernathy's treatment?"

"I'll not raise Frederick's hopes needlessly," Tremont said, his tone curt. "He's been through enough."

"Do you think isolation isn't a trial in itself?" Memories of being bedridden made her hands curl in her lap. And *she* hadn't been shut away. Even when she'd been too weak to leave the room, her siblings had come to her, amused her with stories and games. "Do you know that your son longs to have friends, to have someone to play with? He wants to be normal. He *needs* to be."

"Well, he isn't. He'll never be," Tremont said.

"Perhaps if you didn't lock him away on your estate, he might have a more normal life. He's stronger than you think. And he wants your approval more than anything."

"What makes you think he doesn't have it, Miss Kent?"

The hostility in Tremont's voice goaded her to honesty. "He's afraid of disappointing you, my lord. Of embarrassing you in public with his illness. All he wants is to be able to ride and play sports with you, to do the things other boys do with their papas."

Lightning flashed in his eyes. "Three days has made you an expert on my son?"

"No. Of course not. I didn't mean—"

"My wife did everything possible to cure Frederick. On her deathbed, Sylvia's only wish was that I continue to keep him safe away from the dangers of the world."

"He needs to be part of the world—not shut out from

it," Thea insisted.

"You are gainsaying the wishes of his own mama?"

He said it as if she'd contradicted the teachings of a saint.

Wrangling back impatience, she said, "I do not mean to step on toes; I am merely presenting an alternate point of view. Your wife might have been a paragon, my lord, but *I* have been an invalid." Whoever thought *that* would be a source of confidence. "Trust me when I say I have intimate knowledge of what it is like to live with a condition beyond one's control."

"That doesn't give you the right to interfere," he said in arctic tones.

She teetered on a see-saw of embarrassment and anger. Why did the dashed man keep her off balance and disorder her feelings so? Before Tremont, she'd counted herself patient and even-tempered. She didn't quarrel or provoke or invite conflict. Amongst her siblings, she often played the intermediary, grounded by her natural equanimity.

At the moment, however, her greatest desire was to pluck the vase from the mantel and smash it over Tremont's head. She allowed herself to enjoy the image of him sopping wet, crowned by wilted flowers. Then she rose.

"If Freddy asks for me when he awakens, send word and I will return to keep him company." She gave a cool nod. "Good day, sirs."

That evening, supper was a strained affair.

Given his earlier behavior, Gabriel had expected no less. A part of him had wanted to avoid going down altogether.

Thus far, however, he'd had his meals on a tray with his son and hadn't yet dined with his hosts. Abernathy had been right about the headache passing, thank God, and Freddy had awoken after his afternoon nap feeling much recovered. Good manners dictated that Gabriel should make an appearance at the supper table.

As only the Strathavens, Thea, and he were dining, the long mahogany table had been set cozily at one end.

"No sense in shouting down the table," the duchess said pragmatically.

The duke occupied the end chair, with the duchess to his right and Thea to his left. Gabriel had been placed on Thea's other side. Tonight she looked more like a faerie tale princess than ever in an off-the-shoulder gown of light blue silk. As he cut into his filet of beef, he tried not to notice how the glow of the candelabra slid over her décolletage, kissing smooth, bare skin and creating an intriguing play of shadows. He picked up her sweet, subtle scent the way a bloodhound lifts it nose and scents a fox.

Beneath the table, something else lifted as well.

His lack of control was appalling. Not even the cold shoulder she presented him could dampen his physical reaction to her nearness. On the surface, she was all that was polite, yet the tension between them was downright Siberian and would have frozen a lesser man.

He deserved the chilly reception. Hell, he might be angrier at himself than she was.

You're one stupid bastard. Devil take it, why had he lashed out at her? She'd only wanted to help Freddy. He sliced the beef with a vicious stroke, letting out some of his pent-up frustration, the helplessness of not being able to aid his own son.

Sylvia had consulted quack after quack in search for the cure. He'd stood by as physicians peddled their diagnoses like tinkers with a barrow of second-rate goods. Some termed Freddy's falling sickness a "mental defect"; others cautioned against the contagiousness of the condition—ridiculous when no one around Freddy had developed a similar affliction. When one leech had gone so far as to declare the illness "the work of dark spirits," Gabriel had finally intervened and ejected the charlatan from his property.

He supposed he'd developed a prejudice against the medical profession. As physicians went, he could find no fault with Abernathy, who seemed learned and had more common sense than most. But Gabriel had no intention of subjecting Freddy to further indignities. The cycle of hope and disappointment was too much for a child to bear. Or even an adult.

He must be kept away from others. Sylvia's decision had been weighted with finality. *For his own good and for ours.*

He fought back a sudden, unexamined swell of emotion. He told himself that Sylvia had wanted what was best—for all of them. Her well-bred nature made it difficult to acknowledge imperfections, and when they couldn't be fixed, she avoided them or swept them under the carpet.

Out of sight, out of mind. Closed doors and brief, scheduled visits with one's child. That philosophy had worked well for her.

Guilt gnawed at him. He had no cause to think ill of Sylvia, who'd only wanted peace and harmony, a civilized existence for all of them. His grip tightening on his fork, he blamed his reaction on stress. After all, a murderous spy was on the loose—one who was most likely a former associate of Gabriel's, a treacherous double agent. His son had nearly been kidnapped and suffered another falling spell. And the woman who starred in his nightly fantasies, whose delicate sensuality had been driving him mad for months, was acting as if he didn't exist.

A man could only take so much. He couldn't have Thea for a lover, but he found the idea of them being enemies repugnant. Clearing his throat, he fished for an opening.

"Er, how do you find the asparagus, Miss Kent?" he said.

Her head turned slightly in his direction. Her hair had been simply and elegantly dressed, the chandelier's glow burnishing her honey brown curls. A pair of tortoiseshell combs held those luxuriant tresses in place, and, for an instant, he allowed himself to imagine plucking out those impediments and feeling the silken weight sliding over his palms.

That's a husband's privilege, you bastard—one you'll never know.

Her brows raised. "You care to have my opinion, my lord?"

He winced. He deserved that.

"You must know I do," he muttered. "If I have given you reason to doubt that, then I must ask your forgiveness."

She said nothing, lifting a bite-sized chunk of asparagus to her mouth. The green spear slid smoothly between her coral lips, releasing another debauched image: of her on her knees, taking him that way. Of her eyes, sultry gold, looking up at him as her mouth sweetly received his throbbing length…

A shudder travelled through him. He reached for his wine glass.

She finished chewing. "The truth is, I find it rather hard to swallow."

He choked on his beverage. "Er, I beg your pardon?"

"I don't like to waste time and effort on something that ought to be simple," she said calmly. "Food, like company, ought to be easy and comforting rather than a challenge to enjoy."

Touché. Unfortunately, he was still preoccupied by the outrageously erotic notion of her swallowing what he yearned to give her. Of her willingly submitting to one of his favorite pleasures. *God's teeth.* His napkin tented in his lap; if he got any more aroused, he'd be butting the underside of the table.

"Is something wrong with the asparagus?" Looking puzzled, the duchess sampled some from her plate.

"Don't worry, darling. It tastes fine to me. Then again," Strathaven said, "there's no accounting for a person's appetite. Or lack thereof."

The duke flicked an amused glance between Gabriel and Miss Kent.

At least *someone* was enjoying himself, Gabriel thought irritably.

"Take Tremont, for instance," his host went on. "He's abstemious by nature."

"Perhaps he just doesn't like asparagus." Turning to him, Her Grace said, "Would you care for a different vegetable? I'm sure Cook could whip something up."

"Thank you, Duchess, but I like asparagus," he said quietly. "I like it very much indeed."

Thea's thick gold-tipped lashes lifted. She cast a pointed glance at his plate. "If that is the case, then why have you left it untouched?"

Because my demands would scare you witless. I want to chain you to my bed, have my way with you day and night. And I want you to love it.

"Just because one likes a thing doesn't mean one should have it," he said.

Her shoulders stiffened in their frame of blue silk.

"It's just asparagus," the duchess said, clearly befuddled. "How much harm can come from indulging in a vegetable, for goodness' sake?"

Strathaven, the bastard, looked like he was trying not to laugh. Picking up his wife's hand, he kissed the knuckles. "Have I told you lately how much I adore you?"

This distracted the duchess and gave Gabriel the opportunity to say in an undertone, "May I ask for your forgiveness? I apologize for my churlish behavior earlier. I know you meant well—"

"Frederick is your son, my lord, and I'm sure you know best." Thea dissected a potato into neat pieces. Perhaps as she'd like to do to him. "I won't volunteer my opinion in the future."

But he wanted her opinion. Wanted much more...

You can't bloody have her. Pull it together, man.

Jaw taut, he said, "Whatever you believe, Miss Kent, I do wish for us to be friends."

The hurt that shimmered in her hazel eyes cut him more deeply than her anger had. "I've come to the conclusion that friendship is not possible between us."

"Why not? You must know that I admire you." It was

paramount to him that, if naught else, she knew that much. "The fault lies entirely with me."

"It's not me, it's you?" she scoffed.

"It's the truth. Miss Kent—Thea," he said in a low voice, "I could not admire you more."

A pulse fluttered at her throat. "It doesn't matter. What's done is done, and we must move forward." Her lips fixed in a bright smile that told him they were under scrutiny again. "With the end of the Season fast approaching, I am certain you are as busy as I am."

He did have plenty to do, although not the sort of social obligations she was referring to. He had three old colleagues to investigate and a turncoat to identify. Then he had to eliminate the problem—and avenge the deaths of Octavian, Marius, and all the other good men who'd been betrayed by the double agent who'd hidden himself—or herself—behind the guise of the Spectre.

Cicero, Pompeia, and Tiberius were all currently in London, which made Gabriel's task easier. Direct confrontation would only put them on guard, so he'd called upon old contacts, setting eyes and ears on all three. He didn't expect much to come out of the surveillance, however. From past experience, he knew that the former agents were too careful and cunning to reveal any misdeeds. Thus, he also planned to perform a clandestine search of his ex-comrades' private domains. To find solid proof that one of them was the Spectre.

"Speaking of busy, I do hope your costume arrives in time, Thea," the duchess said.

"Costume?" Gabriel said.

"The Blackwood's annual masquerade. It's tomorrow

night," Strathaven said. "Join us, if you'd like."

It was, Gabriel thought grimly, the rare occasion when Fate was smiling upon him. A costume ball would make his plan so much simpler: he could walk into his enemy's territory through the bloody front door. Conveniently disguised, he could carry out his covert plans during a public affair. The perfect opportunity.

"I have a few appointments, but I might drop by later," he said.

"Excellent. You can help with escorting duties," Strathaven said. "I'll be outnumbered by the ladies."

"As if you've ever complained about that," the duchess teased. Turning to her sister, she said, "What last minute changes did Madame Rousseau have to make? I can't imagine there were many. The swan ensemble was perfect for you."

The vision unfurled in Gabriel's head: Thea, resplendent in a pure white gown trimmed with feathers. She was every bit a swan. Graceful, delicate, so very lovely.

"We came up with a few new ideas. You'll see tomorrow," she said.

Small talk continued, and a wall of politeness once again descended between the two of them. After supper, the duchess suggested that her sister play a few tunes on the pianoforte. Gabriel sat there, riveted by Thea's lithe lines, her elegant movements. Her music wove a spell over his senses, each note penetrating deeper and deeper through the layers he'd built, excavating artifacts of shame and desire...

The years lying alone in his bed, the closed door of his marriage. The agony of unreciprocated desire, the need that no amount of brandy or frigging could ease. The urge bled into the shadowy rooms of a club, the discreet sanctuary where his darkest pleasures could be unleashed. *I've been a naughty slave, milord. Punish me. Ram me harder, fuck me...*

As Miss Kent's slender hands stroked the keys to a crescendo, the dark yearning in him strained, yanking on its tether. He knew it would need to be satisfied soon, and yet the idea of paying a visit to Corbett's didn't seem like much of a solution. Since becoming a widower, he'd gone to the exclusive club on occasion, but he knew from experience that any relief he obtained would be fleeting. There, he would find release but no peace. The depraved games were a mockery of what he truly wanted; in the end, fucking would relieve his lust but leave him cold and empty. The trading of one beast for another.

At the end of the performance, Strathaven suggested withdrawing for port and cigars, and Gabriel accepted with relief. Fleeing was not the most honorable way of dealing with trouble, but at times it was the most prudent. Miss Kent was an unholy temptation. If he wasn't careful, his dark desires would break free—and lead to consequences that he wasn't prepared to face.

Chapter Nine

"They weren't talking about the asparagus, were they?" Emma said as her husband entered her bedchamber from the adjoining door.

Alaric came to the vanity where she was sitting, finishing her evening ablutions. Looking sinfully virile in his black silk robe, he bent and kissed her cheek, his familiar woodsy scent sending a pleasant shiver up her spine. Over a year of marriage and it still amazed her that this gorgeous, dark-haired devil was all hers.

He took the silver brush from her hands. In the looking glass, his pale green eyes were lit with amusement. "I'm afraid the discussion had nothing to do with vegetables, my love."

"Dash it all, I *knew* it." Subtlety had never been her strong point, yet even she had sensed the smoldering subtext. "Why can't Tremont leave Thea alone?"

"Are you certain she wishes to be left alone?"

"After the way he deserted her earlier this Season, I should hope so," she said indignantly.

"I thought nothing happened between them?"

"According to Thea—but she can be as closed as a clam when she wants to be." Worry gnawed at Emma as she thought of her gentle, sweet sister being subjected to Tremont's whims. *Again.* "Something's afoot. He was apologizing to her—what for, I wonder?"

Alaric ran the brush through her hair, and in spite of her agitation, her neck arched in pleasure. Her husband's touch was magical. His firm yet gentle strokes soothed and set off tingles at the same time.

"You mustn't meddle, darling," he said mildly. "Neither Tremont or your sister is likely to thank you for it."

Emma hated that he had a point. She didn't particularly care what Tremont thought, but the last thing she wanted was to upset Thea. That was the dashed difficult thing about family: even when one knew best, sometimes one had to refrain from interfering.

"I don't know what Thea sees in Tremont anyway. They don't suit. She's gentle and lovely, and he's a cold fish." She huffed out a breath. "If he wasn't dealing with an attempted kidnapping and an ill child, I'd give him a piece of my mind for how he has treated her."

"You're being very charitable, pet," her husband said drolly. "As it happens, I agree with you on one thing: Tremont has enough on his plate as it is."

"Hmm. There's more going on than meets the eye. Why is he so adamant about refusing the help of Kent and Associates? Suspicious, if you ask me." Emma narrowed her eyes. "He's hiding something. And I don't believe for a second that the governess was only after money."

"Your feminine intuition at work?"

"My sense of *logic*. If the governess intended to ransom a child, why pick Tremont's? His fortune may be improving, but he's no Croesus. There are plenty of richer, more powerful men—you, for instance."

Alaric's lips twitched. "Tremont's ears are probably

burning. But you do have a point." He paused mid-stroke. "Maybe the governess simply assumed Tremont is plump in the pocket."

"A woman like that isn't going to assume anything. If I were to go to the trouble of kidnapping a child, I'd make certain it was worth my while."

"What a mercenary thing you are. Is that why you married me?"

"I don't give a fig about your money, and you know it. Stop fishing for compliments," she said, "and tell me what you and Tremont talked about over port."

Alaric's eyes gleamed at hers in the mirror. "What is discussed in the study stays in the study. First rule of gentlemen."

"Surely wives are exempt from that rule," she protested.

"Wives are the *reason* for that rule. Sorry, love, my lips are sealed."

She gave him an exasperated look. "You won't tell me anything?"

He set the brush down on the vanity with undue care. "A lot of time has passed since our Oxford days, and we were cronies for only a short time before he left his studies to work for some wealthy relative abroad. I don't know what he was up to in all those intervening years, but whatever it was, it changed him. I suspect he has more than a few skeletons rattling in his closet." Alaric's lips twisted. "Takes one to know one, I suppose."

Not wanting her husband to linger in the darkness of his own past, Emma placed her hand atop his. "You rid yourself of your skeletons."

"With your help, yes." He lifted her hand to his lips.

The warm caress made her nipples bud and jut against her robe. Her breasts were extra sensitive these days. Although most ladies of the *ton* retained a wet nurse for their offspring, the women in her family had always nursed their own infants, and she discovered that she enjoyed that special connection with Olivia. Nursing her daughter kept her breasts full and tender, however, and she felt a slight dampening at the tips.

Flushing, she pulled her wrapper more securely around herself. "Do you think any of Tremont's skeletons might be related to his first marriage?"

"I can't say for certain as he and I hadn't reconnected back then. But rumor has it that his marchioness was above reproach in her behavior and he was devoted to her. Mayhap he still is."

"Don't tell me you believe *The Angel* business." Emma couldn't help but roll her eyes.

"You do not find the moniker fitting?"

"No one is that much of a paragon. Besides, the *ton* is prone to exaggeration and inaccuracy. Look at how they labeled you *The Devil Duke*," she said indignantly, "when you're the most honorable, loyal, and loving man I've ever met."

"I'm glad you think so," he murmured.

"It's the truth. So if the *ton* got you all wrong, what are the chances that they got it right with Tremont? Do you know the wags claim he hasn't had a mistress or lover since his wife's death?"

"I've heard the talk, yes."

"His wife died over four years ago. He's a man in his prime," Emma persisted. "Do you truly think that he'd mourn for that long?"

"If I ever lost you, I'd mourn for the rest of my days." Her husband tipped up her chin, his touch possessive, his eyes hot and intent. "There's no one else for me, Emma. Ever."

Her insides melted. "I love you, too."

His kiss made her senses spin.

"Darling?" he said.

She smiled dreamily up at him. "Hmm?"

"See if you like it."

"Like what?"

With his hands on her shoulders, he turned her to face the looking glass once more. She blinked at the dazzling addition to her reflection. She'd been so absorbed in their kiss that she hadn't felt him fasten the necklace on her.

"Oh... it's beautiful."

She touched her fingertips to the red velvet band, then to the large diamond-encrusted charm nestled in the hollow of her throat. Within the square frame of the charm was the initial "S," also studded with diamonds.

While she was touched by Alaric's gift, his extravagance could be a bit overwhelming. Last year, after visiting their friends' country seat, she'd remarked upon the lovely orangery. Before she knew it, Alaric had summoned architects and builders to their London home and had a miniature conservatory added for her enjoyment. The glass-walled space lush with blooming citrus was now her favorite room in the house.

"The necklace is lovely, but I really don't need more lavish gifts," she said.

"It's not a gift for you. It's for me." His eyes gleamed as

he toyed with the choker. "I want you to wear it with your costume at the masquerade."

Understanding turned her cheeks pink. "It's... a collar?"

"So everyone knows who you belong to, my sweet puss," he said huskily.

A secret thrill shot through her; she did adore his masterful streak. At the same time, she couldn't help but query, "And what will *you* be wearing to remind you who you belong to?"

In answer, he cleared the surface of the vanity with a sweep of his arm, and before she could scold him for the mess he'd made, she was hauled from her seat and plopped on the table. She squealed as her back pressed against glass, an even harder presence wedged between her splayed thighs. Her robe parted, slipping off her bare skin.

Breathless, she stared into her duke's smoldering green eyes.

"I'm not bloody likely to forget who holds my heart. But have it your way, lass," he said, "and give me a reminder."

Her sex fluttered at the emergence of the Scottish lilt, the flush of arousal on his slashing cheekbones. And that was before he cupped her milk-swollen breasts, his long fingers playing with the tender peaks. When he bent his head, the shocking, exquisite suction shot straight to her core, rustling a moan from her throat.

"That's wicked," she managed.

"Aye, and you love that about me," he murmured. "Just as I love doing this to you... and this..."

Under his naughty ministrations, her thoughts blurred into a streak of vibrant red pleasure. Truly, there was no arguing with the man. With her typical pragmatism, she gave up and happily surrendered to His Grace's loving.

Chapter Ten

"I hope you're finding my soiree diverting, Miss Kent?"

Thea turned from watching Emma and Strathaven waltzing together and smiled at her approaching hostess. A supremely attractive and poised lady in her thirties, the Marchioness of Blackwood's inky tresses had been styled *à l'Égytienne*, her violet-blue eyes vivid within an exotic frame of kohl that extended to her temples. Wearing a sleeveless white tunic accentuated by a dazzling ruby necklace, she appeared every inch the sensual Queen of the Nile.

The realm she commanded was no less magnificent. Costumed guests filled the vast mirrored ballroom, conversing under large potted palms and twirling over the dance floor. The lush notes of the orchestra blended with the sounds of gaiety, the tinkling of glasses overflowing with champagne.

"Your party is surely the crush of the Season, my lady. And may I compliment you on your looks?" Thea said sincerely. "The necklace is lovely on you."

"A gift from my husband. He claims my price is far above any jewel." Lips curving, Lady Blackwood touched her fingertips to the web of blood-red rubies and icy diamonds. "But enough about me. The truth is I came over to tell you how exquisite *you* look in your costume. You've attracted quite a few admirers this evening."

"You're too kind, my lady." Thea's cheeks warmed. "In this instance, the feathers do make the bird, I'm afraid. The credit must go to Madame Rousseau."

True to her word, the modiste had created a masterpiece. The gown was everything Thea could have wanted and didn't know how to put into words. The bodice, constructed of crimson satin, was low cut and left her shoulders bare. The gown fitted tightly to her torso and then cascaded into full skirts covered in shimmering feathers of red and orange. When she moved, the skirts gave the illusion of a dancing flame. Matching gloves of scarlet satin and a gold brocade demi-mask completed her transformation.

"What a modest creature you are. Yet not every lady can make a convincing phoenix. Reinvention requires talent, my dear, and my intuition tells me," Lady Blackwood said with a wink, "that you are discovering your own gifts."

"I am trying. But it is difficult to change one's nature," Thea said in earnest tones.

She was putting forth an effort nonetheless. She'd danced more in this one evening than she had all Season. Instead of merely observing or listening in on conversations, she'd made chitchat until her jaw ached. She was determined to do Madame's costume and herself justice.

If this is what it takes to find love, then so be it.

"From what I've observed, your nature has been *very* popular with the gentlemen tonight."

"Oh, that's not truly me," she admitted. "I'm more of a reserved and quiet sort. And my skills in flirtation are altogether abysmal."

"Act with confidence," the marchioness said with a wave of her fan, "and soon it shall become second nature. After all, we are what we repeatedly do."

"Aristotle." Thea recognized the words of her papa's favorite philosopher. "You are well read, my lady."

"Clever and gorgeous. I got myself quite a bargain, didn't I?" a masculine voice said.

The Marquess of Blackwood materialized behind his wife. He was outfitted like a Roman gladiator, complete with metal breastplate and leather sandals, and it suited his military bearing. Steel blue eyes twinkled in his pleasantly weathered face. Sliding an arm around his marchioness' waist, he said, "Although I oughtn't flatter you quite so much, my dear. What if you became vain?"

"Alas, a woman's vanity erodes with time. And children." Lady Blackwood sighed. "Take it from me, Miss Kent: there is nothing to age a woman like three young boys."

"You don't look a day older than when I married you," her husband said.

"Clearly, your eyesight is failing in your dotage, my lord. But I shan't complain." Her lips curved, the marchioness leaned toward Thea and said in a confiding whisper, "As you can see, husbands do have their uses. Are you in the market for one this eve?"

Thea renewed her resolve. "Yes, if I can find the right match."

"No time like the present." Her hostess surveyed the ballroom the way a queen might a map of her kingdom. "Now title or money—which is more important to you?"

Lord Blackwood grimaced. "That's my cue to make myself scarce so you females can get to your mercenary talk."

"Never fear, my lord. I married you for your looks," his lady said in dulcet tones, "and your fortune came a distant second."

"A comforting thought." Smiling, Blackwood kissed his wife, made a precise bow to Thea, and left to circulate amongst his guests.

"Now back to the task at hand." Lady Blackwood's vivid eyes swept over the glittering ballroom. "How about Sir Rathburn? He's in the gold robes, by the champagne fountain. His Midas costume is quite apropos: he is worth twenty thousand a year."

Thea studied the gentleman in question. Although he was handsome and well-built, his smirk reminded her of the rooster they'd had back in the country. The puffed-up bird had paraded around the coop, pecking at the chickens and crowing at ungodly hours... until an exasperated Emma had put him in the soup pot.

"I don't think Sir Rathburn and I are a match," Thea said.

"You're absolutely right. He is a mere baron."

"Oh, it's not that. I'm myself a middling class miss, after all, and quite content to be so," she said earnestly. "In my family, we don't marry for money or status."

"Your sister landed the Duke of Strathaven," Lady Blackwood said dryly.

"Emma would have married him even if he wasn't a duke. In fact," Thea said with a rueful smile, "their courtship might have gone a bit smoother."

"A family of idealists, how refreshing. Tell me, then, what are you after, Miss Kent?"

Tremont leapt into her mind. She blocked out the image.

"Deep, true, and passionate love," she said.

"Well. That does complicate things, doesn't it?" Lady Blackwood's eyes sparkled within their rims of kohl. "As it happens, you are a lady after my own heart, Miss Kent, and I should like to help you. Shall I acquaint you with a few eligible *parti*?"

As Thea was about to answer, awareness tingled over her nape. She glanced over her hostess' shoulder, in the direction of the entryway. Standing by a pillar was a tall man clad in a black domino. From this distance, his hair looked tobacco brown, much darker than Tremont's, yet there was something about him…

She blinked, and he was gone.

Well, that's perfect, isn't it? Not only did I imagine the attraction between Tremont and me, now I'm seeing him everywhere. If I don't get past this ridiculous tendre, I shall turn into a madwoman.

Thea took a composing breath and smoothed her feathery skirts. "Yes, my lady. I would be most grateful for introductions."

Behind the column, Gabriel cursed himself. Although he was a bit rusty at espionage, he still remembered the rules. Losing one's focus was a sure way to botch a mission. Too much was at stake for such foolishness.

He told himself it was just the shock of seeing a swan transformed into a mythical creature of flame. Unable to help himself, he risked another glimpse around the pillar. With each of Thea's movements, incendiary feathers fluttered, a beguiling contrast to the milky skin above her low-cut bodice, the gold-swirled curls piled atop her dainty head. Her gilded mask accentuated the delicacy of her features.

Fragile yet fiery, she was the essence of desire. Answering heat flared in him, the primal urge to claim her as his and his alone. Savagely, he locked away his needs.

You're here for a purpose. Lives—including Freddy's—depend upon it.

Deliberately, he took up conversation with a lady dressed as a nymph. She'd been sending him come-hither looks, and it was always best to blend in. All the while, he discreetly monitored his target for the evening: Pompeia, also known as Lady Pandora Blackwood.

She was doing the rounds, introducing Thea to various guests. Male guests. Gabriel's teeth ground together as Thea waltzed off in the arms of some popinjay dressed like a pirate. He wanted to go over and give the blighter missing teeth to go with the damned eyepatch.

Firmly, he forced his attention back to Pompeia. Her husband was at her side again, exuding genuine affection, the poor sod. Blackwood was an upstanding gentleman, respected and admired for his actions on the battlefield. Which just went to show that even an intelligent man could be blinded by love. If Blackwood ever discovered the true viper he'd married…

The wriggling in the hidden pocket of Gabriel's domino told him it was time. He'd scouted the field well enough. He'd put his next stratagem into play.

Excusing himself from the nymph, he took the hallway into the main foyer, where guests were still trickling in. A pair of footmen was rounding them up, one in front and one at the back to shepherd the tittering newcomers down the corridor to the ballroom. A third servant stood posted at the grand stairwell that led to the upper floors.

As the group headed toward the hallway behind Gabriel, he staggered into their midst like a soused sailor, incurring a few annoyed comments of "Watch it, man!" He slurred his apologies, picked his mark—a man whose scarlet domino matched his bloated face—and dropped the furry decoys into the man's pocket. The harassed-looking footman holding up the rear passed him.

Ten... nine... eight...

Gabriel weaved toward the remaining footman at the stairwell.

"I say," he mumbled in foppish, drunken accents, "where is the blasted convenience in this place? Ain't so much as a chamber pot to be found anywhere, sirrah."

... four... three...

"It is back toward the ballroom, my lord—"

A masculine scream rang from the hallway.

Right on cue.

"Egad, there's mice in my pocket!"

"Vermin!" a lady shrieked. "One just ran up my skirt!"

A wave of shouts and exclamations followed.

"Beg pardon, my lord!" The footman abandoned his post, rushed to the hallway.

Gabriel scaled the steps to the first floor. He walked down the empty corridor, maintaining a drunken stride lest he run into any passersby. He could hear the brouhaha continuing downstairs—a lot of fuss over a couple of harmless dormice.

Gabriel located the master suites in the right wing.

Having surveilled the house from the outside, he knew which room was Pompeia's. He picked the lock and slid inside, closing the door behind him, sealing himself in a darkness of rose and patchouli.

Pompeia's domain.

Moonlight filtered in through the partially parted curtains. The silver light shimmered through the double glass doors of the balcony, limning the feminine furnishings. Methodically, he searched through the chamber. He found a hidden compartment behind the bed's headboard; it contained jewels but no evidence linking Pompeia to Octavian's death or the Spectre.

Gabriel moved his search to the adjoining sitting room. With swift precision, he rifled through the contents of Pompeia's secretaire, careful to return everything to its place. Correspondence, writing implements, a stack of invitations—nothing of note. He trailed his fingertips along the edges of each drawer, and his pulse quickened when he found the concealed switch. A soft click and the bottom of the drawer shifted to reveal a hiding place.

A missive.

He unfolded it, hairs lifting on his skin at the sight of the Spectre's code. It'd been years since he'd seen it, but he'd never forget the spymaster's cypher. His brain worked like a printing press in reverse, stripping off syntax and symbols until the message blazed through.

Fielding's Covent Garden. Thursday 13th of August at ten o'clock.

Had Pompeia written this—was she the Spectre?

Or had she received this message? Was she working for the Spectre, planning to meet him at this time and place?

Possibilities ran through his head. No certain way to get answers except one. Jaw clenched, Gabriel throttled his impatience. Jumping the gun would result in losing the ultimate prey. The meeting was a week from now; he'd bide his time. Then, at the appointed hour, he'd be at Fielding's. He'd capture the Spectre—Pompeia or whoever she was working for—and mete out justice.

His muscles tensed at a rustle in the outside corridor. Quiet, furtive movements, someone acting with deliberate stealth. He replaced the missive, closing the desk drawer. By the time a key scraped the lock of the bedchamber door, he was pulling the balcony doors closed behind him. Enveloped by shadow, he held his back against cold stone, wedging himself against the balustrade. Out of view, he waited.

Humid air clung to his face. The sounds of the masquerade floated up to him. He held perfectly still, slowed his breathing, and focused his senses on what was going on inside the bedchamber.

A slight shuffling from within—Pompeia checking her hiding places, ensuring all was intact? His ears prickled as he strained to hear every little sound. Footsteps... His hands closed around the hilts of his holstered daggers. Someone coming, stopping at the balcony doors. A soft swoosh of fabric, drapery being pushed further apart. He remained still, his back pressed against the chilled wall, picturing Pompeia looking out through the curtains. She was within a few feet of him, but she couldn't see him, not yet. Not unless she decided to step out onto the balcony...

Glass rattled in the panes of the double doors. His blades gleamed dully, poised for action.

Another voice came from within the bedchamber.

Muffled, deep. A man. A moment later, Pompeia gave a laughing reply. Gabriel couldn't hear the exact words, but the tone was flirtatious. She'd been interrupted by her husband—or a lover.

Either way, the curtain twitched back into place. Her footsteps retreated back into the bedchamber, then farther away still. Gabriel didn't move until the voices faded into silence.

He counted to fifty. Then did it again, calculating his next move.

Leaving through the bedchamber was too risky, especially if Pompeia had sensed threat. He had to get out of here now—and quickly. Sliding his knives back into their hidden sheaths, he crouched below the railing to keep out of sight. He crept forward; from between the balusters, he judged the distance to the ground.

Fourteen feet. On the run from enemy agents, he'd once jumped out the window of a hotel in the Marais from twice that height. Nothing to break his fall, either. At least here he could descend down one of the columns supporting the balcony. He wouldn't even break a sweat.

As he readied to cross over the railing, a movement caught his eye.

In the far corner of the garden. A flash of scarlet—

Thea. She was... running? From some fribble dressed in gold. Before Gabriel's disbelieving eyes, the whoreson caught her, flung her slender form against a dark hedge, and *pressed up against her.* Rage splattered across Gabriel's vision, a roar in his ears. In the next heartbeat, he vaulted over the railing.

Chapter Eleven

"Let me go at once!" Thea's lungs strained with effort, yet she forced herself to take a deep breath. To sound strong and firm. "Pray keep your hands to yourself, Sir Rathburn."

"No need to play coy, my dove. You've been fluttering your feathers at me all evening," the baron said with a leer. "Time to pay the piper."

Cringing, Thea turned her head away. Even so, Rathburn's lips landed slimily against her ear, his breath hot and reeking of spirits. So much for being calm. Planting her hands against his shoulders, she shoved with all her might. "Get off me, you *oaf*."

The blighter only laughed. "A miss with sauce, eh? Just the way I like 'em."

"I don't care... what you like!" Thea dodged his slobbering lips. "I want nothing to do with you!"

Why, oh why, had she ignored her instincts and allowed him to take her out for some air? She'd been so intent on turning a new leaf and putting Tremont out of her mind that she'd acted rashly. Traded one disaster for another.

"You need to be taught some manners," Rathburn said, smirking.

"I shall scream if you don't let me go," Thea warned.

"I don't think so. Not unless you want to ruin your reputation. Now be a good girl and we'll have some fun and games with none the wiser—"

Panic flared as he groped her bosom. She struggled, his grip tightening like a noose. When she tried to push him away, the sudden tearing of fabric snapped her to her senses. She couldn't stop him; she needed help. Her virtue was more important than her reputation. She drew a breath to scream—

"What the—?"

The shriek came from Rathburn, his expression startled as he flew backward away from her. He landed against a hedge, groaning; it took her shocked faculties a moment to register that a stranger cloaked in darkness was beating her attacker, his fists connecting with lethal force. The baron flailed, his attempts to fight back ineffectual, like that of a housecat batting at a lion. When her rescuer's knuckles smashed into Rathburn's jaw, the crunch of bone jolted Thea out of her daze.

Dashing over, she grabbed onto Tremont's drawn-back arm. The muscles were rigid, vibrating with elemental power. From behind the black mask, stormy grey eyes sucked the air out of her lungs. Awareness crackled between them.

"Stop it. You'll kill him," she said desperately.

"He deserves to die," he growled in a voice she'd never heard from him before. "He *touched* you."

The violence in his eyes made her swallow. As did the blood dripping from his hands.

"I'm fine. Truly," she said. "Please, let him go."

She didn't care so much what happened to Rathburn, but she didn't want Tremont committing murder because of her. The wrath in his eyes told her that he was fully capable of tearing her attacker from limb to limb. Gone was his skin of civility. With the façade ripped away, he exuded primal power, ferocity barely leashed. Her heart thudded with fear… and devastating attraction.

The admission rushed through her, bringing equal parts resentment and relief. She couldn't hide from the truth any longer. What had been staring her in the face all along.

I want him and only him. If I have to risk getting rejected, then so be it.

If she was facing life on the shelf, she'd rather go with a splat than rot away never knowing what could have been.

"I let the bastard go, you do as I say," Tremont rasped.

Slowly, she nodded.

Tremont loosened his grip on Rathburn. The baron slid down the hedge, slumping on the ground. He appeared unconscious and bloodied—but alive, thank goodness.

Tremont raked his gaze over her, a muscle leaping in his jaw when he saw her ripped bodice. Stripping off his domino, he slung the velvet cloak over her shoulders. He straightened her mask.

"We're getting out of here," he said.

"But I came with Emma and Strathaven—"

"I'll leave them word. We're going straight to my carriage. Now," he ordered.

One look at Tremont's fierce expression told her it was prudent to obey. He led her away, his hand proprietary on the small of her back, and even through the layers of fabric, the potency of his touch sizzled through her. He navigated them through the townhouse, shielding her with his large frame. They arrived at his carriage, the door parting to a dark, plush threshold.

As he handed her in, her belly fluttered with nerves... and anticipation.

As the carriage rolled off, he told himself, *Remain calm. Keep your temper under rein.*

Thea sat on the opposite bench. She'd removed her mask, and, in the faint light of the carriage lamp, shadows played across her fine-boned features. Her neck was white and graceful above the ties of his domino, red feathers peeking through the black velvet. Pins had loosened from her coiffure, her honey tresses tumbling all the way to her waist.

A princess unbound.

So goddamned lovely that his teeth ached.

"Your knuckles are bleeding." She began rummaging through her reticule. "Let me find a handkerchief—"

"I don't need a damned handkerchief." His bloodlust simmered just beneath the surface. "What the devil were you doing in the garden with that bastard?"

She stiffened. Set her bag aside. In cool tones, she said, "Thank you for your intervention, my lord. Sir Rathburn was proving quite a nuisance."

"*Nuisance*, you say? The blighter had his hands on you. If I hadn't arrived when I did..."

His throat clenched at the possibility. A force, deep and feral, drummed in his chest. *No one touches what is mine.*

"As I said, I am grateful. In retrospect, my behavior was a trifle reckless,"—her voice wavered before she plunged on—"but even so, it is of no concern to you."

"It bloody well is my concern. Now see here—"

"No. *You* listen." Her chin lifted, her eyes blazing with golden fire. "I am not some delicate miss in need of a keeper! You have no right to dictate my actions. I will spend time with whomever I choose. You may not want me, but other men enjoy my company."

His vision darkened. "Devil take it, I do want you. I told you, the problem is with me—"

"I'm done with your ambivalence. All your back and forth. If you want me, then I suggest you act upon it now." Her shoulders drew back, the rounded tops of her bosom bobbing like twin lures. "This is your final chance so *make up your dashed mind.*"

Already roused from the night's violence, his primal side reared at the challenge. There was no stopping this. Craving for her saturated him, every muscle throbbing with need. She wanted proof of his desire for her?

So be it.

Tremont hauled her into his arms. *At last.*

Sprawled against his hard thighs, Thea trembled. Finally, she was where she belonged. Where she'd longed to be since their last kiss. He made quick work of the domino, the cocoon of velvet falling from her. His kisses branded her bare throat.

In his arms, she was truly alive. The recognition blazed that no other man could make her feel this way. She wanted him and only him.

"If we do this, we do it my way," he growled.

"Yes," she whispered.

"I'm not going to take you fully, but I will see to your pleasure. If there's anything you don't like, you will tell me to stop. Otherwise, you will do as I say. Are we agreed?"

His masterful tone made her shiver. She dipped her chin.

"I'm not the gentleman people think I am," he warned her. "I'm no angel."

"Just as I'm no porcelain doll." Hesitantly, she said, "Do you truly want me, Tremont?"

"I have never wanted anyone more." He cupped her cheek, his callused touch sending quivers up her spine. "Ready, princess?"

"Yes," she breathed.

He claimed her mouth, and heat flared like a symphony, wrapping her in pure sensation. Only his lips existed, their firmness and warmth, the delicious, drugging friction. It was natural to part her own and welcome him deeper inside. Their tongues met in a glissando of delight that spread goose pimples over her skin. The tips of her breasts stiffened to tingling points beneath her bodice.

Seated as she was on Tremont's lap, she knew the kiss was having a similar effect on him. Through the layers of clothing, she could feel the hard, rampant shape of his manhood. She gave an experimental wriggle, and he groaned.

In the next instant, she found herself lying on her back, her shoulder blades against the velvet squabs. Tremont knelt on the carriage floor, his features austere, his eyes smoldering with possession. The kind of passion she'd dreamed of.

"Beautiful." His voice had a ragged edge. "You set me

afire."

"You make me feel all awash," she confessed, reaching to touch his jaw.

He caught her hand. Placed it above her head, wrapping her fingers around something smooth, made of leather… the passenger strap? Turning her head on the cushion, she saw that he'd indeed made her grasp the black loop attached to the wall beneath the window.

"Both hands, love." He took her other hand and placed it on the strap as well. "I want you to hold on and not let go until I tell you to."

"But… why?"

"Because it is my wish." His hands were a cogent argument, coasting along her spine and unfastening, loosening her very moors. "Because I need to know that you trust me."

She wanted to ask what he meant by the latter, but the question dissolved as his lips traced the curve of her shoulder. Her mind turned hazy as he nuzzled the hollow at the base of her throat. *If this is what he wants*, she thought languidly, *I suppose I'll just have to suffer…*

His kisses roved lower and lower, and she felt a tug on her bodice, exposing her bosom to a man's eyes for the first time. Hunger was a silver flame in his eyes, and it burned away her modesty and shyness. Time later for maidenly concerns and rational thought.

In this moment, all she wanted was him.

"By God, you are lovely beyond words." Reverence hummed in his voice.

His thumb circled one nipple, teasing it to an even fuller peak, and her breath hitched. *Keep breathing*, she reminded herself. *You don't want to miss this.* Somehow, she managed to draw air steadily into her lungs. *Deep breath in, deep breath out.* Her confidence grew as Tremont touched her, telling her how exquisite, how perfectly made he found her.

"Ready for more?" he rasped.

For everything. "Yes. Oh, yes."

"Then hold on tight to the strap, sweeting. Don't let go."

He bent his head, and she gasped, the leather going taut in her hands. The things he was doing with his tongue, his lips... When he licked one of her nipples, then blew softly on it, she felt a quivering tug deep in her center. He drew her into his mouth and suckled, and the sensation spread into her lower belly. Heat liquefied between her legs.

"So sweet and responsive." His breath brushed warmly against the damp tip, making her shiver. "Do you like this, Thea? Like me petting and kissing you... like this?"

His tongue swirled, and she moaned in answer.

"Do you want more?"

Did she *ever.* "I want to experience everything. With you."

He exhaled harshly, and then he was kissing her again. A steamy sharing of lips, tongues, and breaths. Her skirts rustled, his touch gliding up her silk stockings, tracing the skin beneath the garter. When his hand clamped over her bare thigh, a breath whooshed from her.

"All right, princess?" he murmured.

"Don't stop," she pleaded.

His hand wandered higher. "You like me touching you here... and here?"

Words jammed in her throat for he'd reached the apex of

her thighs. He parted her gently, and her cheeks flamed as she realized how damp she'd become. Goodness, was that *normal*?

"You're so soft, wet. Like a flower after the rain." His voice was low and reverent. "You are nature's perfection."

Well, then. Reassured by the heated approval in his eyes, she relaxed and let the wondrous sensations wash over her. At the same time, a strange pressure burgeoned in her belly. A tautness that seemed twined with the pleasure, that matched it beat for beat. Her pulse quickened as if she were in a race... for what?

"Tremont," she said, squirming.

"Gabriel," he said. "I want to hear you say it."

He touched a place that wrung his name from her lips, her hips bucking off the cushions.

"And here," he said huskily, "is the prettiest bud in your garden."

Incoherent sounds left her as he continued to play with that aching peak, circling, stroking, building the tension inside her. She twisted restlessly against the squabs, brimful of sensation yet oddly empty at the same time. She needed something... more. Something she didn't have words for.

"Gabriel, *please*." She didn't even know what she was begging for.

His eyes were dark with triumph. His lips closed over hers, the kiss rougher, more forceful than before. She reveled in his possession. Suddenly, she felt a stretching sensation, and then he was touching her... *inside*. Her breath held, her muscles clenching on unfamiliar fullness.

"Goddamn, you're small. Gripping me so tightly." His chest surged. "Am I hurting you?"

"No." It wasn't painful exactly. "It feels… strange."

"Strange in a bad way?"

"Strange in a strange way. Do it again."

"Like this?"

This time, the exquisite, filling friction made her back arch. "Yes," she sighed.

He groaned her name, and his touch changed. His fingers took on a rough, driving rhythm, the lunging cadence shoving the breath from her lungs. It was so *good*. When his palm met her swollen flesh in a light slap, she whimpered with pleasure. He did it again and again and again. Her head tossed against velvet as the crescendo in her soared…

"Pull on the strap," he ordered. "Pull hard for me."

She clutched the leather and yanked. Every part of her tautened, and his fingers thrust deep, a transcendent surge that made stars blur before her eyes. Her hips arched as he filled her completely, his palm grinding wetly against her sensitive bud.

"Come for me now, Thea," he rasped.

She cried out as she hurtled over the finish line. Voluptuous spasms rippled through her, one after another, strong and unbearably sweet. The tides of bliss rocked her, cleaved her from her old self, and left her shivering with the new discovery.

When she regained her senses, she gazed up at Tremont. For once his expression was unguarded. In his gleaming gaze, she saw her own awe reflected. And the glimmer of something else, too, that might have been… hope.

Chapter Twelve

Gabriel awoke fully alert, a habit from his espionage days. Being groggy could get you killed, and that was no way to start the morning. Lying in the guest bedchamber, the dawn's light seeping in through a crack in the velvet drapes, he was acutely aware of two facts.

First, he'd brought Thea to climax in the carriage last night, and it had been the hottest, most seductive experience of his life. Her passion had rocked him to the core. She hadn't been afraid or repulsed by his lovemaking. She was a lady, an innocent, yet she'd wanted him—hell, she'd *begged* him to give her release. The wanton beauty of her orgasm had stunned him; if they hadn't arrived back at the Strathaven residence, he'd have dearly loved to give her another.

He stared up at the plaster cherubs frolicking along the edge of the ceiling, his heart thudding. Possibility flared inside him. Could she accept his carnal desires?

I want to experience it all with you.

True, her words had been that of an innocent: she had no idea what "all" with him would entail. Yet her openness roused his deepest fantasy, one he'd long ago forsaken. Wanting something that didn't exist was futile, but his old, dangerous desire took root nonetheless: what would it be like to possess a lady entirely? To have her surrender to him, to give him all of her trust, to belong to him and only him?

The prospect fluttered at the edges of his consciousness, as tantalizing as a dream. A hidden floodgate opened inside him, releasing so many needs, of such intensity, that he couldn't register them all. Raw wanting raged through him.

His pulse hammering, he reached below the sheet. He stifled a groan as his hand closed around the stiff, aching ridge of his cock. During the years of his marriage, he'd gotten accustomed to self-pleasure. For better or worse, frigging had become a necessary habit.

But he didn't want to think about the past. He wanted to focus on the future, the fantasy awakening inside him. Closing his eyes, he allowed himself to imagine all the things he wanted to do with Thea. The wicked pleasures he wanted to introduce her to, the limits of her passion he wanted to test... and control.

In his mind, he returned to the darkness of the carriage, to her lovely nude body spread for him on the velvet cushions. This time he saw her hands bound by the passenger strap, her wrists secured by black leather as he fingered her. His breath quickening, he fisted his erection, mimicking the tight, shy clasp of her pussy, the way it had milked him so lushly. By God, she'd been magnificent in her throes. He pictured himself clamping his hands on her downy thighs, spreading them wide as her climax trembled through her.

Lowering his head, he put his mouth on her. Her essence flooded his senses like ambrosia, and he hungrily feasted. To the music of her pleading whimpers, he licked her creamy slit, delving deep, groaning as her fluttering muscles pulled him in deeper. He fucked her with his tongue, and she let him have her this way—in any way he pleased. His cock spurted; he fisted himself harder as he licked upward to her pearl, flicking it.

When he suckled the proud little bud, she cried out again, her thighs tautening around his head. Her crisis set fire to his blood, and the next instant, he mounted her, notching his prick to her wet gash. He drove forward, pleasure rippling down his spine as her passage received him. Her eyes held him as wholly as her untried flesh, hazel pools glimmering with trust. With pure surrender.

Undone by her, he let the animal in him go free. He rammed into the heart of her, into her wet, giving welcome. Her moans accompanied the ferocious smack of his bollocks against her dewy petals. She took him to the balls, and it still wasn't enough, he needed to be deeper yet. Hoisting her ankles over his shoulders, he slammed his hips home. Again and again and again.

Straining against her bonds, she arched to take everything he had to give her. Her breasts bounced with his thrusts, the coral tips erect and proud. She cried out as her sheath began to convulse around his invading shaft. He drove himself home, hitting the end of her with a groan. Her lushness milked him, and his stones burgeoned, his seed climbing. Plunging into her cream-filled cunny one last time, he exploded in a haze of bliss.

Panting, Gabriel lay against the pillows, the bedclothes damp, his heart drumming. As he slowly came down from the release, he felt calmer, his head clearing. The desire between him and Thea last night had been real. True, he hadn't exposed the depth of his proclivities, the extent of his need for sexual domination, but her response thus far had been promising. Was it possible that she could accept him sexually?

Anticipation wound inside him. His sense of honor dictated that he make her a proposal, but he wouldn't go into it blind like the last time. That route led only to misery for both parties. This time, he would learn from his mistakes. He would tell Thea his expectations in full, outline the kind of marriage he had to offer.

Perhaps she wouldn't fall into a dead faint or run screaming from the room. A man could dream. And perhaps, just perhaps, she would want to take him on.

He released a breath. Before he took things any further with her, he had to put his past to rest. He wouldn't let the threat of the Spectre touch her. Six days from now, he'd ambush the villain and Pompeia at their meeting in Covent Garden. He'd put an end to that dirty business and secure the safety of those he cared about. Then, and only then, could he get on with his future.

Hope flickered, illuminating a future that might include Thea.

The skirts of Thea's sprigged muslin swished as she hurried down the steps. It wasn't ladylike to rush, yet she couldn't help herself. She'd slept in far later than usual; if her maid hadn't come in with a breakfast tray, she might have slept until noon. As it was, she couldn't wait to see Gabriel. Her pulse beat a rapid tattoo at the memory of all they'd shared last night.

He wanted her. He thought she was *perfection*.

He was the perfect one, she thought dreamily. Warmth coalesced low in her belly, her intimate muscles fluttering. In his arms, she'd finally experienced the all-consuming passion she'd yearned for. He'd treated her like a flesh and blood woman, and she'd reveled in his deliciously masterful lovemaking.

On the ground floor, she followed the hum of conversation past the library to the billiards room. From the doorway, she saw Emma and Strathaven. At the opposite end of the room, they were bickering over where to hang a circular board that resembled an archery target. A new diversion, Thea thought, hiding a smile. Her sister and brother-in-law did enjoy their games.

Then her gaze shifted, and she saw Gabriel and Freddy sitting in a pair of club chairs. The latter's cowlick had been combed into place, and he was a darling, somber miniature of his papa. The two had the same upright posture; neither of them was talking. She wondered, not for the first time, why there should be distance between father and son. They clearly loved one another. Perhaps what they needed was a nudge to close the gap.

Gabriel looked up as she entered, and the look in his eyes set butterflies swarming in her belly. Gone was the habitual shield of coolness; his gaze was warm and soft as smoke. He rose to meet her, and a thrum of possessive pleasure passed through her. Handsome and virile, he was majestic in a dark green jacket which emphasized his broad shoulders and lean torso. His trousers fit like a second skin over his muscular thighs, tucking into polished Hessians.

"You're up late this morning, Miss Kent. I hope last night's activities didn't overtire you?" His tone was polite;

his eyes had a sensual gleam.

Blushing, she said, "I just needed a little extra rest is all. Did you, um, sleep well?"

"Never better." His mouth crooked up in a rare smile.

Her heart melting, she waved to Freddy. "Hello, dear. It's lovely to see you up and about."

"Dr. Abernathy said a change of scenery would do me good," the boy answered with a shy smile. "And I'm feeling ever so much better today."

"I'm delighted to hear it," she said warmly.

"Thea, you should have found me if you weren't feeling well last night." Emma approached, her brown eyes worried. "Thank heavens Tremont was there to help you. Lord knows these affairs can take one over the edge—"

"There's no need to fuss, Em. I'm perfectly well." Certain her face must be red as an apple by now, Thea sought to change the subject. Looking over her sister's shoulder, she saw Strathaven make a furtive adjustment to the board on the wall. "What are the two of you hanging up there?"

"It's for a game. Similar to archery except one uses darts instead of arrows," Emma explained. "Mr. McLeod has one at home. He and his fellow soldiers used to play it to pass time during their regiment days. And you know Strathaven. Anything his brother has, he has to—" Catching the duke move the target, she said in exasperated tones, "That is far too close to the window, Alaric."

"The board shows up better near the light. It's perfectly placed," her husband said.

"If you don't want glass in the panes." Her lips pursed. "I won't be able to play for fear of breaking the window."

"Fear helps one's aim." Coming over, Strathaven chucked her under the chin. "Now stop worrying, pet, and let's get organized into teams."

Freddy opted to watch, so Thea found herself paired with Gabriel, which was perfect, since she was dying to talk to him. The duke went over the rules: each team was given four darts, tiny spears beautifully ornamented with colored feathers—blue for the Strathavens and green for Thea and Gabriel. From the throwing line, each player had to toss their dart at the target, which was painted with three concentric circles and a red bull's-eye in the center. The team with the dart that landed closest to the bull's-eye was the winner.

As Emma stepped up to take the first turn, Gabriel said in an undertone, "How are you?"

To one who did not know him, his question was merely polite. But Thea saw from the taut line of his jaw that he was genuinely concerned about the aftermath of last night. The fact that this strong, stoic man worried over her made her feel as giddy as if she'd imbibed a glass of champagne.

"I'm well," she assured him. "Better than well."

"You don't regret anything?"

"No." Seeing his seriousness, she couldn't help but tease, "Actually, there is one thing."

"Yes?"

"I regret that we didn't do it sooner."

A breath left him, one that she hadn't realized he'd been holding. His eyes heated, turning to molten steel. "As to that, there is always the future."

Her knees wobbled, her heart thumping. "Is there?"

"God, I hope so."

His tone was fervent, so unlike the emotionless Angel that she had to smile. At the same time, insecurity niggled at her. What had changed for him last night? What prompted him to act on his attraction at last? For so long he'd wavered on their relationship. What guarantee did she have that his feelings wouldn't change again?

Before she could work up the nerve to ask, the duke called her up for her turn. She went to the line and tried to concentrate on the target. Holding the green dart at eye level, she aimed and let it fly. It plunked in the outermost ring, farther from the center than Emma's dart.

She returned to Gabriel. "I'm not very good at this," she said ruefully.

"You just need practice." Though his expression was impassive, his eyes smiled. "I'd be happy to lend a hand with your form, princess."

Her pulse took on a staccato beat. Goodness, a flirtatious Gabriel was even more devastating to her senses than an enigmatic one. Recalling that he'd used the same endearment with her last night, she said shyly, "Why do you call me that?"

"Princess, you mean?"

She nodded.

"Because you remind me of a story. The princess locked in the tower." His low, husky voice made goosebumps rise on her skin. "From the first time I saw you, I wanted you to let down your hair for me."

Thea's breath left her in erratic surges. She felt lightheaded. Any more of this and she might faint with happiness. Luckily, Emma's cheer interrupted them. The duke had landed a dart in the ring closest to the center.

It was Gabriel's turn, but he passed Thea the feathered projectile. "Try again."

"No, you go. We'll lose otherwise—"

"It's just a game." He steered her toward the line. "Bring your arm back a little more, like this." He positioned her arm, so that her hand was near her right ear. His nearness stole her breath, his clean male musk making her giddy. "Try to keep your shoulder and arm relaxed; think of it as throwing from your elbow."

She concentrated, trying to follow his advice. She threw, and the little arrow thudded into the circle next to the bull's-eye.

"Well done, Miss Thea!" Freddy said.

Rather pleased with her improvement, she smiled. "Thank you, dear."

Emma's next throw missed the board completely, landing in the molding around the window, a mere half inch from the glass. She gave her husband an *I-told-you-so* look.

Gabriel handed Thea their third dart. Again, he helped place her arm into position. "This time," he said, "snap your wrist a little to give it extra speed."

Her dart landed even closer to the center than her last one.

"Nicely done," Gabriel said. "You've got the touch for this."

His approval sent a wave of warmth through her.

The duke went last for his team. His arrow landed in the red, just a smidgen left of center. That was that, Thea supposed. No one was going to beat such a shot.

When Gabriel held out the final dart, Thea shook her head. "Please, you take a turn. I want to see your form."

Realizing how that sounded, she blushed.

"If you insist." Smiling faintly, Gabriel didn't even bother to step up to the line. In fact, his eyes didn't leave hers, and in a movement so natural it looked like he wasn't aiming at all, he let their last dart fly.

It hit the board with a decisive thud. Dead center, Thea saw with amazement. The target vibrated from the power of his throw, a few of the other darts loosening and plummeting to the ground.

Freddy let out a whoop. "You won, Papa!"

"Not bad, Tremont." Strathaven's brows lifted. "Done this before, have you?"

"A time or two."

As the duke and Em set about collecting the darts, Gabriel turned to Thea. "Would you care to take a stroll in the garden?" he said quietly. "There is much for us to discuss."

"I would love to—"

She was cut off by the shuffling arrival of Jarvis, the aged butler. "Begging your pardon, Lord Tremont," the loyal retainer said in his Scottish brogue, "but a message arrived for you just now."

Gabriel took the note from the salver. He scanned its contents, his expression darkening.

"News?" the duke said.

"I hired a man to look for the governess, and he's tracked down an old address for her in Shoreditch."

"Do you think she'll be there?" Strathaven said, frowning.

Gabriel's eyes were as hard as steel. "It's a lead I'll have to check out."

"I'll go with you," the duke offered.

"I'd rather you keep an eye on my son. I'll be back soon—with good news, I hope." He paused, his gaze on Thea. "Once this business is over, the future can truly begin."

"Do have a care," she said anxiously. "It could be dangerous—"

He bowed over her hand, murmured, "We'll talk more when I return. Wait for me?"

She nodded. He said a brief goodbye to Freddy and strode out.

"Don't worry, dear." Seeing the fear the boy was valiantly trying to hide, Thea gave his shoulder a reassuring squeeze. "Your papa will be fine."

"I don't like Mademoiselle Fournier. She's not a good person." Freddy's bottom lip quivered.

"No, she isn't, but hopefully this will soon be over. Now would you care to try throwing some darts? I could use a practice partner."

"Oh." Freddy's brow furrowed. "I suppose I can try."

He proved a quick study, the first few tries landing respectably in the middle ring. *Like father, like son*, Thea thought with pride. Freddy's next dart hit the edge of the red, and at that same instant, the windows suddenly rattled with a blast.

He blinked. "I didn't do that... did I?"

"What the devil? That came from the street." Strathaven was already heading out of the room, toward the front of the house. "Stay back here where it's safe."

Emma, of course, followed him, and Thea and Freddy hurried behind her. In the drawing room, Thea went to one of the windows overlooking the street. She stood on tiptoe, craning her neck to see—

Her heart stopped.

At the end of the road, Gabriel's carriage lay on its side, engulfed by flames.

Chapter Thirteen

"Trajan, we have to run. *Now.* I've got horses waiting..."

Marius' voice filtered through smoke and flames. Through burning rage.

Gabriel shoved the other aside. "Not leaving. Not until I kill every last one of these bastards."

"Goddamnit, there's no time—"

The enemy swarmed out of the flaming building, surrounding them. Gabriel bared his teeth, the beast rearing, clawing inside him. Weeks they'd held him captive, beaten and flogged him, laughing as he thrashed in agony.

They're all dead men.

The moon glinted off his knives. The sea roared.

When the haze lifted, bodies lay on the sand all around him. His hands were warm and sticky. Stillness fell like a shroud. Too still. Where was Marius?

His gaze shot to the distance. Two figures near the cliffs. One held a pistol.

The other was Marius.

"No," Gabriel shouted.

The shot shattered the night.

"I'm sorry, my lord. The babe came early. There was nothing I could do for either of them."

Words echoing through an empty corridor. All he could see was the closed door, the barrier that had briefly opened seven months ago. *It is my duty, Tremont, to give you a spare to go with the heir.* Cool words, cooler sheets.

His hand lifted of its own accord, reaching for the knob.

"No, my lord, you mustn't go in. There hasn't been time to—"

Death. The scent of it rousing his instincts, putting them on alert. But danger had already come and gone, leaving destruction in its wake. He ran a trembling hand over matted brown hair, beauty turned into a waxen mask.

Duty had killed her—*he* had killed her. He sat numbly amidst the blood-stained linens, holding the remnants of love.

Gabriel awoke, panting.

His hands clutched... bedclothes. Not the interrogation chamber in Normandy. Not his estate. Flickering dimness, a strange bed—

"Be calm, my love. You're fine. I'm here."

His head turned in the direction of the voice. In the gloom, he saw glimmering hazel eyes, hair spun of gold and honey. Recognition anchored his woozy senses.

"Thea?" he croaked. "What happened?"

Her hand fluttered against his forehead. "You were in an accident this morning."

Panic flared. "Frederick?"

"He's safe," she said soothingly. "No, don't move—"

Too late. Pain clawed his side when he tried to sit up. He fell back against the pillows, black streaking across his vision.

"You must have a care, Gabriel." Her voice quivered with worry, and she pressed something cool against his forehead. "There was an explosion, and you sustained injuries. Luckily, no vital organs were damaged, but you do have bruised ribs. Dr. Abernathy removed a wooden shard from your side."

In a flash, it returned to him: scattered vegetables, the overturned cart blocking the path. He'd opened the carriage door, intending to get out and see what was going on. Then came the deafening blast. Fire shooting everywhere. He'd hurtled through space, horses screaming...

"My driver?" he bit out.

"He's alive," she said quietly, "but his injuries will take some time to heal."

Another innocent hurt because of him. Guilt and rage made his head spin, blackness rising.

"Have some of this." She held a glass to his lips.

The cool, citrus-flavored liquid was a balm to his parched throat. He drank greedily and didn't notice the bitterness until after he'd downed it all.

"Devil take it. You gave me laudanum?"

"Dr. Abernathy said you'll need it for the pain. And to get some rest."

"Don't need rest. Have to get the bastard who did this—"

"When you're better. Right now you can't stand on your own two feet let alone hunt down a murderer," she chided gently. "If you try to move, you'll only reinjure your wounds."

He sagged against the pillows, his mind fuzzing in and out of focus. *Have to protect them... have to tell her... even if she despises me...* He fought off the fog, gripped her wrist.

"Tell Strathaven," he said hoarsely, "he must keep everyone safe. Protect you."

"You needn't worry. There are footmen everywhere."

"*No.* Professional guards." His tongue was thick in his mouth, his eyelids pulling down like lead weights. He grasped the first thing that came to mind. "Your brother's agency—*promise me.*"

"I promise." Her eyes were wide, her lips trembling. "What is going on, Gabriel?"

He tried to focus as her face blurred. "The enemy... dangerous."

"Who is he? Gabriel..."

Her voice came as if from afar. He was falling, falling into a black tunnel.

"Spectre," he whispered.

The dark dragged him down.

Chapter Fourteen

The next afternoon, Thea waited in the drawing room for Gabriel to come down. Upon awakening, he'd insisted on calling a meeting with the others. He'd brushed aside her questions and protests that he wasn't well enough to leave the bed.

It's an urgent matter, he'd said tersely. *I'll explain things when everyone arrives.*

There'd been no dissuading him.

Now Ambrose entered the room, his wife Marianne by his side. His brawny, brown-haired associate, Mr. William McLeod, followed. The Scotsman greeted Strathaven by buffeting him on the arm. The duke returned the favor with equal force; such was the way between the two brothers who were as different as night and day in look and manner.

Thea went to greet the newcomers. "Thank you for coming," she said.

"Of course. How is Tremont faring?" Ambrose said.

Dark-haired and lanky, her brother was a solid, reliable man of principles. He was older than Thea by seventeen years, his mama having been their papa's first wife, yet she'd never thought of him as anything but her full kin. From a young age, he'd provided for her and the family, and his mere presence made her feel safer.

Ambrose's wife Marianne was his opposite, glamorous

down to her very bones. A willowy silver blonde once hailed as an Incomparable amongst the *ton*, she was clever and possessed of a cutting wit. As different as husband and wife seemed on the surface, their devotion to one another was absolute. And more than once, Marianne's knowledge of the *ton* had helped Ambrose in his investigations.

"Tremont shouldn't be getting out of bed," Thea said in worried tones. "I tried to convince him to delay the meeting, but he wouldn't hear of it."

"Given that his carriage exploded, his haste is hardly surprising," her sister-in-law said.

Thea's belly churned with the fear she'd been trying to keep at bay. Gnawing on her lip, she said, "I wish I knew what was going on. Who would be behind such a dastardly attack?"

"That is why we're here. To find out," her brother said with reassuring calm.

Yesterday, she had honored her promise to Gabriel and sent word to her brother's agency. Mr. McLeod had personally arrived to set up what he called a "perimeter," with his trained men keeping watch on the Strathaven residence around the clock.

"We're also here to see how you are faring," Marianne added. "Emma says you've been running yourself ragged nursing the marquess."

Thea shot an exasperated glance at her older sister, who was too busy chatting with Mr. McLeod to notice. "Emma is being a mother hen, as usual. I'm perfectly well."

"With your condition—" Ambrose began.

"I'm *fine*. I'm stronger than I used to be." She huffed out a breath. "Why can't anyone understand that?"

Her brother and sister-in-law looked startled. Even she was surprised by her piqued tone.

"No one doubts your strength, dear. We're simply worried about you," Marianne said.

"I know it." Seeing the pair's genuine concern, Thea felt instantly guilty. "Forgive me?"

"There's nothing to forgive," her brother said. "But I must ask, Thea: what is going on between you and Tremont?"

Thea's face warmed. Since the explosion had curtailed her and Gabriel's discussion of the future, she didn't know how to reply. "May I answer that question later?"

Ambrose frowned. "Why?"

"Because she doesn't know the answer at present," Marianne murmured to him. To Thea, she said, "As long as you know what you're doing, dear."

"I do," Thea said. *At least, I hope I do.*

At that moment, Gabriel entered the room, drawing Thea's attention. His tawny hair was tousled, and his color was still off, the hollows beneath his eyes and cheekbones making him appear more starkly masculine than ever. The slight bulge of his bandage was visible beneath his waistcoat. Even in this state, he was so devastatingly attractive that her heart flipped in her chest.

Yet gone was the tender lover she'd just been getting to know. There was no trace of warmth to him now, nothing but icy resolve. His eyes locked on hers, and they were the cold, lucid grey of dawn. Premonition shivered over her. He'd called this meeting for a purpose, and she had the intuition that she'd soon learn some of his secrets.

Which suited her. Because she yearned to know him, had

been drawn from the start to the dark, passionate soul she'd always sensed just beneath his civilized exterior. *He* was the intensity she'd always craved. He made her feel more alive, more vital than she ever had.

And she was determined to help him in any way she could.

Who was trying to harm him? Was the attempted kidnapping of Freddy related to the carriage attack? What sort of intrigue was Gabriel embroiled in and with what evil enemy?

Everyone found seats around the coffee table, Thea taking the chair next to Gabriel. As tea and refreshments were passed around, he began to speak.

"Thank you all for coming. I owe you my gratitude," he said gravely, "and I'm afraid that I will be further in your debt before the day is done."

"Friends don't speak of debt," Strathaven said dismissively.

"Neither do families," Ambrose said. "Any friend of the Strathavens are friends of ours, Lord Tremont."

Thea felt a rush of love and gratitude toward her brother.

"I am indeed fortunate, then, for I wish to retain the services of your firm." Pausing, Gabriel rubbed the back of his neck. "Forgive me. Asking for help is even more difficult than I imagined."

"Thea told us you have an enemy," Ambrose said. "Perhaps you'd care to begin there."

"Yes." Gabriel drew a breath. "Before I start, there is something you must know. A secret that must remain in this room."

Ambrose inclined his head. "You may be assured of our discretion."

"Don't keep us at the edge of our seats," Emma said.

Thea saw the conflict tautening Gabriel's features.

"Whatever it is," she said softly, "you can trust us, you know."

Gabriel met her eyes. Gave a slight nod, as if coming to some inner decision. "During the war with Bonaparte, I was involved in intelligence operations for the Crown," he said.

As Thea tried to absorb that startling piece of information, he went on, "I was recruited to a group whose primary objective was the covert gathering of information and guarding of national secrets." He exhaled, his gaze never leaving hers. "In other words, I was a spy."

He saw Thea's stricken expression and told himself it should come as no surprise. Spying was seen as a dishonorable activity, something no gentleman would want to be associated with. In seven years of marriage, his past had come up once. He'd been having a nightmare, one so intense that Sylvia had apparently heard him from her chamber. She'd woken him, and in his disoriented state, details of his past had come tumbling out.

She'd cut him off in a soft, trembling voice. *If you act as if it never happened, it will be as if it never did. Put it behind you, Tremont. We'll never speak of it again.*

Although she'd tried to mask it, he'd seen the horror and distaste in her eyes, her embarrassment on his behalf. From then on, he'd kept his past to himself—as he'd always done.

He'd never planned on sharing the sordid facts again, on exposing his filthy secrets to anyone... especially not the woman he craved more than his next breath.

Looking at Thea, he swallowed. She looked so pure in her white frock trimmed with blue ribbon, dangling curls framing her sweet face. His vision of loveliness.

You don't have a choice, he told himself.

As much as he hated to admit it, the danger was too great for him to handle on his own. The attack by the Spectre had slapped him to his senses. He needed help, couldn't defeat the bastard by himself.

"A spy? *You?*" The duchess gawked at him.

"Close your mouth, love," her husband said mildly. "Tremont didn't grow two heads. He merely said he gathered information for his country during a time of war."

"Were you in the military?" William McLeod said.

The strapping Scotsman, Gabriel knew, had been a soldier and scout in the 95th regiment.

"I worked under a different auspice," Gabriel said quietly. "The French had a vast advantage over us when it came to their intelligence efforts. They were more coordinated, efficient, and experienced, which led to their successes on the battlefield. My superior, who went by the codename Octavian, was given the task of developing a similar covert intelligence team for the British. He hand-selected and trained a group of five agents he called the Quorum. I was one of them."

Ambrose Kent's golden eyes were keen. "This enemy who threatens you now—he has ties to your past in espionage?"

The investigator caught on quickly, increasing Gabriel's

confidence that he was making the right decision. He had only one regret… He slanted a look at Thea. Her hazel eyes, which had been filled with such sweet passion the night before, now had a sheen of shock… and disgust? His chest clenching, he told himself to get on with the inevitable.

"A month ago, I found Octavian murdered in his study. I've since discovered that he'd been hunting down a French spymaster dubbed *Le Spectre*. During the war, The Spectre was our nemesis, stealing our secrets, always staying one step ahead. After the war, he began a brisk business selling information to the highest bidder. At one point, he set a trap in Normandy, capturing three of the Quorum, including myself."

Flesh healed; memories didn't. His back quivered with the memory of the floggings, beatings. He forced himself to continue.

"When we made our escape, I spotted the Spectre and thought I'd killed him, but there was no proof as the place went up in flames. Apparently, Octavian continued to search for our enemy through the years and what he uncovered led to his demise."

"What did he discover?" Thea said, her eyes wide.

"Not only is the Spectre alive, but he was one of us. A double agent." Grimly, Gabriel recounted his mentor's last blood-marked message to him and the blade he'd found at Cruik's.

"Bloody hell. A traitor." McLeod raked a hand through his shaggy hair.

"I believe my mentor was killed because he was too close to discovering the true identity of our foe," Gabriel said. "Now I've been targeted as the information was passed onto me. The carriage explosion, the attempted kidnapping of my son—this is all the Spectre's handiwork."

"There were five of you in the spy ring, you say? Minus you, that makes a list of four possible suspects?" Kent was scribbling in a small notebook.

"Three," Gabriel said quietly. "My colleague Marius was killed during the escape in Normandy. The remaining agents—Cicero, Tiberius, and Pompeia—are alive and in London."

"Pompeia." Mrs. Kent's fair brows arched. "A female spy?"

"She was one of our best, and deadliest, agents. She or one of other two could be the Spectre." Gabriel expelled a breath. "With the assistance of Kent and Associates, I plan to unmask the true villain and put an end to this madness."

"We will need to know the identities of the other agents," Kent said.

He'd known this, of course, but resistance rose within him. Exposing a fellow spy went against one of the few codes of honor in espionage and the grain of his own beliefs. Yet he flashed to Octavian lying in a pool of blood, the fear in Freddy's eyes, the cloak of the Spectre descending, bringing darkness and flame...

Do what must be done.

"This information must not leave the room. Reputations, perhaps even lives, are at stake," he said grimly. "As agents, we made powerful enemies, and anonymity is our sole protection."

"Discretion is the policy of Kent and Associates," Kent said.

Glancing at Thea, Gabriel couldn't read her reaction.

Not that it mattered. Before the attack, he'd fallen into a moment of gloriously deluded optimism. He'd let his fantasies cloud his judgement. Now, as he lay bare his past, he saw things through the clear, harsh lens of reality.

Marrying Thea would lead to disaster for both of them. His past had risen yet again to remind him of what he'd been: a spy and cold-hearted killer. A beast through and through. Even though she'd responded to him in the carriage, what he'd shown her there had only scratched the surface of his carnality. His insatiable need for domination.

His blood was cursed. Eventually, if they married, she would get glimpses of the true darkness inside him, and he would repulse her as he had Sylvia. He'd find himself in the same torturous situation as his first marriage—only worse. He'd rather have his guts ripped out than see rejection in Thea's eyes.

Locking away sentiment, Gabriel focused on the hard facts. "Pompeia is Lady Pandora Blackwood."

He heard Thea's indrawn breath and saw eyebrows go up around the room.

"The marchioness?" the duchess said incredulously. "How can that be?"

"As a spy, she had the singular ability to assume any identity. She speaks at least four languages that I know of and can charm or kill a man with equal ease."

"But she was so *nice*," Thea blurted. "I cannot believe it of her. At her masquerade, she chatted with me, introduced me to her guests…"

"Pompeia can seem very nice—until she has her garrotte at your throat," he said flatly.

Thea's hand fluttered to her own throat. Above her

fichu, the tender column was smooth and white. Exquisitely vulnerable.

"Do you think Lady Blackwood is the Spectre?" Kent asked.

Describing the damning note he'd found in her bedchamber, he concluded, "If she's not the Spectre, then she's likely working for him. During our last mission in Normandy, she abandoned our group." The old bitterness welled in him. "Because of her absence, we were shorthanded and captured. During our escape, one of our own fell. If the past is any indication, she cannot be trusted."

"This note you found in her desk—it specified a time and meeting place?" Strathaven said.

"Five days from now. At a place called Fielding's in Covent Garden."

"Sounds like one of the market stalls," McLeod said. "We could set up a watch there and see if this ghost of yours turns up."

"My thoughts exactly," Kent agreed. "And the other two suspects?"

"Cicero is Lord Cecil Davenport and Tiberius, Mr. Tobias Heath."

"Good God," the duke said, quirking a dark eyebrow, "a Tory and a radical with something in common? And that thing being a past in espionage?"

"Davenport and Heath are more similar than you think. Both are ruthless and capable of killing."

"We'll have to monitor them as well," Kent said. "McLeod, do we have the men for it?"

"Aye. I'll put Cooper and Jones on the job."

"That covers the known suspects." Kent's brow lined

with concentration. "Which leaves two other leads: the governess and the carriage explosion. Starting with the former, have you made any progress?"

"I put eyes and ears out for Marie Fournier, but nothing has turned up. She had the foresight to dispose of her belongings from the hotel prior to trying to take my son, so I have little to go on."

"You have the handkerchief she dropped at the zoological gardens," Thea reminded him.

Longing throbbed, deeper than his wounds. Why did she have to be so damned beautiful *and* astute? His every fantasy come true—and now a reality he would never have.

Reaching into his pocket, he removed the item, placing it on the coffee table for all to see. The handkerchief was plain, white, of middling quality. The kind one might find for sale in any shop in the city. Nothing notable about it except the governess' initials, "M. F.," sewn in prominent blue thread at the center.

Kent examined the handkerchief. "It's not much to go on, but I'll ask around at a few shops. If you have the names of her references, I'll follow up there as well; chances are, those, too, are false. Which leaves the explosion as the more viable lead. When I examined your carriage, I found remnants of a gunpowder cartridge attached to the underside. My guess is that the overturned cart was part of a diversion; while you were stopped, someone lit the fuse. Do you have any memory right before the blast?"

Gabriel focused on the minute or so before the explosion. The carriage slowing. Vegetables strewn across the path, the cart tipped over. People starting to mill around the scene. He'd put his hand on the door handle, intending to get out and investigate, but he'd paused because—

"A man. He walked past my door just as I was about to get out. He was dressed in working garb, had brown hair and average features." Gabriel put himself back in time, back in the carriage when he'd glanced briefly at the passing stranger. Why had he looked, what had caught his notice...? Memory glimmered. "He had a limp. Favored his left leg."

"It's a start." Kent closed his notebook. "When we question the witnesses, we'll ask about a man with a limping gait. Perhaps someone will remember something."

"What can I do? I'd like to help," Thea said.

Her words stunned him, warmth flaring in his chest. The flame was extinguished in the next instant by unadulterated horror. His every muscle tensed in denial.

"You are not getting involved," he stated.

"In case you haven't noticed, I'm already involved. I foiled Freddy's kidnapping, after all. Who is to say that I can't be helpful in this instance?"

Aware of their audience, Gabriel strove to hold onto his control. No way in hell would he let his noxious history touch her. Time to nip this in the bud.

"This is a dangerous affair. A woman has no place in it," he said firmly.

"But a woman *is* involved. Lady Blackwood is a suspect." She canted her head. "Actually, at her ball, she was quite friendly to me. I could call upon her, use the opportunity to investigate—"

"Out of the question," he growled.

"Tremont's right, Thea." Her brother, thank God, had the sense to back him up. "This is too dangerous for you."

"Emma works with you. She's in dangerous situations all

the time," Thea pointed out.

The duchess cleared her throat. "That's not entirely true. I do help with cases, yes, but not the ones involving physical peril."

Thea's eyes narrowed. "You helped to find Strathaven's would-be *murderer*."

"In that instance, I had no choice. His life was in danger," her sister said earnestly. "I couldn't stand by and watch the man I love come to harm."

Strathaven put an arm around his wife's shoulders.

Thea folded her arms beneath her bosom. "Then you'll understand why I can't bear to see the man *I* care about get killed."

Her declaration struck the room into silence. A rush filled Gabriel's ears, his heartbeat spinning into an exhilarated rhythm. She cared... about *him*?

She doesn't know all your dark secrets. All that you've done and what you are, his inner voice whispered. *She's too bloody innocent to recognize the beast inside you.*

Seeing the glances being exchanged around the room, he knew he had to act. To protect Thea from a future of disillusionment and pain. Whatever it took, he had to head this off at the pass.

"Your concern over a guest is a testament to your kindness, Miss Kent," he said with chilly civility, "but, I assure you, unnecessary. I have everything in hand."

She stared at him. "Concern over a guest? *That* is how you characterize our relationship?"

"How else would I characterize it?" he said tonelessly. "Your hospitality to me and my son do you credit, but the last thing I need is an interfering female. Especially one with a delicate constitution."

A coral flush spread over her cheeks. "Damn you, Tremont."

He couldn't have been more surprised if she'd slapped him in the face. The Thea he knew never used anything but gentle language. She surged to her feet, and all the men hastily followed, himself included. Even though he towered over her, *he* was the one held captive—by a slender princess with honeyed hair and golden fire in her eyes.

"If you think for *one second* that I'm going to let you face this danger alone, then you don't know me at all." Her voice trembled not with fear but… anger? "For the last time, I am *not* delicate. Play hot and cold if you wish, but I am not going to stand by wringing my hands, waiting for you to get killed."

Her hands clenched in elegant little fists, she walked out of the room.

Well… damn. He suddenly had trouble breathing. Beneath his jacket, he'd gone rock-hard, arousal rushing through his veins.

"He has a point," Kent muttered to the room in general. "It isn't safe for Thea."

"Wouldn't want my wife Annabel mixed up in such business," McLeod agreed with masculine sympathy. "Ladies have no place in murder and mayhem."

Mrs. Kent rose, her skirts swishing. "We *ladies* should make ourselves useful, then, don't you think, Emma?" she said in saccharine tones. "We could, for instance, check on the housekeeping or do some embroidery."

"Or we could just wring hands with Thea," Her Grace said.

As the two swept out of the room, Strathaven muttered, "God help us, gentlemen. Prepare yourselves for battle—on more than one front."

Chapter Fifteen

"I didn't mean to lose my temper," Thea said as she let Emma and Marianne into her bedchamber.

"You had every right. Tremont was being quite boorish," Emma declared.

The understanding in her sister's eyes caused a threatening prickle behind Thea's own. Emma might be overprotective, but she could always be counted on to take one's side.

Thea refused to give into tears. "I am *not* as delicate as he believes."

Surveying the chamber, Marianne chose the chair at the vanity, her skirts draping gracefully as she sat. "All considering, I think your sensibilities are proving rather hardy. I daresay not every lady would handle the news of Tremont's past with such equanimity."

Em sat on the bed and patted the coverlet beside her.

Curling up next to her sister, Thea admitted, "It is shocking. But also not altogether surprising, if that makes any sense."

As difficult as it was to conceive that Gabriel had been involved in espionage, it also sort of... fit. In some ways, she felt relieved because now things made more sense. His carefully controlled façade, the restless power beneath. Why he guarded his passions and secrets so tightly. Recalling the way he'd dispatched Rathburn and his deadly accuracy with darts, she wondered what other hidden skills he possessed.

She didn't find the notion so much disturbing as intriguing. His aura of enigma, of potent self-containment, had always fascinated her. The discovery that he'd done his duty for his country added to her admiration of him. There were so many layers to his complexity, and she wanted to peel them back, one by one, to get to the true heart of him. To the powerful lover in the carriage and the tender suitor in the billiards room.

Dash it all... I'm falling in love with him.

Unfortunately, the tingling revelation was dampened by a healthy dose of annoyance. Why did she have to love a man who'd rejected her time and again? Who couldn't seem to make up his mind about her?

Emma pursed her lips. "The shoe does sort of fit, doesn't it? Spies must be rather cold-blooded to do their work, and I've always thought that Tremont was a bit of an iceberg."

"Only insofar as he has hidden depths beneath the surface." Despite her irritation with Gabriel, Thea jumped to defend him. "He might not wear his emotions upon his sleeve, but he is a man of deep feeling. I wouldn't care about him otherwise."

"Does he return your affection, my dear?" Marianne said gently.

"We came to an understanding the night of the masquerade." She nibbled on her bottom lip. "At least, I thought we did."

Emma's gaze narrowed. "Did Tremont take advantage of you?"

"No. In fact, one might say the opposite occurred," she

said truthfully. "I may have taken advantage of him."

Her sister's brows inched upward.

"It's always the quiet ones," Marianne said. "Has Tremont proposed?"

"Before he was attacked, he said he wanted to discuss our future. Now he's acting as if we're no more than polite acquaintances." Her frustration bubbled over. "From the start, he hasn't been able to make his mind up about me, and it *hurts*. One minute he wants me, the next he's pushing me away."

"Most aggravating," her sister-in-law agreed. "Although, in this instance, I do believe he's trying to do the noble thing and protect you from his past."

"I don't care about his past. I care about *him*."

Emma sighed. "Then I suppose we'd best put our heads together and get him out of this mess." She wrinkled her nose. "Despite assertions to the contrary, I've personally found that the female perspective always comes in handy during investigations. Especially when one of the suspects is a woman."

"And all the suspects are members of the *ton*—of which I am an expert," Marianne added.

Thea had never loved the other two more. "What do you know about Lady Blackwood, Marianne?"

"As a matter of fact, Pandora does have rather mysterious beginnings." A line formed between Marianne's brows. "As I recall, she showed up in Society about a dozen years ago, claiming to be the daughter of one Henry Hudson. Hudson had held a minor title and been an adventurous sort—you know, the kind who lives abroad, digging up things. As far as anyone knew, he and his wife

Flora had died during an expedition years ago. No one knew they had a child, but apparently Pandora had been raised at a finishing school on the Continent all these years. She furnished proof that she was indeed the Hudsons' legitimate offspring and, as it happened, the last remaining member of that family."

"How can you keep all that in your head?" Thea said, amazed. "You're like a walking copy of *Debrett's*."

Lips curved, her sister-in-law continued relating the facts. "Within weeks of her return to England, Pandora met and married Blackwood. Theirs was a whirlwind courtship, but Society was willing to overlook it due to Blackwood's status and position in the *ton*. Nonetheless, there were whispers about his impetuousness—especially when his heir arrived a scant eight months after the wedding."

Thea recalled the genuine affection she'd witnessed between the Blackwoods. She bit her lip. "Do you think Lord Blackwood has any inkling that his wife was a spy?"

"I doubt it," Marianne said. "He is an honorable gentleman and a military man to boot. Such knowledge would not sit well with him."

"And if Lady Blackwood were indeed a double agent? What would happen to her marriage... and her family?" Thea's throat constricted. "She told me she has three young boys."

Marianne's expression turned somber. "It is a disquieting notion, certainly."

Thea's instincts balked at the idea that Lady Blackwood was evil. "At the masquerade, she was so kind to me. And she was clearly in love with her husband."

"According to Tremont, the lady has a talent for

deception," Marianne said.

"As a spy, I imagine that skill was necessary for survival," Thea said. "She—and Tremont, for that matter—performed a great service for our country. They risked life and limb whilst the rest of us slept easy in our beds. And they did so knowing that their valiant efforts would never see the light of day. To me, that makes them heroes."

"You have a point, and yet I fear you underestimate how the business of espionage might shape a person. You don't know what Pandora Blackwood is capable of." Marianne paused. "Or Tremont, for that matter."

Thea stiffened. "What are you implying?"

"No need to get your back up, dear. I'm not trying to impugn your marquess' character. But I do think he may have certain complexities at odds with your own optimistic view of the world."

"I'm not a foolish miss," she protested.

"No, you are a Kent," Marianne said gently, "which means you have a good and loyal heart. I do not wish to see it broken."

Irritation scuttled through Thea. "Why does everyone think I'm fragile? Doesn't anyone see that my health has improved? I'm not as weak and useless as I used to be."

Frowning, her sister said, "Who said you were weak and useless?"

"I know I was once the runt of the litter. But I'm stronger now, and I can help Tremont—"

"You're not a runt. How could you think that?" Emma sounded genuinely surprised. "Dearest girl, you're the rock of the family."

She blinked. "I'm not the rock. You are."

"According to Strathaven, I do have the impact of a boulder when I'm after something," Emma said with a rueful grin, "but when it comes to being the stabilizing presence in our family—that is your role, Thea. It always has been."

"No it hasn't. I'm the sickly one," she said, bewildered. "You're always worried about my lungs, my health... "

"Is this your way of saying that I'm too overbearing?"

"You are especially protective of me. And not without reason." Thea's throat worked. "I know my constitution is not as robust as everyone else's."

"If I'm overprotective, it's a habit from when you were a little girl. In truth, it says more about me than it does about you." Sighing, Emma said, "I *am* trying to be less managing."

"You are caring, loving, and no one could ask for a better sister," Thea said.

"And you, my dear, are even-tempered, kind, and the fulcrum of family peace—just like Mama was." Em's voice grew wistful. "She rarely took sides and saw the best in everyone."

It stunned Thea that Emma saw her this way. "I always thought *you* were the one most like Mama. You're so practical and industrious. When times were lean, you made sure we had food on the table, kept us clean and clothed. We survived because of you."

"And *thrived* because of you. You never complained about anything and set an example for us all." Emma's head tipped to one side. "Remember the year we spent Christmas in the schoolhouse?"

Frost melted from a window of the past. Thea saw that long ago day clearly.

"You'd stretched that cheese and loaf of bread as far as anyone could, even giving up your share," she said in soft tones, "but the younger ones were still so hungry. I can still remember Vi's stomach rumbling."

"The only thing louder was Violet herself." Emma shook her head in fond reminiscence. "The way she was carrying on you'd think she hadn't eaten for weeks. She got Polly and Harry going too, and soon they were caterwauling about *everything*, from the lack of plum pudding to the dearth of presents that year. Christmas might have been ruined entirely if you hadn't remembered the keys."

"Keys?" Marianne asked.

"To the schoolhouse. Papa had just been dismissed from his position as the schoolmaster because of his illness," Thea explained, "but I remembered he had a set of spare keys—"

"And she convinced everyone to bundle up and tromp through the snow to the schoolhouse," Emma reminisced. "There was a pianoforte there, and Thea played Christmas hymns for us all night. Everyone sang along, laughing, forgetting everything but being together."

Thea smiled. "It turned out to be a fine Christmas after all, didn't it?"

"Thanks to you. Which is why you must never doubt your strength," her sister said.

"Emma has a point." Her expression thoughtful, Marianne said, "Moreover, Tremont's concern about your being 'delicate' may say more about him than you. For instance, what do you know about his first marriage?"

Only that it was perfect.

"From what little Tremont has said, Lady Sylvia was the ideal wife and mother," Thea said with a pang. "They were very happy, I think."

How can I compare with such a paragon? Her throat constricted. If the true source of his reservation was his devotion to his dead wife, then Thea could never win his heart. It was ironic, really. Because what she loved about him—the driven intensity of his passion—might be the very thing that kept them apart.

"Your description matches the *on dit* about Lady Sylvia. From everything I've heard, she was the epitome of female virtue. The fact that Tremont has never remarried or taken a lover adds a special shine to her halo." Marianne cleared her throat. "You do know how she died?"

"Yes, in childbirth." The moment Thea said it, the realization struck her. "Goodness. Do you think that is why he's so concerned about my delicate health?"

"That is a question for him, my dear," Marianne said.

Resolution rooted in Thea. Whatever his reasons, she was tired of being led back and forth like a toy on a string. She was a *rock*, according to her sister; from here on in, she would lay the foundation for her own future.

"I'm going to talk to him," she said, "and I'm going to get answers once and for all."

"Spoken like a true Kent," Emma said with approval.

Chapter Sixteen

At midnight, Gabriel arrived.

Thea watched as he closed the door of the conservatory soundlessly behind him. Anticipation lived in the scent of ripening citrus, the hushed secrecy of dark foliage. Moonlight streamed in through the glass that made up three of the room's walls, plating his hair in silver, giving his eyes a predatory light. He prowled toward her, large and sleek. He'd thrown a black brocade dressing gown over his shirtsleeves, and his casual sensuality spun her senses.

She pulled her flannel wrapper tighter around her body. *If you can slip a note under a man's door, you can carry on a rational conversation. Don't lose nerve now.*

Straightening her shoulders, she said, "I'm glad you got my note. I was afraid you were asleep."

"I was up." His expression unreadable, he gestured to a wooden bench surrounded by potted orange trees. "Would you care to sit?"

"I'm fine standing." She took a breath. "We need to talk, Gabriel."

His gaze was dark, unfathomable. "Yes."

'Tis now or never. "I must know where we stand. I told you once before you needed to make up your mind about our relationship," she said, proud of how calm she sounded, "and I meant it. I don't deserve to be toyed with."

"No, you don't. You deserve better." His chest surged. "Much better than what I have to offer you."

Exactly what she'd feared he'd say. Her nerves tremored like the freshly hammered strings of a piano, but she bolstered her resolve. *Don't fall apart now. Get your answers.*

"Because of the Spectre?" she managed.

He gave a grim nod. "I thought I could put the past behind me, but I was wrong. What I was, what I did—it will never leave me. And I won't have you getting hurt because of it."

"What you did, you did for your country. In my eyes, that makes you a hero."

Surprise flared in his eyes; it was gone the next second. "You have no idea of the sins I committed. Espionage is an ugly business. The things I did—it would disgust you. Make you want to run from me as fast as you could."

She didn't back down. "What did you do?"

"I killed," he said. "Dozens of men."

She saw the banked fire in his eyes and knew he was testing her.

Quietly, she said, "Were they innocent?"

His mouth twisted. "Depends which side you were fighting on. But the men I killed—they had family and lovers to mourn them—the same as any British agent or soldier. And I took their lives as easily as a butcher does livestock."

"Not as easily, I think," she said softly, "for the butcher doesn't think of the beast he slaughtered over ten years ago. He doesn't hate himself for doing his job."

Gabriel's lips pressed together. Had she hit a nerve?

"Regardless, I cannot put you in danger." He shoved a hand through his hair. "The Spectre is out for my blood, and no one near me is safe."

"With the help of Kent and Associates, you will capture the villain. I know you will." Squaring her shoulders, she said, "Once the Spectre is caught, would you want to be with me then?"

"Thea, it's not that simple—"

"It is precisely that simple. You've been ambivalent about me from the start—even last Season, before the affair with the Spectre reared its ugly head," she pointed out. "What aren't you telling me, Gabriel? Is it me? Because of my weak lungs, my health—"

"There's nothing wrong with you. Not one bloody thing." His hands closed around her upper arms, his eyes glittering. "You are perfect, princess."

"Then is it because..."—her throat cinched, yet she forced the words out—"because of your wife? Because you love her still?"

He looked briefly startled. "No. That is, I hold her memory in high esteem. I always will. But romantic love... it has long faded."

Relief washed over Thea. She heard the truth in his voice, saw it in his face. Her worst fear was conquered. Placing her hands on his chest, feeling the hard-paved muscles flex at her touch, she whispered, "Why then, Gabriel? Why won't you let us be together?"

Silence hung like ripe and ready fruit.

He released her, took a step back.

"Because," he said in a guttural voice, "I want you too damned much."

She blinked. Of all the things she expected him to say, that wasn't one of them. "I don't understand."

"There are things about me you don't know."

She grasped the lapels of his robe, gave a desperate tug. "For goodness' sake, *tell me.*"

With gentle yet firm authority, he removed her hands and placed them back at her sides. "If we were to marry, I'd want certain things. In the bedchamber," he said bluntly.

Warmth swirled beneath her skin. She still didn't see where the problem was.

"I think… I'd want those things too," she said bashfully.

"Would you?" The corner of his mouth curled and not in amusement. "I'm not talking about the kind of marital relations that exist between most couples. What I want is… more. More even than what would legally be mine, what words on paper could convey. I'd want to possess you, Thea. To have you surrender to my every desire and submit your will to mine."

Heat fluttered between her thighs. Her lungs constricted.

Breathe in, breathe out.

"Could you, um, be more specific?" she managed.

"I'd want your body when I want, how I want. You wouldn't refuse me—unless you were ill or hurt. Even then, you would trust me to take care of you," he said bluntly. "Sometimes I would make love to you tenderly, other times I'd want to rut you hard and fast. I would accept no limits to our sensual life. Restrain you, have you in different positions, anything I can think of. And I would expect you not only to obey my command but wish to."

She felt dizzy. His words swamped her with a wave of arousal—and she wasn't even sure she fully comprehended what he was saying. She moistened her lips. "I… see."

"No, you don't. This isn't something I'd expect a virgin to understand." His pupils were dilated, black edging out grey. "But this is what I want, and I cannot change who I am."

She became aware of two oddly opposite feelings. One was heady, vibrant desire. What would it be like to belong to Gabriel in the way that he described? To finally be *wanted* as a woman and with such unbridled intensity? His masterful possession in the carriage washed over her, and recalling the supple leather between her palms, the way his command had restrained her, she felt a deep, lush tug of yearning.

At the same time, annoyance pricked her. Why did he have to assume that she wasn't able or willing to be what he wanted? After all, she trusted *him*. In spite of the violence in his past, she knew he would never hurt her—would defend her to his dying breath. Why didn't he return her trust, show confidence in her strength? Why did he say the word *virgin* as if her condition were a disease?

Lifting her chin, she said boldly, "And if I say this would not be a problem?"

"Then I'd say you don't know what you're talking about." His eyes hooded, a muscle leaping in his jaw. "You're dainty and innocent, Thea. I don't want to hurt you."

"For heaven's sake, I am tired of you treating me as if I'm a ninny incapable of making up my own mind." He was teaching her that she did indeed have a temper and that it was fully operational. "And I'm even more tired of being treated as too weak and delicate for your manly desires. You were happily married before. If this wasn't a problem then, I fail to see why you think it will be a problem with me."

Lines slashed around his mouth, his features hard as if

carved from granite. His throat worked, as if he wanted to say something and could not. Suddenly, she understood. What he was too much of a gentleman to say.

His marriage… it hadn't been perfect.

That was the reason for his present reservations. Guilt filled her that she'd brought up the topic so carelessly—and even more so that she felt a tiny, terrible spark of relief that whatever she was being measured against, it was not perfection.

"I will not dishonor the past," he said in low tones, "but I have learned from it. I will not place myself in a situation where my needs are incompatible with my wife's. To do so results in misery for both parties."

She swallowed. "And if both parties want the same thing? If I'm willing to try to be the kind of wife you want?"

In the moonlight, his mask of equanimity was ripped away. He was laid bare to her, his expression ravaged. "There's no *trying*, Thea," he said with sizzling scorn. "Marriage is permanent. If we are not suited, you'll be tied to a husband who disgusts you."

"You could never disgust me," she said with conviction.

"You don't know that," he scoffed.

Insight flashed. *He's afraid*, she thought in wonder. Back in the country, one of their neighbors had owned a stallion that had been trapped in a barn struck by lightning. Subsequently, any sign of a storm had caused the animal to react with agitation, to slice the air with its great hooves.

Whatever had happened in Gabriel's marriage had spooked him completely. Was making him lash out and try to scare her away.

Tenderness and a strange calm flowed through her.

Seeing this powerful male quivering with his need for her—fighting against it—opened an inner dam of courage. Strength. *He's yours for the taking*, a voice whispered. *If you're not afraid to reach for what you want.*

Oh, how she wanted him. A daring plan unfolded in her head. It was brazen, wanton—something a frail spinster would never dream of doing. And something a woman in love *had* to do.

She said softly, "The first time we met, I knew I wanted to be with you. You heard the passion in me, and you answered it. That was real, the true music between us. Anything else is just noise."

"In bed, I'm no sonata. By the time I'm finished with you, you'll be hearing a funeral march," he predicted grimly.

She shook off the *frisson* of anxiety elicited by his dire words. "I have a proposal for you, Gabriel. Let me decide for myself if I want what you have to offer. Treat me as the woman that I am," she said steadily, "and let *me* make the choice of whether I want to marry you."

"What you're asking…" He dragged a hand through his hair. "I'm not going to take your virginity without giving you my name."

"Surely there are less irrevocable ways to test our compatibility? In the carriage, you didn't…" Her cheeks pulsed with heat.

"I wanted to. I wanted to take you then and there, hard and fast." His tone was gritty. "Which why I didn't unleash my desires. Why I had you hold onto the strap—so your touch couldn't tempt me to further madness."

She had the sensation of standing on a precipice. Fear and exhilaration made her breathless. All her life she'd been waiting for this moment: to spread her wings and fly.

Taking a breath, she said, "What if we did it that way again?"

Chapter Seventeen

Blood plummeted from his brain and rushed hotly into his groin.

"I beg your pardon?" he said.

His throat went dry when she untied the belt of her flannel wrapper and pulled it free of the loops. The robe hung open, revealing the voluminous folds of her night rail. With care, she folded the wide strip of cloth in lengths and held it out to him.

"Bind me again—make love to me in whatever way you wish. I trust you." Her sweet, reckless faith blasted heat through his veins. "Don't you want to see if this is possible between us? Don't you want me enough to try?"

He said nothing. Didn't trust himself to open his mouth.

"If I don't like what happens, I promise I'll stop you. But if I like what you do,"—even in the moonlight, he could see her blush—"you will promise to give our relationship a chance."

God help him, her words had an unravelling effect. By now, she ought to have fainted, screamed, or run off. Instead, she'd plucked his deepest desires from his chest and presented them to him, tied up in ribbons of courage and innocence.

Innocence is the operative word. She has no idea what she's in store for.

"You'll get no promise from me," he bit out. "It's over between us, Thea. It should have never started. Now do you want to leave first or shall I?"

Her bottom lip quivered. He thought she would turn and flee then, but she remained rooted there, her blasted belt held out like an offering to the Gods. He felt like the veriest bastard—but he'd only be more of a bastard if he stayed. He turned to leave.

"Coward." The accusation echoed like a slap.

He pivoted to face her. "What did you say?"

"You heard me." Her face was flushed, her bosom heaving.

Anger roiled with lust, the tempest battering at his wall of control.

"I've killed men for less than that," he said evenly.

"I'm not afraid of you." Though her voice trembled, there was no mistaking the disdain. "There's only one weakling in this room, and that's you."

"I'm no bloody weakling," he growled.

"You're not protecting me; you're protecting yourself. You're terrified of taking a risk." She crossed her arms. "Of seeing where this relationship could go."

He knew where it was going: straight to hell. But it didn't matter. His vision was already darkening, the beast rearing inside. She wanted proof of what he was? Of how disgusting and degenerate he could be? By God, she was going to get it.

He snatched the length of flannel from her. Hefting the soft weight in his palm, he saw her lips tremble, yet her small chin was set, her expression determined.

"You're certain this is what you want?" he said with

lethal softness.

"Yes." The fire in her eyes made him hotter than Hades. "It's the only way for us to see if we're meant to be together."

We're not, he wanted to snarl. *Why do you keep rubbing my sodding nose in what can't be?*

But there was no fighting this; she'd pushed him too far. There was only one way out, and that was to show her what he was. To force her to recognize the truth: she was too innocent, too good for the likes of him. He circled her slowly, the crackling awareness between them feeding his dark hunger. When he faced her once again, he took her chin between finger and thumb.

"Remove your robe. Let it fall to the ground," he said.

Her wide-eyed gaze shimmered into his. A moment later, she shrugged off the flannel, the soft folds crumpling at her feet. The beribboned white nightgown she wore beneath was even more prim than the layer she'd shed. His pulse raced as he imagined what lay beneath the shapeless, billowing fabric.

But he didn't have to imagine.

"Take that off too," he said.

Her eyelashes flickered, her eyes swirling with a myriad of emotions. Disgust? Fear and regret that she'd started this?

Leave me, he thought in an agony of desire. *While you still can.*

Her fingers fumbled with the tiny pearl buttons on the front placket. In a swift, decisive motion, she pulled the garment over her head and let it, too, fall to the ground.

Devil and damn. His breath lodged in his throat. She was so lovely that it hurt to look at her. Alabaster skin, curves subtle and sweet. Delicate down to her very bones. He reached out and took a tress of her hair, caressing the silk against her right nipple. He heard her soft intake of breath, watched with dark satisfaction as the coral peak stiffened into a tight point.

He moved behind her. Stretching the belt she'd given him between his hands, he placed the wide fabric over her eyes.

"Gabriel, what are you...?"

"Not a word—unless it's 'no.'" He wound it twice and then secured the blindfold with a knot. "Say no, and I'll stop. Say no, and we'll put this madness behind us."

She pinned her lips together. Stubborn wench.

"You wanted this, you're going to get it." He pulled her back against him, against the throbbing column of his erection. Nothing polite about that. Nothing cowardly. Against the vulnerable curve of her ear, he rasped, "Say no, princess. Tell me to stop."

She said... nothing.

He grazed her earlobe with his teeth. Feeling her tremors, he did it again, this time suckling, using his tongue and teeth on the plump flesh as his hands coursed over her front. He cupped her breasts, pinching the stiff tips, and she wriggled against him, her soft pants fueling the inferno inside him.

Taking her hand, he drew her over to the bench. He sat and pulled her, standing, between his thighs. He couldn't help but feast upon the sight of her, trembling and willing. Beauty beyond compare. Primal need heated his blood; he felt like a medieval crusader who'd stormed the castle and claimed his prize.

She's not yours. Teach her a lesson. Show her she's no match for the beast that you are.

He couldn't stop his hands from framing her soft hips, pulling her closer. He kissed the curve of one breast, inhaling her sweet scent. She shivered, her hands clutching his shoulders. He licked her smooth white skin, kissing around the pretty pink nipples that stood so impudently, demanding his attention.

"Gabriel, please," she sighed.

"Please what?" he said.

"Kiss me."

"Where?" He challenged. "Where do you want my mouth?"

"On my breasts," she said shyly.

Disbelief and satisfaction mingled as he gave into her wanton request. He laved one pouting peak with his tongue, took his time sucking the sweet bud as her head fell back. He repeated the action on its twin. She whimpered his name, her fingers curling in his hair, drawing him closer.

Grasping her by the hips, he pulled her back. *Stay in control. Prove your point.*

"Get on the bench. Kneel on it and hold onto the back," he said brusquely.

With adorable awkwardness, she did as he asked.

"Spread your knees farther apart."

She complied, a shiver passing over her elegant limbs.

The sight of her posed with such decadence made his desire swell to new heights. His cock thrust fiercely upward against his abdomen, the head seeping with pre-spend. He ran a hand along the supple length of her spine, riveted by the erotic contrast between her milky paleness and his bronzed skin.

Why couldn't she see the damned difference between them, how wrong he was for her? How could she let him touch her with his filthy hands?

This wasn't some faerie tale. Sooner or later, she would realize that he wasn't going to turn into some prince. The beast was here to stay.

Get this over with.

"Thrust your bottom out," he said grimly. "Be quick about it."

She jutted her arse out, with no hesitation, and in spite of his self-disgust, his nostrils flared at the sight. Pale and trembling in the moonlight, the hills of her derriere beckoned like a field of untrodden snow. Unblemished, unclaimed—inviting him to leave his mark. Arousal pumped through him.

He smacked her on her right cheek.

She squealed in surprise. "What are you—"

"No talking. Not unless you tell me no." He spanked her other cheek. "Tell me to stop this depravity. Tell me to stop debasing you."

Her jaw clenched. She thrust her bottom out further, giving it a subtle wriggle.

Christ. He couldn't believe the spirit in her, the absolute gumption. His balls burgeoned in answer to her feminine defiance. Although he'd hardly used any force—he spanked to arouse not hurt—her bottom bore pretty pink marks. The visible evidence of his possession made him randier, harder than he had ever been in his life. Gritting his teeth, he administered another swat, cupping his hand, minimizing the impact but amplifying the lascivious slap of flesh meeting flesh.

This time she sighed. Bloody *sighed*.

Lusty and anguished, he did it again.

What was it going to take for her to realize what a bastard he was?

Thea was bombarded with sensation. It was like being immersed in music, in a different world where reality was suspended and nothing but feeling existed. She was glad for the cloth covering her eyes; her senses were already overwhelmed, and seeing what was happening would be too much. Here in the darkness, it was easier to let herself go.

To surrender to the wicked percussion of his dominance.

Her hands curled around the cool, smooth back of the bench as Gabriel's big hand smacked her bottom. The contact wasn't painful—quite the opposite. Who knew that being spanked would feel so *good*? His touch made sparks leap from nerve to nerve. Wherever he made contact, tingling warmth and pleasure spread.

"For God's sake, Thea, tell me to stop."

The agitated arousal in his words made her want him even more.

"Give me more, Gabriel," she whispered.

She heard him curse, and for an instant she feared he meant to stop altogether. Then he growled and branding kisses fell upon her shoulder blades, the undulating length of her spine. Strong hands cupped her bottom, kneading, soothing the stimulated flesh. Stars flashed across the dark field of the blindfold as he suddenly delved lower, into her swollen folds.

"*Christ*, your pussy is drenched for me." His words were guttural, disbelieving.

That part of her grew wetter at its naughty name. She gripped the back of the bench, her senses dissolving in a delicious haze as he cupped her, palming her soaking cleft.

"Devil and damn, you *liked* being spanked by me?"

He was catching on.

Shamelessly, she rubbed herself against his hand, sighing, "Oh, yes."

"You want my hand here, petting your pussy?"

"Yes, yes," she gasped.

"And this?" he growled.

His fingers plunged, filling her where she needed him. She moaned, her muscles clenching on the penetration, the fullness shooting fire along her nerves. Then he began to move in deep, masterful lunges that pushed the breath from her lungs.

"Push back on me, princess," he ordered. "Fuck yourself on my fingers."

His wicked words made her giddy with arousal. She obeyed, her need mounting as she rode his hand. His groans melded with the slick sounds of their connection, driving her on, making her wild in her pursuit of that vital finish. She'd never felt more alive, her lungs pumping, her skin burning with need. Suddenly, his touch skated over her hidden bud, and the race careened out of her control.

"Your pearl, your cunny belongs to me," he rasped. "Your pleasure is mine."

"*Yes.*"

He circled her pearl in rhythm to his invading touch.

"Then come for me now."

His forceful thrust propelled her over the edge. With a cry, she flew into the glittering horizon. He caught her, one hand muffling her moans as the other coaxed out spasm after soaring spasm.

The blindfold lifted. Floating on a cloud, she gazed up blissfully into his smoldering eyes as he settled her on the bench. Standing before her, he untied his robe and unfastened the fall of his trousers. Her breath caught as he pulled out his manhood: it was ruddy and thick, prominent veins girdling the length. The upthrust shaft visibly pulsed and strained against the confines of his fist.

"Touch me," he commanded. "Put your hands on my cock."

She'd thought herself well-read, but tonight her vocabulary was increasing by leaps and bounds. Excitement stirred as she wrapped her fingers around him. It was like holding a lightning bolt: a hot, potent rod that she could barely contain between her palms.

"I like touching you," she breathed.

Approval and dark wonder heated his eyes. "Then do it harder. Frig me like this."

His hand closed over hers, tightening her hold on him, urging a new, ferocious rhythm. He was a powerful instrument, and she was eager to learn how to play him properly. To give him the same pleasure that he'd given her. Under his tutorial, she pumped with both fists, lingering at the engorged crown when that seemed to enhance his delight. Moisture leaked from the slit in the tip, lubricating her touch, making him groan aloud.

Suddenly, he pushed her hands away.

"Your eyes, princess. Give me your eyes," he said as his hand jerked over his cock.

Her gaze flew up to his. The glittering possessiveness she saw there thrilled her to the core. The mask of the Angel was gone. Gabriel was baring himself, showing her his primal desires. Trusting that she was strong enough to be his match. The muscles of his jaw suddenly stood out, his teeth grinding as if against a shout.

An instant later, something hot jetted against her skin. She gasped as he climaxed with savage magnificence. Spurt after spurt spewed from the broad head of his cock, heat lashing her breasts, his male scent absorbing into her skin. Shudders wracked his powerful frame as he watched himself mark her with his essence. When he was finished, her heart was pounding as if she'd run for miles.

Wonderingly, she touched her fingertip to the glossy droplet that clung to her right nipple. The slick, circling contact hardened the bud, sent a fresh hum of awareness through her. Her pussy dampened in a rush.

"Devil and damn," he said reverently.

Her gaze raised to his. His chest was surging unevenly, wonder easing the harsh lines of his face. Fastening his trousers, he removed a handkerchief from the pocket of his robe. With gentle care, he wiped himself from her skin, the smoky warmth of his eyes making her throat clench. No words were exchanged, and yet a new connection thrummed between them. He dressed her, then drew her into his arms.

Against her hair, he murmured, "What the devil am I going to do with you?"

"More of what you just did?" she said hopefully.

His laugh was raw with emotion, his arms tightening

around her.

"You're mine now, Thea. Right or wrong," he said fiercely, "I'm never letting you go."

Chapter Eighteen

The next morning, Gabriel met with the men to make arrangements for the ambush at Covent Garden in four days' time. McLeod had secured a stall for them directly across from Fielding's so that they would be able to monitor Pompeia's meeting. They would catch her or the Spectre in the act and nab them.

As Kent and McLeod mapped out the positions where their team would lie in wait, Gabriel couldn't stop his mind from wandering back to the conservatory. To the midnight fantasy that, in the light of day, seemed too preposterously good to be real. Thea had accepted his past. His desires. Hell, she'd redefined eroticism for him, all that he'd known before decimated by the honesty and strength of her passion.

He'd debauched her, and she'd loved it, he thought dazedly. Wanted *more*.

Suddenly, he'd gone from being cursed to being the luckiest bastard in the world.

Because of her. His wanton princess.

"You approve the plan, my lord?"

Hastily, Gabriel drew his gaze to Kent. "Beg pardon?"

The investigator gave him an odd look, tapping the map on the table. "You were smiling as if this were a map to Shangri-La rather than Covent Garden. I assume you find no fault in our strategy?"

"Er, no. No fault," he muttered. "Carry on."

Heat crept up under his collar as the investigator scrutinized him for another moment before continuing on with the plans. If Kent caught wind of his thoughts, the man would more likely than not call him out. Then he would be put in the awkward position of dueling with his future brother-in-law.

For as soon as the Spectre was dealt with, he would offer for Thea. After last night, his honor—and the rest of him—demanded that he claim her as his. She'd provoked the beast; once he'd tasted her sweetness, there was no going back. There was only one problem. In the heat of all the revelations and passion last night, he'd conveniently neglected one topic: love. Specifically, that he wanted no part of it.

His neck heated as he thought of himself in the early days of being a newlywed, when he'd been struck by a mad craving for the emotion. For a closeness that he'd never known before. Embarrassment flooded him as he recalled his needful behavior. He hadn't blamed Sylvia for finding him tedious. He'd chalked it up to a bridegroom's temporary insanity.

He'd regained control, killing the outward signs of the emotion—but it had been too late. The roots had dug deep inside him, leading to misery when Sylvia had no longer wanted him in her bed. Keeping him trapped in a hell of love's making.

Give emotion an inch, and it will take a mile. Octavian had never missed an opportunity to point that out. *In life and in war, Trajan, sentiment only gets in the way.*

Jaw tautening, Gabriel told himself that he would learn

from his mistakes. It was enough—more than he'd hoped for—that Thea could accept him sexually. Desire was real and honest between them. He would possess her, but he wouldn't lose control over his emotions the way he once had. Disaster lay that way. As long as they didn't muddle up the business with unwarranted sentiment, they would rub along just fine.

Resolved, he returned his attention to planning with the other men. After another hour, when they were satisfied that all angles had been considered, they wrapped up for the day.

"If you're set on participating in the capture, you'd best spend the remainder of the time recuperating, my lord," Kent advised. "You're in no shape to be chasing down a murderer."

"I'll be ready," Gabriel said dismissively.

A few scratches weren't going to stop him from personally taking down the Spectre.

After the investigators departed, Gabriel went to find his son. Before he and Thea had parted last night, she'd suggested that he speak to Freddy about what was going on—in general, if not the specifics. Initially, he'd balked at the idea of causing his son distress by talking of villains and murder. He didn't want Freddy to be afraid, to risk triggering another spell.

"There's nothing like the lack of information to foster fear," Thea had countered. "Freddy is a sensitive and intelligent boy. He was almost kidnapped, and you were nearly killed. If you don't give him some reasonable explanation for all that has been happening, his imagination will surely run wild. A child's imagination can be far worse than the truth."

To Gabriel, open communication was a foreign concept. His own parents had not been in the same room often enough to share conversations of any length (he didn't count the occasional shouting matches he'd heard between them). As a spy, he'd learned to hold his cards close for obvious reasons. During his marriage, the times he'd tried to share his inner workings had only annoyed his wife and made him feel stupid and awkward.

Intimacy was not his forte. To his mind, it was preferable to avoid conversations that involved emotions in general. *Let us never speak of unpleasant things,* Sylvia's voice echoed.

But what if Thea was right and silence only led to worsening fears? The idea of Freddy being afraid did not sit well with Gabriel. Moments later, he found himself entering his son's room. Sunshine poured through the open curtains, and Freddy was reading in bed.

"Good afternoon, Papa," he said, politely setting aside his book.

Captain Gulliver again, Gabriel saw with wry amusement. Leave it to Thea to give his son a book about small people who could topple a giant.

He sat in the chair by the bed, searching for the best opening. "How are you feeling today?"

"Much better. I haven't had a headache or a spell," Freddy said tremulously.

"That is good news."

Silence stretched. Gabriel's gaze roamed around the bright chamber, dust motes sparkling in the air when the sun caught them. He cleared his throat. "You are comfortable?"

"Yes, sir. Very."

"Good." Gabriel smoothed an invisible crease on his

trousers, cursing his own ineptness. What if he said something wrong, caused the boy to have a fit? *Get on with it, man.* "Frederick, I've come to say a few words. About what has happened in the last fortnight—namely, your attempted kidnapping and my carriage accident."

Freddy's eyes turned as big as dinner plates. "Yes, sir?"

"It has come to my attention that the two events are not unrelated. I assure you, however, that there's no need to worry. I have everything under control and—"

"Are you going to die, Papa?"

To Gabriel's consternation, his son's eyes filled with tears.

"No, I'm not," he said firmly. "What gave you that idea?"

"I heard the maids gossiping. They said the fire was so big you almost didn't escape. They said it wasn't an accident, and someone is trying to kill you." A rivulet trickled down Freddy's freckled cheek, and the boy gave a sudden sob. "I—I don't want you to die."

"You mustn't get overwrought, Freddy. It isn't good for you…"

Appalled, Gabriel watched as Freddy began to cry in earnest. He fumbled in his jacket for a handkerchief. Held it out. But Freddy didn't even notice, his thin shoulders shaking, tears dripping onto the coverlet. Gingerly, Gabriel sat on the bed and put a tentative hand on the boy's shoulder.

"It's all right," he said gruffly. "Nothing's going to happen to me."

"B-but people die all the time. M-mama died. And if you d-die too, I'll be left alone."

Sudden clarity struck Gabriel. This was the first time Freddy had brought up the subject of Sylvia's death. Gabriel had feared that the topic would cause the boy more distress and worsen the seizures, so he'd never spoken about it. Since over four years had passed, he'd assumed Freddy had recovered from the loss, and no discussion was required. Clearly, he'd been wrong; he had to say something now.

"I don't know why your mama had to die," he said haltingly, "but I can promise you that I will do everything in my power to keep both you and me safe. I am a man of my word, Freddy. I would not lie to you. Do you believe me?"

His chest constricted at the trust he saw in his son's tear-stained eyes.

"Y-yes, Papa," Freddy said, sniffling.

"There's a good lad." Carefully, Gabriel blotted away the tears with his handkerchief. "In several days, I will be going with Mr. Kent and the others to track down the villain. We hope to capture him and end this for good."

"Will that be safe?" Freddy's bottom lip wobbled. "I w-wish I could help you. I w-wish I was normal and not sickly. I'm sorry to b-be a burden—"

"Hush."

Awkwardly, Gabriel tucked the boy's tousled head against his shoulder. As his son's small form shuddered with sobs, he felt an odd tightness in his throat. He remembered what Thea had said to him days ago. *He's afraid of disappointing you... he wants your approval more than anything.*

At the time, he'd snapped at her for daring to interfere. Now he wondered how he could have been so blind. Years he'd spent safeguarding Freddy's physical wellbeing, worrying about the boy's fits. He'd never suspected that his son might be hurting in other ways.

When the crying subsided, Gabriel gently but firmly took his son by the shoulders. "You are not a burden, Frederick. You are my son and heir."

"I still wish I could help." Freddy let out a quivering breath. "Be useful for once."

Gabriel thought quickly. "But you will be useful. You have a part to play as well."

"What can I do?" Freddy said doubtfully.

"Your role is an important one. While the others and I are out capturing the villain, you will be the man of the house. You're to protect Miss Kent and the duchess in my absence," Gabriel said in solemn tones. "Would you be willing to do that for me, son?"

Freddy's lashes lifted. "I'm to protect the ladies? Me?"

Him—along with the coterie of guards posted outside the Strathaven residence. But Freddy didn't have to know that.

"Now Miss Kent, being a female, will likely be worried." Selfishly, Gabriel found that he liked the idea of Thea fretting over him. "So you'll have to be brave and put on a good face. You'll have to set the example. It's not an easy assignment. Do you think you're up to taking it on?"

"Yes, Papa." Freddy's shoulders went back. "You can count on me."

"Excellent." He ruffled his son's hair—and sensed another presence in the room. Turning his head, he saw Thea standing in the doorway with an armful of books. Their gazes locked, and the warmth in her eyes, her rosy blush, made him want to spirit her away somewhere. To have her all to himself.

"I'm sorry to interrupt," she said, smiling. "I brought Freddy some new reading."

"We were just talking about you, Miss Thea." Freddy's chest puffed out. "I'm to look after you and the ladies when Papa is out hunting down the villain."

Thea went to the other side of the bed. Setting the volumes down on the coverlet, she brushed a wayward lock off Freddy's forehead. "In that case, I shall feel extremely safe."

Freddy beamed.

Gabriel looked at Thea over his son's head. His heart seemed to be pounding too quickly, the rhythm as erratic as that of a schoolboy with his first crush. The unpleasant comparison jolted him. *Don't make the same mistakes*, he told himself sternly. *Set realistic expectations.*

Freddy gave a sudden yawn.

"I believe it is time for your nap," Gabriel said.

"Yes, Papa."

"Miss Kent," he said, "I was wondering if you'd care to take a turn in the garden?"

"I'd love to," she said.

Her smile made him lose his train of thought. Offering her his arm, he strove to clear his head. To stay focused. This time around, he'd be damned if he let love get in the way of happiness.

Chapter Nineteen

Thea got permission from Emma to go for a short stroll out back with Gabriel.

She loved the garden, a masterpiece of manicured rosebushes that would make a lovely scene for a landscape painting. As they strolled along the pebbled path surrounded by hedges, she stole looks at Gabriel beneath her lashes. He was the perfect gentleman in a smoke grey cutaway and blue brocade waistcoat, the sun picking out the bronze in his austerely styled hair. He'd be a worthy subject of any portrait.

What was he thinking? she wondered. His features were once again schooled, free of the emotion she'd glimpsed when he'd held his son. Her throat thickened as she recalled that tender scene. So much lay beneath Gabriel's stoicism.

As if she needed proof of that after last night. A swoony feeling stole over her. Goodness, he was a passionate man.

"Penny for your thoughts?" he said.

She collected herself and smiled. "I was just thinking this would be a perfect setting for a painting. I would entitle it, *An English Interlude.*"

"It feels like an interlude, doesn't it? Imagine us with a moment that doesn't involve kidnapping, murder, or mayhem."

"There has been an excess of excitement," she agreed.

"Not the least of which included last night."

Suddenly, she found herself backed against a hedge, leaves and twigs prickling over her back, and Gabriel leaning over her. His pupils darkened, and he didn't look so much like a gentleman anymore. He didn't kiss like one either, she thought dizzily before her thoughts dissolved in the hot, sensual onslaught.

Sometime later, he released her. Straightened his clothing and her own. Tucking her arm in his, he continued to lead her down the path.

"I've been wanting to do that since I saw you this morning," he said in conversational tones.

She was still trying to regain her senses. "How do you *do* that?"

"Do what?"

"Look so proper when you're..."

"Thinking improper thoughts?" His smile was wry. "I was a spy, remember? Concealing one's desires is part of the job."

That made sense. She wanted to know so much more about him, and for once they had the opportunity to talk. Knowing that his marriage was a sensitive topic, she decided to skip over that for now.

"Tell me about your family," she said.

He slid her a glance. "What would you like to know?"

"Do you have siblings?"

"I had an older brother. He's dead."

She'd forgotten that he'd been the spare to the heir. "I'm sorry." She didn't want to imagine the grief she'd feel if she lost one of her own siblings. "That must have been difficult."

"It wasn't."

She frowned. "But he was your brother—"

"Michael and I weren't close. He was five years older than me." A pause. "His favorite hobby was beating me."

"At sports and games?" she said uncertainly.

"With his fists."

The toneless response made her shiver. "Why didn't your parents stop him?"

He paused. "This topic grows tedious."

"Not for me." When he said nothing, she persisted, "This isn't espionage, Gabriel. This is a conversation. What two people have when they're trying to get to know one another."

After a moment, Gabriel said, "My father was the one who set the example. He beat Michael, and Michael beat me. Only fair, I suppose." He shrugged. "My mama stayed out of things by locking herself in her bedchamber. She was a pious sort. Whenever she emerged, she'd announce that a propensity for violence and sin flowed in the veins of all men of the house. 'Twas the Tremont curse, she said. She prayed for us."

His matter-of-fact description chilled Thea. His family was as different from her own loving clan as day and night. No wonder he'd learned to keep to himself; he'd had no one to turn to.

"At least your mama's prayers worked," she said softly.

His brows lifted, his expression sardonic.

"As a spy, any violence you conducted was for a purpose," she said adamantly. "For the greater good. That is not the same as being a mindless brute."

"Octavian told me once that he recruited me because he sensed what I have inside me." Gabriel's lips twisted. "The capacity to do what needed to be done—that was his euphemism for it. He groomed the darkness in me."

"Were you close to him? You called him your mentor," she said tentatively.

Dragonflies performed dizzy, iridescent loops in front of them as they walked on in silence.

"When I met Octavian, there was anger in me," Gabriel said finally. "From the years of living under my brother's tyranny, I suppose. Octavian taught me to control that, gave me skills to put it to a better use. For that, I owe him."

Shadows flitted through his eyes. There was something else he wasn't saying.

"But?" she said softly.

He gave her a wry glance. "But our parting was not amicable. He didn't want me to leave the Quorum, and I refused to stay."

"Why?"

"It's a long story."

"As you said, we've the time." She gave him an encouraging smile.

"There are better ways to pass time."

He stopped on the path, picking up her hand. His lips grazed the inside of her wrist, and her knees wobbled. His smoky gaze promised sinful temptation, yet she wanted to get close to him in other ways as well.

"You're dodging the question," she said.

"And you're more persistent than I realized." His thumb brushed over her lower lip. "What happened to you surrendering your will to mine?"

Heat pulsed in her cheeks. And elsewhere.

"Our agreement was for the bedchamber," she reminded

him. "We're not in one presently."

His slow smile made her toes curl in her half-boots. "I could improvise."

"Even you wouldn't make love to me in the garden… in broad daylight…" The devilish glint in his eyes stole away her certainty. Worried and aroused, she said breathlessly, "Gabriel, anyone could see…"

He laughed. The low, husky sound was the most beautiful music she'd ever heard.

"You should see yourself, princess. Pink-cheeked and fretting." He tipped her chin up, his gaze dark and penetrating. "Tell me, are you afraid that I'm going to make love to you here or afraid," he murmured, "that I'm not?"

His hold on her was mesmeric; she couldn't look away. Couldn't give him anything but the truth. "A little of both?" she managed.

His lips curved with satisfaction. Holding her hand, he led her forward along the path again. "Enough about me. Let's talk about you."

She hadn't learned nearly enough about him. Seeing the impassive set of his features, however, she knew that she wasn't likely to get more from him today. Getting close to Gabriel was like learning an intricate piece of music. Her struggles with Beethoven's Hammerklavier sonata came to mind. She doubted she would ever master the mammoth composition, from the power of its first movement to the deeply emotional nuances of the second to the dizzying complexity of the last.

But she didn't give up trying. One couldn't force music to reveal its true heart. That took patience, practice, and the wisdom to let each piece unfold in its own time.

Sometimes capitulating was a better choice than pounding the keys in frustration.

"You've met most of my family, with the exception of my brother Harry," she said. "He's an aspiring scientist and making quite a splash at Cambridge."

"Your family has unusual interests."

"Our parents encouraged us to follow our hearts, even if that took us off the beaten path."

"In your case, it's taken you straight off a cliff," he said wryly. "You don't know what you've taken on with me, princess."

"I think I got a pretty good idea last night. Wild pleasure, a man who desires me for who I am." She canted her head. "I suppose I'll have to suffer."

"Far be it for me to argue if you think you got yourself a bargain," he muttered. "What I don't understand is why you haven't married before this. Surely you've had offers."

His confidence that she'd received proposals flattered her.

"I'm hardly a Diamond of the First Water, and despite the matches made by my siblings, I'm a middling class miss when it comes down to it," she said earnestly. After a pause, she added, "Then there's my condition. Gentlemen who have shown interest want to treat me like a porcelain doll. An ornament. That's not who I am at all and not the sort of wife I want to be."

He frowned. "You're gorgeous, passionate, and sweet. Everything a man could want."

As thrilled as she was by his praise, she couldn't squelch a bubble of doubt. "You used to think I was too delicate for you."

"The problem was with me, not you. I thought my desires were too much for any virgin." Before she could argue, he amended, "Until you proved me wrong. I think some part of me recognized that you were my match from the first time I laid eyes on you."

"You remember when we met?" she said breathlessly.

"Your sister's engagement party. You were playing a sonata." His lips curved. "I got aroused just listening to you."

Her eyes widened. "You did?"

"I wanted to take you then and there," he said ruefully. "To strip you bare and lay you on the piano, see your soft white skin against the dark wood. I wanted to take my time kissing and touching you... everywhere. And you would lie there and let me do anything I wanted."

She was having trouble breathing. Her nipples tingled; her pussy dampened.

His eyes had a knowing gleam. "At the same time, you reminded me of the princess in the tower. Out of my reach."

"And now?" she dared to ask.

He fingered a loose curl at her temple, his touch proprietary. "I have something to discuss with you, Thea. Something I ought to have said last night."

Her heart began to drum. Was he about to officially propose?

"Yes?" she managed.

"It concerns marriage. To be honest, before you I'd never thought to marry again. I'm not a man suited for that sort of union—"

"I don't agree," she protested.

"Let me finish. I'm not an easy man, and my past—well, you know what it is. Then there are my proclivities in the bedchamber." His gaze was steady on hers. "But you've seemed to take all of that in stride, so the future lays before us. There is a matter, however, that I feel we must address. It concerns love."

This was more like it. Her pulse aflutter, she said, "Yes?"

"I don't believe it has a place in marriage," he said.

She had the sensation of plunging into an abyss. "I... I don't understand."

"Excessive emotion can handicap a marriage and lead to disappointment. I speak from experience," he said quietly, "and it is a mistake I'll not make again."

"Are you referring to your first marriage?" she said uncertainly.

He gave a curt nod. "As I've said, I will not dishonor my deceased wife by discussing details. But love did not serve us well. I'm ill-suited for strong emotion. Perhaps that is due to my time as an agent—but that is neither here nor there. If I were to marry again, I would wish to set clear expectations."

Thea's head was spinning. "What sort of expectations?"

"That my wife and I share physical desire. That we are committed to the same goals: raising a family, making a home of the estate. And that we are honest with one another and develop trust over time."

Slowly, some of Thea's anxiety eased. With the exception of his caveat on love, his description sounded almost exactly like what she wanted. Perhaps this was merely an issue in semantics.

"What about fidelity?" she said cautiously.

"Let me be very clear: you would belong to me. And I would have no need of another." The possessiveness in his eyes was unmistakable and filled her with relief.

Yet a question popped into her head. In truth, it had been tumbling about since he'd revealed last night that his marriage hadn't been perfect, intimating that conjugal relations had been part of the problem.

"Were you faithful to your wife?" she said.

His eyes shuttered. "I told you my marriage isn't open for discussion."

"If I'm to make a decision about the future, then I need to be in possession of the facts." She wasn't about to back down, not about this.

Silence stretched between them.

His jaw taut, he said, "Sylvia told me to take a mistress, and I couldn't do it. I couldn't betray my vows."

This affirmed what Thea believed about him, that he'd been a true and devoted husband. It also raised more questions about his marriage: what sort of a woman would knowingly send her husband off into another's arms? Sensing the emotion churning beneath his controlled surface, she decided not to push about his past. At least, not at the moment.

Instead, she said, "I know extramarital affairs are fashionable amongst the *ton*, but I wouldn't tolerate it. I wouldn't want my husband sharing intimacies with anyone else."

"Possessive, are you?" His eyes softened, as if the notion pleased him. "Don't worry, princess, I won't stray from your bed."

They were approaching a topic, a sensitive and critical one. She hesitated, thinking of how hard it must have been for him to lose his wife in childbirth. Yet it was all the more reason she had to ask.

Steeling herself, she said, "How do you feel about children? Having them, I mean."

Her decision about the future might hang upon his answer. Because she needed—nay, deserved—to be treated as a flesh and blood woman. To have a husband who wanted her as a wife and lover and mother of his children. Being called a princess was one thing; she didn't intend to be shut away, protected in some stupid tower. She'd wasted enough of her life watching the world go by. She wanted to *live*.

With bated breath, she waited for his reply.

His brows came together, his expression intent but not closed off. "I won't lie. The idea of you going through childbirth takes years off my life. There are, er, methods to prevent conception, of course." Before she could speak, he went on, "But I would not insist upon using them if your desire was to add to our family."

"I want any children we might be blessed with," she said tremulously.

After a moment, he gave a curt nod.

Their negotiations gave her hope. Desire, honesty, and commitment to building a family together would provide a strong foundation for their relationship. It was more than most marriages had. And everything he told her solidified her intuition that he wasn't a man incapable of love; he shied from it because it had hurt him before. Over time, if she could win his trust, perhaps she could convince him to give love another chance.

Love couldn't be forced. Luckily, her struggles with her health and her music had taught her patience.

"What do you think about affection?" she ventured.

"A bonus, definitely." His thumb skated along her

bottom lip. "One that I would welcome between us."

This time, she heard a wistful edge to his reply and saw the fierce longing in his eyes. That, of everything, decided it for her. He might speak of love in a dismissive manner, yet he made her feel desired and wanted down to the marrow of her being. He was a man who guarded his emotions, yes, but he could learn to let down his barriers. Look how he'd been with Freddy. He was opening up to her, too—even if he didn't realize it.

In her heart, she knew that they could make each other happy. A future with him was worth any risk. She took the leap of faith.

"At our first meeting, you heard my music—heard *me*. I knew then that you were the husband I wanted. Nothing has changed," she said.

A breath released from him. The fact that he'd been holding it fueled her optimism.

I love you, Gabriel. One day, I hope you'll love me back.

"Then the matter is settled. You honor me, my sweet." He bent over her hand. The gesture was formal, yet primal satisfaction gleamed in his eyes. "Now I suggest we go in before I scandalize my future in-laws beyond repair."

Chapter Twenty

The next three days passed like the calm before the storm. Thea was well aware of the impending danger, the preparations being made, yet even worry couldn't erode the happiness she felt. For almost a year, she'd agonized over whether her affections were returned. Now, to know that Gabriel desired her and wanted to marry her... she could scarcely contain her joy.

Of course, there was his moratorium on love, but once she made up her mind about a thing, she stuck to it. She'd decided not to let a mere word get in the way of their future. After all, his views on the subject might change over time, and she would do everything in her power to sway him. For now, it was enough to know that they would have desire and affection, be true to one another.

Gabriel made her promise, however, not to say anything about their future as yet. He didn't want her tied to him until the threat was over, and nothing she said could dissuade him. *There's no need to rush. You're mine and nothing is going to change that.* He'd given her his slow, heart-stopping smile. *Once I slay the dragon, then I can claim the princess.*

In the interim, he'd made renewed efforts at propriety. He'd put an end to midnight visits, much to her dismay. His reasons were sound. He didn't want to ruin her before they were even engaged. He didn't want to dishonor his hosts and damage her family's opinion of him before he asked for her hand. He didn't want to scandalize Freddy, her future son.

Thea knew Gabriel was right. She didn't like it, but she couldn't fault him for being a gentleman. The time she got to spend with him almost made up for the hiatus in the physical side of things. They were chaperoned by her sister and oft in the company of others, which prevented more intimate talks, yet allowed them to discover more about one another bit by bit. Or at least Gabriel was learning more about *her*.

His abilities as a spy became apparent as he effortlessly culled information from her. He wanted to hear stories about her family, Chudleigh Crest... if any village lad had ever tried to court her. When she admitted that a farmer's son had once shown her interest, the possessive flare in his eyes had pleased her to no end.

When it came to his own past, Gabriel proved more reticent. She gleaned a few more details about his family; it solidified her impression that his childhood had been a cold and solitary one. Certain topics continued to remain out of bounds. He shut down whenever she tried to ask him about his marriage or his espionage days. Whenever she became frustrated with his refusal to share those experiences with her, she reminded herself that a piece wasn't learned in a day. It would take time to excavate emotions that had been buried so deeply.

Then the day of the ambush arrived, and her fear obliterated all other concerns. Gabriel and the men left for Covent Garden before dawn. If all went well, they would catch the Spectre and put an end to the madness. Although Thea trusted in the men's abilities, she couldn't stem the rising tide of worry. Even playing the piano didn't distract her; her fingers felt clumsy and wooden. She hit a jarring, discordant note.

"Do you think Papa will be all right?"

She looked up from the keyboard and saw the anxiety clouding Freddy's blue-grey eyes. He was curled up on the nearby settee. Dr. Abernathy had paid a visit this morning and declared the boy fit as a fiddle. The good physician had imparted other advice as well, sharing a new and exciting treatment that might help the boy's falling spells. Thea couldn't wait to discuss it with Gabriel... when he returned.

Quelling her fear, she managed a smile. "I'm sure that your father is doing just fine. After all, he is with my brother and Mr. McLeod. They are professionals and do this sort of thing every day."

"You mustn't worry, Miss Thea." Freddy's freckled features were adorably fierce. "I will take good care of you in his absence."

"I feel better already." Crossing over, she ruffled the boy's hair and sat next to him.

"Miss Thea?"

"Yes, dear?"

"Are you going to marry my papa?"

She blinked at Freddy's grave expression. Goodness. She hadn't been expecting that.

"Um, why do you ask?" she said, buying for time.

"Because I can tell Papa likes you. He is always looking at you,"—the boy cocked his head—"and he is in better spirits when you are around."

Warmth unfurled. How she wanted to tell Freddy the truth: that they would soon be a family. Yet she and Gabriel had agreed to talk to the boy together after the Spectre's capture, and she didn't want to break her promise.

"We haven't made any decisions about the future as yet," she hedged. "There are too many things going on at present."

"Well, if you were to get married, I wouldn't mind. Actually, I think… I think I'd like having a mama again," he said shyly.

Oh, Freddy, I'd like to be your mama. So very much.

"Would you come live with us in Hampshire?" he asked, clearly warming to the subject.

Gabriel had told her how committed he was to improving Oakhurst, his country seat, and asked if she would mind living away from London and her family. She'd responded with the truth: as long as she could visit with her siblings, she wouldn't mind at all. She enjoyed the pace of country life and wanted to help Gabriel restore his home to its former glory. To undo the damage that the generations before him had done.

Apparently mistaking her silence for reluctance, Freddy said in a small voice, "I know it's not the nicest estate."

"Oh no, dear. It's not that," she said quickly.

"Once, when our neighbor Lord Melville came to talk to Papa about the fences between our properties, his son Horatio made fun of the manor. I overheard him laughing about it. He said, *What a pile of rubble. Nothing works here*,"— Freddy's voice wavered—"*not even the heir.*"

Unfamiliar rage rushed through Thea. She wished Horatio Melville was here so that she could give him a sound tongue lashing and piece of her mind.

"That is utter rubbish," she said hotly. "Only a lack wit

would say such a thing."

"Horatio is the biggest, most athletic boy in the county. He wins at everything." Freddy's gaze lowered to his lap. "And I can't even leave the bedchamber."

"You're not in your bedchamber now," she said.

"Who knows how long that will last?" His shoulders slumped. "When I have another fit, back to the sickroom I'll go."

Thea hesitated, torn between conflicting desires. On the one hand, she knew it wasn't wise to broach the subject of a potential cure for Freddy's seizures before talking to Gabriel... but she couldn't sit by and say nothing whilst Freddy suffered, losing hope by the minute—not when she knew of a way to help. Dr. Abernathy's description of the new treatment ran through her mind.

It may sound unconventional, Miss Kent, he'd said in his Scottish burr, *but I assure you that the fasting cure has been around since antiquity. A colleague of mine in Edinburgh has recently refined the technique, and he's reported astonishing success. My observations suggest that Master Frederick would benefit. His appetite has naturally been down since the attack on his father, and interestingly this has coincided with a reduction in his spells. If you could convince Lord Tremont to consider the treatment, I think it might benefit the young lad greatly.*

Treading carefully, Thea said, "Your papa mentioned that you have tried a great many remedies for your condition. If there was yet another, one that showed some promise but had no guarantee of success, would you want to try it?"

"Does the treatment hurt?"

"No, but it isn't easy," she said honestly. "It involves

following a strict diet—even fasting at times."

"You mean I don't get to eat?" His brow furrowed. "I don't think I'd like that."

"At the beginning, you'd only be given water, beef tea, and the like. If that helps your symptoms, different foods would gradually be introduced to your diet. You'd have to work with the physician to decide what worsens your spells or makes them better."

Freddy's lashes moved rapidly. "Does Papa think I should try this?"

I hope so. Knowing how Gabriel felt about medical treatments, she prayed that he would come around—and not be upset with her for suggesting it.

"First and foremost, he's concerned about protecting you," she said with care. "You've been through a lot already, dearest, and he doesn't want you to undergo any unnecessary hardship or disappointment. As I've said, the treatment might not work."

Freddy's shoulders straightened. "I think I would like to give it a go anyhow." His smile was wistful. "What have I to lose, after all?"

Pride swelled in her. *He's such a brave boy, and he doesn't even realize it.*

Smiling, she squeezed his hand. "Then we'll talk to your father together."

A knock sounded on the door. Jarvis entered and announced the arrival of visitors. Thea had almost forgotten that she'd sent a note to Marianne, asking her to call—and to bring Edward, if she could. Marianne glided in, a vision in a lilac promenade dress trimmed in blond lace. At her heels was her gangly, dark-haired son, who had a wooden box tucked under one arm.

"Good morning to the both of you. Thank you for coming." Thea rose to receive Marianne's kiss on the cheek, and Freddy stumbled to his feet as well.

"With all that is going on today, we could all use some distraction. Edward and I happened to be at loose ends." Removing her bonnet and gloves, Marianne gave her son a little nudge. "Go ahead and introduce yourself, dear."

Edward shuffled forward. He took after Ambrose with his unruly locks, tall, loose-limbed build, and earnest demeanor. His precociousness he'd inherited from his mother, however, and he had her vivid green eyes as well. Her fashion sense clearly had a hand in his smart outfit, which included a checkered waistcoat and trousers tucked into gleaming, boy-sized boots.

"How d'you do? Edward Kent at your service," he said with a grave little bow.

"I'm Frederick Ridgley, Viscount Waverly. But you can call me Freddy, if you like." The boy's face reddened, and after an awkward pause, he blurted, "I'm eight years old."

"You don't *look* eight. I'm eight, and I'm much taller than you," Edward observed.

"Manners, Edward," Marianne admonished.

"But it's true. Why is it impolite to speak the truth, Mama?" Edward directed a puzzled glance at her.

"Because some truths are best kept to oneself. You must consider how your words will affect others before speaking them."

A notch formed between Edward's brows. "You mean I should think things but sometimes not say them?"

"That's the general idea, yes," Marianne said wryly.

After a moment, Edward gave a brisk nod. "My apologies," he said to Freddy, "I didn't mean to be rude. That is, I *am* taller than you, but that doesn't signify anything. My uncle Harry is a scientist, and he and I once performed an experiment with beans."

"Beans?" Freddy said uncertainly.

"We grew them using the exact same amount of soil and water, yet all of the plants sprouted at different rates. Uncle Harry said the nature of the seed is just as important as the conditions in which it is grown. All the beans themselves turned out equally fine, however,"—Edward shrugged—"so in the end it doesn't really matter which plant grows the fastest or tallest, does it?"

Freddy blinked owlishly. "Um, I suppose not."

Thea hid a smile.

"I say, would you care for a game of Spillikins?" Abrupt changes in topic were common with her quick-witted nephew. Edward held up the box he'd brought. "I have my set."

Freddy bit his lip. "I—I don't know how to play."

"It's simple. I'll teach you," Edward said. "Mama, may we be excused?"

"Yes, dear. But don't overtire your host, all right?" Marianne said.

Freddy slid a tentative glance at Thea. She gave him an encouraging nod.

The boys found a place in the far corner. Settling on the carpet, they began laying out the sticks for their game. Before long the two were chatting back and forth, emitting cheers and groans as jackstraw empires rose and fell.

Thea and Marianne watched on from the settee.

"Thank you for coming today," Thea said in an undertone. "Freddy needed the company."

"Edward, too. He could do with a friend his own age. He spends entirely too much time with adults and books. Experiments with beans, for God's sake." Marianne shuddered. "At this rate, he'll be talking about crop rotation before he's ten."

"You're a proud mama, and you know it."

"True." Marianne's lips curved. "You appear to be showing some talent for the role as well."

Fighting off a blush, Thea tried to deflect her sister-in-law's all too astute statement. "Freddy would bring out the maternal instinct in anyone. He's bright and charming—all he needs is the confidence to see the best in himself."

"And you, dearest, are just the one to provide it. Things are progressing nicely with the father, I take it?"

As there was no fooling the other, she might as well be honest. "Yes, they are. But please don't say anything yet. Gabriel and I don't want to make any announcements until after the villain is caught."

"I understand completely. My lips are sealed."

"Thank you." Thea's fingers knotted in her lap. "How do you think the men are doing? I wish I could be there with them."

"I know the feeling, my dear, but we'd only be a distraction. The men would worry about our safety rather than the troubles at hand." Her sister-in-law smiled ruefully. "No, we must let them go about their business whilst we conduct our own."

"Our own?"

Marianne arched a brow. "Solving the case requires

more than physical prowess."

"You have a point. Actually, I've been mulling over the evidence against Lady Blackwood," Thea said thoughtfully, "and I still can't believe she is guilty. I've another hypothesis."

"By all means, do tell," her sister-in-law replied.

Bending their heads together, they got to work discussing the case.

Chapter Twenty-One

Hidden in a covered cart next to the stall, Gabriel surveyed the teeming piazza from a discreet hole bored into the side. On market days, Covent Garden was a site of chaotic industry, and today was no exception. 'Twas as if Bedlam had been contained and put to work within the square bounded by St. Paul's Cathedral to the west and the arched porticoes of the Italianate buildings on the other three sides.

Within the booming market, stalls and barrows overflowed with fresh produce, flowers, and goods of every kind. The scent of violets and lilac mingled with that of savory pasties and fresh green herbs. Merchants cheerfully haggled with passersby from every walk of life, from the bleary-eyed rake just stumbling home from the night's entertainments to the housewife looking for the best bargains to the fine lady whose entourage of servants lugged home baskets of hothouse blooms.

Even William McLeod seemed to be infected by the market's mercantile fever. Sporting a straw hat, an apron over his rough linen shirt and trousers, and a bright silk handkerchief in lieu of a cravat, the brawny Scotsman made a convincing costermonger. With the brashness of a true peddler, he strutted before the fruit-laden table, his Cockney accent ringing with authenticity.

"Fresh melons fer sale," he chanted. "Come get yer ripe and juicy melons."

A pair of painted light skirts stopped in front of the stall, and one cooed out, "Ripe an' juicy as these, my good fellow?" She jiggled the generous wares on display in her skimpy bodice while her companion snickered.

"*My* melons won't get trouble and strife after yer life," McLeod tossed back good-naturedly.

Trouble and strife, Gabriel knew, was thieves' cant for *wife*. Giggling, the prostitutes blew the Scot a kiss before sashaying off to look for customers elsewhere. Once they'd moved on, Gabriel had a clear view of his target again: the stall across the way. He'd been monitoring Fairfield's for the past hour and thus far seen nothing untoward. The flower supplier was doing brisk business, emptying and replenishing buckets of fresh blooms.

Gabriel consulted his pocket watch.

Almost time. Pompeia should be arriving at any moment.

They were ready for her. In his head, he reviewed their strategy once again, the invisible perimeter Kent and Associates had set up around Fairfield's. He and McLeod monitored the stall itself. Kent and his men, all disguised as market goers, roved along the western entrance to the market, covering possible escape routes via King and Henrietta streets. The agency's other partner, Mr. Lugo, masqueraded as a coachman, surveying James Street to the north.

Lastly, Strathaven, whom everyone agreed could not pass for anything but a duke, kept watch over Russell Street to the south from an unmarked carriage.

Everyone and everything was in place. The plan was

simple. They would catch Pompeia and whoever she was meeting in the act. They would discover the Spectre's identity and put an end to the villain's malevolence for good.

Then Gabriel could give his attention to Thea. The thought of her waiting at home with his son gave him hope. He hoarded the memory of her passion like glowing coals against a winter night. She represented a fresh start. He couldn't wait to get back to her and start their future together.

A sixth sense interrupted his thoughts. With trained efficiency, he shut out everything, honing in on the figure walking like a queen down the crowded aisle. The thrill of the hunt rushed through him.

Pompeia had arrived.

She wore a dress of rich amber, her bonnet secured beneath her chin with a blue bow. Ever the excellent actress, she showed no hurry, no indication that she was heading toward a nefarious purpose. She stopped to examine merchandise, smelling this and tasting that. As if she had all the bloody time in the world.

Eventually, she neared Fairfield's. Gabriel pulled back from the viewing hole, counting out twenty heartbeats. Trained by the same spymaster, he and Pompeia played the game by the same rules. If he were about to commit wrongdoing, he'd be conducting a thorough sweep of the terrain before moving forward. He had no doubt that she would take similar precautions. He forced himself to count to twenty again before returning his gaze to the hole.

She was directly across from him now, at Fairfield's, her back to him. The eager flower seller asked if she was looking for anything in particular. She demurred and was invited to browse, which she did with studied deliberateness. She perused the selection of hydrangeas, tulips, and daffodils, her gloved fingers brushing over the petals.

Do whatever you came here to do, he silently urged. *Expose your evil schemes.*

Gabriel's attention suddenly snagged on a man approaching Fairfield's. The stranger came from the opposite direction that Pompeia had, his gait jaunty... *and uneven.* The hairs lifted on Gabriel's skin. He couldn't see the man's face—it was obscured by the brim of a brown cap—but there was no mistaking the slight limp in the stride, the favoring of the left leg. This was the bastard who'd passed his carriage right before the explosion.

The man jostled into Pompeia, muttering an apology, and Gabriel saw it happen.

Pompeia's hand dipped into her reticule. In a movement so quick and sly it would have been lost in a blink, she removed something, slipped it into the pocket of the man's jacket. The transaction completed, the man continued on his way and she on hers, moving in the opposite direction.

Gabriel jumped from his hiding place, fruit flying onto the cobblestones as he hurdled over the cart's edge. He landed on his feet in the aisle, surprised gasps erupting around him. Both Pompeia and her conspirator whirled around; their faces registered shock.

McLeod was instantly at Gabriel's back.

"Who's mine?" the Scot demanded.

"She is."

"Bloody hell, why do I get stuck with the female?" McLeod grumbled. "They don't fight fair, *and* you can't hurt 'em."

Gabriel didn't bother to reply, taking off after the man in brown. The suspect was plowing through the crowd, taking no heed of women and children, shoving everyone and everything out of his way. His limp didn't slow him down a whit.

Feral aggression lengthened Gabriel's stride. He'd chosen to go after the man because he knew Pompeia, knew she was too clever to engage in a tussle. Contrary to McLeod's dire prediction, she wouldn't give him any physical trouble; she'd simply feign innocence, use her status and influential husband as a shield of protection. They couldn't touch her without proof. And the proof lay in the pocket of the bastard Gabriel was chasing down.

He was only several paces behind now, but the man suddenly rounded a corner, pulling down a stack of crates as he went. A hawker's angry shouts in his ears, Gabriel leapt over the boxes, nearly losing his footing on the scattered potatoes but keeping his momentum. He almost caught up to his target, but then the man turned another corner.

Devil take it.

The bastard had chosen a vegetable aisle, one populated by old women in aprons shucking peas into baskets. Cries went up as the scoundrel grabbed the baskets, throwing them behind him as he ran. The morts scrambled forward on hands and knees, blocking the path as they tried desperately to collect the rolling green bits of their livelihood.

Cursing, Gabriel judged the blighter to be halfway down the aisle. Instead of following, he sprinted toward the next row. His lungs burned as he propelled himself forward, determined to head his foe off at the next intersection.

He made it, just seconds after his target, a half-dozen

yards to his left. They'd emerged on the less populated northern edge of the market, and the man took off again, heading east. Gabriel gave chase, his blood pumping as he narrowed the gap between them. Bystanders spared them less than a glance, the chasing of pickpockets and thieves as common as the pigeons that scattered from their path.

Gabriel trailed his target onto a deserted lane. Almost there…

The bastard ducked again, this time into an alleyway between buildings. Gabriel went in right after him, grabbed him by the shoulder, slamming him into the wall. The villain recovered quickly, feigning to the left, a blade suddenly glinting in his grip. Gabriel caught the arcing hand, the tip of the blade inches from his own throat. He gripped hard and twisted.

The man cried out. Steel clattered to the ground.

Just when Gabriel thought he had the upper hand, the bastard landed a blow to his injured side. Pain shot through him, cutting short his breath and loosening his grip. He doubled over, and his foe delivered another swift blow. Through the red-hot haze, he saw the other reach into a hidden holster, pull out another knife. The steel flashed, and even as Gabriel tried to dodge out of the way, he knew it was too late.

A shot rang through the alleyway.

It took Gabriel's befuddled senses a second to comprehend that he wasn't dead. That he was still standing. His opponent, on the other hand, lay gasping on the alleyway floor, blood spurting from a lethal wound.

Gabriel's gaze swung to the end of the alley. He glimpsed what might have been the hem of a greatcoat, the flap of black material vanishing. Should he give chase? His wound throbbed, trickling beneath his shirt, and he knew he was in no shape to catch the other. His mystery savior had too much of a lead.

Who would rescue him—and run afterward?

What in the devil's name was going on?

He staggered over to the unmoving body of his attacker. He'd seen death enough times to know that the other was already gone. Having no wish to explain the situation to a constable, he cast a look around and did a swift search through the dead man's pockets. Nothing to identify the other. His fingers closed around something hard and smooth.

He removed the object. A figurine. The cherubic shepherdess was made of biscuit pottery, no more than six inches tall. Her features were coarsely sculpted and no work of art. Why had Pompeia slipped this to the man?

Footsteps neared. Shoving the figurine into his pocket, Gabriel spun around, his hands reaching for his blades. Mr. Lugo, Kent's partner, filled the end of the alleyway. His pistol was drawn, his chest heaving from exertion.

"Lost you in the crowd there, my lord." The broad-shouldered African eyed the corpse on the ground. "Looks like you handled some trouble on your own."

"I had some help," Gabriel said tersely. "Did you see a man in black just now? Wearing a greatcoat, perhaps?"

"No, my lord. But we oughtn't linger." Lugo gave him a meaningful look. "We have your other suspect in custody."

The investigator was right. Pompeia was the key to this.

One way or another, Gabriel would get his answers from her.

Chapter Twenty-Two

Pompeia gave them nothing.

Sitting in Strathaven's study, she sipped tea as if this were a social visit, and she wasn't here under duress. She was flanked by Kent and McLeod, both of whom remained standing, and Lugo was posted outside the door for good measure. The duke faced her from behind his large mahogany desk while Gabriel leaned against the front edge, his boots crossed at the ankle, his posture as deliberately nonchalant as hers.

"I've told you all I know, gentlemen, which is nothing. I haven't the faintest idea why you've retained me." She put her cup down with a click. "But Blackwood will be expecting me home soon, and I don't like to keep him waiting."

A perfect blend of innocence and threat. She hadn't changed a whit. Her skill at deflection and deceit remained razor sharp.

"You can drop the pretense," he said. "Everyone in this room knows who you are."

She hid behind a puzzled expression. "Of course they do. I am well acquainted with His Grace and the duchess, and I have had the pleasure of chatting with Miss Kent on several occasions." She widened her indigo eyes. "Speaking of which, I wonder why the ladies are not present? I should love to visit with them."

Over Gabriel's dead body. He'd had the duke's full backing when he insisted that Thea and the other ladies stay out of the interrogation. The women hadn't been pleased with the decision, and that was too damned bad. He wasn't letting the viper near them.

"The game is up, Pompeia," he said.

At the mention of her old name, her composure slipped a little. Nothing much—a slight tremble of her lips, her fingers curling in her lap—and she recovered in the next instant.

She laughed. "What an odd thing to say, Lord Tremont."

"I've told everyone in this room about your past and mine," he said with calculated ruthlessness. "There is no hiding. Now what is your connection to the Spectre?"

"How dare you, Trajan." Rage leapt into her violet eyes, her ladylike mask slipping. "You took an oath, the only sacred vow amongst agents—"

"Did you kill Octavian?" He said it point blank to gauge her reaction.

"Did you?" she shot back.

He narrowed his eyes. "He came to me for help. He was on the trail of the Spectre, and somebody killed him for it."

"I hadn't spoken to Octavian in years. That part of my life is done with," she said flatly.

"Then why do you have a note written by the Spectre in your desk?"

Her fingers gripped in her lap. "You had no right to search my things."

"I have every right if you're a turncoat. If you betrayed Octavian and Marius and caused the deaths of countless men during the war."

Her expression was scornful. "You have no proof of that."

"Don't I?" Gabriel said.

He removed the figurine from his pocket and placed it on the desk. Against the rich mahogany, the biscuit pottery looked crude and cheap. Yet it held some vital secret.

"What is the significance of this?" he said. "What message are you passing onto the Spectre?"

"I don't know what you're talking about. I've never seen that before in my life." Her lips curled in derision. "Unless you count those barrows where the hawkers are always trying to sell off their family's last heirlooms."

"This is no heirloom."

Picking up the figurine, he hefted its weight—and smashed it against the desk. Clay crumbled into shards and dust, revealing straw and a small satin purse. He picked up the drawstring bag. It was heavy.

"Give that to me." Pompeia surged to her feet. "If you don't, I vow you will regret it."

He ignored her, emptying the contents into his palm. A fortune of rubies and diamonds glittered in the afternoon light. He dangled the necklace in front of Strathaven.

"How much, would you guess?" he said.

The duke's brows rose. "Ten thousand, at the very least."

McLeod whistled under his breath.

Gabriel faced Pompeia. "Why are you giving the Spectre this? What nefarious schemes are the two of you plotting together?"

"It's none of your sodding business what I do." Her

polished accent slipped a little, revealing an edge of Cockney. "Give the necklace back to me, or you will regret it."

"You're going to hang for treason unless you give me a reason to see you spared."

"A threat from a man. Now there's something new," she spat. "You'll get nothing from me."

He had half a mind to call her bluff and hand her over to the Crown forthwith. Clearly, she was withholding evidence; she'd been caught red-handed giving goods to an infamous traitor. She had guilt written all over her.

The door suddenly opened, and Gabriel's jaw tautened as Thea, the duchess, and Mrs. Kent marched in. He glared at Lugo, who brought up the rear.

"Don't blame Lugo," Thea said quickly. "We made him let us in."

Lugo shrugged his massive shoulders, his broad features abashed. "I tried to stop them."

"He couldn't very well prevent me from entering a room of my own home, could he?" the duchess said. "Hello there, Lady Blackwood."

Uncertainty flashed across Pompeia's features before she said coolly, "Good day, ladies."

"I thought we agreed that the study was my private domain." Going over to his wife, Strathaven tipped up her chin. "What happens here stays here, remember?"

"Which is why we thought it best to be present," she replied, "so we don't miss anything."

"And one misses all sorts of things when one is eavesdropping from the next room." Thea came up to Gabriel, peering at the necklace he held. Her eyes rounded.

"Is that what you were saying was worth ten thousand pounds?"

He gritted his teeth. "You're not supposed to be here."

"I belong here." Her gaze was steady on his. "Let me help."

Aware of Pompeia's scrutiny, he shuffled Thea off to the side, said under his breath, "You can help by turning around and leaving. It's not safe for you to be here."

"For you, either. And from what I overheard,"—her hushed tone matched his—"you're not making much headway. Why don't you let me speak to her, woman to woman?"

"Because she's not just a woman. She's a spy."

"She's both. And a wife and mother as well." Thea touched his sleeve. "Trust me?"

As much as he wanted to argue further, he knew it was too late and that Pompeia was taking everything in. Storing knowledge, information about his relationship with Thea to use against him in the future. In her situation, he'd do the same thing. If he didn't back down, it would only highlight his vulnerability when it came to Thea—and thereby put her at greater risk.

It took all his willpower to step back. "Do what you will," he said indifferently.

Thea smiled at him, her presence so lovely that his chest tightened. Outwardly, he showed nothing. They returned to the larger group, and Her Grace waved everyone toward the sitting area, where she promptly plopped herself onto a settee.

She gestured to the cushion beside her. "Come, Lady Blackwood, you are a guest. This business is awkward enough as it is. No use in being even more uncomfortable."

"Am I a guest, Your Grace?" Pompeia arched an eyebrow.

"Well, yes... unless you are involved in the evil schemes to harm Tremont and his son. If you're involved with the Spectre, then that's a different story altogether," the duchess said. "Then we'll have to see justice done."

One could never accuse Strathaven's lady of being indirect.

"I see." After a moment, Pompeia crossed over to sit next to her hostess, her amber skirts settling around her.

Everyone else took a seat as well, except Strathaven. He stood behind his wife, his posture rigidly protective. Gabriel sat in the wingchair closest to Pompeia, ready to act if she so much as laid an untoward glance on anyone.

Thea spoke from across the coffee table. "Lady Blackwood," she said quietly, "why don't you tell us what is truly going on?"

"Why should I bother?" Pompeia circled the room with a scathing glance. "You'll twist my words, use them against me. If I say I am innocent, no one will believe me."

"I would believe you," Thea said.

"And why would you do that?" the marchioness scoffed.

"Because you have a loving husband and three young boys, which means you have a lot to lose. Why would you sacrifice so much? What could the Spectre possibly offer that was greater than such happiness?"

Gabriel saw the flicker in Pompeia's eyes. Not anger this time, but... fear? She pinned her lips together, remaining silent.

"Do you know what I think, my lady? No spy on earth

could give you more than what you have." Thea paused. "But they could take it away, couldn't they?"

Gabriel frowned at the direction of Thea's hypothesis. Pompeia was no victim; she was cold-blooded and cunning. He remembered the old rumor of how she'd seduced a man—and killed him that same night without blinking. Her marriage to Blackwood had to be a front. A mere cover she'd constructed to protect her from her past. She wasn't capable of decency and devotion.

"Are you being blackmailed, my lady?" Kent's voice was as steady and calm as Thea's. "If you are, extortion is a crime, and we can help you."

"Help me?" Pompeia's lips took on a cynical curve. "What could you possibly do? You cannot change the past."

"No, but we can alter the future—if you tell us the truth." Her gaze earnest, Thea said, "You were wearing that necklace at your ball. You told me it was given to you by your husband, who valued you above those rubies. What could compel you to give up such a priceless gift, a symbol of his love and regard, something I know you must hold dear?"

Pompeia's throat worked. "You know nothing."

"I know you love Lord Blackwood and your three boys. I know you would do anything at all to protect your family."

Damn… she's good, Gabriel thought with a jolt of surprise. With her gentle, natural sincerity, Thea was making more headway than he had with all his threats. He saw Pompeia's stricken expression—and the moment that the fight drained from her.

"It doesn't matter now. Nothing does." Bitterness infused his former colleague's words. "He didn't get his payment today, and he'll carry through with his threat soon enough."

"This is the Spectre you speak of?" Kent said tersely. "He's blackmailing you?"

Pompeia gave a dull nod.

"What hold does he have over you?" the duchess said.

"You know what I was. You have to ask?" Pompeia's smile conveyed the opposite of mirth. "He is threatening to provide my husband and the *ton* with a document outlining in explicit detail my actions during the war. The men I killed, the men I... was associated with."

Gabriel hadn't expected to feel empathy for his old comrade, but the anguish and self-hatred in her eyes... it was like staring into his own looking glass. She might have abandoned them during their last mission and escaped the beatings that he, Tiberius, and Cicero had been subjected to. Yet it seemed even she hadn't emerged unscathed.

"We all do things we regret, my lady." The husky words came from Mrs. Kent, who sat with her husband on an adjacent loveseat. "You were working in service of your country, and in a time of war, right is not always clear from wrong—"

"It is to my husband. Blackwood is an honorable man and knows nothing of my true past. He thinks that I come from a good family, that I was raised abroad until I returned to London that Season when we met. But I've lied to him from the start. From the very beginning, I've deceived Blackwood,"—Pompeia's voice cracked—"and he will never be able to forgive me."

Silence blanketed the room. Gabriel thought Pompeia's assessment was dead on. Chances were slim that her husband—that any man—could forgive such deception.

"When did the Spectre first contact you?" Kent said quietly.

Pompeia's face was bone-white. "Two months ago. An unmarked letter appeared at the top of my correspondence, and I recall opening it at breakfast. I could hardly fathom what I was seeing: Spectre's code and handwriting in front of me… as Blackwood sat not three feet away." Her lips gave a betraying tremble. "The letter named names from my past and threatened to expose me if I didn't bring five thousand pounds to a park near Russell Square three days later."

"You gave the blackmailer money?" Gabriel said.

"A sapphire bracelet to be precise. I didn't have that sort of money lying around and couldn't raise it without Blackwood noticing. But I wasn't about to be bled dry. I went that day prepared to silence our old foe if need be," she said with the ruthlessness he remembered, "but the Spectre never showed. He sent a street urchin to collect, and I tried to follow him, but my skills had gone rusty. The sprat lost me in the rookery." Her lips twisted. "When I received the second blackmail note, I was informed that my disregard of the instructions would cost me. For this next payment, he demanded ten thousand dollars. That is why I had to give him the necklace."

"Forgive me for asking," the duchess said, "but wouldn't Lord Blackwood notice the absence of such expensive jewelry?"

"I had replicas made to wear. High quality glass. My husband is generous but not a connoisseur of jewels," Pompeia said dully.

"But the Spectre didn't get the necklace today." Thea nibbled her lower lip. "How will you prevent him from following through on his threat?"

Helplessness glimmered in Pompeia's eyes even as her hands balled. "I don't know. But I would do anything—anything at all—to protect my husband from my past."

"We will help you," Thea said.

What?

"We have a common enemy, after all, and thus would benefit from working together," she went on brightly. "Don't you agree, Tremont?"

"No," he said.

The fact that he had a twinge of sympathy for Pompeia didn't mean that he trusted her. Even if he believed that she wasn't the Spectre, years of antipathy didn't vanish in an instant. He couldn't forget that her actions had indirectly led to the fiasco in Normandy. To his torture and the death of Marius.

As if reading his thoughts, Pompeia said coolly, "You never were the trusting type, were you, Trajan?"

"I prefer to stay alive," he said.

Pompeia rose. Good manners prompted the men in the room to follow.

"You're the one who brought me here," she said in biting tones. "I never asked for your interference. I can handle the Spectre myself."

"No, you can't," Thea said.

Precisely. Gabriel couldn't agree more. Even though he didn't trust Pompeia, he didn't want her off on her own, potentially scaring off the true prey. It was best to keep her under close watch.

"And neither can Tremont," Thea added.

He scowled at her. "I bloody can and will."

"Is it a rule of espionage that agents must be stubborn?" she said mildly. "The fact is that the both of you need to work together in order to capture this spymaster."

"My sister is right," Kent said. "My agency is here to assist, of course, but in this room the two of you are the experts on the Spectre. My lady, do you know his true identity?"

"I have only suspicions." Exhaling, Pompeia said, "I believe him to be one of ours. That is the only way he would have access to information pertaining to my past activities."

"Octavian found proof of the same thing. The Spectre was a double agent and one of the Quorum," Gabriel said flatly.

Her throat rippled as if she were trying to digest the unpalatable piece of information. The telltale sign suggested that she was telling the truth. That she'd been betrayed just like him.

Her gaze thinned. "So if neither one of us is the Spectre…"

"Then we've narrowed the field down considerably, haven't we?" he said coolly.

Thea beamed at both of them. "Then why don't we put our heads together and capture the villain?"

Chapter Twenty-Three

Thea was relieved at the group's reception of Lady Blackwood. From the nodding of their heads and their looks of concern, Thea could tell that Ambrose and Emma believed the marchioness' story. Thea sensed that even Gabriel was thawing toward his former comrade... although one would be hard pressed to tell from his demeanor.

He'd once again donned his mask of stoicism. Thea was beginning to see how a career in espionage might have shaped that particular tendency for Lady Blackwood, too, had retreated behind a façade of jaded sophistication. To Thea, the two ex-agents treated each other warily, like alley cats ready to attack if either encroached on the other's territory.

Emma rang for refreshments, and Thea made her selection from the silver tiers of sandwiches and pastries before sitting next to Gabriel on the couch. He was summarizing the details of the chase through Covent Garden, concluding with the mysterious shooter who'd saved his life.

"You didn't get a look at him?" Ambrose asked.

Gabriel shook his head. "I saw what might have been the tail of a black greatcoat. It happened too quickly. Whoever he was, he simply vanished."

"Like a ghost," Thea murmured.

"Do you think it was the Spectre?" Lady Blackwood's violet gaze narrowed. "Silencing his own courier? If so, why didn't he just shoot you instead?"

The thought of Gabriel being that close to harm churned Thea's belly. He, however, treated his brush with death with utter sangfroid.

"A good question," he said. "He had a clear shot. If he meant to kill me, I'd be dead."

"Then we must conclude that whoever this stranger was, he meant to save you. It appears you have a secret benefactor," Ambrose said. "A friend who wishes to remain anonymous."

Gabriel's brow furrowed. "I can't think of who that might be."

"Then I suggest we start with the facts we do know and work from there," Ambrose said. "First, we know that the Spectre is after money. His blackmailing of Lady Blackwood is proof of this. It might also explain why he auctioned off Tremont's blade."

"So our suspect has a monetary motive," Strathaven said with a nod. "What do we know about the financials of Heath and Davenport?"

"From what we've gathered, neither appear to be short of funds," Ambrose admitted.

"The Davenports spend lavishly," Marianne added, "and Heath inherited a fortune from an uncle—who was in coal, I believe."

Mulling over the matter, Thea said, "At this point, the Spectre must fear being discovered. Perhaps he is stockpiling money so that he can flee."

"An excellent point, Miss Kent." Gabriel's brows rose.

She heard and saw his surprise. Clearly, it would take time for him to get accustomed to the fact that she meant to be a true partner to him—the way Marianne was to Ambrose and Emma to Strathaven. What little she knew about Gabriel's past led her to believe that his reluctance to involve her wasn't because he saw her as weak; it was because he wasn't used to having support of any kind. Certainly, he hadn't received much growing up, and from what she'd gleaned, his marriage hadn't been as ideal as everyone had supposed.

Was it any wonder that trusting didn't come easily for Gabriel?

Yet a relationship without trust was nothing. Thea felt a *frisson* of anxiety—and pushed it aside. *He said he wanted trust to be part of our marriage. Over time, he'll come to trust me.*

Aloud, she said, "If he is indeed desperate for money, then he will likely contact Lady Blackwood again." She turned to the marchioness. "Your secret may be safe until he gets what he wants."

Lady Blackwood gave a tight nod.

"If he does contact you, my lady, you must let us know," Ambrose said. "Blackmail only begets more blackmail. The only surefire way to stop the Spectre is to capture him."

"I will do whatever is necessary to keep my secret." Menace infused her words.

Gabriel turned to Mr. McLeod. "Have you anything to report on the other suspects?"

"Aye." The Scot gulped down his tea before continuing. "Our ongoing reconnaissance corroborates that Heath's a loaded cannon. His opium habit doesn't help his stability. Our man Cooper infiltrated a meeting of rabble-rousers that

Heath attends regularly. The topic of gunpowder came up."

"The same weapon used in the attack on Tremont," Ambrose said grimly.

"Aye. But according to Cooper, there's no proof that the radicals have actually gotten their hands on any explosives. Mostly they just drink too much and run off at the gob." McLeod popped a ham and watercress triangle into his mouth, chewing vigorously.

"Should we pay Heath a visit and question him?" Ambrose said.

"No," Lady Blackwood said.

"Why not?" Thea asked.

"Tiberius is high-strung and spooks easily. If he scents danger, he's going to run like a fox and then we'll never find him." She shook her head. "I say you wait. Continue to follow him. The minute you have solid proof of anything, you close in."

"Tremont?" Ambrose said.

Gabriel gave a curt nod. "She's right. We'll have to keep monitoring him."

"That leaves Cicero—Lord Davenport." Ambrose sighed. "Now he's a different breed altogether. We've tailed him for days, and his worse offense was a half-day visit to Bond Street while Parliament was in session. He's either innocent or the most careful blighter alive."

"If his speeches in the House of Lords are any indication, he is indeed a master of evasion," Strathaven said wryly.

"So a head-on approach won't work with him either, will it?" Thea said.

"He'd talk circles around us if we tried to interrogate him," Gabriel said. "We'll have to find another way to get proof."

"As it happens, I have a plan."

All eyes turned to Lady Blackwood.

"His wife holds a monthly luncheon for the charity she heads," the marchioness went on. "The next one takes place tomorrow. I will attend and use the opportunity to search Davenport's private domain."

"But won't Lord Davenport be suspicious if you show up?" Thea asked.

"I've done reconnaissance. Ladies who've attended the luncheon in the past say that he is never present. The Davenports are a fashionable couple and do not live in each other's pockets."

"It would be difficult for you to conduct a thorough search on your own. I'll go with you," Emma offered.

"Me too," Thea said.

"*The hell you will,*" Gabriel and Strathaven growled in unison.

Emma sighed. "Now, darling, we've been through this before—"

"This is different. This is a murderer we're talking about," the duke said. "If you think I'm going to permit you to march alone into the lion's den—"

"Emma won't be alone. I'll be there," Thea said, "and Lady Blackwood too. We'll have power in numbers."

"Out of the question," Gabriel grated out. "This plan is far too dangerous."

"Not really. Lady Davenport's luncheon is in the middle of the day, and Davenport won't even be at home," Thea said in reasonable tones. "We'll be with a houseful of society ladies—what could possibly happen to us with all those witnesses? On the off chance that a servant finds me in Davenport's study, I'll just say I got lost."

"I always say that I was looking for the retiring room," Em put in. "In my experience, that prevents further questioning by footmen."

Thea made mental note of her sister's advice.

"I forbid it," Strathaven said.

Emma's chin angled up. Tension thickened in the room. The rustle of jonquil silk interrupted the silent standoff.

"I'll take my leave before this gets bloody," Lady Blackwood drawled. "Let me know what you decide. Even if it's a last minute decision, you'll still be guaranteed entrée."

"Why is that?" Thea asked.

"Millicent Davenport is a snob who married above herself. She's the daughter of George Clemens, one of London's most brilliant legal minds but a solicitor nonetheless. Millicent's most cherished ambition is to leave her roots behind. To have the opportunity to host a duchess at her luncheon?" Lady Blackwood gave Emma a pitying look. "She'll be on you like a vine on a trellis, Your Grace."

"That could be useful. Emma could distract Lady Davenport," Thea said brightly, "while I search Cicero's study."

"You're not going," Gabriel said.

In soothing tones, Thea said, "We'll talk about it later."

"We can discuss it until hell freezes over, and you're still not going."

Thea decided to ignore him for now and talk to him later—in private.

"Let me see you to the door, Lady Blackwood," she said instead.

In the foyer, she lay a hand on the marchioness' arm. Beneath the other's nonchalance, she sensed an agitated spirit.

"All will be well," she said. "You'll see."

The lady's smile was bleak. "I wish I had your faith. Unfortunately, reality has been my religion for far too long."

"You are not alone in this. We're here to help you, my lady."

"Given everything you know about me, you might as well call me Pandora." The raven-haired beauty studied her a moment, then said quietly, "Why do you wish to help me?"

"Because you are innocent. And you deserve justice," Thea said in surprise.

The other's violet eyes glimmered. "I don't think anyone has ever called me innocent before. Even if it is not true," she said, her voice catching, "I thank you for believing it."

"But it is true. You mustn't lose hope, Pandora."

"Hope?" For an instant, the mask slid from the other's face, and what lay underneath caused Thea's heart to constrict. "My dear, that is the least of which I have to lose."

Before she could reply, the marchioness slipped out the door.

Chapter Twenty-Four

On her way back to the study, Thea was waylaid by her sister.

Emma pulled her into the empty dining room and closed the door. "Have you and Tremont come to an understanding?" she said without preamble.

Thea squirmed. "I can't talk about it yet."

"So that's a yes."

"I promised Tremont that I wouldn't say anything until after the Spectre is caught."

"If he doesn't want the world to know, then he shouldn't act as if he has rights over you," Emma pointed out. "His manner in the study was dashed proprietary, if you ask me."

"He's just being protective. He doesn't want me to get hurt." Thea bit her lip. "That's also why he doesn't want to make an engagement official until the villain is captured. He's afraid whomever is after him will target me as well."

"I suppose he gets points for that," her sister said in grudging tones. "But Thea, are you absolutely certain about your feelings for him? That he is the husband you want?"

Yes, he was—with the exception of his aversion to love. But she wasn't about to bring up that topic with her overprotective sister.

"I'm certain," she said.

Emma studied her for a moment. Sighed. "That's that,

then."

"Would you do me a favor, Em?"

"Yes, dear?"

"I need to speak with Tremont in private, to convince him to let me go with Pandora," Thea said in a rush. "Her plan to infiltrate the Davenports' home could provide the key to solving this mystery."

"I agree. And Tremont's not the only one who needs to be convinced. I have my work cut out for me with His Grace." Emma huffed out a breath.

"You'll help me then?"

"If I don't help you," her sister said wryly, "you'll just go about this pell-mell on your own."

Thea's cheeks warmed. "Mama and Papa said we must follow our hearts."

"Well, yours can lead you to the library. I'll see to it that you and Tremont are undisturbed. Seeing as you're practically engaged, I suppose I can turn a blind eye for a few minutes."

"Thank you," Thea said. "For helping me—and especially for helping Tremont."

Emma squeezed her hand. "What are sisters for? I just hope you know what you're doing."

I hope so, too, she thought.

In the library, Gabriel crossed his arms over his chest.

"There's nothing further to talk about. Pompeia's plan is rife with danger," he said.

Had he ever thought of Thea as fragile, weak? Despite

her dainty appearance, she faced him like a warrior princess, battle light in her hazel eyes. Just looking at her stirred his blood.

"This is a charity luncheon, for goodness' sake. Nothing is going to happen to me."

"Forget it," he said. "You're not going."

Her chin lifted. "You can't tell me what to do."

"I can, and I will."

"We're not even officially engaged. You have no rights over me."

"You know damn well that you're mine." A muscle ticked in his jaw. Reining in his temper, he said deliberately, "Or have you forgotten the carriage ride and that night in the conservatory? The promise you made to do everything that I ask?" Hunger for her gnawed at him, amplifying his frustration.

Instead of looking flustered, she seemed… impatient.

"In the bedchamber, yes. But you're not going to dictate everything else in our relationship. If that's the kind of marriage you're envisioning, don't bother to offer for me."

Ice coated his gut. "Is that a threat?"

"No. It's a fact." Her expulsion of breath was slow, deep. "I can't stand by and do nothing when you're in danger. Please don't ask me to." Her beautiful eyes pleaded with him. "One of your expectations for marriage was trust. That goes both ways."

"Trust has nothing to do with this," he said.

Out of nowhere, the dark images assailed him, smoke and fire obscuring his path, black waves churning his gut. A body arching over the cliff, falling, too late to reach…

"Gabriel?"

Her soft voice brought him back.

"Devil take it, I can't put you at risk." His fists balled. "If you get hurt because of me…"

"Nothing's going to happen to me at a society luncheon." Her gaze searched his. "But this isn't just about me, is it?"

He said nothing.

"Tell me," she urged. "I want to know. You can trust me."

"Marius," he said finally.

"You've mentioned him before." Her brow furrowed. "He was your fellow agent. The one who was killed?"

"Because of me." Guilt rushed, dark water under ice. "I got him killed."

"What happened?" she said softly.

"After the defeat of Bonaparte, Octavian remained obsessed with hunting down French spies, including the Spectre. He was convinced that they could do harm to England still, and he was like a mongrel with a bone." Gabriel's lips twisted. "Octavian received information that the Spectre had a lair on the coast of Normandy. He sent the Quorum to capture the spymaster. Pompeia didn't show."

"So that is why there's bad blood between the two of you?" Thea said.

He gave a terse nod. "She abandoned us, left us shorthanded on a critical mission. The four of us went in without her. We were ambushed. Marius escaped, but Tiberius, Cicero, and I were captured. Interrogated." His heart thudded hollowly. "Beaten."

"Oh, Gabriel."

He didn't want her sympathy. Now that he'd reopened

the wound, all he wanted was to let the festering drain out. "Things would have been a lot worse for us if Marius hadn't mounted a rescue. He came back. Risked life and limb to save us."

"He was a hero," Thea murmured.

"Yes. He was the true leader of our group, more of a brother to me than my own had ever been. When I joined the Quorum, he showed me the ropes."

Your temper is a liability, Trajan—unless you learn to harness it. How many times had Marius given him that advice? Gabriel's throat convulsed as his old friend rose in his mind's eye: a wiry fellow with sandy hair, pale eyes that had seen the worst of the world yet still looked for the best. Even in him.

"The night of the rescue, Marius broke into the compound and set off explosives. He set us all free, and we fought our way out. Tiberius and Cicero escaped, but I... I was in a blood rage. Even after I thought I killed the Spectre, it wasn't enough. I wanted all of my enemy dead."

"You weren't in your right mind. After being a prisoner," Thea whispered, "who would be?"

"Marius tried to make me leave. Stayed with me, dragged me out of the burning building," Gabriel said woodenly. "Outside, the enemy surrounded us, and I don't remember what happened next. Only that I killed them, all of them. And when I thought to look for Marius... it was too late.

"He was standing at the edge of a cliff. An enemy soldier had cornered him, pointing a pistol at him, and I couldn't do anything. Couldn't reach him. I watched him get shot and fall over the precipice." His fists clenched at his sides. "By the time I'd killed that last bastard, there was no sign of Marius on the rocks below. The waves must have dragged his body out to sea."

"Oh, my love." Thea hugged him around the waist.

"Marius died because I lost control over my emotions. I lost my head, and my friend paid the ultimate price for it." Slowly, his arms went around her, absorbing her warmth, letting her honeysuckle sweetness sustain him through the rest. "Around that time, my brother died, and I inherited the title. I decided to focus on my estate and duty. I wanted to put espionage behind me, to never spill another's blood again. Octavian was not happy with my decision, but I didn't give a damn. Our parting was not amicable."

"God knows you'd given enough to your country." Thea's words emerged muffled from against his chest. "And you mustn't blame yourself for doing your duty as a spy."

"I murdered men in cold blood," he said flatly. "You don't find that abhorrent?"

"I find war abhorrent. I find what it does to good men abhorrent." The golden warmth in her eyes flowed through him. "But never you, Gabriel."

He surrounded her face with his palms. "Then don't put me through hell. If you ever got hurt because of me... it would destroy me, Thea."

"But the situations aren't the same. I'm going to a tea party not an enemy stronghold." She placed her hands over his. "No one is safe while the Spectre is at large. The best way to protect me is to let me help you catch him."

Christ, she had the grace of a princess—and the brain of a barrister.

"The best way to protect you is to keep you away from harm," he said.

"What tower do you plan to lock me into, Gabriel?

What place do you know of that the Spectre cannot reach? How will you guard me every moment of every day?"

Her words struck a deep chord of truth. Released a resonating fear.

"If you truly want to protect me, then let me go with Pandora and Emma tomorrow to Lady Davenport's. I promise we'll be careful... and you can monitor the proceedings if you wish," she said quickly.

Her logic battled his denial. Was she right? Was allowing her to participate in the investigation the best way to protect her?

His spy's mind analyzed her plan, broke it down to various angles. If he kept watch during her visit to the Davenports—had all entrances to the townhouse monitored—it was unlikely that anything could happen to her or the other two ladies. It was a luncheon, after all. The presence of the other guests would add a layer of safety.

But he would require more. He looked into Thea's earnest eyes and came to a decision. He would do everything in his power to keep her safe. Even if it meant trusting in her strength.

"You will have one hour," he said. "If you're not out by then, I will go in and drag you out myself."

"Oh, Gabriel, thank—"

"I will be circling outside in the carriage. I'll post men at the front and back of the house. If anything so much as feels amiss, I want you to leave immediately."

"Of course—"

"Finally, you're not going in unarmed," he said.

She flung her arms around him. "You won't regret this, I promise. I'll carry anything you like. A pistol, knife, explosives—"

"You don't need an arsenal." His lips twitched at her crestfallen expression. "Beginners are more likely to hurt themselves with their weapons than their opponents."

Her brow furrowed. "Then how do you plan to arm me?"

Although it went against his fundamental desire to keep her safe under lock and key, the best protection, he'd concluded, was to teach her how to defend herself. Unbuttoning his jacket, he placed it over the back of the couch.

"I'm going to show you how to fight, princess," he said.

Chapter Twenty-Five

Exhilaration thrummed through Thea as Gabriel led her behind the couches to an empty space in the library. He'd agreed to her plan. He was learning to trust her instead of just pushing her away, and he'd shared more of his painful past. Even as her chest clenched at all the guilt he'd buried, the ordeal that he'd suffered, she also felt a surge of hope. Short of having his love, his trust was the next best thing. Who knew where it would lead?

We're making progress. Happiness bubbled inside her as he positioned her at the center of the round Axminster carpet, a vibrant green field abloom with a floral motif.

Facing her, he said, "What would you do if you were attacked?"

"Scream for help," she answered promptly.

"What if there was no one to hear you?"

"I'd struggle… and pummel him if necessary."

In a flash, he moved. She gasped as she found herself caged, her back against his hard chest, his arm hooked around her neck. Instinctively, she tried to get loose, her hands grasping at the muscular limb that held her captive. It was like trying to lift a fallen column of the Acropolis. Trapped by his superior strength, she could do nothing. She wriggled as haplessly as a pinned butterfly.

"First lesson: don't fight an attacker on his terms."

Gabriel's words warmed the sensitive curve of her ear, and in spite of the situation, sensual awareness shivered over her. "He's going to be stronger than you physically; trying to match him in brute strength will only waste your energy."

It was true. Her strength *was* draining from her. She stopped squirming.

"Good. Now can you move my arm?"

She realized that she was still futilely grabbing onto the sinewy limb around her neck. "No."

"Which leads to the second lesson: don't be predictable. Your attacker will expect you to follow a victim's instinct, so take him by surprise instead. The best defense can often be an offensive move. Let go of my arm."

She let her hands fall to her sides.

"Now he's stronger than you, but he's got his weaknesses as well. You use those against him, along with the element of surprise, and it can buy you precious seconds of freedom. Ready to learn three simple steps?"

She nodded.

"First, bring your left elbow back as hard as you can, straight into his solar plexus. He'll double over or at least be surprised," Gabriel said. "You then execute the second step: stomp on his foot, aiming for the instep to maximize pain. That should free you of his grip and then you have a choice with the third step."

Thea's mind spun with the startling information. It went against every ladylike behavior that she'd ever been taught. But being a lady wasn't helpful when it came to dealing with an enemy spy, was it?

"Choice?" she said.

"Run or spin around and knee him in the groin."

Thea reviewed the steps in her head. "It seems simple enough."

"Try it."

"But I don't want to hurt you," she protested.

"I'll be fine." His voice was dry. "Give it a go, princess."

Before she could respond, his arm tightened around her neck. The choking sensation set off an inner alarm. Her hands went immediately to the source of her confinement, but then Gabriel's instructions kicked in. In a swift movement, she brought her elbow back instead, heard his breath whoosh as she made contact with the wall of muscle. In the next second, she stepped on his foot with all her might. His grip loosened enough for her to whirl around, bring up her knee.

At the last instant, he deflected her attack with his hands.

They stood facing each other, their breaths heavy in the air.

He rubbed his chest, said ruefully, "You're a quick study."

Energy flowed through her. The sizzling sense of power was not unlike what she experienced when Gabriel made love to her. She felt vital, amazingly strong.

"Show me more," she said.

His lips quirked. With a bow, he said, "As you wish."

Ten minutes later, she'd practiced several techniques that not only defused an attacker's strength but used it against him. Gabriel showed her that, with the right leverage and maneuvers, she could defend herself against a larger, stronger opponent. The knowledge empowered her. Brimming with new confidence, she decided to try a variation on the theme. When Gabriel came at her, she ducked and instead of using her elbow as he'd taught her, she stuck out her leg to trip him.

The world tilted. She found herself flat on her back, her hands pinned above her head, Gabriel's muscled length crushing her into the silky carpet. Panting, she stared dazedly up into his face.

His eyes glinted. "Nice try, princess. Here's a final lesson: being overconfident can land you in trouble."

She became aware of the heavy weight of his manhood against her thigh, the heat rushing beneath the surface of her own skin. With startling speed, battle fever transformed into desire. Arousal sparked along her every nerve.

"Maybe I have you just where I want you," she said daringly.

His nostrils flared. "Is that so?"

With her hands trapped, she couldn't use them to touch him. So instead she softened beneath him, welcoming his weight, cradling his body with hers. His response to her surrender was immediate: his pupils enlarged, his cock an iron bar pressing through the layers of her skirts.

"Don't move," he said. "Keep your hands where they are."

She stilled, the erotic command in his tone causing her temperature to soar. He was once again her masterful lover, his features carved with stark intensity. Perhaps given his recent capitulations to her, he needed to reinstate his dominance in other ways. She would gladly give him whatever he wanted. Indeed, she yearned for their sensual connection... but a niggling voice reminded her that they were in the library, the midday sun streaming through the tall windows.

Breathlessly, she said, "Anyone could come in—"

"We're hidden behind the couches. Now hush and let me have my way with you."

Her nipples strained against the confines of her corset as his touch roved in a proprietary path down her body, and she lay there, brazenly stretched out for his perusal. Her lungs seized when he pushed her skirts and petticoats up in one swift motion. Air wafted against her stockinged calves, her bare thighs, her damp and aching sex. His shoulders wedged up against the back of her legs, spreading her wide. She trembled as he held her open and vulnerable, gazing at her with ravening hunger in his eyes.

"My wanton princess," he murmured, "I've been dreaming of this."

He lowered his head.

Oh my goodness.

Shock and pleasure spiked through her. This was unthinkable. Unspeakable. What he was doing with his tongue... She had to bite back a moan.

"You taste like nectar," he said thickly. "Give me your sweetness, love. I want it all."

Resistance dissolved in a honeyed rush. She gazed up dreamily at the plasterwork on the ceiling as his mouth claimed her. Cherubs frolicked amongst flowers as he wickedly licked, suckled, and consumed her sex. *Lift yourself to my mouth. Let me feast on what is mine.* Her head lolled against the carpet as sensation after sensation swamped her. She felt him part her humid folds, his tongue skillfully gliding to her eager peak.

Ecstasy swelled and broke. Pleasure spilled inside her like a bowl full of sugar, sweetness scattering into every nook and cranny. She lay there, boneless, steeped in bliss and sunlight.

"Time to get up." His voice drifted through her stupor.

Languidly, she thought she probably ought to do so... if she could figure out how to get her limbs to move. Then the world shifted, and she found herself on her feet, Gabriel's arm steadying her around the waist. Her hands came to rest against his waistcoat, feeling his strong heartbeat as he set her to rights.

"Good as new," he said.

He gave her a gentle, almost courtly kiss. She tasted herself on his lips, and despite her satiated state, sensual awareness rippled through her.

Glancing down, she saw his bulging arousal. "You didn't..."

He donned his jacket with studied carelessness, the charcoal superfine covering the affected area. "Today it was my pleasure to see to yours. At a time of my choosing, you will see to mine."

Said with utterly male confidence, his words sent intriguing possibilities flashing through her head. She blushed—it was amazing that she could still do so after what had just transpired on the library floor. Even more amazing was how perfectly civilized he looked, with nary a hair out of place, his cravat pristinely knotted. He was every inch the proper Angel—unless one looked in his eyes.

Dark grey and devilish, they gleamed with satisfaction.

"We'd better go." He offered her his arm. "I think you've had enough lessons for the day, hmm?"

Chapter Twenty-Six

Why the hell did I allow this?

The next day, the question circled in Gabriel's mind just as his carriage was circling the block of the Davenport residence. He saw nothing untoward about the Palladian mansion, yet his gut was knotted with tension. Around the corner, his conveyance pulled to a stop. The door opened, and Strathaven stepped in. Under the pretense of taking a stroll, the other had been surveying the townhouse up close.

Scowling, the duke dropped onto the opposite seat, tossing his hat onto the cushions. He parted the curtain, his pale gaze centered on the quiet house. "All I saw through the window was a gaggle of ladies gossiping over tea. No sign of Emma and the others. They're probably searching the place."

At the thought of Thea prowling through the premises like a seasoned agent, the knots in Gabriel tightened. "Devil take it, I can't believe I let her talk me into this."

"Trust me, I know the feeling. But if you intend to marry Dorothea,"—the duke arched a brow—"you might as well get used to it."

"Of course I intend to marry her." Moodily, Gabriel rubbed the back of his neck. "As soon as this affair with the Spectre is over, I'll talk to Kent. Or you, I suppose."

"We could talk now. Seeing as we have time on our

hands."

Hearing the trace of humor in the other's voice, he said stiffly, "I'm glad you find the situation entertaining. Considering the ladies may be in peril, I find little amusing about it."

"I'm not amused; I'm resigned. It's a common condition when one is wed to a Kent. You'll learn soon enough," the duke said mildly. "So why do you want to marry Dorothea?"

"What do you mean *why*?"

The other gave him an innocent look. "If you're asking my permission for her hand, you ought to at least come prepared with some convincing arguments."

He was on edge enough as it was and in no mood for the duke's sardonic wit.

"First of all, I'm not asking you for anything. I'm telling you that Thea and I have come to an understanding. The moment this bloody business is over, I will make her mine." His gaze snapped to the window as they once again passed the townhouse. Still no sign of movement—devil and damn, what was taking so long? His last thread of patience snapped, and he reached for the door handle. "I'm going in."

The duke stopped him. "We promised them a full hour. Hell, aren't you supposed to be the cool-headed one? I thought you spy fellows had ice flowing through your veins."

"This is different," he gritted out.

In the old days, he'd been known for his composure. He'd been cold and methodical in his work, shutting out inconvenient things like emotions. But this was different. Personal. Thea was involved, and if so much as a hair on her head was disturbed—

Calm down, and get a bloody grip.

"Love does complicate things, doesn't it?" Strathaven said.

"This isn't about love," he said testily, "but common sense. I should never have let my future marchioness take such a risk."

"As you say." Strathaven studied him. "I must confess I'm surprised that you've decided to give marriage another go. I thought your first experience had ruined you for all others."

Gabriel's jaw tautened. He wouldn't dishonor Sylvia by speaking the truth aloud. Yet as much as it shamed him to admit it, he was discovering that perfection didn't hold a candle to a flesh and blood woman. One whose feminine strength and tender vulnerability beguiled him. He'd choose honest passion over tormented love any day.

"One moves on," he said.

"That I can understand." The duke's gaze vigilantly scanned the street as he spoke. "You know that I, myself, wasn't keen on getting caught in the parson's mousetrap a second time."

Gabriel knew the vile rumors that had been spread by the other's vindictive first wife. If anyone had had reason to be wary of marriage, it had been Strathaven.

"And yet you succumbed," he said.

"Not easily. I gave the good fight." His friend smiled faintly. "But I soon realized that resistance was futile—another thing you learn when dealing with a Kent."

"I'm not resisting Thea. I want to protect her."

"Do you think I feel any differently when it comes to Emma?"

"You agreed to the present asinine plan," Gabriel

muttered.

"Because I know how to choose my battles. When my duchess sets her heart upon a thing, it is near impossible to persuade her otherwise. Why waste the effort?" Strathaven shrugged. "I'd much rather she try to persuade me."

"I don't follow."

"Let's just say Her Grace spent a great deal of effort yesterday evening trying to convince me of her plan. She easily made concessions that would have taken me forever to negotiate: she agreed to my escort, a set time frame to carry out her little plot, etcetera. Trust me, I've learned that it is preferable to have *her* be in the position of winning *me* over rather than vice versa."

Gabriel's brows rose. "You mean you forbade her all the while *intending* to concede? For the purpose of gaining the upper hand?"

"I prefer to think of it as creating a situation in which both parties win. Emma gets to have her way, I reap the benefits of being the best of husbands,"—the other's pale green eyes gleamed—"and, most importantly, safeguards are in place for her wellbeing."

Gabriel shook his head. "That's Machiavellian, old fellow."

"Machiavelli had it easy. He didn't have to protect Emma from herself." The duke gave him a knowing look. "You'll have your hands full, too, my friend."

"Thea's not like the duchess." Realizing that might sound insulting, he said hastily, "No offense meant. Your lady is lovely, I'm sure, but Thea is less... strong-willed."

Strathaven's brows arched. "Are you quite certain of that?"

Gabriel frowned... because he wasn't. He was discovering that beneath Thea's sweet, gentle exterior was a spine of finely wrought steel. She was more than he expected, more, in truth, than he'd known to hope for. Her courage and mettle aroused him as strongly as they warred with his own instinct to protect and take care of her.

"Dorothea may be the gentlest of the Kents," the duke said, "but she is still a Kent. They have strong hearts and wills, and you must respect that. Fighting the essence of who they are... well, that's like trying to stop the tides. Why do that when you can instead harness that energy toward more satisfying uses?"

Gabriel mulled it over. What Strathaven was saying made sense. In fact, he was surprised to find that the other was proving to be a veritable trove of advice. Being private men, neither had spoken so frankly about personal matters in the past. Gabriel found the open conversation novel... and not unwelcome.

Since proposing to Thea, he'd been struggling with a question, and it nudged its way forward now. At present, he and she seemed so well-suited, yet how did one ensure that compatibility lasted in a marriage? His relationship with Sylvia had seemed promising at first too... before he'd managed to make a wreck of things in the bedchamber and beyond. There was no better person to discuss this problem with than Strathaven, a former rake whose exploits had once titillated the *ton*, yet who now, by all appearances, was a model husband.

Gabriel cleared his throat. "On that topic, may I ask something of a personal nature?"

The duke quirked a brow.

"Before you were married, you had a certain reputation when it came to females. Specifically when it came to your, ahem, activities with them."

The duke's brow rose another fraction.

His neck heated, yet he bumbled on like an idiot. "What I mean to say is, after one is wed, one must obviously consider a wife's sensibilities. Whatever his past, a gentleman must make certain adjustments for the long term health of his marriage. Maintaining a lady's, er, contentment cannot be easy."

The duke studied him for a moment before saying, "I won't discuss what happens in my bedchamber."

Gabriel felt himself turn red. "No, of course not. I didn't mean to suggest—"

"But I will say this. I've made only one adjustment, as you put it, and that is to conduct all my activities exclusively with my duchess."

"That's it?" It couldn't be that simple.

"My lady has no complaints. Trust me, if she had, I'd have heard them."

Would it be that easy to keep Thea happy? Gabriel brooded. He had no problems with fidelity. He'd remained true to Sylvia even when she'd asked him to stay out of her bed. No, faithfulness hadn't been the problem in his first marriage: *he* had been. He'd repulsed Sylvia with his bestial excesses, the curse of his blood.

With Thea, however, he'd headed those problems off at the pass. She had accepted his past and his carnal desires; she wasn't going in blind. As long as love stayed out of the mix, there was no reason to doubt that their marriage would be a success.

Don't be pathetic and needful, and things will be fine.

Strathaven was regarding him with something akin to compassion. "Whatever your previous experience with marriage was, don't bring it into your future. Drink from a clean cup, my friend. A Kent is a rare vintage and should be enjoyed for her unique qualities."

Could he put his past behind him? Lock away the demons for good? For Thea's sake and his own, he would have to try.

"Of course, some of these rare qualities—namely a propensity for recklessness—may also drive you to Bedlam," Strathaven went on, "but you'll get used to it."

He frowned. "I am not going to get used to Thea taking risks."

Today would be the one and only exception, he told himself. She might have swayed him this one time, but that didn't mean he would permit his future marchioness to endanger herself again. He'd taught her a few defensive moves as an emergency precaution only. He sure as hell didn't want her in situations where she'd actually have cause to put them to use.

"You think I like Emma running about pell-mell?" his friend said. "But short of chaining her to the bedchamber, all I can do is support her and trust in her abilities."

The thought of chaining Thea to his bed held a lot of appeal.

"A man must be master of his own house," Gabriel said firmly.

"Right," the duke said in wry tones. He consulted his gold pocket watch. "Speaking as Her Grace's lord and master then, she has precisely forty minutes left before I break down that front door and haul her out of there."

Gabriel nodded in agreement. The two of them withdrew into shared silence, their eyes locked on the townhouse.

Chapter Twenty-Seven

Despite being labelled an informal luncheon, Lady Davenport's event was a lavish affair. Three rows of dining tables had been laid out in the ballroom, an abundance of crystal, china, and silver glinting beneath the chandeliers. Ladies in elaborate day dresses gossiped in the buffet line as a half-dozen footmen served out delicacies such as roasted turbot, pressed beef tongue, and vegetables molded in aspic.

Waiting in queue with Emma and Pandora, Thea whispered, "Should we go and conduct the search now?"

"Not yet, dear." Em's brown eyes took in the environs with an experienced sweep. "We'll wait until everyone's seated and occupied with eating before we make our move."

"Lady Davenport will give a speech. That should buy us fifteen minutes of distraction," Pandora said in an undertone. "We'll go then."

"Your Grace? Miss Kent?"

The timid voice came from behind them. Thea turned and saw a plump, red-haired girl with bright blue eyes and the face of a pixie. Gabriella Billings was the sweet and artless daughter of a wealthy banker. Emma had met Gabby last year and brought her into the Kent fold. Thea liked the girl tremendously.

Exchanging greetings, Emma introduced Gabby to Pandora, who acknowledged the girl's diffident curtsy with a nod before returning to her vigilant perusal of the ballroom.

Thea gave Gabby's hand a squeeze. "How nice to see you."

"It is a *relief* to see you and Emma," Gabby said with feeling. "I thought I was going to have to muddle through another one of these *ton* affairs alone. Papa secured me the invitation, you see. He's donated oodles to this charity since he's been friends with Uncle George forever—"

"Uncle George?" Used to Gabby's free-flowing conversation, Thea knew the other didn't mind being cut off now and again.

"Well, he's not really my uncle, not by blood, but he and my father are old cronies. They've done business together forever. Papa says Uncle George is the best solicitor in London, and every banker needs a good solicitor. And vice versa. Uncle George is Millicent's—I mean, Lady Davenport's—papa, so I've known Lady Davenport for ages, too. When she was Millicent Clemens, that is. Now I don't see her all that much." Gabby's brow pleated. "At all, actually."

"It must be nice to see an old friend," Thea said.

Gabby sighed. "Papa says I must model myself after Lady Davenport. After all, she caught a title, and in two Seasons all I've attracted are fortune hunters."

"It can't be as bad as all that."

"Believe me, it's *worse*. Most of them are as old as Papa, missing their teeth and hair, and they all have a depressing tendency to forget my name." Gabby mimicked an aged, aristocratic voice. "*You there, the ginger-haired chit. Pass me my walking stick, won't you?*"

Chuckling, Thea said with sympathy, "I know the

feeling. You must take care, however. I hear fortune hunters are clever at getting what they want."

"Not as clever as my father. When it comes to money, Papa knows best," Gabby said cheerfully. "He's protected my inheritance with a trust."

"What's a trust?" Thea asked.

"I'm not sure exactly. Some sort of legal rigmarole that Uncle George helped with. The gist of it," Gabby said brightly, "is that I'll retain control over my own money after I marry."

"How extraordinary," Thea mused. "That sounds like something every woman should know about."

Before Gabby could reply, a thin, brittle voice cut through the conversation. "Ladies, how lovely to see you!"

Lady Davenport was thin and short, and what she lacked in stature, she made up for with the voluminous layers of lace on her gown. Her hair was a mousy shade, her dark gaze beady and assessing. She gave an impression of twitching energy.

"La, a *duchess*," she exclaimed in tones that carried, "at my own little luncheon! You honor us with your presence."

"Thank you for having us, Lady Davenport." Looking discomfited, Emma said, "Um, may I introduce my sister, Miss Dorothea Kent?"

Thea made her curtsy.

Gabby opened her mouth to speak but was cut off.

"A pleasure, Miss Kent, I'm sure." Their hostess hooked her arm through Emma's. "I'm so *pleased* to have you here, Duchess. I feel as if we are kindred spirits, and I know we shall simply be the best of friends." To Lady Blackwood, she said, "And my dear marchioness, how exquisite you look! I simply adore your necklace."

"Your own is very fine. New?" Pandora said casually.

Lady Davenport preened, brushing her fingers over the rope of large, unblemished pearls dangling over her scant bosom. "As a matter of fact, yes. Davenport spoils me terribly, you know."

Thea thought a necklace such as that must cost a pretty penny. And the lady's gown looked expensive too. If the Spectre was indeed in need of money, then Lord Davenport might not be a likely suspect after all.

"I'm about to give a few words. You must take the place of honor next to me, Duchess," Lady Davenport said. "I insist."

"Um, hello, Lady Millicent," Gabby blurted.

Lady Davenport's brows formed thin arches. "Miss Billings. I didn't see you there."

Gabby's face turned scarlet.

Turning her back to the girl, Lady Davenport said, "Ladies, shall we proceed to the head table?"

Thea was aghast at the lady's rudeness. Seeing Gabby's bottom lip tremble, she said firmly, "Miss Billings is in need of a seat, too."

"I'm afraid there isn't room at my table." Lady Davenport's mouth turned down at the corners. "I'm sure Miss Billings can find a seat elsewhere."

"It's all right, Thea," Gabby said anxiously. "I'll just—"

"Miss Billings can have my seat," Thea said.

"You cannot mean to sit on your own, Miss Kent?" her hostess said in a hard voice.

"I'll go with Miss Kent," Pandora drawled. "Miss Billings can accompany you and the duchess."

Lady Davenport's face rippled with ill-temper... and then smoothed into pragmatic lines. Her hand closed on Emma's arm, holding on to her ultimate prize. "This way, Your Grace."

She led Emma toward the table at the front of the room, Gabby trailing timidly behind.

"Good work," Pandora murmured. "That was a narrow escape."

Thea had only been reacting to Gabby's snub, but she realized that Pandora was right. It would have been far too conspicuous to leave and conduct a search if they had been seated with their hostess. She followed Pandora to a pair of seats closest to the exit. A bell rung, bringing the room to order.

Lady Davenport stood at the front of the room, clearing her throat importantly. "Welcome, dear ladies. How good of you to take time out of your busy schedules to attend my luncheon. Even the Duchess of Strathaven herself, a close personal friend, is here to join us in our worthy endeavor. Please welcome my distinguished guest."

At the polite applause, Emma turned beet red.

"But, as you know, not everyone has been blessed with the same good fortune as you and I," Lady Davenport went on, "and it is for the benefit of these Unfortunates that we gather here today. Through our good works, we shall lift these Downtrodden from their doomful fates. Our moral strength will fill them with virtue. Our shining example will teach these poor, diseased creatures to disavow their lives of sloth and turpitude."

A coal began to smolder beneath Thea's breastbone. Having known hunger herself, she was quite certain the

Downtrodden needed food more than moral condescension. And if the poor ought to be taught anything, it was the skills of an honorable trade that would earn them a fair living wage. According to her papa, the true antidote to poverty was education.

Give a man a fish and you'll feed him for a day, he'd say. *Teach a man to fish and you'll feed him for a lifetime.*

"To that end, I am proud to present my newest charitable cause." Lady Davenport gestured imperiously at the footman posted at the entryway. "Send her in."

The door opened, and Thea's stomach churned as a young woman in a mobcap shuffled awkwardly toward the beckoning Lady Davenport. She was dressed in a tawdry, low-cut gown that bore the stamp of her trade. Gasps and titters went up as the woman stood slouched at the front of the room.

"Behold," Lady Davenport said with a self-satisfied cluck, "a Woman of Loose Virtue."

Thea's jaw tightened. Beside her, Pandora stiffened almost imperceptibly.

"Our mission today is to rescue slatternly creatures such as this from a life of sin. How, you ask?"

Lady Davenport waited, smiling, as murmurs rose in the room. Then, with dramatic flourish, she produced a piece of white cloth. Bustling over to her model, she made a great show of tying and tucking in the fabric, so that the scarf covered the woman from bosom to chin.

Stepping back, Lady Davenport declared, "I introduce my newest pet project, which I like to call *Fichus for the Fallen.*"

Thea blinked as applause broke out, excited murmurs

rolling through the room.

"After lunch, we will retire to the sitting room to sew these mantles of modesty," their hostess went on. "Thanks to our efforts, these Fallen Women will regain dignity and virtue—and be an eyesore to civility no more."

A lady dressed in blue satin waved her hand.

"Yes, Miss Simpson?" Lady Davenport said.

"I was thinking we might add a touch of embroidery to the fichus. Perhaps a cross—or some other reminder of piousness?" the lady said in simpering tones.

"An excellent suggestion." Lady Davenport beamed. "Any others?"

Why not sew hair shirts for the poor and be done with it? Thea wanted to snap. But she restrained herself. She couldn't afford to attract attention when they were on a covert mission.

"Time to go," Pandora whispered.

Thea gave a quick nod. As the crowd debated vital issues such as embroidery designs and thread color, she and Pandora slipped unnoticed from the room. Outside, she drew a breath, trying to put the scene of smug pretension behind her. She must concentrate on the present task.

If Pandora had been affected, she showed no sign, leading the way through the hallways with focused intent. They rounded a corner into another corridor, and, as they approached the end, voices could be heard coming from the intersecting hallway. Pandora pressed against the wall, and Thea immediately did the same, waiting with bated breath until a pair of maids passed. Once the servants disappeared, the marchioness turned right, and moments later she and Thea arrived at a set of double doors.

Pandora tried the door—locked.

"Keep watch," she murmured, removing a length of wire from her reticule.

Nerves prickling, Thea did so as the other worked on the lock. A minute later, there was a click, the soft sweep of the door giving way. Pandora went inside first, and Thea followed, closing the door with damp palms.

With the curtains drawn, Davenport's study was dim and cavernous. It seemed ordinary enough with its dark wood and leather furnishings, the book-lined shelves. The large portrait over the fireplace dominated the room. It depicted Lady Davenport sitting beneath an oak tree in a gown of frothy lace, her hat dripping with plumes. Thea presumed that the man in the painting—the one Lady Davenport gazed up at with wifely adoration—was Lord Davenport. The viscount was a distinguished-looking man in his forties, with slight greying at the temples and a tall, fit figure.

Yet there was something disturbing about his eyes, which met the viewer's straight on. That pale gaze seemed so penetrating and life-like that Thea had the sudden panic that she was being watched. A shiver chased over her nape.

"We don't have much time." Pandora's urgent tones broke the spell. "Both of us will have to search. You start with the desk. Try not to disturb anything."

With a quick nod, Thea padded over to the desk, its surface neatly organized with a silver tray of writing instruments and a thick leather blotter. With trembling hands, she pulled open the top drawer and carefully rifled through the contents. Nothing remotely suspicious. She continued onto the two other drawers. Still nothing, not even a hidden compartment.

If I were Davenport and had something to hide, where would I put it? As she mulled, she drummed her fingers against the desk… and awareness prickled over her at the faint hollow vibration. The resonance was similar to the sound she made when tapping against the lid of a pianoforte. Crouching, she placed her ear close to the top of the desk, repeating the rhythm of her fingers, and she heard it again—a muffled echo coming from within. *There's an empty chamber inside.* Heart thumping, she ran her hands under the ledge of the desk, her fingers encountering a hidden button. She pressed it, and the entire blotter slid to the side, revealing a hidden cache.

Excitement rushed up her spine at the sight of papers.

"Pandora," she called softly.

The marchioness arrived just as Thea lifted out the top document for inspection. Written in a bold hand, the string of words was strange and nonsensical. She heard the other's sharp indrawn breath.

"*Spectre,*" Pandora whispered.

Chapter Twenty-Eight

Thea and Pandora returned just as the ladies were beginning to file out of the ballroom.

Emma hurried toward them. "Find anything?" she whispered.

Thea nodded, barely able to suppress her excitement.

Em huffed out a breath. "Thank heavens. Let's get out of here. Because if I have to listen to one minute more of this patronizing claptrap, I swear I'll—"

"La, there you are!" The voice rang shrilly from behind her. "Oh, Duchess!"

Em froze like a hunted deer.

Lady Davenport hurried over. "We're just about to begin sewing the fichus. You shall have the seat of honor in my circle, Your Grace."

"That sounds lovely, but I'm, um, getting rather tired—"

"I shall call for caviar and champagne to keep our energies up. I won't take no for an answer." The viscountess' hand wrapped like ivy around Emma's arm. "You wouldn't want to let down a good cause, would you?"

"No," Em said, looking desperate, "but truly I have to go—"

Thea let out a gasping breath, grabbing her sister's free arm.

"What is the matter, Miss Kent?" Lady Davenport said,

looking alarmed.

"I… I c-can't… breathe."

Emma's brown eyes rounded with worry, her arm going instantly around Thea's waist. "Breathe deeply, dear. In and out. Just as Dr. Abernathy taught you."

Seeing Lady Davenport take a step back, Thea wheezed, "Yes, stay back. It might be catching."

Instantly, the hostess retreated farther. "Er, can I have anything fetched for you?"

"Air… just need… air…"

"Let's get you outside," Em said.

"Thank you for your hospitality, Lady Davenport," Pandora said.

The three of them left the townhouse.

"We'll get you home straightaway," Emma fretted, "and call for Dr. Abernathy—"

"I'm fine," Thea said in her normal voice.

"You are?" Her sister blinked. "But back there… what happened?"

"I was improvising." Thea felt absurdly proud of herself.

Pandora's lips curved. "As I suspected from the first, you are a lady of hidden talents."

Just then, Thea caught sight of a mob-capped figure leaving from the servant's entrance several yards away. The woman paused, tugging the fichu from her neck, crumpling it in her hand. Shoulders hunched, she began walking in the opposite direction.

Thea gave her sister a hopeful look. "Couldn't you use another maid?"

"Let's talk to her," Em said.

Thea and Emma approached the young woman, who

bobbed a startled curtsy and identified herself as Sara Tully. Miss Tully eagerly accepted Emma's card and direction, promising to come by the house for an interview. They were saying goodbye when Gabriel's carriage arrived. He jumped down from the vehicle with predatory grace. His grey gaze went from Thea to the departing Miss Tully.

"Who was that?" he said, frowning.

"A new acquaintance," she said.

He tipped her chin up with a gloved hand, his eyes radiating concern. "How did things go in there?"

"Splendidly, thanks to Miss Kent's ingenuity," Pandora said. "She'll explain in the carriage."

"Lord Davenport will see you now."

The secretary led Gabriel, Strathaven, and Kent into well-appointed chambers paneled in dark wood. Sun shone through the mullioned windows, gleaming off heavy furniture and the burgundy carpet of Oriental design. The secretary closed the door discreetly behind him.

Rising from a carved desk, Lord Cecil Davenport came over to greet them. Tall, fit, possessed of patrician features made even more distinguished by the greying at his temples, the viscount was every inch the polished politician. His light blue eyes showed polite curiosity and nothing more.

Cicero had always been a master of disguising his true intent.

"Gentlemen." He bowed. "To what do I owe the honor?"

"We're here to talk about blackmail," Gabriel said.

Davenport's brows lifted, his gaze skirting for the briefest instant toward Strathaven and Kent. He adopted a puzzled smile. "Is this some sort of jest, Lord Tremont?"

"No jest, Cicero," he said steadily.

The other's tone remained light. "I'm afraid I don't follow. Now I'm a very busy man and—"

"We found the blackmail notes in your study. In the hidden compartment of your desk." Despite the volatile situation, Gabriel felt a flash of pride at Thea's cleverness. She continued to amaze him with the depth of her spirit and strength. "You are being blackmailed by the Spectre," he said.

A faint crack showed in Davenport's composure. At his sides, his manicured hands curled.

"There had better be a good reason for you betraying our code of anonymity. What do you want, Trajan?" he said in level tones.

"Your help in catching the Spectre. With the help of Strathaven and Kent here, I've been hunting down possible suspects," Gabriel said.

Davenport's eyes narrowed. "You've just confessed to breaking into my study and ransacking my personal effects. Why should I trust you?"

"Because someone tried to kill Tremont," Kent said, "and succeeded in murdering your mentor, Octavian. You could be next."

Davenport's lips thinned, and Gabriel understood the other's struggle. They'd had the same teacher, after all. *Keep your guard up, and trust no one.* After a taut silence, the viscount gestured to the sitting area.

The men took their seats, and Gabriel gave a terse

summary of the facts. Out of habit, he gave the least amount of information necessary. Octavian's summons and death. The recovery of his dagger at Cruik's. The extortion of Pompeia. All the while, he monitored Davenport's expression and saw nothing but bleak acceptance.

"When did you begin to receive the blackmail notes?" Kent had his trusty notebook out.

"Around two months ago," Davenport said after a hesitation. "The first one appeared with the morning mail, out of nowhere. For a moment, I thought I was hallucinating."

Gabriel exchanged swift glances with Kent and Strathaven. What Davenport described was almost identical to Pompeia's experience with the blackmailer.

"The note threatened to expose my activities as a spy. To ruin my reputation, political career, and all I have built if I didn't pay him five thousand pounds." Anger simmered in Davenport's voice. "I had no choice. I have a wife—I couldn't let him destroy her life as well. So I paid."

"What happened next?" Strathaven said.

"More demands came." Davenport's jaw clenched. "I should have known better. Blackmailers are never satisfied."

"Do you have any culprits in mind?" Kent said.

"My first thought was one of the Quorum." The politician's cool, assessing gaze centered on Gabriel. "Only one of our inner circle would be in possession of such facts about me. Thus, I made inquiries into the activities of my three former colleagues."

Cicero had had him investigated. That came as no surprise.

"And?" Gabriel said.

"Of the three, you're the one who could use money the most. It seems your circumstances have improved, however, since your business venture with Strathaven last year." The suspicious gleam lingered in Davenport's pale eyes. "Still, one can never have too much money."

"I'm no blackmailer," Gabriel said coolly.

"Apparently not. If you were, I doubt you'd have hired on an investigator and exposed the secrets of espionage to those outside our world." Davenport's eyes formed pale slits. "So that leaves Pompeia and Tiberius. The lady was always a treacherous sort. After all," he said, his tone darkening, "she was the only one of us who managed to avoid Normandy."

The mention of the hellhole awakened the ghosts in Gabriel, the muscles of his back tautening. Kent and Strathaven, whom he'd told about the ambush, sat in somber silence.

"Apparently she had her reasons," Gabriel said curtly. "She's being blackmailed by the Spectre too."

"If Pompeia isn't a suspect and assuming for now that you and I are also innocent,"—Davenport smiled without humor—"then that leaves one clear culprit, doesn't it?"

"Heath," Gabriel said.

From the moment Thea and Pompeia had shared their discovery—that Cicero, too, was a victim of extortion—he'd been contemplating the fact that Tiberius, also known as Tobias Heath, was the sole remaining suspect. It made sense. Unstable at best, Heath had always lived life by his own moral compass; it wouldn't have taken much to steer him in a criminal direction.

Yet some part of Gabriel resisted the notion that Tiberius was the Spectre. He wondered if a fellow on the brink of madness could be capable of such calculation. Then again, sanity wasn't a requirement of being evil. He'd encountered his share of crazed despots during the war. And maybe Tiberius had been faking his mental instability all along.

"Recall how Tiberius escaped imprisonment unscathed?" Davenport murmured. "Unlike the two of us."

The memory trickled into Gabriel's awareness. Spectre's men had kept the three of them in separate cells, yet they could hear each other's screams. Gabriel and Davenport's cries had echoed through those stone caverns but never Heath's. The latter had emerged dirty, nonsensical, and terrified... but he hadn't been beaten. Gabriel had assumed that the younger man had broken down and blurted out secrets or had simply been deemed too cracked for torture tactics to do any good.

Now another explanation raised its ugly head. Could Heath have been deceiving them all these years, pretending madness whilst all the while he'd been double crossing them? Was he even now blackmailing and killing off his former comrades one by one?

"We'll still need solid evidence that he's the Spectre," Kent said.

"If he's the guilty one, I don't want him slipping from the noose," Gabriel agreed darkly.

"Heath keeps a place near Lincoln's Inn Fields," the investigator said. "According to my men, he's got a meeting with the radical group tomorrow night. We could take the opportunity to search his place."

"Are you in, Davenport?" Gabriel said.

The other inclined his head. "Anything to prevent the

ghosts of the past from rising."

"The Spectre's already risen. Tomorrow night," Gabriel said with grim determination, "we put him down for good."

Chapter Twenty-Nine

That night, Thea made her way stealthily down the dark hallway of the guest wing. A sense of urgency fueled her flight, the hem of her wrapper whispering over the carpet, her lamp casting a moving shadow until she found the door she sought. Casting a furtive glance this way and that, she drew a breath and rapped softly.

Heartbeats passed. She leaned in, pressing her ear to the door, listening for any sounds from within. She couldn't hear anything above the thudding in her ears. Her hopes fell. Perhaps he was already asleep—

The door opened so suddenly that she toppled forward.

Strong arms caught her, dragged her inside. Her lamp was summarily deposited on a table. Breathless, she found herself with her back against the closed door, Gabriel towering over her, his hands planted on either side of her shoulders. He'd clearly just risen from bed. A tempting expanse of hair-dusted muscle rippled in the vee of his hastily donned robe. His hair was tousled, his eyes glinting silver in the semi-darkness.

He looked dangerous, deliciously predatory. Her desire for him saturated her being like a watermark through fibers of parchment.

"What are you doing here?" he said in low tones.

"I missed you," she whispered back. "I wanted to see

you."

He ran a finger along her jaw, his touch rasping over her nerve endings. "As much as I appreciate and return the sentiment," he said huskily, "you can't be here. You'll be ruined if we're caught."

"I don't care. Everyone knows we're getting married anyway." Earlier, he'd told her that he'd broken the news to Strathaven. Which meant Emma already knew and the rest of the family wasn't far off. "You're going to capture the Spectre tomorrow, and life is too precious to waste. I don't want to lose a single moment with you."

"There's nothing to fear, princess." He took her hands, kissed them one by one. "You're not getting rid of me that easily."

How could she convey the desperation she felt? Knowing that he would be out there tomorrow night, chasing after evil—she wanted to give him a part of her, a talisman for safekeeping. If he didn't want words of love from her, then she would show him how much she cared. Whenever they made love, she felt the bond between them strengthen.

"We could just lie in bed together," she coaxed, "and not do anything but hold each other."

"Yes, and hell could bloom with roses." He sounded wryly amused.

"I *need* to be with you tonight." Impassioned, she reached for him—only to have him grip both wrists, this time pinning them above her head.

"No, sweetheart," he said. "I'm going to see you back to your room."

Whereas once she would have been hurt by his refusal,

attributing it to some failing in herself, now she saw his protectiveness for what it was, and it only made her love him more. With her wrists still anchored by him, she couldn't use her hands, so she leaned upward on her toes, feathering her lips over his in soft persuasion. She felt like the mouse of Aesop's tale, seeking clemency from a lion—the moral of the tale being that even smaller, frailer creatures have their power.

And Gabriel had helped her discover hers.

When his mouth remained stubbornly closed, she licked the hard seam. She felt his coiling tension, and sensing her advantage, delicately nipped his firm bottom lip. He shuddered—and then all hell sprung loose.

One moment Thea was standing against the door, the next she was swung up into Gabriel's arms. His mouth ravaged hers, and she thrilled in the rough possession. When his tongue plunged with voluptuous force, she opened further, holding nothing back. He tasted of desire, dark and primal, and she couldn't hold back a whimper of excitement.

He set her on her feet by the edge of the bed, his gaze glittering in the lamplight. "Do you know what happens to naughty minxes who disobey orders?"

She didn't... but she had hopes.

He sat on the mattress. The hem of his robe stopped beneath his knees, revealing his sleekly bulging calves. With his thighs slightly splayed and his eyes heavy-lidded, he radiated male power. "Take off your clothes," he said. "Be quick about it."

His clipped commands filled her with heady, feminine triumph. She loved this demanding, intense side of him—loved even more that she had the power to bring it out.

Following his instruction, she shed her wrapper, letting it pool at her feet. She kicked off her slippers and pulled her nightgown over her head. Her hair fell in a silken curtain to her waist, but she was otherwise laid bare.

Naked and blushing, she held his gaze.

He crooked a finger at her. "Come closer."

She took the two steps forward into the lee of his thighs. She could smell his clean scent, nothing but soap and male, and her nipples hardened, straining for his touch. Her toes curled in the soft fibers of the bedside rug.

"Get on your knees, princess."

Her startled gaze flew to his; her breath lodged at the wicked challenge she saw there. Her knees trembled so badly that she couldn't have remained standing even if she wanted to. Uncertain and stimulated, she slowly lowered herself so that she was kneeling at his feet.

"How lovely you are," he murmured.

He, she thought with pulsing arousal, was more along the lines of magnificent. Eye-level with his groin, she couldn't miss the massive bulge beneath the dark brocade. The words he'd uttered in the library suddenly echoed in her head.

Today it was my pleasure to see to yours. At a time of my choosing, you will see to mine.

She moistened her lips. What would it be like to pleasure him in the same manner that he had pleasured her? To kiss his most intimate parts, the way he had done to her?

She had the shocking, almost overwhelming desire to find out.

He lifted a lock of her hair and rubbed the glinting strand between thumb and forefinger. "You could be made of spun gold."

"But I'm not." The last thing she wanted to be compared to was a weak, malleable metal. Lifting her chin to look at him, she said, "I'm not delicate. I helped find the blackmail note in Lord Davenport's desk, remember?"

"How could I forget? It took years off my life." he said wryly. "But don't confuse delicacy with weakness, love. Sometimes the softest things can have the most profound impact."

His acknowledgement of her power sent a buzzing thrill through her. As did the way he was stroking the silky length of her hair back and forth against her nipple, titillating the sensitive point. The feather-light sensation caused a hot rush between her legs. She squirmed, pressing her knees together as desire burgeoned.

Her cheeks flushed. "Please, Gabriel. I can't stand it."

"I like the way you look at me," he murmured. "With those big hazel eyes of yours. You make me feel as if I'm the most powerful man in the world. As if I could share the darkest corners of my soul with you. As if I'd kill to have you."

His words elicited another gush of dew.

"I like the way you look at me," she said. "You make me feel as if I'm the most desirable woman in the world. As if I could give you everything you need. As if I'd do anything to please you."

They stared at one another, their breaths surging in unison. In that moment, Thea felt something shift between them, as intangible and powerful as an electric current. She saw her own awareness reflected in his stormy eyes.

"You are the most desirable woman in the world," he

said, "and you're going to give me everything I need."

He shed his robe, tossed it aside. It was the first time she'd seen him completely naked—and the sight made her dizzy with want. His masculinity overwhelmed her, virile strength in every aspect, from the muscled slabs of his chest to the carved ridges on his taut belly. His manhood stood fiercely, hugely erect.

"Pleasure me, princess." His words held both a command and a dare.

Eager yet uncertain exactly how to proceed, she came up on her knees. Ignoring his rampant cock for the moment (not the easiest to do since it clamored for her attention), she ran her palms over his chest, savoring the texture of his satiny skin, the light scratch of bronze hair. He bore a few faint scars, mementos of the life he'd led, and it added to his tough potency, his uniqueness. Leaning forward, she pressed her lips to the thin ridge of knitted skin below his right nipple. He made a raspy sound.

"Does it hurt?" she said in surprise.

His eyes smoldering, he gave a slow shake of his head.

Relieved, she continued her exploration. She kissed his flat nipples, guessing from his uneven breaths that he liked it. Her hands smoothed over his leanness, learning his edges, his hidden corners, before arriving at the part of him where desire was not concealed at all.

Carefully, she wrapped a hand around his bold member. The thick stalk pulsed with life as she caressed it, moving its velvety cover over the rigid core. Remembering what he'd taught her before, she tightened her grip and increased her pace. She heard his quickened respiration; a drop of liquid beaded upon the burgeoned crown of his cock.

With great daring, she leaned forward and licked it off. His salty clean essence infused her senses. He tasted wild and raw, and she wanted more.

She lapped at the tip, circling it with her tongue. She heard him groan, and determination filled her to please him, to be everything he wanted. She pressed kisses down the length of his shaft, following a veiny ridge down to the root, where his bollocks hung heavily over the edge of the bed. She gave the dusky sac a tentative lick... and his hand speared into her hair.

"Enough." He guided her head up. "We don't want this over before it's begun."

She looked at him, puzzled.

He gave a dark chuckle. "My sweet innocent, let me have you the way I want." With his palm at the back of her skull, he brought her lips back to the blunt head of his rod. "Open your mouth, and take me inside."

With sizzling excitement, she followed his instruction. Fitting her lips around the fat dome, she mouthed him and gently sucked. That had an instant effect, his fingers tightening against her scalp, a hiss leaving him.

"Christ, that's good." His eyes were heavy-lidded, his features stark with arousal. "Take me deeper, princess. As deep as you can."

Giddy with newfound knowledge, she obeyed. It was thrilling to make love to him this way, to hear his grunted breaths as she tried to take as much of him in her mouth as possible. His dark encouragement inflamed her. *Relax your jaw, love. Breathe through your nose. Swallow my cock—God yes, like that...*

Given his size, the task wasn't easy. When she went too

far, she choked, her throat convulsing around his thickness. A groan ripped from Gabriel's chest.

An instant later, he dragged her head up, and before she could catch her breath, she was tossed upon the bed, his mouth between her legs. His tongue stabbed deeply into her drenched core. He ravaged her sex, licking, sucking. The storm broke inside her, robbing her of all control.

She bucked against his mouth, the climax wringing mindless words from her. "*I love you, Gabriel.*"

In the next instant, she was flipped onto her belly, his fingers thrusting into her from behind. The sudden fullness made her gasp, building on the rippling spasms of her orgasm. He penetrated her forcefully, slick hard pumps that sent her soaring toward another peak. He rammed into a place deep inside, and with a startled cry, she went over again. Suffused in bliss, her cheek pressed against the coverlet, she felt his fingers glide along the valley of her bottom, spreading her wetness there.

She jolted at the thick, weighted slide of his cock along the crevice.

"So good, princess." His voice was thick, urgent. "Let me have you this way."

Heart pounding, she let her cheek fall back onto the silk. His palms pressed the hills of her bottom together, and her breath hitched at the decadent friction of his erection gliding between. Panting, he began to thrust in a bold rhythm, his hardness rubbing against her delicate tissues, his bollocks slapping against her softness.

Unbelievably, she felt yet another climax building within her. Her pussy throbbed, his plunges grinding her against the mattress, but not stimulating the place where she needed it most…

"Touch yourself." His voice poured over her. "Come for me one more time."

It was so easy to obey. Her hand slipping beneath her, she found her pearl, pressing it, letting his rocking motion do the rest. He groaned her name, and she felt the scorching lash of his seed on her back as ecstasy claimed her once more.

The moist sweep of a towel brought her back to her senses. As he tended to her, she lay there, her body limp with pleasure but her pulse pounding. She hadn't meant to let slip those words of love, but it was too late to take them back. How would he react to her confession? She felt vulnerable, naked beyond her uncovered skin: it was her heart that she'd bared to him. Their future felt balanced upon his reaction, the next moment.

He turned her over and tugged her to her feet. Eyes impassive, he brushed his lips over her forehead. She waited, breath held.

"We'd better get you back to your room," he said.

Chapter Thirty

London was always a hodgepodge of sights, sounds, and smells. Nowhere was this more apparent than the neighborhood in which Tiberius lived. From a tavern window, Gabriel watched the mix of affluence, poverty, and a distinct criminal element jostling together in the streets of Lincoln's Fields Inn. It was nearing dusk, businessmen and laborers returning home from their day's work just as pickpockets and thieves began to ply their trade. Already Gabriel had spotted two well-to-do merchants being relieved of their wallets.

Across the table from him, Pompeia smirked. "Easy pickings if I ever saw. Pigeons like that deserved to be plucked."

It was easy to forget that she was a marchioness. A brassy wig, paint, and disreputable gown covered up any glimpse of the fashionable Lady Blackwood. She looked like someone who belonged in this smoky public house filled with the smell of roasting meat, the tables sticky with spilled ale.

Gabriel himself was also disguised. He'd darkened his hair, donned a moustache. His clothes were the kind one wore to convince a customer that the goods one was pimping were worth the price and wouldn't give you the pox.

It was altogether strange to be on a mission with his one-time colleague. He didn't entirely trust Pompeia, but the enemy of an enemy was a friend. At present, under the guise of pimp and prostitute trolling for the night's work, he and Pompeia occupied a window seat at the tavern, keeping watch on the second-storey flat across the street. The light in the apartment window, the occasional shadow flitting behind the shade, told them the subject had not yet left the premises.

"It's getting late. Why hasn't Tiberius left?" Pompeia said under her breath.

An echo of his own thoughts. To lure Tiberius out from his lair, they'd laid out bait. Cicero had sent Tiberius a note, saying they had urgent business to discuss. Gabriel didn't know what Cicero had planned, but whatever it was, it would be good. More than once, Cicero's silver tongue had come in handy. Tonight, they were depending on him to keep Tiberius occupied whilst Gabriel and Pompeia performed the search.

"There's still time." Gabriel sipped his ale. It tasted like piss.

"I have until midnight. Blackwood expects me home when he returns from the club."

"How domestic you've become."

Her eyes had a dangerous spark. "Don't mock me, Trajan. He's the only reason I'm here. I couldn't give a damn about spy business otherwise."

"You proved that years ago," he said coolly. "After all, you jumped ship right before it capsized. With the rest of us in it."

"I owed you nothing. I gave years to Octavian, the obsessed bastard, and in return he bled me dry." To an outsider, Pompeia's expression was so bland she might have been discussing the quality of the beefsteak. "I wasn't about to let him take what remained of my soul. You chose to stay—that was your problem, not mine. Don't lay the consequences of your misguided loyalty at my door."

He tore off a chunk of bread. "I wouldn't expect you to know anything of loyalty."

"Because you don't know me." Her smile was cold. "Amusing how with all your knowledge and experience you can't understand the simplest facts. Unlike your little Miss Kent."

"Don't bring her into this." Warning edged his words.

He didn't like her even speaking Thea's name. For an instant, the memory of Thea's soft confession and their tempestuous lovemaking blazed; he snuffed it out just as quickly. Later, he would examine the damnable tangle of his feelings. For now, he needed to remain focused and in control. Sentiment had no place in the night's work.

Or in your private life, you sod. One torturous marriage wasn't enough for you?

"Touchy, are we?" Pompeia's brows arched. "I don't blame you. It's not easy for people like us to fall in love."

Why was the world so obsessed with the blasted emotion?

Before he could tell her to mind her own business, Heath's disheveled figure emerged from the flat. *Finally.* Standing on the landing, Heath was dressed in the rough, casual clothes of an artist, his cravat carelessly knotted, his wild black curls completing the Byronic look. Gabriel angled his head away as Heath scanned the street. From the corner of his eye, he saw Heath descend the steps into the street.

"He's headed west. On his way to Davenport."

Pompeia's eyes were razor sharp.

"Let's go in," Gabriel said.

They exited the tavern, him with swagger and her with a saucy stride that made them blend with the crowd in the street. The cooling night air was a welcome change from the humidity of the tavern. They headed for the alleyway next to Tiberius' building.

Kent and McLeod arrived moments later. The pair had been circling the neighborhood in a carriage, keeping an eye on things.

"Subject's headed west on Holborn. Hackney," McLeod said without preamble. "It'll take him a half-hour just to get to Davenport's club and back. Depending on how long your friend can hold him up, you'll have an hour tops."

"Let's not dally," Pompeia said.

"We'll keep watch here." Kent tapped the whistle he wore around his neck. "I'll sound a signal if Heath returns."

Once the coast was clear, Gabriel led the way up the creaking steps to Heath's flat. On the landing, Gabriel took out a set of wires and set to work on the lock. Heath being Heath, the mechanism was absurdly complicated but finally yielded with a click.

He opened the door, motioning for Pompeia to stay behind him. He waited until his eyes adjusted to the gloom—and then pointed to the slightly raised floorboard to the right.

"Avoid that," he said.

"Ah, yes. Tiberius always did like to surprise unwelcome visitors," she drawled.

The surprise, as she put it, had tended to take the form of an explosive or other life-threatening device. Heath's paranoia was trumped only by his creativity. With an eye for his former comrade's old tricks, Gabriel crept cautiously into the room.

Pompeia found a lamp, lit it, and set it on the ground to keep the bulk of the light from the windows. It cast shadows over the floor and just enough of a glow to see the chaos of Heath's apartment. Books, maps, and piles of paper littered most surfaces. The kitchen occupied a far corner, a pyramid of dishes standing precariously on a multipurpose table. In another corner stood an easel, several half-completed canvases lying around it. Finished paintings hung on the wall at crooked angles.

Gabriel followed a hallway to a single bedchamber. He searched the sleeping pallet, piles of strewn clothing, floorboards. For all that Heath was a man of means, he lived like a resident of Bedlam. Gabriel returned to the main room to find Pompeia gingerly picking through the pile of papers and oddities on Heath's desk.

"How the devil are we going to find anything?" Gabriel muttered.

"I don't know. But something just *moved* under here," she said.

Rolling up his sleeves, Gabriel dug in. In silence, he and Pompeia methodically searched every filthy nook and cranny of the place... and found nothing.

"It's been nearly an hour," Pompeia said at last. "We don't have much time left. Do you think it's possible there's nothing to find?"

"We're missing something." Gabriel circled the room, trying to see it from Heath's eyes. "Tiberius always was a clever bastard. If he wanted something hidden, it wouldn't be easy to find."

Pompeia made her own loop around the cluttered chamber. "He'd hide evidence someplace accessible to him but not others. Someplace that might have some meaning to him." Her eyes narrowed. "Someplace hiding in plain sight..."

They arrived at the easel at the same time. Gabriel examined the incomplete canvases piled on the floor; the agitated strokes of color could have been the beginnings of a flower field or a nightmare—memories of Normandy blazed through Gabriel's brain. Perfect, now Heath's madness was rubbing off on him. Grimly, he lifted the canvases and found nothing hidden behind them.

He joined Pompeia, who was staring at the paintings hung on the wall. Four in total, the small framed portraits all depicted the same pretty, doe-eyed woman. They were so radically different from the unfinished canvases that one would assume they'd been executed by a different artist. Yet Heath's signature was upon each one.

"Do you know who she is?" Pompeia said.

"No." Gabriel's nape prickled. "But do you see what I see?"

"That these were painted with an affection that I did not think Tiberius capable of?"

He shook his head impatiently. "Look here. Along the edge of this one." He stepped closer to the portrait in the middle, ran a finger down one side of the frame. "The paint on the wall here is darker." As if it had been previously covered, shielded from the sun.

"The portrait has been moved," Pompeia said.

When Gabriel tried to remove the portrait from the

wall, it wouldn't budge.

"It's bolted." He produced a blade.

"Wait, you're going to cut it?" For an instant, he thought that she wanted him to spare the portrait out of sentimentality. But her next words proved her to be the Pompeia he knew. "If you destroy that painting, Heath will know for certain that someone has been in his flat."

Gabriel was already running the tip of the blade along the seam where painting met frame. "If there's nothing behind this painting, I'll apologize to him personally."

He cut along the top and sides, and the canvas peeled down.

A safe was embedded in the wall behind.

Gabriel quirked a brow at his former colleague.

"Iron boxes are my specialty, I believe." Pompeia removed a pair of lock picks and set to work. Within moments, a click sounded, the door of the safe swinging open.

Papers, stacks of banknotes. And…

Pompeia reached in, withdrawing a string of sapphires. Even in the dim light, the stones glittered with dark fire. "My bracelet," she said. "The one I gave to the Spectre."

At that moment, a whistle sounded shrilly. Footsteps pounded up the stairwell. An instant later, Heath burst into the room, his hair and eyes wild.

"You *bastards*." He waved a pistol. "Come to get me, have you? Not if I get you first."

Gabriel was already running, tackling Heath before the other could take aim. They both hit the floor with a thud, the gun skittering out of reach. They grappled, rolling over papers and books, until Gabriel managed to get the upper hand. His fist cracked against Heath's jaw. The other man groaned, his head lolling to the side, his grip on Gabriel slackening. Gabriel grabbed his opponent by the lapels.

"You bloody turncoat," Gabriel snarled.

"I'm going to kill you." Heath thrashed wildly.

Gabriel slammed the other's head against the floor. Images exploded in his head. Marius falling. The smoke-choked interrogation chambers. Octavian bleeding out on the carpet. Control snapped, the need for vengeance roaring free. His fists made contact again and again. He gripped Heath's windpipe, crushing...

Strong hands yanked at his shoulders. He shook them off, refusing to relinquish his prey.

"Tremont, let go. You'll kill him."

Kent's calm voice cut through the haze. Gabriel looked down and saw his hands wrapped around Heath's throat. Saw the other's bulging eyes, bloodied face. With effort, he loosened his grip, and Heath's head thudded to the ground. The other moaned, eyes closing. Unconscious but not dead.

Looking up, Gabriel saw the ring of faces. Pompeia was staring at Heath, her face hard with fury. McLeod had a pistol aimed at the man on the ground.

At Tiberius—the Spectre. The perpetrator of evil. A comrade who'd betrayed them all.

Numbly, Gabriel rose to his feet. His hands curled and uncurled, something sticky dripping from the knuckles. His senses were as acute as an animal's; his mind was curiously blank. In some distant part of his brain, he remembered this sensation. It was as familiar as slipping into an old skin, watching it happen from the outside.

Rage hollowed him. Made him empty and cold.

"Rest easy, my lord," Kent said. "We have him now."

"Yes," he said tonelessly.

He waited for the relief to come. To feel anything at all.

Chapter Thirty-One

Two days later, hearing Gabriel's voice in the distance, Thea set her cup down, tea sloshing onto the saucer as she did so. She folded her trembling hands in her lap. Told herself she was being silly.

There was no need to be nervous around Gabriel. They were an officially engaged couple now. After the Spectre's capture, he'd kept his word and spoken to Ambrose. The exquisite diamond and topaz engagement ring he'd given her sparkled on her finger even now, casting a confetti of light. A tangible symbol of their future together.

But what if he never loves me?

Lately, the panicked thought had been fluttering in her head like a trapped bird. It wasn't fair of her, she knew, to expect something that he'd told her from the beginning he wouldn't give. Yet his lack of response to her words of love had hit her like an icy splash of reality. To make matters worse, his behavior had become increasingly aloof since then. Now that the danger was finally over, she'd thought that their relationship would have a chance to progress and blossom.

Instead, he was shutting her out.

Oh, he was going through the motions. He was unfailingly polite to her, and to all who didn't know him, everything a proper, attentive fiancé should be. But she knew him better. The shields were up in his eyes, and even his sensual heat had been banked.

When she'd finally gotten up the courage to ask him if anything was amiss, he'd replied shortly, "I'm fine, Thea."

Is this all because I told him I loved him? Because he doesn't want that from me? Have I been fooling myself all along that he could love me?

Her insecurities and fears had come rushing back. Just because she and Gabriel had a strong physical connection didn't mean that he'd find her worthy of his love. Maybe for him sensual attraction and love had naught to do with one another. Maybe, in his mind, they were two separate things. After all, he'd loved his paragon of a wife despite their apparent incompatibility in bedroom matters.

Dread took up a palpitating presence in Thea's chest, yet she knew it was too late for regrets. She'd signed up for all of this. She'd agreed to his terms, said that she was fine with a marriage built on honesty, common goals, and commitment. Their engagement had been made public, wedding preparations were underway, and Freddy, the little dear, was overjoyed. Hearing footsteps in the hallway, she steeled herself with her mama's words.

You must lie in the bed of your own making.

The door opened, and Gabriel walked in. He looked lean and powerful in somber grey, a fitting shade for his visit to Newgate. Despite everything, the sight of him made longing pulse within her. *I do love him so,* she thought with a trace of resentment.

She forced a smile. "How did things go?"

"Heath still hasn't confessed." As usual these days, his expression was impassive. He joined her on the settee. "But he's not denying being the Spectre either. He just keeps carrying on about the plot against him."

She poured tea and filled a plate of sandwiches for him. "He doesn't sound in his right mind."

"I agree." Gabriel polished off two triangles of bread stuffed with eggs and chives. "Heath keeps insisting that we're out to kill him—that he's going to get us, all of us including the King, before we get him. To be honest, he seems more like a madman than an infamous spymaster."

"Perhaps he's gone insane because of everything he's done," she suggested. "Like Shakespeare's Lady Macbeth, perhaps Heath's conscience has overtaken his sanity."

Gabriel's smile was wry. "There's a difference between fiction and reality. The fact is Heath's rationality has been precarious since I've known him. Would such a man be capable of masterminding espionage, of eluding capture all these years?"

She mulled it over. "Papa always said there's no great genius without madness."

"Perhaps it is so. Moreover, one can't argue with the evidence we found in his vault. He had plans and letters containing military secrets that guarantee that he'll be found guilty of High Treason and put to death. In fact," he went on quietly, "there was sufficient damning evidence that none of our names—Lady Blackwood's, Davenport's, or mine— need to be drawn into this. The Crown is to reward us by safeguarding our reputations."

"I'm so happy for Pandora," Thea said with genuine relief. "Her marriage and family are more important to her than anything."

"Yes, you saw that from the start, didn't you?" Gabriel

curled a finger under her chin. "And for yourself? Aren't you happy that you won't be known as the wife of a notorious former spy?"

His touch made her heart pound, and she couldn't help but speak the truth. "I don't care what anyone thinks. I know what a hero you are, and I would be proud to be your wife."

If only I could be your love as well.

He dropped his hand. "In that case, we'll have the banns read and be married within a month's time," he said brusquely. "I'll need to be here that long anyway to see the business with Heath come to a close. Afterward, I'd like to take you and Freddy back to my estate. I've been gone too long as it is."

Her belly fluttered at the thought of the future. In truth, this was just the beginning of their journey together. Perhaps his aloofness would fade, she told herself. Perhaps he was just having pre-wedding jitters. Perhaps over time, with honesty and trust growing between them, love would flourish as well. She had to believe all that would be true.

In the interim, she would try to be a good wife to him... and mama to her soon-to-be-son. No time like the present to address the latter. With all the brouhaha in the past five days, she hadn't found the right time to speak to Gabriel about treating Freddy's spells.

Be honest. You've also been avoiding it.

She pushed aside her qualms. "Speaking of Freddy," she said brightly, "there's something I've been meaning to discuss with you. I had a talk with Dr. Abernathy at his last visit. About a treatment for Freddy."

Gabriel frowned. "I thought I made my feelings quite clear on the matter."

"Yes, but this new cure isn't painful and doesn't involve taking any dangerous substances. Dr. Abernathy says he's seen quite a bit of success with it." She paused. "And Freddy says he'd like to try it."

The crease deepened between his brows. "You've spoken to Freddy about it?"

"He's going to be my son too." Something in his voice made her lift her chin. "And I think he should have a say in his own future."

"He is a child. He doesn't know what he wants." A muscle jumped in Gabriel's jaw. "I specifically told you that Sylvia tried everything and decided that his hopes were not to be futilely raised."

Anger swelled with dizzying speed. Trying to hold onto her equanimity, Thea said, "I disagree. Freddy needs hope. He deserves it."

"Sylvia said that disappointment could worsen his spells," he stated flatly.

"Maybe Sylvia didn't know everything," she shot back.

"I beg your pardon?"

His icy tone incensed her beyond rationality. Leaping to her feet, she said, "You heard me. Maybe your marchioness wasn't as perfect as you make her out to be. Maybe she didn't know every blessed thing under the sun."

He rose slowly, his eyes flinty hard. "I find both your manner and your words distasteful. This is the last time I'll say it: my marriage is not up for discussion."

"Why? Because you're afraid the truth will knock your sainted wife off her pedestal?"

Oh my goodness, where did that come from? The moment Thea said the words, she wished she could take them back.

Mortified, she saw Gabriel's expression grow colder than she'd ever seen it.

"That," he said evenly, "is unworthy of you."

Shame stole her voice. Her face blotched with heat.

"I take full responsibility for the problems in my marriage. Sylvia was not to blame for my proclivities. She was a good wife and a good mother," he said.

"I know." With helpless embarrassment, Thea mumbled, "I didn't mean to imply…"

"She is off limits for discussion. Do I make myself clear?"

She bit down on her bottom lip to prevent it from trembling. Gave a nod.

"Good." He straightened his waistcoat. "Now as for this treatment—I might consider it. But I will be the one who decides, not you. What steps are involved?"

Her lashes fanned as resentment joined the confusing fray of her emotions. Frustration clouded her mind, tied her tongue in knots. Somehow, she got the words out.

"The protocol requires a period of fasting followed by a strict dietary regimen. Apparently, this method was first described by Hippocrates and has recently been rediscovered. Dr. Abernathy says it has met with excellent success," she said flatly.

"Other than fasting, there's no pain? No medicines or other concoctions involved?"

"No."

"As you've already brought the subject up with Freddy, we will give it a try. This one time." Gabriel's eyes were distant and cool. "In the future, I expect that you will discuss any ideas you have regarding his health with me first."

"Yes, my lord." Her jaw tight, she said, "Is there

anything else?"

"There is not."

"Please excuse me, then. I have errands to attend to."

She left and managed to reach her chamber before she gave into tears.

Chapter Thirty-Two

"It's lovely for all of us to be together again," Emma said, beaming.

It was five days later, and the Kent clan had come together to celebrate Thea's upcoming nuptials. Everyone was present: Marianne and Ambrose with their children, Rosie and Edward, all of the Kent sisters, and even their younger brother Harry. They occupied an entire corner of Gunter's Tea Shop in Berkeley Square, the waiters pulling together three tables to fit them all.

Being with her family was a balm to Thea's spirits and just what she needed. Since her and Gabriel's argument over Sylvia, things between them had remained at a cool impasse. Gabriel seemed to have retreated further behind invisible walls, beyond her reach. Frustration and despair simmered inside her, but she didn't know what to do about it.

"Penny for your thoughts, sis."

Tucking away her ruminations, she managed to smile at Harry, who'd returned yesterday from Cambridge. He'd become a grown man, she saw with sisterly affection, and a handsome one at that. His rawboned frame had filled out, his height now balanced with sleek muscle. With his dark curling hair and spectacles, he had a scholar's earnest charm; combined with his athletic physique, he was sure to attract the attention of young ladies everywhere.

"I'm so glad you're here, Harry," Thea said tremulously. "I've missed you."

"I wouldn't miss your wedding for the world," he said.

"You've grown, lad," Ambrose remarked. "Added at least another two stone since we've seen you last. I presume you're not holed up in the laboratory the entire time?"

"In between blowing things up or setting them on fire, the fellows and I find time to get in the ring," Harry said with a raffish grin.

"I bet I could still take you in a race," Violet said from beside him.

Harry and Vi had always been close, their bond taking the form of spirited sibling rivalry.

"You're a lady now, Vi. I don't race ladies. After all," Harry said, "where would the sport be in beating a female? Not gentlemanly by far."

Thea wasn't fooled by his bland tone. He was deliberately baiting Vi... who, of course, fell for it with her usual aplomb.

"You couldn't beat me with a stick." Her caramel-colored eyes narrowed. "The day I can't outrun, outclimb, or outride you, I'll... I'll eat my corset."

"Careful not to choke on the bones," Harry said.

"Let's do it then. Right now. Out in the square, we'll—"

"Before you challenge our brother to games worthy of the ancient Greeks," Emma put in, "perhaps you'd care to recall that we're here to celebrate Thea's upcoming marriage? Bloodshed is no way to mark the occasion."

"Actually," Polly said, her aquamarine eyes serious, "I've read that certain ancient tribes performed blood sacrifices as part of the wedding ritual. It's supposed to guarantee fertility."

Thea's cheeks heated. "Goodness, Polly, where did you read that?"

"In one of Papa's books on the history of civilization," her youngest sister said.

"It's best not to volunteer such information in polite company, dear," Em said.

Polly bit her lip. "People will think I'm peculiar, won't they?"

Back in Chudleigh Crest, Polly had had a reputation for being different due to a certain acuity she possessed that went beyond her tender years. Knowing how much her shy sister feared being an outcast, Thea said gently, "I wouldn't say peculiar exactly. But people might be taken aback by your unusual fount of knowledge."

"Pish posh to what others think." This came from Rosie, who patted Polly's hand. "I, for one, would much rather be an Original than some milk-fed debutante."

"That bodes well for your come out," her mama said dryly.

The waiter arrived with plates of Gunter's famous confectionaries. The family exclaimed over the luscious treats: small cakes iced with marzipan and fresh cream, jellied fruits, and cookies decorated with violets made of sugar. This was accompanied by strong, steaming tea, and they all dug in with customary gusto.

As Thea nibbled on a bit of cake soaked in elderflower syrup, she reflected on how things had changed. There was a time when the family could scarcely afford bread and cheese never mind a luxury such as Gunter's. The ritual of eating and talking together, however, felt exactly the same. She experienced a sudden, bittersweet pang; soon she'd not be a Kent in name any longer.

Morosely, she wondered if she and Gabriel would ever achieve this level of ease and comfort with one another. The distance between them was ever widening, and, since their argument, he'd made no physical advances upon her. She, already feeling at a disadvantage in the relationship, wasn't about to make any on him. She now realized how much she'd come to depend upon their lovemaking to feel the connection between them.

"Things are coming along nicely with the wedding plans," Marianne commented.

If only the same could be said of the relationship between the bride and groom.

Pushing aside her worries, Thea said, "Thanks to you. If it weren't for you, Madame Rousseau would never have made my wedding dress on rush order."

"Marianne has a knack for wedding planning." For some reason, Ambrose's eyes gleamed with humor as he looked at his wife.

"We all have our talents," Marianne said demurely, "and I think our rose garden will make the perfect spot for the wedding brunch. It was your father's favorite place."

Thea remembered how much Papa had loved having his tea outside, surrounded by the bright blooms and humming insects. She knew she would feel his presence when her special day came. Her throat thickened.

Please watch over me and Gabriel, Papa. Please don't let us make a terrible mistake.

"Since Marianne has the wedding itself in hand," Emma put in, "Strathaven and I wanted to contribute something different. We thought you might enjoy a stay at our hunting lodge in Scotland. It's a beautiful and private place, perfect for a wedding trip. And as Freddy is doing so well, he could make the trip too."

That had been the one bright spot in Thea's week. Dr. Abernathy's fasting and dietary protocol seemed to be working wonders. The physician had predicted that if there were to be positive results, they would be immediate. Like a miracle, Freddy hadn't had a single spell since he'd begun treatment. Even Gabriel had evinced grudging surprise and guarded hope.

"Freddy could stay with us at Strathmore," Emma went on. "It's just an hour away from the lodge, so you can check in on him whenever you'd like."

"May I come too, Aunt Emma?" A dab of cream clung to Edward's upper lip. "I could keep Freddy company. We'll be cousins, after all."

As expected, he and Freddy had become fast friends. In fact, they were so inseparable that Violet had nicknamed the pair "Fredward."

Marianne motioned at her lip, and Edward hastily wiped his mouth.

"Of course you may," Emma said, "if your parents agree."

"As lovely as it sounds, a trip to Scotland will have to wait," Thea said. "Tremont wants to return to Hampshire once the business in London is complete."

"After all the man's been through lately, I can't blame him. I'm sure all he wants is to settle in with his new bride," Ambrose said. "To enjoy some much deserved peace and domesticity."

To her horror, Thea felt her smile wobble.

Her brother frowned, his gaze darting swiftly to Marianne. Time and again, Thea had seen the pair engage in such wordless communication, as if they could read each other's thoughts.

What if Gabriel and I never achieve such intimacy? Or any intimacy at all?

"Ambrose, darling, why don't you take everyone outside for a stroll in the square?" Marianne said. "Emma, Thea, and I have wedding matters to discuss."

Ambrose put down his napkin. "Capital idea, my love. Come along, everyone."

The younger Kents tromped out after him, leaving Thea with Marianne and Emma.

Without preamble, Marianne said, "How are you, dear?"

To Thea's dismay, heat pushed behind her eyes. "Why do you ask?" she said, fumbling for her reticule.

Emma passed her a handkerchief. "Because you've looked on the edge of tears all week. Having a case of the bridal jitters, dear?"

Knowing that her feelings had been visible to all made her feel even more wretched.

"I don't know if it's jitters or not," she said, her voice hitching. "But Tremont and I—we had an argument. And I don't know... I don't know if he'll ever love me."

With that, she burst into tears.

Emma rubbed her back. "There, there now. Let it all out. We're here to listen."

In between halting breaths, Thea shared the marriage pact she'd made with Gabriel. She had to edit out the intimate details, of course, but she disclosed that she'd let words of love slip out and his reaction to them. She spoke of his increasing coldness, their recent disagreement.

"The gist of it is, I thought he was falling in love with me and just couldn't say the words," she concluded, sniffling. "I thought because he'd been a spy, he'd learned to block out his emotions to survive, and I believed it was just a matter of unlearning the tendency. I thought if we had honesty and trust, he'd come to love me eventually. But now I'm wondering if all of that was wishful thinking on my part."

"His reaction to your declaration of love *was* rather Siberian," Marianne said.

"I know." Her despair grew.

"But perhaps that's not the only explanation for his recent behavior," her sister-in-law went on. "Perhaps it's not your love that he's reacting so badly to. Or not entirely that, anyway."

"What else could it be?" she said miserably.

Marianne's expression was pensive. "Ambrose mentioned that Tremont was quite forceful in the way he took Heath down. As if he were possessed by some inner demons. Ambrose said he had to stop Tremont from killing the man and that, afterward, Tremont seemed shaken and withdrawn. Not at all himself."

Gabriel's words echoed in Thea's head. *I wanted to put espionage behind me, to never spill another's blood again.* Understanding began to spread like sensation returning to a limb that had fallen asleep.

With prickling awareness, she said, "What he was forced to do during the war eats at him. He may seem stoic, but guilt festers inside him. To come face to face with that time in his life, to re-experience that betrayal and horror…"

Dear God, is this why he's been so distant? So cold?

Marianne gave her an intent look. "Be that as it may, your brother wanted to make sure that you are safe."

"Safe?" Thea said, blinking.

Marianne gave a firm nod. "In a physical sense."

"Tremont would never hurt me physically. If anything, he's overprotective." Thea pursed her lips. "Emotionally, however, he may drive me mad. He hasn't spoken a word about his capture of Heath. I've tried to ask him what the matter was, but all he'll say is that he's fine."

Emma snorted. "If I had a penny for every time I heard that from His Grace, I'd be richer than Croesus."

"What you've told me explains so much, Marianne." A wave of hope surged through Thea as she saw the situation through a new lens. "If only Tremont had talked to me. If I had known, I wouldn't have pushed... wouldn't have gotten so frustrated. Perhaps we wouldn't have fought..."

"You mustn't take the blame, dear," Em said crisply. "You can't read his mind."

That *was* true. Thea gnawed on her lower lip. "I just wish I hadn't brought up his wife. That wasn't well done of me at all."

"Are you having second thoughts, dear?" Marianne said quietly. "Because if you are, we will support—"

"No." Thea's feelings suddenly clarified. Things between her and Gabriel were far from perfect, but as long as the possibility of love remained, there was hope. "I want to marry Tremont. I love him."

"And if he's not able to give you his love in return?" Em said. "What then?"

The truth blazed.

"That's the risk I'll have to take," she said.

It was called *falling* in love for a reason, she realized. There was no guarantee of safety. One could gaze out longingly from one's window in a tower... or take the jump.

Chapter Thirty-Three

That evening, Gabriel broodingly watched the gaiety going on around him. Kent and his wife were throwing him and Thea an informal engagement party, and he was struck by a sense of unreality as he observed his betrothed's laughing, boisterous kin. Their warm affection, the way they bantered back and forth so freely with one another... he'd never known families such as this existed.

His own parents had led separate lives. Papa had been off whoring or gambling, whilst Mama had spent hours praying, presumably to make up for her husband's sins. Gabriel had a faint impression of his mother emerging from her cocoon. *You mustn't dirty Mama's dress*, she'd say in her cool, lilting voice. She would flutter out of reach like a beautiful butterfly whose wings must never be touched.

Much like... Sylvia.

He frowned as he made that connection for the first time. His first wife, too, had shied away from open affection. Visits with Freddy had been formal, conducted twice daily: a half-hour after breakfast and a half-hour before supper. She and Gabriel had taken their meals separately from their son; with a twinge, he recalled how stilted their conversations had become, the two of them dining at the opposite ends of an empty table.

Presently, the Kents were arranged with haphazard

coziness on the furniture or on the carpet in front of the merrily burning hearth. Harry, the brother Gabriel had met for the first time that evening, had started off the festivities with a demonstration of his latest scientific creation: a batch of invisible ink. The vial of liquid was a clear, light pink that was nearly colorless; when Harry wrote a sentence on a piece of parchment, the paper appeared blank and untouched. When he held it near the flame of a lamp, however, his message appeared as if by magic:

Things are not as they appear.

After a resounding round of applause, Harry explained the chemical mechanism behind the mysterious ink. Ruefully, Gabriel thought Harry's invention would have come in handy back in his espionage days. The younger Kents were tickled to pieces... and Freddy was too. When Harry presented the boy with a small vial of ink, Freddy's eyes turned as big as saucers. He took the bottle as reverently as if it were the crown jewels.

As soon as the demonstration was done with, the boy plopped down on the carpet with Polly, Primrose, and Edward. The four proceeded to play a game involving a great quantity of sticks and even more hilarity. As Freddy whooped with joy when he successfully removed a stick without disturbing the pile, Gabriel could scarcely credit the change in his once timid son.

In a short span of weeks, Frederick had blossomed. Not only were his falling spells improving, but the warmth of Thea and her family had infused him with new vitality. Freddy was now a boy like any other. Glancing at Thea— talking quietly with Kent by the pianoforte—Gabriel experienced a spasm in his chest. It took him a moment to recognize his feelings as longing and gratitude... mingled with bone-deep fear.

He knew that he was being a bastard. Making a bloody hash of things. Day by day, he'd felt the chasm widening between him and Thea. It had started when she told him she loved him. The fierceness of his response had taken him aback; he hadn't known how to answer. His inner voice had whispered, *Begin as you mean to go on. Don't set her up for disappointment.*

To compound matters, the business with Heath the next day had... unsettled him. Resurrected a part of himself that he wanted nothing to do with. The mindless, bloodthirsty animal who had gotten Marius killed. No way in hell was he letting that near Thea. He had stayed away from her, couldn't risk touching her, tainting her while the darkness raged inside him. When she'd pushed to get closer, he'd lashed out at her.

Guilt and self-hatred crept over him as he thought of how badly he'd treated her... again. She'd only wanted to help Freddy, and he'd acted like a damned blighter. When she'd left the room, a part of him had wanted to chase after her, to fall on his knees and apologize. The other part had kept him rooted in place, paralyzed by a growing sense of inevitability.

How could she love him, after all? When no one had done so before?

As the days had passed, thankfully the darkness in him had subsided, and finally, tonight, he'd felt in control again. The numbness had faded; he was back in his own skin. With crystal clarity, he realized that he needed to talk to Thea, to beg her forgiveness for his behavior. The only thing holding him back was fear. What if he'd bungled things up beyond repair? What if she no longer wanted him?

The advice that Strathaven had given him in the carriage suddenly echoed in his head. *Drink from a clean cup.*

The duke was right. Thea wasn't Sylvia. She was unique, rare.

Stop acting like a namby-pamby fool, he told himself. *Go and bloody talk to her.*

Expelling a breath, he headed over to Thea and her brother.

"May I join in?" he said.

"Of course." Her voice was light, her hazel gaze guarded.

"How are you finding our family affair?" Kent said.

"It's lively," he said honestly.

The investigator shared a wry glance with his sister. "We've certainly been called worse."

"I meant no offense. By lively, I meant kind and welcoming—" he began.

"Ambrose is just teasing." Thea's smile chased away some of his emptiness. Hungrily, he absorbed her sweetness, her radiance, everything about her. "It's a Kent tendency, I'm afraid."

"Sometimes we can take it too far." Kent's gaze was directed at Harry and Violet, whose competitive game of cards had devolved into out and out war. "As Marianne loathes bloodstains on the carpet, I'd best put an end to that. Excuse me."

Alone with his betrothed, Gabriel found that his heart was pounding.

"You look beautiful," he said finally.

Her ivory gown clung to her exquisite bosom and

slender waist, flaring into full skirts. With her golden brown hair arranged in cascading ringlets, she looked like a faerie princess. He felt like a dark goblin who wanted to spirit her away so that he could have her all to himself.

"Thank you," she said politely. "You look very handsome yourself."

There was a time when he masked himself in civility. But it suddenly felt like a tiresome barrier, something he wanted to rip away so that he could get close to Thea again. To her warmth and generous vitality. He resented having anything between them... even if he'd been the fool who'd put the wall there in the first place.

His chest tight, he said, "I wish to apologize."

Her golden eyelashes flickered. "What for?"

Mentally, he reviewed his sins. Settled on the safest one. "For being an ass."

She studied him, her expression so somber that dread crept through him. Then her mouth twitched. "You'll have to be more specific," she said.

He screwed his courage to the sticking place. "I know I've been... difficult this past week."

"Yes," she said, "you have."

"I am sorry for it. For being disagreeable about Freddy's treatment. For... everything." He dragged the words out. "The whole business with Heath, discovering the nature of his betrayal—it disquieted me. I did not handle it well, and you did not deserve to bear the brunt of my behavior."

After a moment, she said softly, "Anyone would be disquieted by such a shock. And I know how much you want to put your past behind you."

"But it always comes back." The returning warmth in her

eyes made the truth tumble out of him like rubbish from a bin. "The things I despise about myself, the killer I was... During the capture, I lost control. I could have killed Heath. Wanted to."

"But you didn't. You stopped." With gentle palms, she held his jaw, focusing him on her. His present. "You did what you had to in the past. One day, you'll forgive yourself. You're a good man, Gabriel."

Her faith humbled him. He couldn't speak.

"And I want to thank you for sharing what you just did. For talking to me," she said in a rush. "The truth is it's been a difficult week for me too. When you blocked me out, I didn't know why. I can't read your mind. I thought perhaps you were having second thoughts about marriage or me—"

"No, Thea." Appalled at the conclusions she'd drawn, he said, "I *want* to marry you. More than anything. I can hardly wait to make you mine."

"Truly?" Her eyes glimmered.

"Truly." He took her hands, kissed her soft knuckles. "What I wouldn't give to be alone with you right now, princess."

"Oh, Gabriel," she said tremulously, "I've missed—"

"Papa! Miss Thea!"

They both turned their heads as Freddy ran toward them. Sliding a longing, apologetic look at Thea, Gabriel said, "What is it, son?"

"We're to play a new game. A spelling game." His boy's eyes were bright with excitement. "We need to make teams. Will you both be on mine?"

Gabriel and Thea exchanged amused glances.

"We'd be delighted," she said.

When she made to follow Freddy, Gabriel took hold of her hand. She didn't pull away, instead lacing her fingers with his. He held on tightly as they went over to the fireplace where the game was taking place.

The party had been divided into four groups. According to the rules—gravely presented by Edward—the object of the game was to gain the most points possible by accurately spelling a word. Each player had the chance to pull a scrap of paper from a box; the paper contained a single letter. The player had one minute in which to come up with a word beginning with that letter and to spell it properly. Each letter of the word equaled one point.

With things back on course with Thea, Gabriel found himself able to relax for the first time in days. Perhaps it was Freddy's delight or the air of crackling competition, but he was actually drawn into the game. When he selected the letter "M" and correctly spelled out the word "meticulousness," Freddy and Thea cheered aloud.

"That's *fourteen* points, Papa!" Freddy crowed. "We're in the lead!"

Gabriel smiled at his son's enthusiasm.

Not to be outdone, Strathaven pulled the letter "F" and proceeded to spell out a word.

"*Farfetchedness* isn't a word," his duchess argued (she was on another team).

"Indeed it is," the duke said loftily. "It refers to the quality of being farfetched."

"Like your *word*," she said, rolling her eyes.

Nonetheless, after some good-natured debate, Strathaven's team was awarded fourteen points. The play continued, with the competition becoming fiercer and the words more outlandish. When they reached the last round, Gabriel and Strathaven's teams were in the clear lead, head to head. Edward declared that there would be a final round between the two teams. Each player on the team would get the chance to spell one word.

Strathaven won the coin toss, and his team went first.

Harry correctly spelled "ambitiousness" for thirteen points.

Gabriel felt a moment's worry when Thea pulled the letter "O." But she, clever girl, provided the word, "orchestration," tying them again.

Strathaven and Gabriel kept the scores even with their respective entries.

Then it was the turn of the final players, Violet and Freddy.

Violet drew her letter. "Q!" she said indignantly. "Dash it, that's not fair. Who put a "Q" in here?"

"Forty-six seconds and counting," Edward intoned.

Wearing a look of panic, Violet blurted, "Quinces!"

Her accurate spelling garnered her team seven points. As she accepted congratulations, she muttered, "Gadzooks, I hope that's enough. But Q! That's like boxing with an arm tied behind your back!"

It was Freddy's turn. Sensing his son's nervousness, Gabriel said, "You'll do fine."

"Remember 'tis only a game." Thea ruffled Freddy's hair. "Just do your best and have fun."

With a nod, Freddy reached into the box. He unfolded the slip.

"T," he said.

Gabriel waited, breath held, as his son frowned in

concentration. Countless words flitted through his head, and he wished he could somehow put them into his son's. But this was something Freddy had to do on his own. With half a minute to spare, Freddy spoke.

"Tenterhooks," he said. "T-E-N-T-E-R-H-O-O-K-S."

Eleven points. They'd won.

As cheers and congratulations went up all around, Thea said to Freddy in admiring tones, "You were brilliant, dear. However did you think up that word?"

"It just came to me," Freddy said happily. "In one of our lessons, Mademoiselle Fournier..." He trailed off, as if he'd just realized what he'd said.

Gabriel tensed at the mention of the villainous governess. As far as he knew, she was still at large. He'd questioned Heath about his partner in crime, but the man had refused to talk.

"She taught you the word?" Thea said gently. "It's all right to speak of her, if you wish. In fact,"—her gaze met Gabriel's—"sometimes it is best to talk about things even if they are unpleasant."

Freddy swallowed and nodded. "She was explaining how cloth was made. They used tenterhooks, she said, to stretch the fabric after washing. To make it dry flat and smooth. She said that the tentergrounds near where she lived were as colorful as a field of wildflowers."

Gabriel stilled, his nape prickling. His gaze shot to Thea's; though he saw the awareness in her eyes, she subtly shook her head. Warning him not to frighten Freddy.

"Did she mention which tentergrounds in particular? There are a few in London," she said.

"No. All she said was that the tentergrounds had closed

recently so that buildings could be put in..." Freddy's eyes widened. "Do you think... is this a clue? To finding her?"

"Did she say anything else, son?" Gabriel said.

Freddy's forehead furrowed. "I can't recall anything else. I'm sorry."

Thea patted his shoulder. "You've been incredibly helpful, Freddy. Now run along and play with the others."

With an uncertain look, Freddy scampered off.

Thea said, "Are you thinking of continuing the search for the governess? After all, you have the Spectre in custody already. "

"Let's talk to your brother," Gabriel said.

Thea asked Violet and Harry to take charge of the younger ones as Gabriel quietly assembled the others. They gathered in Ambrose's study, closing the door just as sounds of "Hide the Slipper" could be heard from the drawing room. The four couples arranged themselves in a circle: Emma and Mrs. McLeod on the settee, their husbands standing behind them, Thea in a wingchair and Gabriel pacing behind her, and Marianne at the desk, Ambrose at her side.

"So Freddy said Marie Fournier lived near tentergrounds?" Ambrose said alertly. "Did he remember anything else?"

"That she said those grounds had recently closed and buildings were put in," Gabriel said.

"She's talking about Spitalfields." Mr. McLeod's shaggy head lifted like that of a hound on the scent. "The area bordered by White's Row, Wentworth and those two lanes, what are their names…"

"Bell and Rose," Mrs. McLeod supplied. "The area is the heart of the rag trade. Weavers, seamstresses, button makers—they're all there, so crowded together that the streets are fairly bursting at the seams. No pun intended."

Thea had always liked Annabel McLeod, whose sensual auburn beauty belied a generous and practical spirit. From the snippets that Thea had gleaned over the years, Mrs. McLeod's life had not been easy before her marriage, and she was never one to hold airs. Since Ambrose and Mr. McLeod were partners, the two families socialized frequently, and the warmth of Mrs. McLeod's home had always reminded Thea of the cottage back in Chudleigh Crest. The Scotsman and his wife raised their two redheaded girls with the same cozy affection that Thea had grown up with.

"Finding Fournier there would be like searching for a needle in a haystack," Mr. McLeod said.

"It's not much to go on." Lines of frustration were carved into Gabriel's face. "It might not even be important, given that we have the Spectre."

"Information is always important. We at Kent and Associates do not like loose threads," Ambrose said.

"Heaven help us with the puns." Tapping her chin, Emma said, "What do we know about Fournier at this point?"

"All her references were false," Ambrose replied. "She must have been educated, however, as her lessons appeared to have been of good quality. She spoke French and English fluently. And we have this."

Opening the drawer of his desk, Ambrose removed an item. Thea recognized the handkerchief she'd found that day at the zoological gardens.

"I took it around to a few shops. None of the clerks recognized its origins," Ambrose went on. "They all agreed it is a commonplace handkerchief of middling quality and that her initials are rather overdone."

"May I see it?" Mrs. McLeod said.

Ambrose brought it over.

Mrs. McLeod ran a finger over the large letters sewn in blue thread at the center of the handkerchief. Her expression turned pensive. "I don't think those are her initials."

"They're not?" Ambrose's brow furrowed. "What are they then?"

"The mark of the manufacturer," the redheaded beauty replied. "The clerks you questioned wouldn't know this because they work in a shop, not a factory. But for a time I was a seamstress, and I know it is the practice of some factories to have sample items for the seamstresses to follow. A yardstick, if you will, to measure the goods they produce. To prevent these pattern items from being stolen, the manufacturer would mark the piece with their insignia. The mark renders the item valueless; if one were to remove these letters, for instance, it would leave a handkerchief full of holes." Her violet gaze circled the room. "In any case, I think what you may be looking for is a manufacturer with the initials M. F."

"Annabel, you are brilliant," Emma declared.

Mr. McLeod's large hand came to rest on his wife's shoulder. "Who'd have thought that that damnable time would prove useful, eh lass?" he said with tender gruffness.

Mrs. McLeod smiled, her hand covering her husband's. "Since that time led me to you, I have no complaints."

"How would Fournier have gotten such a handkerchief?" Thea asked.

"A good question. Samples are meant to stay in the factory." A line deepened between Mrs. McLeod's auburn brows. "My best guess is that Fournier once worked at this place and filched it. Since her own initials happen to match that of the manufacturer, she could use the item herself."

"So we're looking for a handkerchief factory in Spitalfields. One with the initials M. F.," Thea said eagerly. "There can't be too many of those."

"I'll pay a visit to Spitalfields tomorrow," Gabriel said, his eyes grim.

"No, my lord. *We* will," Ambrose said.

Chapter Thirty-Four

The next morning, Gabriel managed to get Thea alone in the library. He shepherded her in between the bookcases. They didn't have much time; Kent and the others would be arriving shortly to accompany him to Spitalfields, and he wanted a moment alone with her.

"You'll be careful today?" Thea said.

"Yes." He rubbed a thumb over her bottom lip, savoring its softness, the contact between them once more. "We're probably just chasing our own tail."

"You never know." She shivered. "I just wish this business was truly over."

"It will be soon. All evidence points to Heath being the Spectre, and, if anything, finding Fournier will just put the nail in his coffin. Now stop fretting, princess," he murmured, "and give me a kiss goodbye."

He bent his head, intending only to give her a little peck. But after a week of going without, desire roared over him... along with potent, heady relief when she responded.

She still wants me. I haven't bungled things up beyond repair.

Before he knew what he was doing, he'd backed her into the shelves, her palms flattening against the leather spines, her lips parting in sensual surrender. Her taste, the feel of her so soft and giving, overwhelmed him. The need burgeoned in him to be closer to her, as close as he could possibly be.

He threw up her skirts, his hand finding the curve of her knee and upward, past the frill of her garter. Her thighs were down-soft, tempting as hell. But he didn't have time to linger.

"Gabriel, anyone can see," she protested.

"Then you'll have to decide, won't you? Whether the risk is worth it."

"I can't possibly—*oh*." Her eyes closed, pink suffusing her cheeks.

Triumph surged within him. "Open your eyes, princess. Look at me when I touch you."

Her lashes lifted, the hazel depths swirling with passionate gold. He rewarded her by circling his thumb over her pearl, his other fingers surging upward into her voluptuous warmth. She was so snug and wet around him that he could hardly breathe.

"Did you miss this?" he said against her ear. "My fingers inside you?"

"Yes. Oh yes."

He withdrew, drove upward again. "You've got two of them now. Can you take another?"

She whimpered, and a gush of dew dampened his palm. He'd take that as a yes.

It was the work of a moment to give her more, his cock rock-hard with envy at the way her sheath clutched his driving touch. Oh, to be balls deep in her pussy... heaven for another day. For now it was enough to reestablish that he owned her pleasure, that she was still his. This was real between them. Intimacy he knew how to give.

His teeth ground together as she came. He endured the

exquisite torture of her cunny convulsing around his fingers, milking his thick digits before the flutters subsided. Only then did he pull free of her and settle her skirts back into place.

Smiling into her bliss-glazed eyes, he said, "Now give me a goodbye kiss, and I'll be off."

She looked at him and, in the next instant, sank to her knees. To his astonishment, she went to work on the fastenings of his trousers. When his heavy erection fell into her hands, he came to his senses.

"Thea, love, I don't think—"

The rest of the sentence evaporated from his brain as her lips closed around him.

Christ. Holy Mother of God.

His knees nearly buckled as she took him hard and fast, her fist pumping him as she sucked on his shaft. Her taking control like this wasn't their agreement, he thought dazedly, but at the moment he couldn't give a damn.

Her curls bobbed prettily as she took him deeper and deeper. As she endeavored to swallow his prick whole, to consume every living inch of him with her wildfire. His hands clenched in the silk of her hair; his hips thrust with animal volition, fucking her beautiful mouth, and she didn't pull back. Raw words tore from his throat.

"I need this," he growled. "I need *you*."

She moaned in response, the moist vibration making his neck arch. Her hot, wet sucking drove him to the edge. When his cockhead nudged the silken end of her throat, lights streaked across his vision. Heat rumbled up from his balls, and with his last ounce of sanity, he tried to pull away.

She wouldn't let him. Feeling her fingers dig into his

buttocks, holding him in place as she had her wicked way with him, he lost all control. He came with a roar, the hot load rushing from him and into her generous keeping.

He staggered backward, his shoulders sagging against a bookcase. As he tried to catch his breath, she refastened his pants and rose. Through the haze of pleasure, he saw that she looked perfectly pristine and ladylike... unless one looked at her eyes. They were slumberous and sultry, brimming with feminine satisfaction.

The merging of lady and siren, the glowing wholeness of it, made his senses spin.

"That," he said hoarsely, "was the best goodbye kiss I've ever had."

"Consider it an incentive." Her smile beguiled the hell out of him. "Because my hello kisses are even better."

After Gabriel and the others left, time seemed to drag by at a snail's pace. Thea tried practicing at the pianoforte, but she couldn't concentrate. She was too distracted by thoughts of what might be happening in Spitalfields... and of the sensual encounter between her and Gabriel this morning.

I need you.

She hugged the words to herself. It was the closest he'd come to saying that he loved her. He'd trusted her enough to let her take the lead in their lovemaking, and it had felt glorious to be in command of his pleasure. More importantly, last night he'd apologized for his behavior and opened up to her. He'd reaffirmed his desire to marry her.

Things *were* progressing between them.

Her previous worries began to seem like the bridal jitters after all.

Seeing that she was getting nowhere with practice, Thea went to check in on Freddy. The boy was sitting at the desk in his room, his tawny head bent over a piece of parchment. He had a half-finished tray of roasted beef and carrots beside him.

Freddy's health had continued to make excellent progress. Dr. Abernathy had begun to experiment with various foods in order to see their effects on the boy's ailment. Thus far, they'd discovered that Freddy tolerated meats and fatty foods without any problem, while breads and sweets could trigger a megrim. Though the process required trial and error, Freddy remained full of hope, his resilience filling Thea with pride.

"What are you doing, dear?" she said.

Freddy looked up, his eyes bright with excitement. It was a common expression for him these days. "Edward and I are playing a game. We're pretending to be spies," he said eagerly. "I'm writing him a secret message using the invisible ink Harry gave me."

Thea hid a grin. *I wonder what Gabriel would think of this new game.*

"That's lovely," she said. "Shall I see if Edward is available for a visit today?"

"Oh, yes," Freddy enthused. "But I must finish my message before we go."

Leaving him to the task, Thea sent a note to Marianne and received an affirmative reply to call. Thea debated sending for the carriage, but the idea of stretching her legs and getting some sunshine and fresh air seemed preferable to the trouble. It was less than a ten-minute walk away, and they'd take a pair of footmen with them. She decided to let Freddy make the choice.

"Let's walk," he said. "That way I can test the ink outdoors. I want to see if I can leave secret messages on fence posts for Edward to find."

"I'm afraid that would be vandalism, dear."

"How is it vandalism if you can't see it?" Freddy said in reasonable tones. "Unless someone puts a flame near it, the ink will remain invisible. And if the ink does become visible, Harry says all you have to do is put water on it to make it disappear."

Thea opened her mouth—then closed it.

"Just don't let anyone see what you're doing," she said with a sigh.

Chapter Thirty-Five

It took them less than an hour to find what they were looking for.

Maison de Fortescue, a factory specializing in handkerchiefs, occupied a squat building in the heart of Spitalfield's Petticoat Lane. It sat on a street crammed with shops on both sides, garments of every kind strung up along the low-hanging eaves. In this heart of industry, rules of civility gave way to commerce. A lady's used corset dangled side by side with a pair of gentleman's smalls. Morts sold stockings and garters from baskets on the street. Customers jostled one another as they tried on items, tugging them over their clothes.

Accompanied by Kent and McLeod, Gabriel entered the shop. Inside, Fortescue's was more spacious and cleaner than its exterior might suggest. The front counter was polished, and the man who came to greet them had the glistening pink mien of one who never missed his meals. His waistcoat, patterned in a loud stripe, strained at the buttons. His thinning black hair had been meticulously combed to cover his balding pate.

He sized them up. His gaze gleamed like that of a man who'd been presented with a feast. He waddled over and performed an unctuous bow.

"James Fortescue, at your service." Despite the French

surname, the man's Cockney accent was several generations thick. "How may I be o' assistance to you fine gents today?"

Gabriel removed the handkerchief from his pocket. Placed it on the counter.

"Is this one of yours?" he said.

"As a matter o' fact, it is, and it don't belong outside the shop." Fortescue frowned. "Don't know as 'ow it fell into such fine 'ands as yours, but rest assured that that is a rough sample only. I've much finer examples if you wish to order a supply—"

"What I wish to know is if a woman by the name of Marie Fournier worked here."

"Don't know no Fournier," the proprietor said. "But perhaps I could interest you in some o' our fine merchandise—"

"She may have used a different name. The woman I seek is of average height, thin, dark hair and eyes. She is well-educated and speaks fluent French and English." Seeing the sudden dart of the other's eyes, Gabriel said evenly, "This is a matter of import, and I am offering a reward."

Fortescue licked his lips. "A reward, you say?"

Gabriel removed a coin purse, letting the contents jingle.

"I might know the woman you're lookin' for." His eyes on the purse, Fortescue said, "'Ad a seamstress by the name o' Manette Fontaine workin' for me."

Gabriel's nape prickled.

"How long ago?" Kent said alertly.

"She disappeared around three months ago. Left without a word." Fortescue huffed. "Should 'ave listened to my gut and turned the hussy away from the start."

Gabriel traded glances with the investigators. The

timing matched with when Fournier—or Fontaine, rather—
had started in his employ. This had to be the woman they
were after.

"Why should you have turned her away?" Gabriel said.

"'Er manner. Hoity-toity, she was. Because she had a bit
o' book learning, she thought she was better than the rest."
Fortescue grunted—his comment on educated females,
apparently. "Claimed she'd been a governess for a rich family
and 'ad been let go when the children went away to school.
Only a fool would believe that tale when she didn't have a
single reference to show for it." Fortescue's thin brows rose.
"My guess is that Miss High and Mighty got herself
compromised and was shown the back door."

"Then why did you hire her?" Gabriel said.

The proprietor's eyes slid away. "I've a big 'eart, I do."

The heart wasn't the part of the anatomy that had made
the other's decision, Gabriel thought with disgust. "After she
left," he said coldly, "you heard nothing else?"

"I've said all I know." Fortescue held his hand out for the
purse.

Gabriel kept it back. "We will need to speak to your
employees who knew Fontaine."

"My seamstresses are busy. They 'aven't the time to—"

Gabriel emptied the purse, the gold clinking onto his
gloved palm.

Fortescue's avarice got the better of him. "All right. You
may speak to Alice—she and Manette were as chatty as
magpies." He took the gold, stuffing it into his pocket. "Ten
minutes only, mind you. I've a business to run."

∞

The woman named Alice was more than happy to talk.

"Well, beats bein' up in that bleedin' garret room, don't it?" Batting her eyelashes, she untied her fichu, making a great show of fanning her exposed décolletage. "La, it's so *hot* up there."

Gabriel observed that the woman's milkmaid looks were already showing signs of wear. Fine lines were etched around her eyes and mouth, and her gaze was as jaded and assessing as that of any trollop. In fact, her coy manner suggested that she had at least some experience in the world's oldest trade.

He'd sent Kent and McLeod back to the carriage so as not to intimidate their only lead to Fontaine. He and Alice were out in the alley behind Fortescue's. Squeezed between buildings, the corridor was stifling and reeked of garbage. The back doors of the other businesses swung open now and again, letting out people or buckets of refuse.

It was the most privacy they were going to get.

"I'm told you know Manette Fontaine," Gabriel said.

"Knew. 'Aven't 'eard from 'er since she left this place." Alice gave him a flirtatious smile. "What'er she did for you, sir, I reckon I can do better."

"Manette is a prostitute?"

"You're not one o' 'er fancy coves?" Alice's eyes thinned. "Who are you then?"

"Someone who wants to find her." He held out a quid. "This is yours if you answer my questions."

"Double that, and I'll tell you everything I know," she said.

He gave her half of what she asked. "The rest when you're done. So you and Manette—you both worked in the streets?"

"I ain't no common streetwalker. I'm a good girl, I am," Alice said unconvincingly. "Work my fingers to the bone in my God-given trade, but sometimes it ain't enough and if there 'appens to be a job or two on the side…" She shrugged. "A girl's got to make ends meet, don't she?"

"Manette was doing these side jobs as well?"

"*She's* the one who 'ooked me onto the idea. We started 'ere 'round the same time and got friendly like. One day she says to me she knows o' a way to make some extra blunt and am I interested? I says, do birds 'ave wings? That's when she tells me o' this 'igh-kick place in Covent Garden called the Tickle and Fancy. There, a girl can work whene'er and howe'er much she wants. The nobs there like it that way; they don't fancy long-toothed whores." Alice smirked. "They prefer fresh goods—seamstresses and maids wot only do it now an' again and nicely like. Pay more for the likes o' us, they do."

"You said Manette knew some fancy coves."

"She was a favorite, she was. The gents liked 'er since she was pretty and clever." Alice arched a brow. "Why, before all this she used to work as a governess—but the masters, she said, they all 'ad wandering 'ands. *Why give it away for a governess' wages, when you could make 'em pay properly for what they're getting?* Manette always said. 'Ad brains, that one."

"Do you know the names of the gentlemen she kept company with?"

Alice shook her head, her fat brown curls flopping beneath her cap. "Manette kept as quiet as a clam about 'er affairs. Discretion, she said, is the difference between us an' the common run whores. Gor, she 'ad class, make no mistake about it. Makes sense that she'd land 'erself a nob."

Gabriel stilled. "What nob?"

"Don't know 'is name—like I said, Manette knew 'ow to keep her gob shut. But one night, she and I got a bit top 'eavy, and she said she'd got 'er ticket to a better place. Some toff 'ad given it to 'er. Thought it was the bottle talking, but sure enough, a fortnight later she was gone. Gor, by now she could be a Lady-So-And-So," Alice enthused.

Gabriel did not share the other's optimism. "You can recall nothing else she said about this man?" he said tersely.

"No, sir. I've said all I know."

Gabriel handed over the rest of the money. "Thank you for your time."

"Are you certain I can't 'elp you with anything else?" Alice said coquettishly.

"That is all," he said firmly.

"Well, you know where I am if you change your mind." She gave a good-natured pout, sashaying back into the building.

The door closed behind her. Gabriel remained, his thoughts racing.

Was Heath the nob Manette/Marie had met? Had he been the one to hire the Frenchwoman, not for carnal purposes as Alice believed, but to spy and kidnap? Gabriel's gut told him that the governess was somehow the key to everything. He would go next to the Tickle and Fancy and see if anyone there knew Manette's whereabouts or could identify Heath as one of her customers.

The door to the adjacent building swung open. A sandy-haired man emerged, and as he turned, shock spread like frost through Gabriel. He stood, frozen, as the vision closed the distance between them.

The familiar face bore a wry smile. "Hello, Trajan."

"Marius?" Gabriel whispered.

Quick as lightning, the other moved. Even as Gabriel's arm came up instinctively, he knew it was too late. Powder wound into his nostrils and lungs, choking, inescapable. He staggered backward, away from the ghost, and this time he was the one to tumble into oblivion.

Chapter Thirty-Six

The world came into focus.

Gabriel's mind analyzed his situation even as he remained perfectly still.

Windowless room. Lying on a bed, hands and legs manacled. Don't let him know you're awake. Marius. My brother—my enemy.

"Welcome back, Gabriel."

Devil take it. Slowly, he sat up, the chains between his wrists rattling. Marius emerged from the shadows, and Gabriel's gut twisted as he beheld the face that had haunted him for so many years. Time had been kind to the bastard. A few more lines in the tanned skin, grey sprinkled in with the short brown hair. The keen blue eyes were the same. Sharp as a blade.

The kind one found in one's back, apparently.

"How?" Gabriel bit out. "Why?"

Marius smiled. "With two words, you open a universe of questions, my friend."

"I'm not your friend."

"And I am not your enemy."

"Prove it," Gabriel said calmly as he seethed on the inside. "Unchain me and then we'll have a discussion about friendship."

"I'm not a fool. In hand to hand battle, I never could best

you. Which is why I had to arrange this *tête-à-tête*." Marius shook his head. "I won't free you until you listen to what I have to say. And you will listen carefully, Gabriel. I came back from the grave to convey this message."

"Devil take your message." Rage incinerated Gabriel's composure. "And speaking of the grave—why in damnation aren't you in one?"

Marius sighed. "I suppose there's no getting around history. I'll have to start from the beginning. But I warn you: we may have little time."

"I don't need your warning, you backstabbing blighter. You're the Spectre, aren't you?" Gabriel was on his feet in a second, forced to shuffle his manacled feet as he advanced toward his former friend. "All along, it was *you*. For years, I lived with the guilt of your death. But there's no blood on my hands, is there? It's all dripping from yours!"

Marius withdrew a pistol from his pocket. Aimed it at Gabriel's heart. "Come any closer, and I'll be forced to kill you. I don't want to, but I'll do it."

"Damn you to hell," Gabriel snarled.

"Sit down. In that chair." Marius motioned with his gun.

Chest heaving, Gabriel forced himself to comply. *Get in control. Find a way out of here.*

"One move and I will put a bullet through your heart," Marius said. "Understand?"

I'm going to rip you from limb to limb. It required all his inner resources, but Gabriel gave a terse nod. He would bide his time.

"Since you brought it up, we'll start with that last mission. From the start, I tried to talk Octavian out of it, but he wouldn't listen. Hardheaded bastard, he was."

"Is that why you slit his throat?" Gabriel said through his teeth.

"I tried to hand Octavian my resignation," Marius continued as if Gabriel hadn't spoken. "By that time, I'd had more than enough of espionage and all the ugliness it entailed. But Octavian wouldn't have it. He reminded me of what I owed him, how he'd plucked me from poverty, the pile of shite I'd sprung from, and made a blooming gentleman of me." Marius' lips twisted. "He convinced me to do this one last mission. To put my neck, and those of my fellow agents, on the line because of his obsession with capturing the Almighty Spectre. And I did it—because I could never bloody say no to the man. He was a master of manipulation, our mentor."

Don't listen to Marius. He's a lying bastard. What does he want?

"The night of the mission, everything went wrong. It was a trap. I escaped by the skin of my teeth, and I waited for three days at our agreed upon meeting place in Rouen. When no one showed, I knew you'd all been captured." Marius' bronzed features were harsh in the dimness. "I'll be honest: I was tempted to run. To let Octavian think that he'd lost all of us that night and to start a new life, free of him at last. But I couldn't."

"Why should I believe anything you say?" Gabriel bit out.

"Because I came back for you and the others when that was the last bloody thing I wanted to do," Marius said tightly. "Like a madman, I argued with myself—and was damn pissed with the side of me that won. But I couldn't leave you in the hands of the Spectre, knowing what the bastard was capable of."

"Loyal to a fault." Gabriel's voice dripped with sarcasm even as his heart thudded.

"Call it loyalty or stupidity—it doesn't matter. The fact is, I came back, freed you all. And when you and I were fighting our way to freedom and that bugger pushed me over the cliff, I had but one thought in my head: *Damn, this is all it's come to.*" Marius' throat worked. "I was going to die in the middle of bloody nowhere, with no one knowing or caring, and for no purpose whatsoever. This was how it was going to end for me—and it didn't even come as a bleeding surprise."

Don't listen to him. Don't be fooled again. "That would all be very touching—if you were dead. But you're not," Gabriel said acidly. "You're alive and pointing a gun at me."

"I wouldn't need the gun if you weren't so bullheaded." Marius expelled a breath. "There was a ledge on the cliff, hidden beneath a larger outcropping. On my way down, I managed to grab hold of it and hoist myself up. I lay there, bleeding from the shot in my arm, and in that moment, I knew that Marius had died. He'd fallen into the ocean to his unmarked grave. But I, John Malcolm, was going to live. The universe had given me a second chance at life, and I was damn well going to make it one worth living."

Gabriel hated that he heard the truth in Marius' words. Hated even more that he understood those sentiments all too well.

"I thought you died because of me," he said, his voice gritty. "For over twelve years, you've let me live with that guilt."

Marius had the gall to look surprised. "Why would you think that my death was your fault? You didn't push me over the cliff."

"I was the reason we were slow getting out of that hellhole." The memory seared through Gabriel like lava. "You kept telling me to run, to go, to get out of there, but I wouldn't listen because I was out of control, caught up in bloodlust. Instead of running, I stayed and fought and killed. By the time we reached the outside, the enemy surrounded us. If I'd listened to you, we'd have had a good ten minutes start on them. You wouldn't have been forced to have a stand-off on the cliffs."

Comprehension shifted over Marius' worn features. "You thought that the delay you caused led to my death?"

"Not now that you're standing there as alive as I am," Gabriel bit out. "But for all the years before—yes, goddamnit, I thought it was my fault. You died because I let my emotions rule instead of my head. Because I lost control. Because I failed to heed Octavian's teachings—"

"Control was *never* the problem." Now Marius' eyes glowed with anger. "Don't let our mentor's so-called lessons blind you to the truth. To block out all emotion is *not* normal. To kill, to see the things we've seen, and pretend that that doesn't affect one's soul is bloody *wrong*. That was why I needed to get out. I didn't want to become a deadened, soulless soldier. An empty shell of a man."

A vise clamped around Gabriel's chest. He couldn't speak.

"I'm not the Spectre, Gabriel," Marius said quietly, "and I've lived a life of peace—some might say boredom—since I started over again. I've no reason to be here today except to pay a debt that's owed."

"What debt is that?" Gabriel said hoarsely.

"Loyalty I owed to you—to the comrades I'd left behind. Normandy has continued to niggle at me over the years, like a pebble in my boot. Or, more aptly, like a snake in the grass. How did the Spectre know our group's inner workings well enough to set such a trap?" Marius' eyes narrowed. "There was only one answer, of course. When I got word of Octavian's death followed shortly by your own carriage 'accident,' I knew unfinished business had risen. As much as I tried, I couldn't ignore it. So I came back. As it turns out, my apparent death has given me a great advantage when it comes to spying. I've been monitoring events for the past fortnight with no one the wiser. And I was able to step in when needed."

"The shooter in the alley," Gabriel said suddenly. "That was… you?"

Marius nodded. "I followed you and Pompeia to the market that day. And when it looked like you could use a hand, I gave it."

"You always were a crack shot." Swallowing, Gabriel said, "Why didn't you reveal yourself to me then?"

"Because at the time I still didn't know who the Spectre was. I needed the benefit of obscurity to watch things unfold. To see who would finally show themselves as the guilty one."

"You know who the Spectre is?" Gabriel said.

"Yes."

He read all he needed to know in the other's somber expression. What his gut had been trying to tell him all along. "It's not Heath."

"No, it's not."

"Devil take it." Anger blazed through him. "Davenport."

Marius gave a grim nod. "Cicero always had the cunning

of a fox, and he's suspicious by nature too. Several times I followed his carriage from his offices—only to discover later that it had been a decoy. He'd hired another to pose as him, running errands on Bond Street and the like, whilst he was off God knows where making trouble. Only by accident did I catch his true scent. I was also watching Heath, the other viable suspect, and who should show up at Heath's place but Cicero. Heath wasn't home, but Cicero let himself right in. I knew he was up to no good; I just didn't know what exactly. Then three nights later, you 'discovered' the Spectre's plans at Heath's home, and I deduced that Cicero had framed our mad friend."

"Why didn't you come forward then?"

"Because I wanted tangible proof. Not just speculation. And I got it finally. Two nights ago, Cicero, believing that he was in the clear after Heath's capture, was finally careless. I was able to follow him all the way to a cottage in Camden Town where I found the missing link." Marius took a key from his pocket. "I'll show you—if you vow not to waste time trying to kill me."

The past was done. Gabriel found he no longer gave a damn. What mattered was that Marius' explanations and revelations made sense and pointed a way to the future: to ending the Spectre's evil reign once and for all.

"Unlock these damned chains," he said.

After the manacles fell, Marius said, "Follow me."

Gabriel trailed him down the hallway to a closed door. Marius unlocked it. "After you."

A woman sat on a bed, her hands chained, her mouth gagged. Her pretty features were pale, her hair dyed a lighter shade, but Gabriel would recognize her anywhere.

His hands balled at his sides. "Devil take you, Fournier or Fontaine or whoever the hell you are."

Her words were muffled; she shrank back against the headboard.

"She happens to be Davenport's mistress as well, but you can hear her confession later. Come, my friend." Marius ushered him out and locked the door. "We haven't much time. If Cicero discovers she's missing, it will send him into a panic. He may strike out."

Freddy. Thea. An icy hand gripped Gabriel's insides. "I have to get back."

"Yes. Do you want to take—"

A loud crash cut through the house. In a flash, Marius drew out a pair of pistols, tossing one to Gabriel. They moved in the old pattern, Gabriel going high, Marius low, both of them aiming at the figures storming down the dim hallway. As the intruders rushed closer, their faces became clear.

Gabriel shouted, "Hold fire. Everyone."

"Tremont, are you safe?" Kent came forward, his gun aimed at Marius. "Drop your weapon, whoever you are. We have the place surrounded."

"Everyone put down your guns," Gabriel said. "This is Marius… a friend."

Slowly, Marius lowered his firearm.

Kent followed suit, muttering, "You've interesting friends, my lord. Do all of them abduct you in broad daylight?"

"Marius found the governess. She's Davenport's mistress and his accomplice," Gabriel said grimly. "I'll explain everything in the carriage. We need to get back to

Strathaven's immediately."

As they pulled up in front of the duke's residence, Gabriel knew something was wrong. The door was open; servants and men in uniform were milling about. He hit the ground running before the wheels came to a complete stop. He shouldered his way through the small throng and saw Strathaven and the duchess standing in the foyer.

The duke was giving orders to a circle of men. Runner types. Beside him, the duchess was pale, her face etched with worry.

"Where are Thea and Freddy?" The words left Gabriel in a shout.

"Tremont, you're back." Strathaven strode toward him, put a hand on his shoulder. "We'll talk in my study where it's calmer—"

"Tell me what the hell happened."

"They were taken." This came from the duchess. "Sometime this afternoon. They were on their way to Marianne's, and from what we've been able to piece together from witnesses, an unmarked carriage pulled up and shot the two footmen who were accompanying them. Thea and Freddy were grabbed." Her voice hitched, and the duke's arm circled her shoulders. "We don't know who's behind this or where they've been taken."

"Davenport." Blood was rushing through Gabriel's ears. "He's the Spectre."

"What?" Strathaven and the duchess said as one.

Images bombarded him of Thea and Freddy, locked

away in some hellhole. His beloved fighting for her breath, his son falling... Gabriel shook off his panic.

They're strong; they'll manage until you get there. Focus on getting them back.

"Gather everyone in your study. We're going to rescue Thea and Freddy from the Spectre," he said in clipped tones, "and every bloody minute counts."

Chapter Thirty-Seven

With Freddy's head cradled in her lap, Thea took stock of the ominous situation. The boy was still unconscious from the noxious substance in the handkerchiefs that had been pressed over their faces during the abduction. She had regained her senses about a quarter hour ago and still felt woozy from the aftereffects. She had no idea how much time had passed, how long that carriage ride had been, or where they'd been taken.

At present, there was only the small, windowless room. The darkness suggested that they were in a basement. Both she and Freddy had metal cuffs on their ankles, with heavy chains connecting them to an iron ring in the wall. They sat on a thin pallet of straw, and her skin crawled at the skittering beneath her skirts.

Don't panic. Try to figure out where you are.

Squinting into the dimness, she made out a small brick-lined alcove darkened with ash. A cooking area. This had functioned as a kitchen at one time. Sniffing now, she picked up the scent of stale grease and coal smoke steeped into the wooden walls. There was another smell in the air... brackish like seawater and sewage. She heard muffled, distant sounds from beyond the room. A boat's horn, perhaps? Were they near the Thames? But it didn't sound like the city; the hush here was different from the cacophony of London.

Freddy's head shifted. His eyelashes fluttered, his unfocused eyes looking up at her.

Relief spread through Thea. "Are you all right, dear?"

"What h-happened?" he said groggily.

"We were taken. I don't know by whom." Feeling him tremble, she stroked his little freckled cheek. "I know it's frightening, dear, but we mustn't give into fear. We must focus on getting out of here. Your papa and my brother are surely on their way to find us."

Freddy nodded, wide-eyed.

"Now do you think you can sit up?" she asked.

"I—I think so."

With her assistance, he managed to prop himself up against the wall.

"Good job, dear. Now I'm going to take a look around the room, all right? You can help me by trying to see if there's any way out of here."

Getting to her feet, she walked the short perimeter of the chamber, no more than ten feet on each side. She tried to move as stealthily as possible to minimize the telltale clinking of the chain. She placed her palms on the walls; they were solid wood and thick. As far as she could tell, the only way out of the room was through the door, and she could hear the heavy footfalls of someone just outside. A guard, probably. Even if they could somehow get through the door, she hadn't a chance of getting past a cutthroat.

As she stood there, despairing, a slight whistling sound caught her ear. At first, she thought she might be imagining it, but then it came again. Low and mournful as a funeral march.

"Do you hear that?" she whispered to Freddy.

"Hear what?" he whispered back.

"A whistling sound."

He shook his head.

Nonetheless, she closed her eyes and focused just on listening, the way she sometimes did during practice. She heard her own heartbeat, the shifting of the world outside— and there it was. That noise again. It was coming from... the cooking area.

She hurried over to the nook. Ashes formed a thick carpet on the ground, and the brick walls of the cove were darkened from years of exposure to a cooking fire. *Fire, smoke* ... Her heart began to thud. *It has to go out somewhere.* Stepping carefully onto the hearth, she peered into the darkness above.

And there it was.

A thin board had been nailed over the old opening for the flue. It didn't cover the hole completely, and the whistling sound came from the wind seeping in around the edges. She could see the thin lines of light above and below the board. Freedom was suddenly not as far away as it had seemed just a moment ago. The hole was set about six feet high—reachable if she could hoist Freddy onto her shoulders. She judged the opening just big enough for the boy to fit through... if they could pry the wood loose. And if Freddy wasn't chained to the wall.

At that instant, she heard footsteps approaching. Men's voices. She hurried back toward Freddy, plopping herself next to him just as the door creaked on its hinges. A man in a greatcoat walked in. She recognized him from the painting she'd seen in his study. In the light of the lamp he held, Davenport's patrician features had a distinctly menacing cast.

Two lackeys hovered behind him, roughly dressed, hyenas eager to scavenge.

"Miss Kent and young Master Ridgley," Davenport said in polished accents, "I do apologize for the humble lodgings, but I'm afraid I ran short of time. Unexpected circumstances, you see. But never fear, we shall only be here for a short time."

Thea stood, her shoulders straight. "Why have you taken us, Lord Davenport?"

He showed no surprise that she knew his identity. Instead, he smiled, and a chill slithered down her spine. "Why, for your charming company of course."

"If it's money you want—"

"Oh, I *do* want. But you, my dears, are even more valuable than gold."

"Why?" Thea said.

"I have Trajan's son and his fiancée as my guests." The venom in Davenport's voice injected her with paralyzing fear. "I'll have him at my mercy and pay him back for ruining my plans."

"You... you're the Spectre?" she breathed.

His mouth curled. "My reputation precedes me, I see."

"I don't understand. Why are you doing this? You have position, status, wealth—"

"None of which will protect me when my secret is out. Octavian just wouldn't give up, and Trajan was always an apple off the old tree. Because of them, I am going to lose the privileged life I've been leading. Since Octavian has already cashed his chips, so to speak, there's only Trajan left to compensate me for my inconvenience." His mouth curled with malice. "We travel soon."

He turned, his black cape whirling behind him. His henchmen followed, casting covetous, hungry glances back. The door closed, and Thea felt the starch dissolve from her knees. She put a hand to the wall for support.

"Thea?" Freddy's thin, frightened voice penetrated her daze.

She sank to her knees beside him. "I'm fine, Freddy."

"Why did you call that man the Spectre? And when he said Trajan, did he mean Papa?" Lines pleated the boy's brow as he said in a quivering voice, "Is he going to hurt Papa? Is he going to hurt us?"

She swallowed, not knowing what to say. She was no fool. The Spectre was a bloodthirsty and remorseless villain who had no intention of bargaining for anything. He meant to get his money—and his revenge too. And there was one sure way of bringing Gabriel to his knees.

She looked at Freddy's small, dear face, and love and resolution rooted in her.

"Nothing's going to happen to you, my darling." She took him by the shoulders. "I have a plan. And I'm going to need your help."

"Where did he take them?" Gabriel demanded.

"I don't know." Sitting in the duke's study, Manette Fontaine was white-lipped. "He did not tell me his plans."

"He has my sister and the marquess' son." The duchess stood in front of the prisoner, her hands fisted on her hips. "If anything happens to them, you will be an accomplice to murder. Actually, you're already an accomplice to high treason. You're going to hang."

"Tr-treason?"

Seeing the blood drain from the woman's face, Gabriel surmised her surprise was genuine.

"Didn't Davenport tell you?" he said in lethal tones. "He's a spy. He's been selling British secrets for years. He's been using his position in Parliament to facilitate his trade in treason."

"I know nothing about that," Fontaine gasped.

"Do you think anyone will believe you? You impersonated a governess and tried to abduct an innocent boy. You plotted to assassinate me in my carriage," Gabriel said ruthlessly.

Her chest rose and fell in panicked waves. "I swear I know nothing about an assassination."

"No one's going to believe you. You're going to swing for your crimes—unless you help us now. Unless we plead leniency for you."

He saw reality sink into Fontaine, the fight leaving her.

Her shoulders sagging, she said in a low voice, "Davenport, he trusts no one. He never told me the plans, where we were going, only to be ready when he came for me."

"That's not enough to save you from the noose." There was no time for her blasted dithering; Thea and Freddy's lives were at stake. "If you have nothing better, you can rot in Newgate until you hang," he snapped.

"No. Wait." Fontaine licked her lips, her gaze darting around the room. "Perhaps... perhaps I do know something."

Gabriel waited, his heart beating furiously.

"Davenport sent word to me to wait for him in that cottage in Camden Town. He told me to prepare for a journey by water. He was supposed to send for me at half-past eleven tonight."

"Where is he taking you?" Gabriel demanded.

"I don't know. I swear that is the truth." Fontaine's hands clasped in her lap. "All he said was to pack lightly and take only what I needed as there were to be several legs to the journey."

Finally, a lead. Gabriel exchanged swift glances with the other men and saw his own hypothesis reflected in their pensive expressions. Fire lit in his belly. *I'm coming, princess. Tell Freddy not to be scared. Wait for me.*

He gestured to one of Kent's men. "Take the prisoner out of here. Keep her secure."

"You'll keep your word about clemency?" Fontaine said.

"If Miss Kent and my boy are returned safely," he clipped out.

When the door closed behind her, Kent said, "He's going to use the Regent's Canal."

Gabriel's thoughts exactly. Davenport had chosen Camden Town for its location by the canal. From the lock, he could take a barge to reach the Thames and, from there, get out to sea. If he got that far... there would be no finding him. Gabriel's gut clenched. He had to get to Thea and Freddy before they were put on a damn boat.

"My guess is that he's got Freddy and Thea tucked away somewhere in Camden Town. Not far from Fontaine's cottage," Gabriel said tersely. "Sneaky bastard took the precaution to keep them and Fontaine separated in case the latter was found."

"Do you think he knows we have her?" Strathaven said.

"He's not supposed to come for her until half-past eleven. We have four hours yet, so he might not know. But there's no time to lose." Gabriel parsed out the strategy. "We'll need three teams in Camden Town. One to monitor the cottage, one to comb the area for Thea and Freddy, and one to set up watch by the lock."

"My men and I will take the cottage," McLeod said.

"I'll send word to my old colleagues at the Thames River Police," Kent said. "They can help keep an eye on the lock and the barges along the canal for any sign of Thea and Frederick."

"I'll search the town," Gabriel said.

"I'll come with you," Strathaven offered.

"And I as well," Marius said.

Gabriel gave a curt nod, his hands curling. He was going to get Thea and Freddy back safely. After that, he'd deal with the Spectre—and deliver the justice the blighter deserved.

Chapter Thirty-Eight

"Help! Someone please help us!" Thea cried. "My boy is ill!"

She heard a muffled curse from outside the door, someone fumbling to insert a key into the lock. A minute later, the door swung open, and one of the lackeys stormed in. He took one look at Freddy shaking on the ground, and his eyes bugged.

"Mary's tits, wots the matter wif 'im?" the cutthroat said.

"He's got falling sickness. The stress of being kidnapped—it's too much for him," Thea said tearfully. "I've never seen him in such a bad way before."

Freddy's eyes rolled back, and he began making gargling noises.

The cutthroat crossed himself, stepped back. "What the bleedin' 'ell am I supposed to do about it?" he said with clear panic. "Master ain't back yet, and 'e'll 'ave me 'ead if anything 'appens to the l'il bugger!"

"Unchain him so that I can make him more comfortable," Thea said urgently.

The lackey removed the key from his pocket. Hesitated. "Do I 'ave to touch 'im?"

"Oh, for God's sake," Thea said in disgust. "Just throw me the key."

The guard dropped the key to the ground and kicked it

over. Heart pounding, Thea grabbed it and unlocked the manacle on Freddy's shaking foot. The open shackle clanked to the ground. Breath held, she reached as casually as she could toward the heavy cuff on her own ankle...

"Just 'is," the guard commanded.

That would have been too easy. Tossing the key back, she said, "He needs some water."

The guard shuffled off.

The second he was gone, Thea whispered, "You're doing an excellent job, dear."

Freddy stopped shaking. Flashed an impish grin.

When the door opened again, he took up the convulsing movements with verve. Thea took the water from the terrified guard and told him that only rest and quiet would help the boy now. The cutthroat seemed more than happy to get away from them. He slammed the door shut, the lock clicking.

Listening to the boot steps fade away, Thea said, "Let's go. We don't have much time."

She and Freddy made their way stealthily toward the alcove. It took some effort, but she managed to get him onto her shoulders. Perched there, he could reach the boarded-up flue.

"The top of the board's loose," he whispered. "Hold me still, and I'll give it a pull."

Perspiring under the boy's weight, she nonetheless held him firmly below the knees and braced them both. He yanked hard. The plank gave way with a crack. They both froze at the sound... and at the sudden, stunning whoosh of crisp night air. When the guard didn't come bursting in, Thea craned her neck, trying to see out the hole.

A patch of gravel. Beyond that, nothing but darkness. As much as she fretted over sending Freddy out there alone, he would be in far greater danger if he remained here.

"Go quickly now," she urged. "Climb through."

Tossing the board out onto the gravel, Freddy grabbed onto the edges of the hole. Thea's lungs strained with effort as she gave him as much of a boost as she could. An instant later, his weight lifted from her shoulders, and she watched, her breath hitching as the soles of his boots disappeared through the opening.

A moment later, his anxious face peered back down at her. "I don't feel right leaving—"

"Remember what we discussed. Keep moving until you can find a hackney to take you home or a public place where someone can help you. You're a strong and clever boy: you can do this."

"I'll bring Papa back. We'll come back for you," he said, his bottom lip trembling.

"I love you, Freddy. Now *go*," she said urgently.

At last, he obeyed. She couldn't see him, her ears straining for any sounds that might indicate that he'd been spotted. But no cry came up, nor any sounds of scuffling. She slumped against the brick, looking up into the exposed night. Worry filled her as she thought of Freddy alone in the dark world, but at least out there he had a chance.

Her head bowing, she prayed that he would find the way home.

Night saturated the country sky like indigo ink,

darkening Gabriel's spirits. For the past hour, he, Strathaven, and Marius had been canvassing the quiet streets of Camden Town, a village just north of London. He'd stopped through this bucolic hamlet several times before on his way to Hampstead or Highgate and had thought it rather quaint. Never in a million years had he imagined that he'd be here on a desperate search for his son and Thea. That somewhere in this sleepy town a treacherous spymaster was hiding, preparing for the final game.

"There's another tavern up ahead," Strathaven said. "The Bedford Arms. We can ask if anyone there has seen Thea and Freddy."

They approached the bustling building. To the side of the tavern was an arched entryway with a painted sign above reading, "Tea Gardens." The raucousness of the crowd beneath the strings of lights indicated that beverages significantly more fortifying than tea were being served.

"You two take the gardens," Gabriel said. "I'll inquire inside."

He entered through a door that badly needed oil on its hinges. Patrons were elbow-to-elbow at the rough trench tables. He honed in on the barkeep behind the scarred counter, a beefy ginger-haired man pouring out tankards as fast as the harried-looking barmaids could scoop them up onto their trays. Gabriel approached and laid down a quid.

The barkeep didn't lift his eyes from his task. "What'll it be, sir?"

"I'm looking for two people. A woman and a young boy," Gabriel said.

"Can't say I've seen any boys in here."

Hope dwindled, yet Gabriel tried again. "The woman,

she's pretty. Thick golden-brown hair, slender, with delicate features."

"Gor, I'd have noticed a female like that." This time, the barkeep raised his head to give Gabriel a man-to-man wink. "But, sorry, guv, I haven't seen her."

Fear and desperation gripped Gabriel. His temples throbbed, the creaking door and jovial crowd a dull roar in his ears. *Where are you, princess? If you're here somewhere, send me a sign—*

"Guv, this boy you mentioned… could he look a might young for his age?"

Gabriel's attention snapped back to the barkeep. "Yes. He's slight."

"Tow-headed? Bran-faced?"

"You've seen him?" Gabriel demanded.

The barkeep pointed over his shoulder. "Standing behind you, guv."

Gabriel spun around. Couldn't believe his eyes.

There, standing on the threshold, was Freddy. He was pale and disheveled, dirt smearing one cheek and a rip at the elbow of his jacket. But he looked otherwise unharmed.

"Papa?" he said in a quivering voice.

"*Frederick.*" Gabriel was over there in three strides, his arms enfolding the boy, holding the small, trembling body close. "How did you get here? Where's Thea?"

The boy gave a sudden sob. Pulled back.

"We have to go back for her, Papa. Now," he blurted.

Ice coated Gabriel's gut. "Where is she?"

"Back at the house where they took us. The bad man, Davenport. She told me to pretend to have a fit and helped me escape through a hole, but she couldn't get free because of the chains. They still have her, Papa!"

"Slow down, son. Take a breath." Gabriel took hold of his boy's shoulders. "Now tell me where this house is."

"I don't know the address."

Frost spread into Gabriel's blood.

"But I think I can find it again." Exhaling, Freddy reached into his pocket and pulled out a small vial. Eyes wide, he said, "I left a trail with the invisible ink. If we follow it, it will lead us back to Thea."

Chapter Thirty-Nine

"I think this is it," Freddy whispered, pointing at the fencepost.

Gabriel held the lamp close to the whitewashed wood. Seconds later, a blue cross flared into sight. His muscles tautening, he said in a low voice, "Excellent work. I'm proud of you, son."

Freddy's smile was wobbly. "Are we going to get Thea now, Papa?"

Gabriel eyed the brick building beyond the fence. A number of such small country manors were spaced along the banks of the canal. This one was partially hidden by trees, the crumbling stone a spectral silver in the full moon. No lights shone from the windows, and the property had an eerie, abandoned feel. A place where ghosts lurked. Behind the house, water flowed as dark and steady as a vein.

"She's in the basement?" he said.

"Yes, Papa. To the right side of the house. I got out through the venting hole, but I don't think you'll fit through," Freddy said in a worried voice.

"I'll figure it out." He turned to the others. "Strathaven, take care of Freddy, will you?"

The duke nodded gravely. "He'll be safe with me."

"Ready, Marius?" Gabriel said.

His comrade nodded, pistol in hand. "Let's finish this

once and for all."

"Papa, you'll be careful won't you?" Freddy said with a quiver.

He cupped his son's cheek. "Always. Now be a good lad and keep watch with His Grace. We'll be back in no time."

He jerked his chin at Marius, and the two of them set off. They crossed over the fence, approaching the house by the field rather than the pebbled drive. They moved stealthily, in the old, coordinated pattern, covering one another as they neared the house. They paused behind a hedgerow. Through the leaves, Gabriel had a view of the right side of the manor and saw the bushes Freddy had described. The hole must be behind them.

He made the gestures. *I'm going in. You cover.*

In answer, Marius nodded and cocked his pistol.

Gabriel rounded the hedge and sprinted toward the side of the house. He made it to the bushes and crouched, parting the brush. The hole was there, just as Freddy had said.

His blades drawn, he called softly, "Thea?"

Silence. His heart raged. *If anything's happened to her...*

A rustling. Chains clanking. Seconds later, he heard her tremulous reply.

"Gabriel?"

Relief shot through him. "By the window, love."

Her face surfaced from the darkness, her eyes wide. "Gabriel, you must run. He's back—"

He heard a thunderous crash. Thea whipped around, screaming, yanked from sight an instant later. In her place, metal glinted, and Gabriel threw himself to the side just as a blast came from the hole, the shot tearing through the bushes. He rolled to a crouch, pressed against the wall of the house, knives ready; he couldn't let them fly for fear of hitting Thea. He heard scrambling from within, Thea crying, *Let me go*, the sounds of her being dragged from the room.

"Marius, take the front. No one gets out," Gabriel shouted. "He has Thea!"

Marius was already clearing the hedgerow toward the front entrance.

Gabriel raced to the rear of the house. The windows were shuttered, preventing him from seeing inside. Dead brush surrounded the courtyard, trunks piled upon the graveled path that led to a small dock some fifty yards away. A barge bobbed on the dark waves. Cicero's escape route.

Over my dead body.

He heard sudden blasts of gunfire from the front. Marius at work.

The rear door opened, two cutthroats charging out, their guns blazing. Gabriel ducked the fire, rolling smoothly behind the trunks. In the instant his enemies took to reload, he aimed, releasing his blades simultaneously. The men fell to the gravel. Gabriel paused to yank his weapons from their unmoving bodies before continuing on.

He crept through the open door, his senses on high alert. A room of empty shelves. No movement here. Footsteps overhead. The floor above. His blood pumping hot and fast, he headed out of the room toward the sounds.

In the paneled corridor, he saw the darkness lightening up ahead. The foyer and access to the upper floor. Two doors between him and the foyer. He moved on, knives at the ready. Floorboards creaked, doors opened, and two brutes tore into the hallway. Gabriel went in low and fast, his right blade slicing cleanly upward, his left crossing his body in a deadly arc. Blood slid hotly over his fingers, bodies thudding to the ground behind him. He kept right on moving toward Thea.

Toward the only thing that mattered.

He took the stairwell up, following the sounds. He kicked open the door at the top. A ballroom. The balcony windows were open, white curtains whipping against the dark sky, ghostly reflections dancing along the mirrored walls. At the far end...

Thea. *My love.*

Cicero stood behind her, an arm around her throat and a pistol held to her head.

Options flashed. Flick of the wrist and Gabriel would have the blade embedded in the soft giving spot between Cicero's eyes. Or a curving throw to that place in the side of the neck, the one that made a man bleed out within a minute. He could do either before Cicero even pulled the trigger.

And Cicero knew it. Which was why the lily-livered bastard was using Thea as a shield.

"Let her go," Gabriel said, "and I'll kill you quickly."

"That was always your problem, Trajan. Talented killer,"—Cicero shook his head mournfully—"terrible negotiator."

Gabriel's fingers itched to make the kill. But he couldn't risk Thea getting harmed.

Keep Cicero talking. That's his weakness. Wait for an opening.

"I haven't your talent for selling our country's secrets to the highest bidder," he said evenly.

"But you do have a rare aptitude for ruining my plans." Cicero's smile bared his teeth. "Normandy still wasn't enough to teach you a lesson, it seems."

"Clever of you," Gabriel said, "pretending to be taken prisoner along with me and Tiberius. Screaming so loud we believed you were being tortured."

"I had a sore throat for days." Cicero's grin widened.

"How did you survive my dagger? I saw you fall."

"I was wearing a vest of chainmail. In such situations, I always take precautions." The spymaster shrugged. "For years, your knife made quite the souvenir. Pity I had to pawn it."

Gabriel's grip tightened subtly on the hilts. "Money? Is that what this is all about?"

"My dear fellow, money is what everything is about."

He had to distract Cicero, get Thea loose...

"You have money," he said evenly. "You married an heiress."

"Alas, my access to her fortune is not as I had hoped." Cicero smiled thinly. "I would have managed, however, had Octavian not caught my trail. The codger never knew when to stop, so I had to stop him. For good. But then you got on the scent."

Half a foot—that was all it would take. If Thea was just half a foot away from Cicero, Gabriel could safely go in for the kill. He willed her to recall the moves he'd taught her.

Surprise the bastard. Attack him. Free yourself.

"You've led me on a merry chase," he said.

"It *is* rather refreshing to share my triumphs. Seeing as how dead men and women don't talk,"—Cicero dug the gun's muzzle deeper into Thea's temple, causing her to wince and Gabriel's fingers to twitch around his blade—"I suppose there's no harm in indulging a little, is there? I planted the documents you discovered in Tiberius' safe. And the blackmail note, supposedly from the Spectre, that you found in my desk. Do you honestly think you could find something of mine if I didn't intend for you to see it?"

"Why try to kidnap Freddy?"

"For leverage over you—you'd do anything I said with your boy's life on the line. Eventually, I would have ransomed him back to you." Cicero's arm tightened around Thea's neck. "But now I have someone just as good, don't I? Enough parleying. Throw your weapons toward me, or I'll put a bullet through her pretty head."

Gabriel made the calculation. He couldn't risk Thea. He tossed down one knife, and it skittered across the floor toward his enemy.

"No, Gabriel, don't—" Thea's cry was choked off by Cicero. Her hands grasped futilely at the arm crushing her windpipe.

His heart thundering, Gabriel urged her with his eyes. *Come on, princess. You're strong. Remember what I taught you.*

Her eyes widened—from lack of air or awareness?

"The other one, too," Cicero snapped.

With no choice, Gabriel threw away his remaining weapon.

At that moment, Thea acted. In a flash, she let go of the arm choking her and brought her elbow back, connecting with Cicero's solar plexus. He grunted in surprise, and she lifted her right foot, stomping on his instep. His hold on her loosened, and she jerked free, stumbling to the side.

"Little bitch—"

Before Gabriel could get to his knives, Cicero recovered, taking aim and firing at him. Gabriel dove out of harm's way, the bullet shattering a mirrored wall, glass raining everywhere. He rolled, his fingers closing around a jagged shard. Twisting to face his enemy, he let it fly.

The glass glittered in the darkness, a deadly star, and it hit true.

Gabriel staggered over to Cicero. The other lay blinking, the shard planted in his neck, crimson bubbles gurgling from his lips. A dark, glossy pool spread beneath him. Gabriel watched, unflinching, until the traitor's eyes went blank and unseeing.

"Gabriel?"

Thea ran up to him, and he wrapped his arms around her. Held her close.

"Are you all right, love?" he said.

"I'm fine." She was trembling all over. "Just a bit shaky at the moment."

"'Tis the aftermath. It'll pass." He looked into her beautiful eyes. "I'm proud of you, my fierce princess."

"What about you? I know you never wanted to kill again—"

"I did what I had to. And that is what I've always done." He kissed her softly on the forehead. "I'm at peace, knowing you and Freddy are safe and that no one will suffer at the hands of the Spectre again."

Her gaze shimmered. "I love you."

"And I love you. With everything that I am." Emotion swelled, and he didn't try to fight it. He cupped her precious face in his hands. "It killed me, thinking that I might not have the chance to tell you. I was a fool not to recognize what was in my own heart. But I swear I'll make it up to you. You're going to tire of having a husband who tells you day and night how much he adores you."

"I don't think I could ever tire of that." Her smile warmed his soul.

The romantic moment was shattered by the sound of gunshots in the distance.

"Damn, I'd best check on Marius," Gabriel muttered. "He must be losing his touch."

"Marius?" she said in surprise.

Retrieving his weapons, Gabriel flashed her a quick grin. "I'll explain later."

Chapter Forty

The next afternoon, Thea found herself safe and snug in her sister's drawing room. Gabriel sat to the right of her on the settee, Freddy to the left, and the entire Kent clan was present. Surrounded by the ones she loved, she felt as if a Bach hymn was soaring through her. Her heart was so full it was nigh bursting at the seams.

"All three of you were so brave," Emma was saying. In her arms, she cradled Olivia, who cooed and tried to grasp her mama's hair with tiny fists. "A family of derring-doers."

"Freddy especially," Thea responded with pride. "Not only did he manage to get into town for help, but he had the forethought to use the invisible ink. He was brilliant."

Freddy's face flushed as the others added their nods and words of agreement.

"Like father, like son." This came from Strathaven, who was busy trying to pry one of Emma's dark curls from their daughter. "Now, my little angel, don't grab at your mama," he admonished.

"Like father, like daughter," Gabriel said.

They all laughed. Gabriel's grey eyes were smiling.

"There are a few details we ought to wrap up," Ambrose said, his mien serious. He turned to his son. "Edward, why don't you and Freddy go play a game for a bit?"

"But Papa," Edward protested, "we're just getting to the

interesting part."

"That's exactly why you're leaving," his father said dryly.

"How am I to become an investigator like you if I can't learn from your cases?"

"You want to be an investigator like me?" Ambrose's brow furrowed, his gaze shifting to Marianne. She just smiled and shrugged.

"Yes, I do," Edward affirmed, "and what is more, Freddy and I have decided to open an agency together. When we're a bit older, of course."

"Of course," his father said solemnly. "Until Fredward and Associates comes to fruition, however, I'm afraid you'll have to occupy yourself with something more suited to your age. Spillikins or quoits, for instance."

"But Papa—"

"Boys," Harry interrupted, "I've a new invention I want to test out in the garden. Care to lend me a hand?"

The boys looked at Harry and then at each other.

"Yes, please," Fredward said as one.

"C'mon then." Harry waved them to the door, and they scampered out.

Then he crooked a finger at Violet, Polly, and Primrose.

The girls groaned in unison.

"We're not children, Harry," Violet said, crossing her arms. "You can't distract us by simply dangling a carrot."

"No? What about this then?" Withdrawing a leather pouch from his pocket, Harry let it swing enticingly by the strings. "I guarantee it's something none of you have *ever* seen before. It'll be a spectacle for the ages. Men would sell their soul to see it."

The three girls consulted amongst themselves. Then

they, too, got to their feet and headed for the door.

"Gadzooks, you've better showmanship than the ringmaster at Astley's," Violet grumbled as she passed him. "This had better live up to your claims."

Thea smiled at her younger brother. "Thank you, Harry. Out of curiosity, what is in the bag?"

"A new substance I'm tinkering with. Chemically, it's similar to gunpowder," Harry said, "but with a bit more oomph."

The door closed behind him.

Strathaven looked at his duchess. "Should we worry about the neighbors?"

"If we hear an explosion, yes," Emma said.

"Before Harry blows us all to smithereens, I suggest we return to the case at hand." Ambrose tented his fingers in front of him. "There are a few new facts I'd like to share. As it turns out, you were right, Thea."

"About what?" Emma said.

"The state of Davenport's finances," Ambrose replied. "At Tremont's request, I spoke with Davenport's father-in-law, Mr. George Clemens, this morning. I gave him the barest details, keeping identities anonymous. A sharp man, Clemens, worthy of his reputation as London's brightest solicitor. He was shocked at the nature of Davenport's activities, but not with the character of his former son-in-law. He said he never trusted Davenport's suit of his daughter, but when Lady Davenport threatened to elope, he relented and gave in. Not, however, without protecting her interests first."

"He created a trust for her?" Thea said.

Ambrose nodded.

"How did you know that, Thea?" her sister wanted to know.

"At Lady Davenport's luncheon, Gabby told me that Mr. Clemens had helped her father to set up a trust to protect her inheritance from fortune hunters," Thea explained. "When Davenport said he didn't have access to his wife's fortune, I put two and two together."

"Through brilliant legal maneuvering, Clemens managed to fool Davenport into signing the trust. Under its terms, Davenport has no access to the bulk of his wife's fortune. She could withdraw from her accounts, but Clemens put limits on that too. If anything should happen to her, the money went to the designee of the trust, a distant cousin. Killing her would accomplish nothing for Davenport; in fact, he'd lose the use of her generous quarterly spending account."

"Mr. Clemens thought of everything," Thea said.

"He loves his daughter very much. Indeed, he wished to express his gratitude to the anonymous benefactor,"—Ambrose's eyes crinkled at the corners—"who rid her of her dastardly husband."

"All's well that ends well," Marianne murmured.

"As to that, any news on Heath?" Kent asked Gabriel.

Gabriel nodded. "Malcolm and I spoke to the magistrates. They're releasing him."

"Not that Heath seemed too overjoyed about it. Poor chap's not in his right mind." John Malcolm—formerly known as Marius—spoke for the first time.

Thea liked Gabriel's old friend. Especially since Gabriel had admitted to her privately that he understood why Malcolm had faked his own death all those years ago.

Malcolm had only wanted to escape the nightmare of espionage and hadn't realized that Gabriel would be wracked with guilt over his death.

Malcolm had apologized; Gabriel had accepted.

The two had come to terms with the past.

"The opium's not helping," Gabriel said soberly. "I hope Heath will take our advice to heart. Try for a fresh start with a clear head."

"I'll be here to keep him in line if he doesn't." Malcolm's countenance was set into determined lines. "It'll be just like the old days, only without the spying, killing, and betrayal."

"I'll be here, too," Gabriel said.

Thea smiled, and when Gabriel looked over at her, she saw that the shadows had lifted from his eyes. One by one, his ghosts were being vanquished.

Just then, there was a knock on the door, and Jarvis entered to inform them that Lady Blackwood had arrived. She swept into the room a minute later, wearing a dashing aubergine-and-cream striped carriage dress. Thea noted, however, the slight redness of Pandora's eyes and the puffiness underneath.

Going over to her, Thea said worriedly, "Has something happened?"

Instead of answering, Pandora absently kissed the air near Thea's cheeks. "I'm here because I received Tremont's note this morning. I had to come see for myself." Her gaze landed on Malcolm, who'd stepped forward. "So Tremont wasn't hallucinating after all."

"Hello, Pandora." Malcolm bent over her hand. "It is a pleasure to see you again."

"It is a *shock* to see you." Despite her tart words, there

was a catch in Pandora's voice that she couldn't quite hide. "To think, I may have shed a tear or two over your demise. Where have you been hiding all these years?"

"In places you wouldn't care to know about, my lady." There was humor in Malcolm's faded blue eyes. "Now that you're a marchioness, I'm sure you don't want to be rubbing elbows with us common riffraff."

Pandora's violet eyes shimmered. Her lips trembled.

"I meant no offense," Malcolm said hastily. "'Twas a jest—"

"No, it's nothing you said." Pandora allowed Thea to lead her to an empty chair. Her face crumpling, she said, "It's my marriage. I think... it is over."

"What happened?" Thea said with concern.

"Blackwood knows everything. About my past." Between halting breaths, Pandora said, "Cicero, the bastard, couldn't resist a final act of destruction. He sent my husband an anonymous letter, and it arrived this morning."

"How dastardly of him." Crouching, Thea took the other woman's hands. "But perhaps honesty is not the worst thing that could happen. Surely if you clear the air now—"

"It's too late." Tears tracked down Pandora's cheeks. "He's left me. He had his valet pack his things, and he left Town. I don't even know where he's gone."

"Perhaps he needs time to cool his heels. And his head." This came from Gabriel, who brought Thea to her feet, his arm around her waist. "We men sometimes let our tempers get the better of us."

"Not my husband. He's a proud, loyal, good man." Pandora took the handkerchief Thea offered and dabbed at her eyes. "And I've deceived him from the start."

Heart wrenching, Thea turned to Gabriel. "Can't you speak to Blackwood, darling?"

"Me?" He looked as appalled as a stoic man could look.

"You and Mr. Malcolm together. You were her colleagues, after all," Thea said encouragingly. "Surely if the two of you pled Pandora's case, told her husband what a true heroine she was during the war, he'd listen."

"If he doesn't shoot us dead first," Malcolm muttered. "Trust me, no man wants to hear about his wife's past from other men."

"But we'll do it." Gabriel cleared his throat. "If you wish us to, Pandora."

"Thank you, but no. I made this mess, and it's up to me to fix it." The marchioness sat up straight, her face tear-stained but determined. "I shall find a way to win my husband back."

"You always were a fighter," Malcolm said, "and a damned fine one at that."

"Enough of my woes. Let us talk of happier news." With determined cheer, she said, "When is the wedding to take place?"

Gabriel's arm tightened around Thea's waist. "Next Saturday."

"You're invited," Thea hastened to say. "Everyone here is. We haven't gotten around to invitations given... well..."

"You've been a bit busy." Pandora's tone was dry.

"You'll come, won't you?" Thea said anxiously. "Pandora? Malcolm?"

"To see our old boy embark upon the most important mission of his life?" Malcolm winked. "We wouldn't miss it for all the secrets in the world, my dear."

Chapter Forty-One

A week later, Gabriel knocked, and the sound of Thea's lovely voice granting him entrance filled him with satisfaction. Anticipation simmered in his blood. Beneath his silk dressing gown, he was already hard for his wife. His love.

Opening the adjoining door, he entered the lavish chamber done in shades of ivory and gold. He'd secured them the finest suite at Mivart's for their wedding night. There wasn't to be much of a honeymoon trip as they were heading back to Oakhurst in three days, so he thought they could make do with a weekend stay at the hotel. The Strathavens had offered to look after Freddy, so that Gabriel and Thea could have time alone.

Gabriel intended to make the most of the time. His chest warmed at the pretty picture Thea made combing her hair before the vanity. She looked like a princess in her snowy robe with a fall of lace at the neckline and cuffs, her hair a shining cascade down her back. When he went to stand behind her, she smiled at him in the looking glass.

He threaded his fingers through her luxuriant tresses. "I like your hair down, Lady Tremont," he murmured. "Especially since I'm the only man who gets to see it this way."

"Possessive, are you?" Her eyes twinkled up at him.

"You know that I am." He took the brush from her

hands. "And you know that you love it."

Her blush was a glorious thing, sunset spreading up her smooth white throat and porcelain cheeks. He ran the bristles through her locks, savoring the way she shivered at his touch.

The domesticity of the moment struck him. He was combing his wife's hair. He wasn't holding a blade, pistol, or other instrument of killing; that time was finally over. Because of Thea, he was finally getting his fresh start. And he was determined to begin this chapter right.

"Goodness, that's nice." She sighed, her neck arching a little. "The wedding went well, don't you think?"

"Hmm," he said absently.

He was searching for words, the best way to share the results of his soul-searching over the past few days. Intimacy still didn't come easily for him; perhaps it never would. For Thea, however, he was willing to try. Willing, in truth, to do anything.

"My favorite part was the throwing of the bouquet. Did you see Violet's face when she caught it?" Thea chuckled. "She looked like she'd bitten into a lemon."

Amused in spite of himself, he said, "Didn't she want to catch it?"

"She wanted to *win*. This will teach her that there are consequences to being competitive." Thea swiveled around to look at him. "Which was your favorite part of the wedding?"

"The part that made you my wife." He set the brush down with a decisive click. "Thea, there's something I wish to discuss."

"Yes?"

"I wanted to tell you... you were right." He let out a breath. "About Sylvia."

Color stained her cheeks; her gaze slid away. "We don't have to talk about the past. It was wrong of me to pry about your marriage that time and—"

"No, love." He tipped her chin up, and the embarrassment in her eyes made him want to kick himself. "You've done nothing wrong. Of course you wanted to talk about my past. I'm sorry I was a bastard about it. The truth is I don't want anything between us. Not even old secrets."

Her smile almost reached her eyes. Gave him the courage to go on.

"I've been thinking about what you said, about my keeping Sylvia on a pedestal, and I've come to realize that you were right." He rubbed the back of his neck, admitted gruffly, "It was the only way to connect with her. She was so ladylike, so... untouchable. I never felt like I deserved her."

"You were a good husband to her," Thea said softly.

"I thought I loved her, but I realize now that I loved an idea of perfection that wasn't real. Or maybe it was real, but it wasn't what I truly wanted. What I needed." He let go of the final truth. "It never made me happy."

"Oh, Gabriel." Thea's eyes shimmered. "I'm sorry."

"No, princess, don't be. Don't you see?" Going down on one knee, he cupped her precious face in his hands. "I know what happiness is now because of you. Because you've shown me that my desires and who I am are worthy of acceptance. Your sweet love and wanton passion have made me whole, brought me the peace that I never thought to find. You've freed me from my curse."

Two droplets spilled from her eyes, but he thought they

were tears of joy.

"You're everything I've ever wanted," she said with a sniffle. "I love you so much."

"As I love you, my dearest wife," he said.

Their lips met in a tender, searing kiss. He tasted salt and sweetness, the addicting contrast of cherished bride and sultry lover, the seamless interweaving of love and desire. One thing led to another, and before he knew it, he'd lifted her onto the vanity, her back against the glass, his lips wandering down her elegant throat. One tug of her belt, and her robe parted, slipping off her shoulders to reveal a garment that made his temperature spike. Made of powder blue satin and creamy lace, the slip plunged deeply over her bosom and had no sleeves. It was held up by a satin bow on each shoulder.

He slid his finger under one bow. "I like this," he murmured.

"I thought you might."

His hands skimmed the lithe curve of her hips. "Actually, I'd prefer you in nothing at all."

"I think that can be arranged as well."

"Minx." Holding her eyes, he took a step back. "Take it off for me, then."

There was no hesitation in her gaze. Just love and feminine desire. A breathtaking acceptance that he would remember for the rest of his life. In a graceful movement, she slid off the vanity. Standing, she tugged first on one bow and then the other. The satin cascaded off her skin like a wave, pooling at her feet. A dewy flush spread over her creamy skin, and she kept her eyes on his. Innocent and sensuous, she was his own Aphrodite rising from the sea.

Tonight he would claim her fully.

Wonder and lust flowed through him. In a smooth motion, he lifted her into his arms and carried her over to the canopied bed. He lay her on the satin sheets and just feasted on the sight of her. She was delight in every aspect, her hair spread in a decadent fan, her nipples hard and blushing coral, gilded floss peeping between her slender thighs.

Kneeling on the bed, he bent and kissed her soft mouth. "You're so beautiful, my princess in the tower."

Her smile brimmed with seductive promise. "But I'm no longer in a tower, am I?"

"No. You're right here with me," he said huskily. "Where you belong."

As he said the words, the need to claim his prize overwhelmed him. He kissed her throat, its vital warmth leaping beneath his tongue. Her breasts came next, the pouting peaks begging for his attention. He lingered there, licking and suckling her tits, captivated by her moans, her abandoned response to his loving. Then the other fragrant hills and valleys of her beckoned, and he continued his journey downward.

He worked his way along the graceful length of one leg, savoring her silky skin. He discovered that she was ticklish behind her knee, her infectious giggles making him grin. This playfulness was new to him, a delightful ease that somehow complemented the intensity of his feelings. He kissed her sweet calf, the delicate turn of her ankle, the instep of her dainty foot. When he sucked one toe into his mouth, her laughter gave way to a sultry gasp.

He kissed each and every one of her pretty little toes.

Then he made his way up along the inside of her other leg, reaching her shy petals. His heart thumped as he found her wet and delicately swollen. Parting her, he eased two fingers inside, groaning at the snug clasp of her pussy. Her hips arched in supplication, and he had to make sure she was completely ready for him this first time.

Besides, his mouth watered for a taste of his wife.

Burying his head between her thighs, he ate her cunny with all the ravening need inside him. Her scent maddened him, as did her flavor, rich and heady as the finest wine. Sighs left her as he stabbed his tongue deeply. He diddled her pearl while he fucked her this way, and her hands clenched his hair, urging him on. She stiffened, her passage rippling around his tongue, her lips chanting his name.

"So good," he muttered thickly. "Come for me, sweeting."

As her climax broke, he tore off his robe. His erection was huge, dripping at the tip. Leaning over her, he notched the flaring head to her slit and drove slowly forward. A groan ripped from his chest. Hot, tight bliss—a pleasure that merged body and soul, that obliterated everything he'd known before. He felt her virgin cunny stretching to accommodate him, flowering around the meat of his shaft, and he knew that he'd come home at last.

Gabriel's face hung over her, his cheekbones flushed, his features held in tight concentration.

He was inside her.

His presence overwhelmed her senses. Thick and hard,

his cock was tightly wedged. Each breath she took seemed to intensify the contact until she fancied she could feel each ridge and prominent vein, each throbbing inch. He stretched her, filled her, overwhelmed her with feeling.

My husband, she thought in wonder. Her vision grew blurry.

"Princess?" A crease formed between his brows. "Does it hurt? Are you—"

"It doesn't hurt. It feels right. Oh, Gabriel," she whispered, "you're a part of me now."

The adoration in his eyes lured more tears down her cheeks. Tenderly, he wiped them away.

"I never want to part from you." His gaze radiated passionate intensity as he began to move. "I want to be inside you, fucking you, loving you always."

She sighed as each lunge spread her further, opening her to discovery. She ran her hands over his bunching shoulders, the rippling muscles of his back. Beneath her palms, she felt the faint lines of scars, but she knew they could hurt him no more. His sinewy body caged her as he stroked his cock deeper and deeper inside. Surrounded by his strength, his scent, his love, she felt need blossoming in her again. Wanting to be closer to him still, she circled the hard grooves of his hips with her legs. She arched, intuitively meeting his thrusts, moaning at the friction of the new angle.

"Yes, darling," he growled. "Move with me. Make love with me."

His thrusts became harder, the erotic sounds of their meeting flesh filling the room. The pounding rhythm overtook her heart, and she lost herself in the primal beauty of their music. Her body heaved against his in slick and urgent counterpart, the chorus of their passion soaring.

"I'm close," he gritted out. "Take it from me, princess. Take your due."

His words triggered a tremor deep in her core. The voluptuous shock spread to her pussy, the muscles convulsing, gripping his plunging cock. The finale made her cry out, and he shuddered, his eyes rolling back in his head as he flooded her with endless, rapturous heat.

With a groan, he collapsed atop her, and she savored the crushing weight. The knowledge that he'd finally given her everything that he was. And she'd given the same to him.

After a while, he rolled onto his side, keeping their bodies joined. Brushing his knuckles against her cheek, he said, "How do you feel, love?"

"Like your wife." She loved the contentment glowing in his eyes. "And you?"

"Like your husband." He kissed her softly. "The luckiest man in the world."

Epilogue

Gabriel paced before one of the windows in his study. Normally, the sight of the flourishing lands outside brought him satisfaction. Today, he felt nothing but a bone-deep chill.

"Why is it taking so long, Papa? Do you think Mama is all right?" Freddy was walking up and down the length of the study, his stride coltish due to his recent growth spurt. "Why hasn't Dr. Abernathy come down yet?"

"These things take time, son." He tried to sound confident, his heart palpitating with fear.

Strathaven spoke up from the wingchair, where he was reading a paper. "No need to worry, the both of you," he said complacently. "The Kents are a robust lot."

Recalling how white-knuckled His Grace had been during the recent delivery of his heir, Gabriel stifled a sarcastic rejoinder. Instead, he turned back to the window, staring out blindly as memories of the past year flitted through his head. Everyday moments like laughing with Thea and Freddy at the dining table. The three of them visiting the tenants together or taking swimming expeditions at the estate's pond. The simple joys of creating a home together.

Private moments, too, rolled over him. The time he'd surprised Thea with a new piano... and the sweet, hot way she'd thanked him. He shivered, seeing her pale curves bent over the dark wood, his hands gripping her hips as he rutted her hard and fast from behind, her ecstatic cries mingling with his. There were the long, steamy nights, too, where in the sanctuary of their shared bed no avenue to pleasure was left unexplored, nothing forbidden.

His throat constricted. *If anything happens to her...*

Just as he was vowing eternal celibacy (or at least the use of certain preventative measures), the door opened.

Dr. Abernathy stepped in, and Gabriel's breath held.

"Congratulations, my lord. Your wife is doing well. You have a new son..." Just as a tide of relief washed over Gabriel, the physician added, "And a new daughter."

Holy Christ... twins?

Freddy let out an excited whoop. "I have a brother *and* a sister!"

"Congratulations, old boy." Strathaven strode over and slapped Gabriel on the back.

Gabriel stared at the doctor. "My wife," he managed, "you're certain she's..."

"She's doing exceptionally well. She and your babes are ready for a visit, although we ought to make it a short one. Your marchioness is a strong lass, but she has put in a good day's work," Dr. Abernathy said with a twinkle.

Dazed, Gabriel headed up to Thea's room, their son behind him. He entered, and, at the sight of his wife, emotion broke inside him. His eyes wet, he staggered over, his hand shaking as he smoothed a curl from her cheek.

She smiled up at him, looking tired but happy. The most beautiful sight he'd ever seen.

"How are you, princess?" he said hoarsely.

"There were a few surprises," she said ruefully, "but I think I weathered them rather well. Would you care to meet the newest members of our family?"

The duchess came forward then; in his haste to get to his wife, he hadn't even noticed his sister-in-law standing there. Smiling, she held a white-flannel bundle in each arm; she gave him one and Thea the other.

"I'll leave you all to your introductions," she said softly and closed the door behind her.

With wonder, Gabriel cradled the precious weight, taking in the puffy, wrinkled face of the sleeping babe. The miracle that he and Thea had made together.

"Would you like to hold your new sibling, Freddy?" Thea said.

Their son gingerly took the bundle Thea held out to him. She ruffled his hair as he rocked the newborn, his expression awestruck. He peered over at the babe in Gabriel's arms.

"Papa," he said, "is this my brother or sister I'm holding?"

Gabriel realized that he hadn't the faintest clue. "Er…"

Thea laughed. "You're holding your sister. Your papa has your brother."

"What are their names?" Freddy asked.

Gabriel cleared his throat. "I was thinking we might name the boy after your father, Thea."

"Little Samuel." His marchioness' eyes glowed. "And our daughter?"

"Whatever name you'd like," he told her.

She looked at Freddy, who'd snuggled his cheek up against his sister's. "Would you like to name your sister, dear?"

"Me?" Freddy breathed. "Truly, Mama?"

"Truly." Thea's smile was broken by a yawn.

"Time to let your mama get her rest," Gabriel said.

He rang for the nursemaid, who came and took the twins. Tagging at her heels, Freddy left the chamber muttering, "What do you think of Frederica... or Fredelina... or *Fredwina*..."

Closing the door, Gabriel undressed and got into bed. Carefully, he drew his wife into his arms. "Thank you, princess," he whispered.

She nestled against him. "You're welcome, darling," she said drowsily. "You know I wanted them as much as you did."

He wasn't thanking her just for the precious lives she'd brought into the world. But hearing his wife's soft, even breaths, he knew that she needed rest more than his professions of love just then. So he tucked her against his heart, his body sheltering hers as she slept, no barriers between them. Eventually, his eyelids got heavy too. He drifted into the peaceful fog, knowing that his dreams would still be there when he awakened... because she'd made them all come true.

Author's Note

Readers may be wondering about Dr. Abernathy's fasting cure for seizures. It is a fictionalized account of the ketogenic diet, a treatment for certain epilepsy and seizure disorders. In an instance of fiction intersecting with real life, my knowledge of the ketogenic diet comes from using it to treat my son's generalized intractable epilepsy.

The ketogenic diet is a carbohydrate restricted, protein sufficient, and liberal fat diet. It is a mainstream treatment that may be prescribed by neurologists, particularly in cases where seizures have been refractory to medications. The ketogenic diet isn't easy; it involves rigorous adherence to a stringent protocol (e.g., we calculate and measure our son's every meal to the tenth of a gram) and must be done under the guidance of a specially trained medical team. In my family's experience, the commitment and effort has been well worth it, leading to benefits we hadn't seen with medications and other procedures.

For more information on ketogenic therapies, consult with your medical provider. Additional resources may be found through www.charliefoundation.org and the Johns Hopkins Epilepsy Center website, under dietary therapies.

**Please enjoy a peek at
Grace's other books...**

The *Heart of Enquiry* series

Prequel Novella: *The Widow Vanishes*
Fate throws beautiful widow Annabel Foster into the arms of William McLeod, her enemy's most ruthless soldier. When an unexpected and explosive night of passion ensues, she must decide: should she run for her life—or stay for her heart?

Book 1: *The Duke Who Knew Too Much*
When Miss Emma Kent witnesses a depraved encounter involving the wicked Duke of Strathaven, her honor compels her to do the right thing. But steamy desire challenges her quest for justice, and she and Strathaven must work together to unravel a dangerous mystery ... before it's too late.

Book 2: *M is for Marquess*
With her frail constitution improving, Miss Dorothea Kent yearns to live a full and passionate life. Desire blooms between her and Gabriel Ridgley, the Marquess of Tremont, an enigmatic widower with a disabled son. But the road to love proves treacherous as Gabriel's past as a spy emerges to threaten them both... and they must defeat a dangerous enemy lying in wait.

Book 3: *The Lady Who Came in from the Cold*
Former spy Pandora Hudson gave up espionage for love. Twelve years later, her dark secret rises to threaten her blissful marriage to Marcus, Marquess of Blackwood, and she must face her most challenging mission yet: winning back the heart of the only man she's ever loved.

Book 4: *The Viscount Always Knocks Twice*
Sparks fly when feisty hoyden Violet Kent and proper gentleman Richard Murray, Viscount Carlisle, meet at a house party. Yet their forbidden passion and blossoming romance are not the only adventures afoot. For a guest is soon discovered dead—and Violet and Richard must join forces to solve the mystery and protect their loved ones... before the murderer strikes again.

The *Mayhem in Mayfair* series

Book 1: *Her Husband's Harlot*
How far will a wallflower go to win her husband's love? When her disguise as a courtesan backfires, Lady Helena finds herself entangled in a game of deception and desire with her husband Nicholas, the Marquess of Harteford ... and discovers that he has dark secrets of his own.

Book 2: *Her Wanton Wager*
To what lengths will a feisty miss go to save her family from ruin? Miss Persephone Fines takes on a wager of seduction with notorious gaming hell owner Gavin Hunt and discovers that love is the most dangerous risk of all.

Book 3: *Her Protector's Pleasure*
Wealthy widow Lady Marianne Draven will stop at nothing to find her kidnapped daughter. Having suffered betrayal in the past, she trusts no man—and especially not Thames River Policeman Ambrose Kent, who has a few secrets of his own. Yet fiery passion ignites between the unlikely pair as they battle a shadowy foe. Can they work together to save Marianne's daughter? And will nights of pleasure turn into a love for all time?

Book 4: *Her Prodigal Passion*
Sensible Miss Charity Sparkler has been in love with Paul Fines, her best friend's brother, for years. When he accidentally compromises her, they find themselves wed in haste. Can an ugly duckling recognize her own beauty and a reformed rake his own value? As secrets of the past lead to present dangers, will this marriage of convenience transform into one of love?

The *Chronicles of Abigail Jones* series

Abigail Jones
When destiny brings shy Victorian maid Abigail Jones into the home of the brooding and enigmatic Earl of Huxton, she discovers forbidden passion ... and a dangerous world of supernatural forces.

About the Author

Grace Callaway's debut novel, *Her Husband's Harlot*, was a Romance Writers of America® Golden Heart® Finalist and went on to become a National #1 Bestselling Regency Romance. Since then, the books in her Mayhem in Mayfair series have hit multiple national and international bestselling lists. She's received top-starred reviews from *Love Romance Passion*, *Bitten by Paranormal Romance*, and *Nightowl Reviews*, amongst others.

Grace grew up on the Canadian prairies battling mosquitoes and freezing temperatures. She made her way south to earn a Ph.D. at the University of Michigan. She thought writing a dissertation was difficult until she started writing a book; she thought writing a book was challenging until she became a mom. She's learned that the harder the work, the sweeter the reward. Currently, she and her family live in California, where their adventures include caretaking an ancestral Buddhist temple, exploring the great outdoors, and sampling local artisanal goodies.

Grace loves to hear from her readers and can be reached at grace@gracecallaway.com.

Other ways to connect:
Website: www.gracecallaway.com
Facebook: www.facebook.com/GraceCallawayBooks
Twitter: @Grace_Callaway

CPSIA information can be obtained
at www.ICGtesting.com
Printed in the USA
FSHW010138290119
55331FS